THE MURAL

Borgo Press Books by MICHAEL MALLORY

The Mural: A Novel of Horror

THE MURAL

A NOVEL OF HORROR

MICHAEL MALLORY

THE BORGO PRESS

MMXII

THE MURAL

THE MURAL

CONTENTS

PROLOGUE
SEVENTY-FIVE YEARS AGO

The town had sprung up out of the ground like a bush.

City hall, market, school, restaurant, auto garage, and houses all stood on a plot of Colonel Henry Jackson Breen's land that only two years before had shown nothing but trees and bramble. More trees surrounded the buildings and those trees, as well as the soon-to-be-built lumber mill they would supply, were the reason for the fledgling town's existence.

Breen's mill; Breen's town. Soon Breen's workers would come here to operate the mill and live in the town, which had been christened "Wood City." They would arrive on the just-completed highway that hugged the coastline and overlooked the Pacific, and he hoped Old Man Hearst up on his goddamned mountaintop just a few miles away would choke on his silver spoon every time he saw the signs of industry that he wasn't any part of, and never would be, damn the man.

Stepping out of a battered Buick sedan that had been purchased specifically for his visits to Wood City, having concluded that there was little purpose in pummeling his Duisenberg town car on the rough washboard road that accessed the site, Breen surveyed the brick and wood buildings. Most of the civic section had been completed, though there was still a good deal of work to do on the residential sections. But since the level of construction on the houses would be far cheaper, it would move quickly. People could start to move in even before the running water hook-ups were complete.

It was Sunday, which was why the town was devoid of workmen. It was a cooler, crisper day than Colonel Breen had expected, though he knew well enough how the fog and wet mist could settle over the coast, and Wood City was only a few miles inland. Shivering, he pulled the fur color of his overcoat tighter around his neck, jammed his hat down further. Leaving his sense of satisfaction trailing behind him, like so much cigar smoke, he made his way straight to the city hall building. His visit today was a surprise one, which is why he had come up here alone. He had to find out for himself what that Bolshevik painter from Roosevelt's damnable public art program was up to (or, rather, *Rosenfeld's*, since the bastard in the White House was rumored to be a secret Jew intent on carrying out an international cabalistic agenda).

Breen could not even remember the painter's name, but he knew the type: temperamental, argumentative, with a tendency to use his talent—real or imagined—like a weapon, pulling it against a "lesser mortal" like a dueling saber. Worst of all, all reports from his staff indicated that he was one of those born with a misplaced sense of entitlement, as though the world owed him a free lunch.

Breen had not even wanted the damned mural in the first place. He had seen examples of this so-called art and had hated it. It was nothing more than unrealistic, distorted figures that looked as though they belonged on the walls of some ancient tomb in Egypt rather than in a modern American building. It had been one of Breen's subordinates who had encouraged him to take advantage of the program, since it was, in effect, free to him. But even at that price it was no bargain, since the "artist" was stalling, refusing to show up for work for days at a time, insisting that he could not create while hampered by a timeline.

Well, by god, there *was* a timeline, and it would damned well be met! No force on Heaven or earth was going to prevent Colonel Henry Jackson Breen from dedicating Wood City on schedule, at the first of the month. If the damnable mural was not finished, then the wall would be painted over and the lazy

Communist hired to create it could be thrown into the ocean, for all Breen cared.

There was a light on inside, indicating the rotter was there. All of the town's public buildings had already been wired for electricity, and all of the workmen had been using floods to finish their interior work. The front door was unlocked, another sign someone was here, since Breen had personally ordered that all buildings were to be locked once the day's work had been completed (though he himself held a key to every building in the town, even the houses).

"Hullo!" Breen called out, stepping inside. For some reason, the floods had been turned toward the entrance, leaving the rest of the interior in the shadows. "Is anyone in here?" He received only silence in return. "I said, is anyone in here?"

The smells of drying plaster and paint permeated the interior, barely overriding another earthy, slightly foul odor, like decay. From somewhere inside the building came a sound, almost like a voice, but not quite. Could an animal have gotten in from the woods? Could the damnable thing have come inside and died?

He swung one of the floods around and washed the side wall of the building in a bright, white glow. Breen looked around but could see no one. "Well, let's have a look at what the genius hath wrought," he muttered to himself, repositioning the light so that it faced the back wall, and the mural. At his initial glance, it looked to be complete: a massive painting crammed with imagery and overpopulated with figures, like all other Socialist art. At second glance, though, Colonel Henry Jackson Breen saw it for what it really was. It was not the expected depiction of American business and industry; rather it was a monstrous tapestry made up of scenes of misery, degradation, and horror.

In one scene rows of women, their faces twisted into expressions of agony, sewed on ancient Singer machines in what was clearly a depiction of a sweat shop. The cloth on which they worked was a rich crimson, which contrasted with the more muted pastel colors of the scene, drawing the eye to it. The ghastliest touch, however, was the fact that all of the women's fingers were literally worn away, revealing white bone underneath.

Next to it was a scene in a machine shop, with agonized looking men struggling against what appeared to be a mechanical monster that literally rent their limbs from their bodies.

Overtop was a panorama of agriculture, with terror-stricken looking farmers plowing a grave yard, the loose earth beginning to reveal its contents.

At one side was the depiction of a meat packing plant, showing miserable, blood-splattered drudges cutting up living animals whose faces bore horrific expressions of pain. Below was the depiction of a man grinning dementedly while sodomizing a headless sheep.

This is a vision that could only come from Hell itself! Breen thought, feeling his gorge rising even faster than his anger. Still, he continued to look.

The painted scene of an automobile factory depicted corpses on the assembly line, and thrusting from it, in a horrifying realistic simulation of three-dimensional art, was the remnant of a faulty car that the dead workers had created, overturned and burning on a road, with a family of four trapped inside, their flesh blackened from the fire, all shrieking in terror and anguish. Breen could almost hear the screams.

Next to it was a scene in a department store, but instead of merchandize such as clothing or toys or books, the shelves were stocked with body parts, including a display of severed human genitals.

This was a goddamned abomination! Breen attempted to dismiss the mural as a sickening practical joke, but too much work had been on done on it to make that explanation credible. The only explanation was that the "artist" was a raving lunatic!

Breen had already made the decision to obliterate the mural before looking at the last section. When he did gaze upon it, it caused his blood to rise to the point where there was a pounding in his ears.

It depicted a lumber mill, well populated by workers, but

instead of the dead, hopelessly pain-stricken expressions seen on every other figure in the painting, the men shown here were clearly insane. Each one beamed out of the painting with wild eyes and hideous grins as they manned the huge saws, which were not being used to rip tree logs into lumber, but rather dismember people and turn bodies into carrion.

Breen pulled his handkerchief from his pocket and held it tightly over his mouth. Once the wave of nausea had passed, he used it to mop his sweating face. That undetectable foul odor was becoming stronger now and was intermingling with another smell, an acrid one like that of a freshly-struck match. He had to get out of this place.

He heard another noise, and it seemed to come from directly in front of him. *Don't look at it!* Breen ordered himself, but he was powerless to stop. As if not under his own power, his head slowly rose and he faced the mural again. He heard a shout of terror, unaware that it came from his own throat.

Every face in the painting was now staring directly at him, their agony intensified a thousand times by the fact that their wide, pain-informed eyes burned straight into his.

Breen felt the fingers of his left hand go numb and heavy. The numbness spread up his arm and then stabbed him like a dagger under his armpit. He began to reel, his eyes wandering all over the mural. Finally, though, they came to light on one particular spot, which he would swear had not been there before: it was the scene of the dead farmer plowing the graveyard. There were two distinct bodies, half-emerged from the loose soil. A futile cry escaped his lips as he recognized the faces.

But nobody knows this, he thought, madly. *Nobody alive knows.*

The figures in the painting were two men he had known years ago, rivals in business. Both of them had been dead for decades, which Breen knew for a fact, because it was he who had them killed. *That was twenty years ago....*

Then as Breen watched, the two figures slowly, painfully turned their painted heads until they stared straight at him.

They shook their heads and smiled. The lips of one dead face formed the words, *Hello, Breen*, so clearly that the colonel actually heard them.

Breen's bladder gave way and the stream of urine coursing down his leg felt like lava against his cold flesh. A white hot spear of pain shot through his chest. There was a similar sharp jab in the side of his head, and the flood illuminating the room seemed to turn pinkish-red. Clutching at his chest, he started to fall and tried to regain his footing, but it was too late. Like one of the trees that had been cut to make him wealthy, he toppled sideways, hitting the stand of the floodlight on the way down, knocking it to the floor, shattering the lamp and throwing the building into total blackness.

A moment later, writhing on the floor in the darkness of the yet-to-be dedicated city hall, wracked by a greater sense of terror than he had ever known, Colonel Henry Jackson Breen's heart ceased beating.

The mural's work had begun.

BOOK ONE

CHAPTER ONE
TODAY

Jack Hayden did not believe in miracles, but nothing else could explain his getting cell phone service out here in the middle of the woods. Somewhere amidst all these towering genuine trees there must be a cell tower disguised as a pine. Startled as he was by its ringing, Jack did not bother to answer it. He did not want to talk to Marcus Broarty.

Jack Hayden rarely wanted to talk to his boss, but out here, in the heart of the misty, piney forest on the central coast of California, he particularly did not want to talk to him. After all, it was supposed to be Broarty who was taking charge of this job, not him. But Broarty had absolutely no idea what he was doing, which meant that he would endlessly pester Jack for up-to-the-second reports about what he was finding in the old California ghost town, which he could parrot it back to the client, giving the illusion of being knowledgeable.

"Go to hell," Jack said, and the phone stopped ringing as though it had heard him. If Broarty made an issue about being unable to connect with him, he could always claim he could not get a signal, which, by all rights, he should not be able to.

Jack continued to trudge through the woods, glad he had worn his old boots, since the earth was moist and wet. He glanced again at the damp surveyor's map, which really was not much help in locating the ruins of the town. It had taken him long enough to find the turnoff from the highway, which after so many years was virtually imperceptible, particularly at sixty miles an hour. Only by driving along the shoulder of Highway 1 had he managed to spot the entrance to the old service road. Jack had barely been able to squeeze his pickup through the opening. The road beyond was as runnelled and rutted as any he had seen, and it sloped uphill, which prevented the engine from dropping out of first gear. The density and height of the trees created a canopy that all but blocked out the sun, casting an eerie perpetual twilight over the woods. The moss that hung down from the tree branches like sea foam cobwebs only added to the effect. Jack was not expecting the old site to be this desolate, and he prayed he would not meet up with a bear.

After about ten minutes in first gear, Jack came to an impasse in the road: a large tree had fallen over the rustic path, preventing him from taking the truck in any further. He stepped out of the cab and looked around. The old road seemed to vanish altogether. What's more, there was no sign in any direction that any kind of village or two once stood here. He could continue on foot, and *should* continue on foot if he wanted to conscientiously do the job for which he was being paid, but at the moment it looked like a fool's chase. If Wood City had ever existed, it was now long gone.

Jack had just taken out his compass to check it against the map, when his cell phone rang again. "Christ," he muttered. "Okay, you asshole, you win." Pulling out the phone and flipping it open, he hit the proper button and said, "Yeah, Hayden."

"Hi, Daddy!" a voice came back, and Jack smiled broadly.

"Hey, punkin! How are you? Did you call earlier?"

"Yeah, but you didn't answer," Robynn Hayden replied, with the kind of hurt, accusatory indignation that only a five-year-old could summon.

"I'm sorry, punkin, but I'm here now," Jack said. Then he checked his watch. "Hey, aren't you supposed to be in school."

"Mmm-hmm, but I'm sick today."

"Oh, no, what's wrong?"

"I dunno. I have spots on my back and face. Mom's taking me to Dr. Ari."

"Boy, I'm sorry to hear that. Can I talk to Mom?"

"Mm-hmm." Then the line went vacant for a moment, a sign that the phone was being passed. The next voice that came on was that of his wife, Elley.

"Where have you been, Jack. I've been trying to get through to you for a half-hour."

"Sorry, but it's pretty astonishing you're getting through now. I'm in the middle of the forest. So what are these spots all about?"

"On the phone the doctor thought they were probably nothing more than hives, but I'm taking her in just to make sure. You know how schools are when it comes to red spots."

"So you're taking the day off work?"

"Half day," she said. "I had to cancel a morning meeting, but there's one in the afternoon that I can't blow off by playing hooky." While Jack did not consider staying home in order to take care of a sick child to be playing hooky, he held his tongue. "I called Nola and asked her to come by early so I can leave." Nola was the nanny they had hired at the beginning of the school year to pick Robynn up after kindergarten and take care of her until Elley got home. Elley (whose name was not short for anything, but rather was the phonetic form of *L.E.*, her mother's initials) had a high-pressure job. She was a senior account executive in a big marketing firm and as such she was far more dedicated to her work than Jack was to his job as a building inspector. She was also paid a great deal more, though that was not a factor in her devotion. Elley was a career woman, one who savored every write-up in a business journal, while Jack viewed work simply as the price for having a life, a home, and a comfortable environment in which to raise a child. For him, five o'clock was quitting time and five-thirty signaled the start of Happy Hour.

"Do you know how long you're going to be up there?" Elley asked him.

"I haven't even found the place yet, but I'm hoping I'll be back home by Wednesday at the latest."

"*Wednesday?*"

"That's worst case scenario. I'm shooting for tomorrow."

"I'd prefer that."

"So would I," Jack said, silently adding: *I think.* "Can you put Robynn back on?"

"Don't talk too long, I have to get her to the doctor."

That emptiness was heard again, and then his daughter's voice said: "Daddy, can I have a turtle?"

"A turtle?" Jack laughed. "What put that idea into your head?"

"There was a show on turtles last night. Did you know they can live a hundred years?"

"Well, the big ones can, like the ones they have at the zoo, but we're not getting one of those."

"So we can get a small one?"

"We'll talk about it when I get home, okay?"

"Okay. I love you, Daddy."

"I love you too, punkin."

The line then went dead. With a smile, Jack Hayden replaced the phone in his pocket and forged through the woods until he finally came to what was clearly the continuation of the old road he had lost earlier, illuminated by a shaft of light that bled through the treetops. "All it takes is a beam of pure sunshine to light the way," he said, thinking more about his daughter's golden face, which was lovely, despite the prominent crimp on her upper lip, than of the sun itself.

Jack was encouraged by the fact that Robynn remained unaffected by the scar on her face, which was the result of an operation for a severely cleft palate when she was less than a year old. He hoped it would always be that way, but in his heart he knew that would not be the case. Someday, confronted by the cruelty of other children or society in general, Robynn would be forced to accept the fact that her face was, in the eyes of the world, blemished. The thought of that impending kept him awake some nights. He tried to push it out of his mind now.

The loud crunching sounds Jack's steps made as he trudged

up the nearly overgrown dirt and gravel road were the only sounds around him. He was beginning to wonder whether or not he would be able to find his way back to his truck when he spotted the ruins of some kind of structure. Jack jogged up to it, his breath now coming in visible spouts. Reaching into his breast pocket, he pulled out the small microcassette on which he recorded all his notes, impressions and figurings, which were then later transcribed onto paper back in the office. He knew from looking at the original plans for the layout Wood City that this building would be residential, and even a cursory examination of this structure told him occupancy would be impossible. "Residential structure number one, single storey," he said into the tape recorder, "roof missing, chimney collapsed. Doors missing, glass missing, completely out of square and noticeably listing to one side." Carefully, he crept to the open windows and peered in. "Interior walls open, studs revealed," he recorded, as he shined a flashlight beam over the walls. "Construction is very cheap. There appears to be more than two feet distance between some of the studs. Overall, the structure looks unsafe for entry. If you're listening in, Marcus, nobody in their right mind would inhabit this dump."

Shining the light around, he saw nothing of value inside, except for a stack of wood that was obviously for the fire, and a white object on the floor. Training his light on it, Jack saw that it was a ruined child's doll, a baby figure dressed in a filthy, ragged cloth nightgown. Had it been in better shape, he might have rescued it, cleaned it up and had it appraised. It was not everyday that one stumbled over a 1930s era toy. But this one was in such a state of decay that it could not possibly have any value. Jack's thoughts shifted to the doll's original owner, whoever she was. Living in this glorified lumber camp couldn't have been easy for a kid.

After circling the house and dictating a few more notes, Jack Hayden slipped the microcassette back in his jacket pocket and from another one pulled out his digital camera, and photographed the place from each side. He had sat in on only one client meeting with the unsmiling wealth monkeys from Resort Partners, LLC, the Las Vegas firm that was committed to the notion of turning the ghost town of Wood City into a new getaway resort, but it was enough to know that they would never believe that the existing buildings could not be salvaged without photographic proof.

Once finished, he slid the camera back into his pocket (and even though people had been bugging him to get a camera phone, which took up much less pocket space, Jack preferred a separate camera) and went off in search of the other buildings. What he found were mostly footprints and artifacts, a collapsed fireplace here, a foundation block there, even a small sink at one site. Five cabin-sized houses still retained walls though their roofs had fallen in. For all his diligence in trudging through the dirt and pushing through tangles of brush, Jack had come upon nothing that was salvageable for future use. Nothing. The entire site would have to be razed.

His phone rang again, and this time he answered it immediately, fearing that it might be Elley calling to tell him that Robynn's spots were not simply hives.

"Hi, Jack, it's Yolanda."

Damn. "Hey, Yoli, what's up? Or do I want to know?"

Yolanda Valdera was Marcus Broarty's personal secretary. She was a pleasant, professional, and highly competent young woman with the patience of a horse and the kind of beauty that stopped traffic, even in L.A.. The latter, Jack knew, was the primary reason she was hired, despite her efficiency as a worker and ability to get along with anyone inside Crane Commercial Building Engineering, even assholes like Marcus. Jack sometimes wondered if it was not really Yolanda who kept the company running.

"I have Mr. Broarty for you."

"My empty life is now complete," Jack said, and at the other end of the line was the sharp snort that meant Yolanda was stifling a laugh.

"I'll put him through," she said.

You can put him through the sewer line to clean it, Jack thought.

Marcus Broarty's voice came on the line. "I'm a busy man, Jack, so don't keep me in suspense. Tell me what you're finding up there in our central coast paradise."

"Not much, I'm afraid."

"Those are discouraging words, Jack. I don't want to hear any negativity."

Christ. "I know, but believe me, Marc, it isn't good." Jack Hayden gave his boss a rundown of the notes he had recorded. When he was done, Broarty asked: "Can't anything be fixed up?"

"When I get back to the motel, I'll email you the pictures and you can see for yourself."

"And you inspected each building, right?"

"I haven't found the commercial area of the town yet, but the residential structures can't even be called buildings anymore."

"Shit. Those are what Emac was most hoping to rehabilitate."

Emac was Egon McMenamin, the director of expansion for Resort Partners, and the man who was responsible for Jack's firm being brought in on the project. That nickname was what McMenamin insisted with forced joviality that all his acquaintances call him. If Jack's parents had been so sadistic as to saddle him with a name like *Egon,* he'd probably be insisting on a pseudonym too.

"These are wood structures, Marc, and they don't look like they were made very well to begin with. They've been exposed to the elements for more than seventy years, so you can't expect them to hold up. Emac has to understand that."

"That kind of attitude is not being helpful, Jack."

Jack closed his eyes, feeling a headache coming on. "I'm not giving you attitude, Marc, I'm giving you the truth. I'm standing here looking at unsafe, unsound ruins. I wish I could change that fact, but I can't."

"Well, then, Jacko, I guess you'd better start thinking about how you're going to break the news to Emac."

"How *I'm* going to break the news?" Jack said, a little more sharply than he had intended.

"You're the one who's seeing the conditions of these buildings, not me. You're the one with the first-hand knowledge."

Right, and if someone has to take a hit for telling the truth, it's certainly not going to be Mr. MBA, which within the company stood for *Marcus Broarty, Asshole.* "All right," Jack sighed. Right now, all he really wanted was to get Broarty out of his ear. "Maybe I'll find something more encouraging closer to the business district."

"That's the spirit. I want to hear good news when you call back, as I'm sure Emac does. I don't have to tell you that this is a big client for us. We can't screw it up. Bye, Jack." The line cut off.

Jack exhaled loudly. "If a man contemplates killing his boss in a forest, and no one is around to hear it, can he still be charged with criminal intent?" he asked the woods. Slipping the phone back in his shirt pocket, Jack trudged on to find if anything at all was left of the tiny commercial area of Wood City. He could see nothing ahead of him that could be construed as shops or office buildings. In fact, a quarter-mile or so up from the last house foundation, the road appeared to stop at a small grove of uncut trees and brush. The mist now seemed to be heavier, wetter, and Jack lifted up the collar of his jacket in a futile attempt to keep the cold air from going straight down his neck.

Leaving the identifiable path, Jack began hiking through the brush, squeezing through the tangle wherever he could. *I should have brought a frigging machete*, he thought. It was hard, tiring work, particularly in the chill and dampness, and Jack was on the verge of giving up and going back, at least for the day, when he saw it.

Through the foliage he could make out a high, square, official looking stone building, looming out of the green like a lost Incan temple. As he fought his way to it, traces of the old road once more became visible beneath his feet. According to the surveyor's map, there should have been eight structures in the downtown district, though he could only see this one. The closer he came to it, though, the more visible the ruins of the others became; they were mostly foundation blocks poking up out of the ground every here and there like a wino's smile.

Apparently, every other building except this one had been constructed of wood, like the houses, which meant they suffered the same fate, though the skeletal remains of iron playground apparatus identified one of them as a school. The stone building, which had managed to defy the decades of neglect and punishing weather, was identifiable by the carving in the granite lintel above the arched front door: *City Hall*. The doors themselves were gone, and the portal in which they had once hung gaped blackly like a cave entrance.

Retrieving his recorder as he walked around the structure, Jack Hayden said into the mike: "City hall building appears to be largely intact, with no visible cracks in exterior walls. Windows and doors are gone, not surprisingly, though as near as I can tell through visual inspection, the foundation looks sound." Clicking the pause button, Jack trained the beam of his flashlight into the opening and, taking careful steps, walked into the dark building.

The interior was a complete mess. The floor was covered with layers of dirt and chunks of plaster that had fallen from the ceiling. A ruined chandelier hung down like a forgotten criminal's body from a gibbet. Amidst the rubble were fragments of broken furniture and partitions, which once defined offices in the building. Some of the interior walls had fallen away to reveal the outer stone layer while others still retained traces of wood paneling.

After making as thorough an inspection as was possible under the circumstances, Jack switched his recording back on and said: "Interior of city hall in an extreme state of distress, but cannot see anything that indicates structural instability. With enough people dedicated to the effort, and enough cleanser, this building probably could be rehabilitated for use again." *But Jesus*, he thought, *I'd hate to be responsible for cleaning this place up.*

Clicking off the recorder, Jack set the flashlight down on a heap of plaster chips and pulled out his camera, checking it against the light bema to make certain it was set for flash. Pointing it at one side wall, he clicked the button and waited until the flash went off, then checked the screen to see if anything had been captured. It had: the picture showed the stained, moldy paneling quite clearly. He took a few more shots from different angles and then turned to the other wall the floor and the ceiling. Last to be shot was the back wall, which oddly appeared to be made of poured concrete. Training the camera on it he clicked the button and peered through the viewfinder as the flash went off.

What Jack Hayden saw in that lightning second through the camera made him jump back and cry out, involuntarily. Tripping on a pile of rubble, he fell backwards, landing hard on his backside. He did not even notice the pain, however. He was still too shaken.

He had seen a face in the momentary flash. A human face, looking back at him.

Struggling to his feet, Jack rushed back to the open door, his heart pounding, and cried, "Who's in there?"

There was no answer.

"If you're there, show yourself. I'm not going to do anything to you."

No one responded.

Jack called out again, and then began to wonder if his imagination had not gotten the better of him. There was one way to find out. He pulled up the last shot he had taken. Staring into the small screen, tilting it back and forth to catch the best light, Jack Hayden once more saw the face, though this time it was clear that it was not the face of a living being. Its stylization revealed it for what it was. "Oh, good god," he laughed.

Moving back into the dark building, he picked up his flashlight and held it up to the wall. The face he had seen was a painting, though it was not inside of a frame. It seemed to be painted directly onto the wall. As he approached it, he could see that it was the face of a woman, one that stared out from behind a curtain of gray, and for the first time Jack realized that the wall was not made of concrete, but plaster that had been painted over with heavy gray paint. A chunk of the ceiling sat on the floor directly in front of it, and Jack guessed that it had fallen in just the right place as to shave away the paint on the way down. With his fingernail he chipped away at the gray covering, enough to reveal more painted surface underneath. After a minute's worth of chipping, this time using his keys, he uncovered a portion of another face.

"I'll be damned," he whispered. The style of the artwork was the kind he had seen in Depression-era public works projects. Into the tape recorder he said: "The back wall of the city hall building is decorated with what appears to be an old WPA mural, which at some point in time was painted over. From what I can see of it, this mural appears to be in good enough condition to warrant restoration. Note...be sure to bring this up with Emac since this definitely adds a few new wrinkles to things. Get the preservation people involved and maybe they'll pay for the restoration."

Who knew? Maybe there was some potential life in Lost Pines Resort after all. Maybe once word got out about the discovery of the mural artwork, if it's really something special, Resort Partners could obtain grant or foundation money to build the resort from scratch, with minimal out-of-pocket expense. Wouldn't they love that! Suddenly Jack was no longer dreading having to confront Emac McMenamin.

Clicking the machine off, he slipped it back into his pocket and picked the camera back up, taking several additional shots of the revealed mural. Maybe he should get his marketing whiz of a wife involved to get her take on how to hype this thing. *An historic, lost icon of California's progressive past; a masterpiece newly discovered and brought to you by Resort Partners, LLC! And now you can own two weeks of this miraculous discovery every year—*

"Who am I kidding," Jack said, laughing. Even though Elley

had the marketing ability to sell abstinence brochures to sailors on shore leave, Resort Partners would never pay for her.

Surprisingly, it had not been a bad day's work. The buildings were still rubble, but at least he now had an angle, and Jack knew from experience that angles were also acceptable in lieu of reality, particularly if Marcus Broarty was involved. Not bad at all, and he was already tasting the cold beer waiting for him at the hotel.

As he was making his way out of the city hall building, Jack Hayden also realized that he was hungry, too. The trek back to his truck made him even more so, despite the fact that it was much easier to walk downhill out of the woods than it had been to fight his way in. The fog had lifted, too, warming the day considerably, and even the thicket across the road seemed less of a problem to get through. His only discomfort came when slid behind the wheel and realized how much his tailbone still hurt from his pratfall back at the city hall.

Turning the truck around in the woods was a challenge, but once he had managed, Jack made it back to the highway in no time. From there it was only six miles to his motel, a comfortable, if slightly sterile, place called the Tide Pool Inn, which was on the beachside tourist strip of San Simeon, a couple of miles from the original tiny village that had once serviced William Randolph Hearst and the creation of his legendary palace of opulence high above the ocean.

After bolting down a burger and a few beers in the motel restaurant, Jack returned to his room and set up his laptop on top of the bed. After powering it up, he plugged in his camera in order to download the photos. While waiting for the two digital devices to do their thing, he phoned Elley at her work number.

"How's the patient?"

"Impatient is more like it," she replied. "It was hives, just as I suspected, but we had to wait forever before we saw the doctor. Half the day was shot."

"Well, she probably enjoyed having a surprise morning with her mom."

"Look, I have to go into a meeting. Is there anything else?"

"I guess not."

"Okay. Bye."

"Bye," Jack said to the disconnected phone line. Turning back to his computer, he saw that the download had been completed. Setting it for a slide show, he watched one picture after another, still somewhat amazed that the lighting was so good, only through flash illumination. When he came to the first picture of the back wall, he laughed all over again at how frightened the sight of the painted face had made him, and gave thanks that Broarty, or anyone else for that matter, had not been there to hear him scream like a girl and fall on his ass. But when the closer pictures of the mural figure's face came up, he paused the slide show, stopping it to study them carefully. Jack frowned. The face in the photos did not look quite the same as it had when he looked at it in the building. It was still a woman's face, but the expression now appeared slightly different. The figure's eyes now seemed to bore into his. It had to be a trick of the light flash, but it was a damned weird one. Even weirder was the fact that even the feature seemed to have subtly changed. They looked a little more refined, a little sharper; certainly different than before.

The picture now changed to the next sequential image in the slide show, and Jack leapt backward off of the bed.

It was a painting of Elley, his wife, staring back at him from his laptop, her eyes wide and insane, her mouth twisted into an evil grin.

"My god!" he panted, covering his eyes, groping his way backward until he collided with the wall. A moment later he felt like a fool. *This is stupid*, Jack though. *There had to be a photo of her already on the memory stick and it just popped up.*

Then why did she look so thoroughly evil?

My mind; or else fatigue; or maybe too many beers; or maybe not enough; I don't know.

Slowly Jack cracked open one eye, then the other, and forced himself to look at the laptop. The woman's face remained on the screen, but it was not Elley. It was the face in the mural, altered, if at all, only by the combination of the flashlight and the camera flash, being used simultaneously. "God," Jack muttered. He was a pussy. For the second time that day, he was glad to have been alone in his moment of supreme cowardice.

Going back to the bed, Jack closed the slide show, put the pictures in a file, and as quickly as he could, emailed them to Broarty. Then he powered off the machine and vowed to leave it off for the rest of the night.

It was not even six o'clock yet. Jack had already eaten, and nothing on the television appealed to him. He decided to go down to the motel shop and see if they had a pair of swim trunks in his size (they would probably be exorbitant, but he'd find a way to expense them), and then check out the pool area. Maybe what he needed most right now was to soak his aching butt in some warm water. Maybe it would relax him enough so that he could get a good night's sleep.

Maybe the vision of his wife as some kind of horror movie creature that his mind had generated, for whatever perverse reason of its own, would not come back.

CHAPTER TWO

The pool area seemed like it was the furthest point possible from his room, forcing Jack to traipse in his swim trunks through every hallway of the motel's first floor, but the welcoming, warm chlorine smell that greeted him as soon as he passed through the double glass doors leading to the recreation area brushed that concern aside. The Jacuzzi was empty, a situation he quickly remedied. Lowering himself into the hot, steaming, initially stinging water, Jack leaned back, closed his eyes and let it lap up around him. He was getting thirsty again, but was trying to ignore that for fear that more alcohol would bring back the frightening vision of Elley, not drive it away.

He concentrated on other thoughts. This was only Monday (though it seemed like the week should be over already): he could leave first thing tomorrow morning and be back in L.A. by the early afternoon, or he could return to Wood City in the morning, now that he knew exactly where it was, and make a second inspection, just to ensure that there were no structures he had missed. By doing that, he could be on his way by lunchtime and back in town by late afternoon—not soon enough to pick Robynn up from school, but certainly in time for a dinner. Sticking around for another day would also deflect any questions that Marcus Broarty would undoubtedly come up with, all of which would begin with: *Since you were already there, and we were paying for you to be there, why didn't you...?* That was Broarty's way of letting you know what *he* would have done differently, had he been the type who actually did things instead of talk about them.

Both the soreness in Jack's backside and the memory of the damp chill that had infiltrated his bones out in the woods were being massaged away by the swirling water. To rid his mind of the image of the pink, piggish face of Marcus Broarty, he closed his eyes and thought instead of Robynn. He missed her terribly whenever he was away, though just the mental picture of her beautiful face brought a smile to his lips.

"Must be awfully good, whatever you're thinking," a voice near him said, and Jack opened his eyes.

He saw a woman standing at the edge of the Jacuzzi across from him. She was young—about twenty-eight, he guessed—tanned, blonde, and form-fitted into a satiny blue one-piece. The woman's freckles were completely disarming. So were her eyes, which were a rich green color. "Sorry," she said, flashing a perfect smile, "I didn't mean to startle you. Mind if I join you?"

"No, not at all."

The woman stepped into the Jacuzzi, her tanned legs melting into the water. "Wow, this is warm."

"It takes a few seconds to get used to it, but once you do, you won't want to leave. At least I don't. I may spend the night in here."

"I could tell you were having a good time from your expression when I walked up."

Jack smiled. "Well, it was also because I was thinking about my daughter. She's back in L.A."

"What's her name?"

"Robynn, and I'm Jack. Jack Hayden." He extended a wet hand to her and she shook it.

"I'm Dani Lindstrom."

"Danny? Like Danny Glover?"

"D-A-N-I. It's short for Danica. So, Jack Hayden, what brings you all the way up here from L.A.?"

"Work. I'm a structural engineer and building inspector, and I had to come up to check out an old ghost town a little south of here."

"Around here? Really? You're not talking about Glenowen, are you?"

Glenowen, California, was a small, quasi-Victorian village several miles down the highway. "No, this one is called Wood City. It's the ruins of a company town that was built in the thirties to service a lumber mill that they never got around to opening. I guess if you've never heard of the place you're not from this area, either."

"I'm from San Diego," she said. "But I travel a lot. I'm a freelance DJ."

"For parties?"

"No, on the radio, for smaller towns, mostly. I do vacation gigs, or go in if someone leaves a station altogether and they're suddenly stuck for a DJ. I stay as long as they need me, and then go onto the next gig. It's a little like being a temp, but instead of typing or filing, I play songs and talk."

For the first time Jack became conscious of her voice, which was low and pleasing, and had the promise of sounding sexy as hell. "How does one even get into that kind of work?" he asked.

"Are you really interested or just being polite?"

"I'm interested. It sounds like an unusual job."

Dani Lindstrom stretched out her legs and leaned back against the rim of the Jacuzzi, so that her breasts appeared to float on the water like twin buoys. Jack tried not to leer. "It's not that fascinating a story," she said. "I got an internship at a station when I was in college, and decided I liked radio, except for the politics that always seems to come with it. It's show biz, so you're dealing with egos and people who were fixated on their career trajectory, and I have a kind of allergy to that sort of thing. I had just about decided that radio wasn't for me after all when a little station asked if I'd fill in for a few weeks, and I realized that was it. The regular staff wasn't threatened by my temporary presence, so I started advertising in radio journals as a professional replacement, then an agent contacted me, and here I am."

"So you just travel around the country going from station to station?"

"Pretty much. I'm ready to spin whatever they need, classical, country, rock, anything."

"You must know an awful lot about all music."

She smiled. "I learned early on that if you read the liner notes in the CD, you can become an instant expert."

"I don't think I could take all that travel," Jack said.

"Oh, I enjoy it. It was Perry had the problem."

"Boyfriend?"

"Husband."

"Ah. I can see where constant travel could be hard on a marriage."

"Not as hard as being married to a total jerk. My marriage was the biggest mistake of my life, but now it's over, as of last Wednesday. That's why I'm here. I'm taking two weeks off to celebrate." She sat up and leaned closer to him, her green eyes shining, and for the first time Jack realized that Dani Lindstrom was not wearing make-up of any kind, nor did she need any to look stunning. "But I'd rather hear more about this ghost town of yours. Where is it?"

"You know where the highway goes to two-lane and seems to be cut through the forest just south of here, before you get to Glenowen?"

"No, but I'll take your word for it."

"The remnant of an old access road is right there. Follow it in for a mile or so and you eventually come to Wood City, or what's left of it. It's largely ruins. There was one thing that happened that was kind of scary, though."

Dani slid closer, so close that her hand could have easily touched Jack's arm. "What?" she asked.

He told her about the exposed mural fragment in the building, and she listened raptly. After he was finished, she said: "I'd love to see that."

"There's not much to see, and it's in a filthy, dilapidated old building. I'd be a little nervous about bringing someone else in there. Besides, you can't drive all the way in because of the foliage, and once you get out it's an uphill, difficult hike to the city."

"Sounds like fun to me."

Jack shook his head. "Okay, look at it this way. The guy I report to is the type who gives idiots a bad name. If I took you to the site and you got injured, he would fire me immediately for reckless negligence and then sue you for trespassing. I'm sorry, Dani, I just can't take the risk."

"Then what about the pictures? You said you took pictures while you were up there. Can I at least see those?"

"You're really interested in this, aren't you?"

"You were really interested in my story. I want to see the pictures. Are they in your room?"

"Yes, on my laptop."

Her smiled nearly blinded him. "Then let's go." As she climbed out of the Jacuzzi, Jack couldn't take his eyes off her body. Dani Lindstrom was slender and amply-breasted, and without a trace of the cellulite that Elley was forever fighting. "Coming?" she asked, looking back at him.

Damn close to it, lady, he thought, watching her nipples rise through the one-piece. When it was no longer embarrassing for him to stand up, he climbed out of the water and reached for his towel.

Halfway back to his room, Jack said, "You know, I'd hate for you to be uncomfortable in your wet swimsuit."

"Jack Hayden, that's the cheapest, sleaziest pick-on line I've ever heard!" she said. "So what, you want me to go to your room at take it off?"

"No, no, that's not what I meant! Honest!"

She began to laugh loudly at his distress, and Jack now realized that she had set him up. He could not help but grin in response. "Man, a guy's got to watch his guard around you, lady," he said. "But just for the record, I'm painfully out of practice with pick-up lines."

"Because you're married?"

"Yes, because I'm married. What I meant was that perhaps

we should both go to our respective rooms, dry off, and change clothes so that neither of us will be wet and cold."

She smiled. "How about we hook up in neutral territory, like the lounge? I'll be there, dry and clothed, in a half-hour. You bring the pictures."

"It's a date."

Jack raced to his room, toweled off, dressed, and then waited the remaining twenty-one minutes before grabbing his laptop and heading down to the lounge, which was dubbed "The Pines." It was typical of motel watering holes: dark, wood paneled (not pine, Jack noticed, most likely veneer), with a television, permanently tuned to a sports channel, anchored into one corner at ceiling level, but with the sound muted so that those who cared had to rely on the closed captioning crawl. Only four people were in the bar, which made it even easier to spot Dani, who was seated in a booth. As alluring as she looked in a wet bathing suit, she was even more so in a simple white blouse (with no bra underneath, he could not help noticing). She smiled as he approached laptop in hand, and slid in across from her. "Have you ordered?" he asked.

"No."

"Then can I get you something?"

"Are you on an expense account?"

Jack nodded.

"Great. Then I'll have the Ridgewood Chardonnay."

Jack flagged down the waitress and ordered her wine and a microbrew draft for himself, a local kind with which he was unfamiliar. Then he opened up his laptop and powered it up. By the time the drinks had been delivered, he had the photo file up.

"You want to run a tab, hon?" the waitress asked, and Jack nodded. To Dani he said, "Cheers," and picked up the beer, which at first bite was a bit dark and hoppy for his taste.

Dani, however, appeared to savor the chardonnay. "A dark room, good wine and spooky pictures—do we know how to have a good time or what?" she asked.

Jack smiled. "I hope you won't be disappointed." He began

clicking through the photos on his screen. "You're probably not interested in the pictures of the ruins so I'll cut to the chase. They should be right...hey."

"Something wrong?" Dani asked.

"They aren't here," Jack said. "They have to be here. Shit."

She took a sip of wine. "I hate computers. They always let you down."

"This is a first for me. Let me go back and check the directory, they've got to be there someplace." Jack spent the next minute clicking and typing, all of which was mystifying to the woman next to him, and then stopped, his head shaking. "Maybe I managed to delete them when I emailed them to my boss. I guess it's a good thing I was planning to go back tomorrow morning."

"Maybe what you need is someone to go with you and help this time."

"Dani, I've already told you, I can't take the risk." Jack took another swig of beer, which got better with the second and third swallows. But he lowered the glass from his lips when he saw her puppy dog eyes. "Oh, for god's sake, Dani, don't do this to me."

She actually began whimpering.

Finally Jack began to laugh. "Okay, okay, you can come! Jesus Christ, with your ability, I don't know why you need an agent. You could just go to the station manager and give him those eyes and he'd give you the drive time slot."

Dani Lindstrom blinked but maintained the puppy dog look. "*Now* what?"

"I was just thinking that some dinner might be nice, as long as we're here."

Jack laughed again and signaled for the waitress. He was not particularly hungry, having eaten an early dinner, but he wanted to stay there in the booth in the bar with this woman, yet did not want to simply keep drinking until he was buzzed, or worse. So Jack got the Pines Burger (for which the kitchen cleverly mixed a few pine nuts into the patty) while Dani ordered the

California Salad, which consisted of alternative lettuces heaped with avocado slices.

As they picked at their meals they made small talk: Dani about her interest in radio, to the exclusion of any other media (clearly despite her film-and-television looks), and Jack about his dick of a boss. In the process Jack learned that she was older than he had assumed—thirty-three, only five years younger than he—and was interested in art and history. When Jack finally glanced at his watch he saw that it was nearly nine. "Good lord, I should probably be getting back to my room," he said, killing his fifth beer. "I need to check in at home before turning in, and I have to get up early to get all this stuff done."

"Well, I've enjoyed this evening, Jack Hayden," she said, sliding out of the booth. Then leaning close to him, she whispered: "I'm in room 207."

"Umm, why did you tell me that?"

"So you know where to come to tomorrow morning to pick me up so we can head on out to your ghost town. Why do you think I told you?"

"Just that," he said, too quickly.

"Tomorrow morning, then," she said, flashing that damned perfect smile before turning around and striding out of the bar like a model in search of a ramp. Jack exhaled loudly and contemplated ordering another beer before heading back but decided against it. Instead he asked for the check. Like most motel bars, the drinks and food weren't cheap, and Jack had to put it on plastic. He wrote in a generous tip (Broarty could choke on it) and slid out of the booth. Standing upright, he was a little further gone from the beers than he realized. The damned stuff probably had a higher alcohol content that he realized. Nevertheless, he managed to stagger to the door and was almost out the lounge before the waitress hollered after him to tell him that he had left his laptop in the booth.

Once back in his room, Jack dutifully called home to resume the truncated conversation with his wife from earlier in the afternoon. This time he used the room phone instead of his cell phone, which was charging.

"Well, the hives are gone, like they were never there," Elley told him. "It was pretty much a Chinese fire drill."

"Still, you didn't know that at the time," Jack said, concentrating on his enunciation.

"No. But I had a bitch of an afternoon, and all I want to do now is soak in a hot tub."

"Go ahead."

"How can I do that and deal with Robynn both?" she asked.

"Why don't you put her in with you?" Jack asked.

"What?"

"I said, put her in the tub with you. She'd probably love it."

"The entire point of a hot soak is to take it by yourself. It's personal time. It's the only 'me' time I have, Jack, and I have to forego it tonight."

"Maybe after she's in bed you can take a bath."

"Then I'd be laying there in the tub worrying that she'd wake up at any second and call for me," Elley argued. "It wouldn't be the same."

Jack hoped his sigh didn't register loudly on the other end of the phone connection. "I should be home tomorrow early evening. Then you can go to the spa if you like."

"I just might."

"Fine. If there's nothing else exciting, I have to be up and out early tomorrow and go back to the site for some more pictures. The ones I took today somehow got shrewd...*screwed* up. I should be home by dinner tomorrow, barring any disasters."

"All right. She misses you, you know."

"I miss her, too."

"And me?"

Jack did not answer right away. He knew he was taking too long. He knew the pause between the end of her question and his response was so great that there could be no other interpretation except that he was forcing himself to say how much he missed her. But for some reason, he could not force his tongue to make the words. *Say something, dammit,* he demanded of himself.

"You've no idea how much I miss the woman I married."

"Why do you turn sweet only when you're away from me?" she asked, oblivious to the irony of his words. "See you tomorrow." Elley hung up without saying goodbye, as was her fashion.

"Right," Jack said to the dead phone line.

Room 207. She's there. She's there now. Elley will never know. Why else would Dani have given you her room number? That business about knowing where to find her in the morning was just a chess move. Why are you waiting? Jesus, Hayden, that smile, those eyes, those freckles, those legs, those tits!

Jack sighed deeply, then said, "No." Disappointed or not, he would leave Dani Lindstrom to her business in her room. Most men, he knew, would not. Most men would have torn a leg muscle getting down to the motel sundry shop for a package of condoms, and then be slavering at her door like a wolf smelling meat. Broarty, for instance; he was forever making comments about what he would do, or had done, with women inside if he ever had the chance. So far as Jack knew, Yolanda had managed to deflect any non work-related demands from her horny boss. He also knew, but Broarty didn't, that she kept journal of all Marc's dirty little comments and casual pats on the bottom in just in case she ever needed to file a sexual harassment suit complaint.

Perhaps that was why he was staying put, so as not to be like Broarty. It was as good a working definition of "conscience" as any: *to act in such a way as Marcus Broarty, Asshole, wouldn't.*

Jack picked up the phone and called the bar, and ordered another beer to be delivered to his room...hell, *two* beers...and Broarty could damn well pay for the room service charge. Then he set his travel alarm for 6:30, switched on the television and settled in for the night.

Room 207. Just upstairs.

"Shit," Jack muttered, getting up off the bed and walking into the bathroom where he splashed cold water on his face and waited for the beers to arrive.

CHAPTER THREE

Strangely, Althea Kinchloe found herself in her parent's house, the home that had been destroyed by fire more than fifty years before. But now the house was back and in its former glory. Actually, greater than its former glory: the colors on the walls and the drapes seemed richer and brighter than at any time when she was still living there, and it was certainly cleaner than her last memory of the place.

There were no sign of Althea's parents, both of whom died in the conflagration, though there was another figure with her. It was Althea's sister Bernia, but not Bernia the way she had been the last time Althea saw her, withered and emaciated from the cancer. It was Bernia as she was when they were young girls during the Depression.

"You need to go somewhere," Bernia was saying, directing Althea's attention to a door set in one wall of the living room, where a door had never been before.

My heavens, am I dead? Althea thought. Then the truth came to her. *No, it has to be a dream; a very peculiar one, but a dream nonetheless.*

Althea Kinchloe had always possessed the ability to recognize when she was experiencing a dream, which this most definitely had to be. But before she could step outside of her experience any further, the door opened. Behind it was a staircase leading down to the basement. She went down.

It was dark at the bottom, but not so dark that Althea could not see. A washing machine sat to one side, the old fashioned kind that looked like a drum on legs and had a hand roller to squeeze out the water, the kind her mother had used, and which she herself had used for the first several years of her marriage. Beyond the laundry room was a long, dark corridor, which she started down. The basement corridor reeked of musty dankness, which was hardly surprising. But as she walked, the musty smell was overwhelmed by another one—it was unmistakably the scent of oil paint. It was a familiar odor from her younger days; the smell of an art studio, like the one in which she and Howard used to meet, using the cover story that she was posing for one of his paintings. If her father had known what had really gone on in that studio, he would have taken a shotgun to both of them.

How Althea had loved Howard Kearney. When he became one of the tens of thousands who did not return from the Great War, so young and suddenly so dead, she thought her life was over. That, though, had been seven decades worth of life ago; seven decades that had encompassed a forty-eight year marriage to a fine, if unexciting, man, two children, five grandchildren, and now two great-grandchildren. Her life had not ended when Howard died on the battlefield any more than it had when Barry, her husband, suffered a heart attack and died while on a fishing trip two months before his eightieth birthday. Both tragedies had changed her life, though she often mused that overcoming Howard's death when he was young had in some way prepared her for Barry's death when she was old. The fact that both had been separated from her at the times of their passing left her each time with feelings of emptiness that was painfully hard to overcome, but ultimately she had overcome them. As her grandmother used to say, it was amazing how much people were able to bend in the wind without breaking.

Althea Kinchloe, *née* Dorneman, had done a lot of bending in the wind.

She continued to walk down the dark corridor, the walls of which were covered with paintings of people, all engaged in some kind of activity. She recognized the artwork instantly, and her pulse raced. A figure stepped out from the shadows. "Howard!" Althea cried, rushing toward him. "Oh, Howard!"

Howard was as big and tall and strong and youthful as the last time she had seen him alive, in 1942. He smiled as she approached and held his arms out, and Althea melted into them. He smelled of paint and tobacco, as he always had, but now there was a faint new odor, that of gunpowder. "I've missed you, darling," Althea said, her voice shaky, not with age, but with emotion. "Howard, have you come for me? Am I dying?"

"Not yet, Pookie," he answered softly, and her heart melted. That had been his private name for her. No one else on earth knew of that name. "I've come to tell you that there is something you must do first."

"Tell me and I'll do it, Howard. I'll do anything for you."

"You must help defeat it."

"What must I help defeat?"

"The legion."

"What legion?"

"We thought we took care of it way back when, but the gateway has been opened again."

"I don't understand."

"You have to make yourself understand," Howard replied. "It will not be easy, but you will have help. You will not be alone. There will be a little girl."

"Howard, please tell me what are you talking about!"

"It's fighting me...the legion...I don't have much time. Look for the little girl at Tarelton, California." Howard said, stepping back from her. "And be brave, Althea. Don't give in to it."

"Howard!"

Her long dead love was gone now, like he had never been there. The only signs of life in the basement room were simulated ones: the painted figures on each wall, which had been rendered in the style of a public art mural, the kind Howard used to create before the war. Althea looked from one face to another, and then put her hand to her mouth to stifle a cry.

The painted figures all slowly turned to face her.

I'm dreaming I'm dreaming I'm dreaming I'm dreaming, she chanted to herself, but that did nothing to eliminate her fear.

A shadow in her peripheral vision caused her to look down the seemingly endless corridor. Another figure was standing there, one that was all black. She could not make out features of any kind, but she could see that the shadow was moving. It was coming toward her, very quickly. Althea began to back up, keeping her eyes on the dark figure. As the black figure passed the pictures, the painted figures within them withered and rotted.

That was when Althea screamed. She turned and started running down the corridor, never daring to look back, too frightened to slow down. She ran as fast as she did when she and Bernia used to have races up the drive from the street. Ahead now she could see the stairs leading up to the mysterious door of her house. Behind her, she could hear the footfalls of the dark figure chasing her, as well as the moans of the figures on the wall.

Why can't I wake up?

She got to the base of the stairs and sprinted up, taking two steps at a time, until she reached the top. Althea was about to bolt through the door, when it violently slammed shut in her face. She felt the pressure of the wooden door hitting her flesh, but no pain. Then she fell backwards.

She expected to hit the steps with her back at any moment, but that moment never came. Instead she continued to fall helplessly through the air, like she was falling down a mine shaft. She opened her mouth to cry out....

But Althea Kinchloe did not cry out as her eyes opened and she bounced tensely on her bed, as though she had just landed there from a height. Her nightgown was sopping wet, but it was from sweat, not one of the bladder accidents she occasionally had in her sleep. She reached for her forehead and found that her hair was wet as well, like she had just emerged from the shower. Her heart was pounding almost audibly. "Dear Lord in Heaven," she moaned, closing her eyes again, and wondering whether or not she should call the emergency room.

No, that would be foolish, she decided. There was no pain, only discomfort. And fear. In fact, in her ninety-three years of life, she could not remember a dream that had been so thoroughly terrifying. She glanced at the digital clock beside her bed: it was 4:37 a.m.

"I doubt I'm going to get back to sleep," she told herself, getting out of bed and shuffling to the bathroom to dry herself off. Putting her damp nightgown into the sink, Althea clad herself in her cotton robe, walked into the dark living room and seated herself on the sofa. She searched the cushions for the television remote, finally found it, and switched on the new, impossibly large set that her grandson had bought for her, more for light and noise than entertainment. The programming choices were nothing special this time of night, anyway, mostly those thirty-minute commercials for real estate classes or vacuum cleaners or weight-loss programs. But just having something with sound in front of her might help her to forget the terrible dream.

No. You mustn't forget, you cannot forget, my darling, I will not let you, a voice whispered in her mind.

"Lord, have mercy," Althea uttered. Fine; she would not forget. Rising, she walked into the dining room, where she had a small desk and an upright typewriter that she had had since business school. Taking a clean sheet of paper, she fed it into the roller of the Underwood. There was no doubt that she was awake. She was in her dining room, wide awake. And Howard's voice had just spoken to her.

"If remembering that dream is that important to you, Howard, I guess I'll have to do it," she said aloud, and then reprimanded herself. She had better be careful about talking to empty rooms, or letting anyone, particularly the kids, know that she was following the instructions of her long-dead lover, or else they might declare her senile and put her away into one of those horrible living facilities. If that happened, she would not be able to help anybody. *Dying* facilities was what they were.

As she started to peck out the details of her nightmare onto the paper, Althea's fear began to subside, and a welcoming calm came over her. She felt that she was doing the right thing. She still did not understand what the nightmare meant, if it really meant anything at all, but if it was important to Howard, it was important to her, too. He would not lie to her.

He was still the one she would have trusted above anyone else on earth.

Alive or dead.

CHAPTER FOUR

The tall trees blocked out a good portion of the sun, making it seem much darker, though Jack was relieved that the misty fog that had made yesterday's visit to the woods so uncomfortable had gone. He and Dani Lindstrom had bumped and bounced their way to the spot where the road was blocked by the fallen tree and then got out. "We'll have to fight our way through a tangle of brush a ways up," Jack told her, "so I hope you're not wearing anything delicate."

"I left my chiffon prom dress back at the motel," Dani said, grinning.

The hike seemed easier this time, perhaps because Jack knew where he was going, though the new day revealed nothing that Jack had not noticed before. The city hall building was now more visible from other parts of the ghost town, but that could be attributed to the lack of fog. Jack snapped pictures all the way along as they hiked into the main part of the village. Once they had reached the city hall, Dani said: "Wow, look at this place." She started to trot up the steps, but Jack stopped her.

"There's no light in there," he said, pulling out his flashlight, "and you have to be really careful. Debris is everywhere." Holding the light in front of him, he crept inside, while Dani followed.

"This is like a mausoleum," she commented, her voice echoing in the large empty building.

Jack shined the light on the back wall. "There. You can make out a woman's face."

Dani moved closer to it. "She doesn't look very happy."

"I hadn't noticed that before, but you're right." Jack started snapping a few more shots of the exposed part of the mural. In today's light the face did appear to be in some sort of discomfort, even pain.

Dani reached out and touched the dull gray overcoat. "Why do you suppose they painted over it?"

"Maybe all the figures looked unhappy," Jack said, checking his last picture on the tiny digital screen. "Maybe the effect of the mural on the viewer was depressing, something people back then didn't need."

Dani continued to explore the wall with her fingers. She pulled off a loose gray flake which revealed more of the picture. She touched the painted image, but pulled her hand back, like the wall was hot. "This is wet!"

"That's not surprising," Jack said. "It's been exposed to the elements for quite some time."

"Not the wall, Jack, the paint itself." Dani held up her hand to the flashlight beam, and revealed smudges of reddish-brown on her fingers. "How can the paint still be wet?"

"Certain kinds of paints take forever to dry, particularly if the pigment is not properly mixed with the base. The moisture in the wall might have so permeated the paint layer that it has combined with the pigment." He reached into his back pocket and pulled out a handkerchief, and tossed it to her so she could wipe the paint off her finger.

"Do you really believe that?" she asked, blotting her hand.

"Why wouldn't I? Why else would it be wet?"

In the dim light, Dani examined her stained index finger and then said: "Don't you feel it, Jack?"

"Feel what?"

"Don't you sense that something just isn't right here?"

Jack smiled. "Ruined buildings sometimes have that effect on people. You said it yourself: this place is like a mausoleum."

"Jack, let's get out of here, okay?" Dani said.

"Sure. Let me take one more shot of the face in the mural, for safety, and then we'll go."

"Hurry, please."

As Jack stepped over to the wall, camera in hand, he told himself that this was exactly why he was reluctant to let Dani in here. Like most people, she viewed a building as some kind of living thing. A house with lights and a family living in it was full of life; a house with no lights, no family, no human activity, was somehow "dead," and therefore creepy. While he had grown accustomed to the sentiment, because it was so common, he could not accept it himself. A building was a building, period. A foundation, floors, walls, and a roof, none of which were inherently alive. Buildings were erected by men, maintained by men, and demolished by men.

Buildings did not have souls.

Jack crouched slightly to get a good eye-level view of the woman's painted face and snapped the flash, then checked it to make sure he had it. But before stepping back, he reached out and lightly touched the image. Dani had been right, the paint was wet. Perhaps it had been improperly done, and had started to deteriorate, so was covered up. Maybe it was never even finished.

"Jack?"

"I'm coming, let's go."

Whatever bad vibe Dani was feeling inside the city hall abated with each step she took back to Jack's pickup. "You're going back to L.A. today, right?" she asked, climbing into the passenger seat.

"As soon as I drop you off at the motel," he said, closing the driver's door, but not starting the engine.

"I think I'm going to miss you."

Jack desperately tried to think of a soothing, polite lie, but could not. "Truth be told, I think I'm going to miss you, too."

Her green eyes drew him toward her. He tried to fight it, but could not.

"Dani, I'm not going to lie to you," Jack said, leaning closer to her face, her body. "I'm attracted as hell to you." His breathing was getting heavier, deeper. "When you climbed into that Jacuzzi with me last night, what were you thinking? Be honest."

Her lips parted. "My first thought was, 'Maybe I should go over there and take that guy and drag him back to my room and give him the screwing of his life, because I now can. I'm free. And I want to see if I still have it.'"

Jack swallowed hard. It seemed like the temperature inside the pickup cab was rapidly rising.

"Then I saw the expression on your face. You looked so happy, and you said you were thinking about your little girl, and I realized you didn't deserve to be led on, rolled, and dumped, just because I'm pissed at my ex. Okay, my soul's bared. Now it's your turn. Did you want to come to my room last night?"

"Hell, yes."

"Why didn't you?"

Jack sighed. "Maybe I'm all thought and no follow-through. Maybe that's why my wife is more successful than I am."

"Do you still love her?"

"Don't ask hard questions."

"How about me, Jack?" Slowly, deliberately, she started unbuttoning her blouse. "Do you love me?" She slid her blouse completely off. "Or is that a hard question, too?" With one smooth move, she pulled her bra up over her head, revealing flawless breasts.

Jack tore his shirt off so violently he lost a couple of buttons.

They were on each other like vampires. Alone, in the middle of the woods, unseen by anything human, they tore the rest of their clothes off and made wild, head-banging love in the driver's seat of Jack's pickup. Dani straddled him, her back pressed against the steering wheel, and Jack feeling the bounce of the truck with each and every thrust. After both had climaxed, they held each other, Jack still inside her, Dani's sweat-covered breasts both warming and cooling his chest. Finally, Jack panted: "What do we do now?"

"More of the same, if you're up to it."

"I mean in the long run. I don't want to leave you. But I have to."

"Something will bring us back together. We'll find a way." She began wiggling in his lap, and ten minutes later they were both once more crying out in ecstasy.

It took another hour for them to separate and get their clothes back on. For Jack, it was a revelation; the intensity of the sex had been something he had never felt before. Somewhat shakily, he started the truck back up and drove onto the highway.

After a few silent miles, Dani started to giggle. "You need me to sew some buttons back on your shirt before you go?"

"I'll just change shirts, but thanks."

"Won't your wife become suspicious when she does the laundry?"

"Elley doesn't do the laundry. We have a housekeeper."

She reached over and began to massage his chest under his open, buttonless shirt, hardening his nipples.

They barely made it back to the hotel in time.

Literally running to Jack's room, they made love once on the bed, once on the floor, and finally in the shower. It was there, with the hot water streaming down their linked bodies that Jack asked her: "How much longer are you planning to stay here?"

"Another couple of days. I might hang around longer and see if there are any local historical societies before heading back down to San Diego. If you want, I can see if anyone knows anything about your mural, or the old city."

"I'd hate to put you to any trouble."

She slowly knelt down, following the contour of his body with her tongue. "I think I'd enjoy it," she said.

"There's nothing left," Jack moaned as she took him in her mouth.

He was wrong.

* * * * * * *

Several hundred miles away, Marcus Broarty leaned back in his executive office chair and scored a paper ball hoop in the circular file. Seconds earlier the ball had been a follow-up thank you letter from some hungry kid he had interviewed last week. He could not even remember the kid's name, which did not make much difference, since he was not planning on hiring him. Job-hunters annoyed him. They were nothing but street beggars with neckties instead of cardboard signs, wandering around from company to company pleading for a chance to impress you with their "accomplishments," then following-up any meeting with the kind of brownnosing missive that he had just used to score two cosmic points. He had never stooped to that sort of thing. His MBA was his ticket. Some of the pricks around here thought it was simply because his aunt was the wife of the chairman of Crane Commercial Building Engineering, but Marcus knew better. He still had to prove that he had the executive stuff after he was installed.

His firing of the man who wrote *MBA: Marc Broarty, Asshole* on one of the washroom walls was just one example of his strength. Ditto for the miserable little shit that came up with the joke, "What's the sound of a buzzard vomiting? *BROOOOOOOARTY!*"

The intercom on Marc Broarty's desk buzzed. Pressing it, he said, "Yeah, babe."

"Mr. McMenamin is on line two," Yolanda's voice said.

What the hell does he want now? "Oh, god, tell him I'm...no, no, that's okay, Yolanda, I'll take it." Wrapping pudgy fingers around the receiver, he put it to his ear and jabbed the button. "Emac, how the hell are you? I was thinking about giving you a call."

"I'm here now," Egon McMenamin said at the other end of the line, and since he was using the speakerphone, he was likely not alone in his office. "I was wondering if you'd heard back from your guy up at the site yet."

"I don't have his official report yet," Broarty answered. "He'll be in the office tomorrow. I'll get him on the stick as he gets back."

"Well, Marc, I could really use some information now, even

if it's preliminary, anything you've got."

"Sounds like you're in kind of a rush."

"Not me, Marc, the board. Can't you call your guy?"

"I suppose I could," Broarty said, "though when I talked to him yesterday—"

"Oh, you've already spoken with him, then," Emac said.

"Well, yes, but he had not completed his review at the time, and—"

"Marcus, I'm going to confide in you. It looks like the budget on this project is going to be revised downward, so I need to be able to report back absolutely everything that can be salvaged."

Broarty took a deep breath. "Well, the thing is, Emac, it's starting to look like the buildings out there might need a lot of work."

"Meaning what?"

"Meaning, um, all this is based on an unconfirmed early report, you understand, but, well, the conditions of the structures apparently aren't what I'd call great."

"I need you to be a little more specific than that, Marc," Emac said. "If they aren't great, what are they? Good? Satisfactory? What?"

Broarty started to perspire. "Well, we might be in a situation where it could take a lot of work for the houses to be brought up to code—"

"What code are we talking about?"

"Uh, you know, the building and sa—"

"Jesus, Marc, don't tell me you people are using the building codes of Los Angeles to judge those structures by," Emac snapped. "Most of the castles in Europe couldn't meet L.A. standards."

Rivulets of sweat were running down Broarty's temples. "I'm sure Jack Hayden is taking that into account," he said. At least Broarty hoped to hell Hayden was taking it into account, since this was the first time he had stopped to consider such matters.

"I hope he does, Marcus, because I'd hate to think that we engaged a firm that didn't have a complete grasp of the requirements of the job."

"Emac, Emac, c'mon, you know we're here for you."

"I'd like to think so, but what I'm hearing from you is a lot of vagaries. I have to go into a meeting this afternoon with the men who are paying my salary and your fee for working on this particular project, and I have to be able to tell them either that the Lost Pines Resort development is completely within reach and on track, or that it is going to be prohibitively expense and they should pull the plug. Now which is it?"

"Emac, those are kind of extreme choices, aren't they?" Broarty said. "I mean, isn't there something in the middle?"

There was a brief pause before Egon McMenamin replied, "You want option number three, Mr. Broarty? Here it is: that Resort Partners severs its contract with Crane immediately and sues to recoup the moneys already allotted, and then hires another inspection firm that understands what's at stake and knows what the hell they're doing."

Shit! Broarty had glanced at the photos Hayden had sent but had not studied them. Frankly, he was hoping to stay out of this altogether, except to sign his name on the cover letter of Hayden's report.

"I'm sorry, Marc," Emac was saying, "but I didn't hear your reply."

Broarty coughed. "Actually, Hayden is supposed to be in the office first thing tomorrow mor—"

"Jesus, Marc, who's in charge down there? Hayden or you?"

"What do you want? Do you want me to sign off on the buildings as they stand?"

"What I want is for you to tell me whether our goal of rehabilitating the existing town is doable. If you sincerely believe it is not, Marc, based on your expertise, then for Christ's sake tell me. I'd be disappointed, as would the board, but I would accept it. I would, however, hate to find out later that it was a judgment based on faulty information, just like I would hate to offer a good report to the board and then find out that's not true either."

Broarty's head was spinning. Jack had emailed something

to him, presumably photos of the place, but he had not actually looked at them yet. *Hayden's the one who should be dealing with this.* But Jack was not back, and the decision, like it or not, was his to make. "First, Emac, I want you to understand that I have not personally been to the site. I do, however, trust Jack Hayden's judgment implicitly, and based upon the very sketchy details he has sent down, prior to his arrival back at the office and the filing of his report, I think you should be able to reach your goal."

"So that means I can go to the board and assure them that based on your inspection the plans to rehabilitate the structures in the town are both sound and cost effective."

Marcus Broarty closed his eyes and said: "Yes."

"That's all I wanted to know, Marc," Emac said, his voice suddenly cheerful. "That wasn't so hard, was it? Send along that full report as soon as you can."

"You can be sure of it."

After a few lame pleasantries, the two men hung up. Broarty replaced the receiver with one hand mopped his brow with the other. Then he turned to his computer and pulled up the emailed photos Hayden had sent him, this time really studying them. By the third one, Marcus Broarty's stomach felt like a chunk of dry ice had lodged in it. Picture after picture showed ruins of buildings and still-standing structures far beyond redemption, except for the city hall structure. Christ, what was he going to do now? He could hardly call Emac back and tell him that he had bluffed his way to a decision that turned out to be the wrong one.

There was only one thing to do.

Broarty pulled up the file on his computer to which he had saved the images and, one by one, began deleting them, sight unseen, as though he had never gotten them. When he was finished, he would go back in and delete Jack's email as well. This would be his story: he had talked to Jack, but had never received his photos. As for Hayden's verbal communication to him, well, verbal communication wasn't worth the paper it was written on. Besides, what was the last thing that Jack said? That he was going to investigate further and hopefully find something more encouraging? The word *encouraging* was good enough for Broarty.

If the shit really did hit the fan, though, there was always the fact that Jack, if office parties were any indication, was a drinker, so his judgment could be impeached.

You mean you sent a drunk out to do the inspection? Broarty could hear Emac's snap.

Of course I knew about Jack's problem, he'd reply, *but his work in the past, before his drinking got out of control, had always been professional, and, well, I believe in giving people every chance possible. That's just the kind of manager I am. But of course, in light of this situation, he will be fired immediately.*

Whatever Jack might say in protest would have to be taken against Broarty's own word; the testimony of a goddamned drunk versus that of an MBA.

He was starting to feel better as he continued eradicating his system of the photos, finally coming to the last one. On a whim, this one he opened, and was surprised to see the face of a woman, turned out so that she appeared to be facing him directly, looking straight into his eyes, if not his soul. She appeared to smile at him. *Goddamn Hayden!* Broarty thought, grinning at his computer screen, *he emailed the wrong pictures in the first place!* Jack was supposed to be photographing buildings, not paintings, or whatever the hell this was. "Goodbye, my dear," Marc Broarty said softly, as he tapped the mouse to delete it, and in a flash, it was gone.

No more evidence.

Broarty sat back in his chair and took a deep breath. Things were going to work out, he felt confident of that. He had protected himself.

He was about to get up and go to the washroom to freshen up, when he looked back at his computer screen and noticed that the image of the painted woman was still there. "That's odd," he muttered. Perhaps Hayden had sent two shots of the painting and he had not noticed before now. Aligning his cursor to the corner of the image, he selected Delete and clicked again. Then his head snapped back.

Broarty sat looking at the empty screen for a few seconds, then chuckled. A digital glitch; that was all it was. When he keyed for the image to be deleted, some pixels shifted right before it disappeared.

How else could he explain the illusion that the woman in the painting had just winked at him?

CHAPTER FIVE

"Daddeeeee!" Robynn squealed when Jack walked in the door. She ran and launched herself into his waiting arms. "I missed you I missed you I missed you!"

"I missed you too, punkin," Jack said, hugging her tightly. Glancing over at their nanny, he added: "Hi, Nola, how's everything going?"

Nola Gutiérrez answered by rolling her eyes. "Can I talk to you, Mr. Jack?" she asked.

"Sure. Just hold on a second."

Once Jack was able to peel himself away from Robynn, he took Nola into the kitchen. "What's wrong?" he asked. "Is it something with Robynn?"

"No, no, not with him," she said in heavily accented English. It always amused Jack that Nola confused her gender pronouns. "Daniel was sent home from school again." Daniel, Nola's son, had just started middle school and was not having an easy time of it. He had been sent down to the principal at least once a week over the past month, usually for fighting. Jack had seen Daniel enough to know that he was not a bad kid, but like so many others he was dealing with pressures coming in from all sides, while living in a neighborhood that was heavily gang-influenced. Nola was a strong woman and was handling it the best she could, but Jack knew she had her hands full with the boy, particularly since she had to devote so much of her time and attention to Robynn. "I'd like to go home now, if that's all right."

Normally, Nola did not leave until Elley arrived home, even if Jack was already there, but today he said: "Go on ahead. Robynn and I will be fine here. I hope everything is okay."

"*Gracias.*" Nola grabbed her purse and headed out as Robynn pulled Jack back into the dining room and showed him a drawing she had made that morning. It depicted her in the middle holding the hands of two big stick people, standing out in a field next to a house, under a bright yellow sun. Jack easily recognized himself—Robynn always used an orange ochre color crayon to color his light chestnut hair—while the other figure's dark hair and enormous red lips signified Elley. Jack was always amused by the way his daughter managed to make her mother look like The Joker. Robynn's own self-portrait was all eyes and hair and teeth and a line under her nose representing her scar. The three stick people walked happily in the sunshine with huge smiles on their face.

If it could only be like this. "This is beautiful, punkin, can I keep it?"

"Mm-hmmm."

Once she had started in on another drawing and was working on it intently, Jack snuck away and called in to the office. At the other end of the line Jonelle, the receptionist, flipped through his messages for the last couple of days. None were terribly important, so Jack asked her to hold them until he came in tomorrow. "Does Mr. Broarty need to ask me anything?"

"Let me check," Jonelle replied, and transferred the call to Yolanda Valdera, who greeted him warmly and then said: "I don't know if Mr. B. needs you or not. He's had the door closed most of the day. I know that Emac called earlier."

"Do you know what he wanted?"

"Not a clue, but right after the call was when the door closed."

"Oh." Jack could not decide if that boded well or ill. Marcus might have worked up the balls to tell Emac that Wood City was a disaster zone, and if so, he was probably basking in his new-found authority. Or he might have been browbeaten by Emac for something or other and went into hiding, should anyone else call. "I guess we'll find out tomorrow," Jack said. "I'll be in early." He hung up and went to the kitchen and grabbed a Sam Adams from the fridge. It was 4:39...close enough to five-thirty. Then Jack retrieved his laptop, which was still by the front door, and carried it into the dining room, setting it up on the other end of the table Robynn was using to draw. He winked at her when she looked up. Powering up, he then pulled his microcassette out of his pocket, plugged in the earpiece, and played his notes back, transcribing them on the screen, minus the bits of commentary that were nobody else's business. A slow typist, Jack had to rewind and play back certain parts over and over again, but two beers later, he was finished. He would put the notes on CD and take it into the office to finish his report there. Before powering the laptop down again he made sure that he also had copies of the pictures on the CD.

It was nearly seven by the time Elley got home, and by that time there were five empties lined up near the sink. "Looks like I missed the party," she said, glaring at them.

"Hi, Mommy!" Robynn called, racing into the kitchen, her new drawing in hand.

"Hi, sweetie. This is a lovely picture, Robynn. Now go in the other room, okay? I need to talk to Daddy."

Jack Hayden had never felt so busted in his life. It was not simply the beers, though they were bad enough when he was supposed to be watching Robynn. But he harbored an irrational fear that Elley had somehow found out about Dani, and what they had done up in San Simeon...and done, and done, and *done*...until Little Jack had throbbed like it he'd stuck it in a hornet's nest. Maybe he had. As soon as Robynn was gone, he said: "Look, if it's about the empties—"

"I have to go to New York for several days," Elley interrupted. "I have to leave tomorrow."

"That's a bit sudden, don't you think?"

"It doesn't thrill me to the marrow either, but we've just landed a big new account and the company is based in Manhattan, so we're throwing a kind of welcome party for them. I've been working on it all day."

"Shouldn't they be throwing the welcome party for you?"

"They're paying for it. I'm not sure they realize that yet, but the cost of the party comes straight out of the fee they're paying us. It's our way of showing what we can do for a new client, impress them with a dog and pony show."

"How long will you be there?"

"The event's on Friday, so we've got a few days to make the final arrangements and set everything up, and then I'll have to stay the weekend, maybe even into next week, to meet with all of the executives."

"You the only one going?"

"Of course not. Blaise is coming as well."

Jack looked at his wife. He had no proof that his wife was servicing Blaise Micelli, the founder of Orbit Marketing, but the thought had occurred to him quite regularly ever since that incident at Orbit's office Christmas party last year, when Micelli had spilled a drink on his lap and mopped it up with a napkin, which picked up traces of bright red lipstick—Elley's shade—from his zipper area.

"You'll have no trouble taking care of Robynn while I'm gone, I presume?" Elley was saying.

"Why would I have trouble?"

Elley examined the five dead Sams by the sink, then gathered them all up, walked to the trashcan, and loudly dropped them in. "I can't imagine."

"All right, all right."

"No, it's not all right, Jack. I come home from a grueling day at the office followed by a miserable drive from Santa Monica to find you alone with our daughter, having consumed the better part of a six-pack. What proof can you give me that it won't be a six-pack and a half tomorrow night, and even more while I'm gone? And where the hell is Nola, anyway? She's supposed to be here."

"Daniel's in trouble again, so she had to go. And I'm sorry, really. I had a grueling day, too, and I just lost count. I'll be good while you're gone, promise. Is my word good anymore?"

Elley couldn't hide her surprise at his rolling over so quickly and easily. "I'd like it to be," she said, then: "Yeah, it's good."

He approached her and took her in his arms. "You know I'd never deliberately to anything that would hurt Robynn, or you."

"I know that," she said, hugging back. "It's the accidental things I worry about."

That makes two of us, he thought.

"Mommeeee," Robynn called from the other room, "can I come back in yet?"

"Of course, sweetie," Elley called back, pulling away from Jack as the girl rushed in to excitedly tell her that she had learned a new word from Nola today: *basura*.

"*Basura*, doesn't that mean 'trash?'"

"Mm hmmm. She was taking out the garbage when she said it. What's for dinner?"

"Robynn, Mommy just got home. I was sort of hoping maybe Daddy would have fixed something, because Mommy's got to pack tonight to go away tomorrow."

"Why do you have to go away?" the girl whimpered.

"It's Mommy's work, sweetie. Sometimes I have to go."

"Sounds like a take-out night to me," Jack said, feeling a rush of guilt over sitting and drinking and pretending to work and not even thinking about providing dinner. "What'll it be? Pizza? Chinese? Frog salad?"

"Yuuuuck!" Robynn cried, giggling.

"I'm not in the mood for Chinese and I don't want the calories of pizza," Elley said. "There's a new fish place down on San Vicente. I drive by it nearly every day. I think the sign says they do take-out."

"Do you remember the name?"

"Seafood something. Seafood Hut, Seafood Crate, I don't know."

"I'll find out," Jack said, scurrying back to his laptop, linking onto the web and putting in a search for *Seafood West. L.A. San Vicente*. Three choices popped up (including, for some reason,

Amazon.com), but only one seemed like the candidate. "Could it be Seafood Shanty?"

"Yes, that's it," Elley said. Using the number he found online, Jack called in an order for the three of them: fish and chips for Robynn, salmon for Elley and sea bass for himself.

"Do they deliver?" Elley asked

"Yeah, but I'll go pick it up," Jack replied. "It will get here quicker that way." The truth was, he wanted to get away and on his own, if even for a few minutes.

"Why don't you take Robynn with you? I have to start packing, and she'd only get in the way."

Jack sighed. *She's your child, too, for Christ's sake*, he wanted to shout back, but didn't. Instead he turned to Robynn and said, "Hey, punkin, want to go catch some fish?"

Her face lit up? "Really? Like on a lake?"

"No, from a restaurant. But I'll bet they have a lobster tank there." *Wouldn't it be fine if the place had a bar, too? He could grab a quick one. Just one more would be okay.*

"Okay!" Robynn cried.

Jack scooped up his daughter and carried her out to the driveway. "Let's take Mom's car," he said, opening the back door of Elley's silver Lexus to let Robynn in, and carefully buckling her in the car seat that lived there. Only when he was behind the wheel and sticking his key in the ignition did Jack Hayden begin to feel something of the five beers. He was not buzzed, exactly; rather it was a sensation he usually enjoyed that he could only describe as *comfy*. While he felt perfectly aware and in control—it took more than five for him to start to wobble—he wondered if he might be over the legal limit. Then again, who would know as long as he gave them no reason to suspect? "I'll drive carefully," he muttered aloud, starting to back out of the driveway.

"What, Daddy?"

"I said, 'Here we go.'"

"Didn't sound like it."

"I was speaking another language, punkin, the language of

Dad."

"Oh. I don't know that one 'cause I'm a girl."

Jack smiled. "You're the best girl." he said, wondering if there wasn't some way he could wrap up all the *basura* in his life, take it out and dump it in a can, where it would be picked up and taken away.

They had gone only two blocks before Jack's confidence suffered a serious challenge: a black-and-white police cruiser was coming toward him. He slowed down, giving the policemen no reason to watch him or follow him, and he made certain that the Lexus came to a complete stop at the stop sign. He even counted to five before starting through the intersection. The police cruiser passed through as well without slowing. But once it was behind Jack, he heard the siren blare on and saw in his rearview mirror the flashing lights as the cop car made a fast U-turn and charged up behind him.

"Shit!"

"Hmm?"

"Nothing, punkin." Jack's stomach dropping as he pulled over to the curb. *Just fucking swell*, he thought, bitterly, *pulled over, probable DUI made worse by the fact that there's a child in the car.* If he had to call Elley from the police station, she would probably come down to retrieve Robynn and then leave him there to die. But to Jack's tangible relief, the police car did not pull up behind him. It did not stop at all, or even slow. Instead it sped past him, apparently responding to a call that had nothing to do with him or his good buddy Sam Adams. He was guilty of nothing more than being a good citizen and pulling over to let the cop car zoom past on its way to an emergency. "Fuck me," Jack exhaled.

"What, Daddy?"

"Nothing, Robynn."

"You're talking a lot of Dad stuff tonight."

"Sorry. I'll try to talk punkin from now on."

"Where was that policeman going?"

"Off to catch a criminal, I guess. We just had to get out of his way so he could go." Jack pulled the Lexus away from the curb knowing he had been spared by whatever cosmic court bothered to look down his way, but not knowing whether he deserved the pass. But having been spared, he would not temp fate further by having another one at the restaurant while waiting for the food.

That became moot since the Seafood Shanty—a dreadful name for a fairly upscale fish market and grill—did not have a bar. It was, however, packed with customers. As he had figured, Robynn was captivated by the lobsters in the slightly scummy water tank, their claws bound with rubber bands so that they would not fight. It was not a consideration for the safety of the animals, which were, after all, about to become dinner, but so that they did not mar or damage any of their succulent meat. Jack had never quite gotten used to the idea of popping a living thing, even one so ugly, into a vat of boiling water and letting it scald to death in the name of fine dining.

While waiting for his order, drinking in the enticing aromas circling around him, Jack tuned in and out of various conversations in the waiting area. Most of it was static, but one thing cut through the buzz: the word *split-face*. Turning around into the direction of the word, Jack spotted an older couple sitting on a bench and waiting for a table. The woman was at least seventy, badly made up, and speaking with the kind of clarion voice that indicated she was partially deaf. The man sitting with her was of equal age and appeared bored to tears. "I said, she'd be such a cute little thing if not for that hideous scar on her mouth," the woman was shouting to him. "Looks like someone took a tomahawk to her." Jack quickly glanced over at Robynn, who was still studying the lobsters, and he was relieved to see that she had apparently not heard the comment.

He looked back at the couple. Blood pulsed and pounded in his ears. He had taken a step toward her to confront her callousness head on when he heard his name being called. His order was ready. Collecting Robynn, Jack went to the register and paid, then picked up the bag of hot food and started to leave. But at the door he stopped. "Hang on a second, punkin, there's something I've got to do," he told Robynn. "I'll be right back." He walked to the table with the old couple and interrupted the woman mid-sentence. "Excuse me, lady," Jack began, "but I heard what you said about my beautiful daughter."

The woman looked startled. "What?" she said.

"Now you can listen to what I say. I read somewhere that three-thousand people each year die from choking on fish bones. I'm hoping that you'll make it three-thousand-and-one, you miserable dried-up cunt."

Even as it came out of his mouth, Jack could not believe what he had said.

The woman's face dropped in total shock. "You...why... Harold!" she screamed at her husband. "Are you going to sit there and let this animal talk to me like that?"

Jack looked over at Harold and thought the old man was trying to stifle a grin.

"Where's the manager?" she hollered, and Jack took that as an opportunity to head for the door. He had delivered his message, quite more forcefully than he had really intended to. Rushing back to Robynn, he took her hand and ran out to the car.

Driving back, Jack felt a rush of conflicting emotions: exhilaration at having actually taken a stand and shut the old cow up, but guilt at having done it so rudely. Mingling with those was something else: a touch of fear. His level of vituperation had shocked even him; where had it come from? Residual anger at Marcus Broarty? Or could he excuse it away by claiming that while it had been Jack Hayden speaking, the lines had been written by Sam Adams?

Ten minutes later Jack pulled the Lexus into the driveway, and then reached back and unbuckled Robynn, letting her slide out of the seat herself like a big girl. Grabbing the bag of food, he marched into the house, calling "Dinner!" upon entering. He set the bag down on the dining room table, which sat at the center of the pristine, white-walled dining room. Elley was on the other end of the table, standing like a statue. "Got your salmon," Jack said.

"There was a phone call for you while you were gone," she replied, frostily.

"Not Marc Broarty, I hope."

"It was someone named Danica Lindstrom."

"Oh...um, what did she say?"

Elley stared at him for a moment. "Not as much as the expression on your face."

"Look, Elley—"

"I have to go pack. I'll eat later." She spun around and headed up the staircase, disappearing into their bedroom, whose door closed with a resounding slam.

Jack sighed.

"I'm hungry, Daddy."

Turning, he looked at his daughter, whose warm brown eyes were opened wide like those of a cartoon character. "I'm hungry too. Let's eat."

Getting plates from the kitchen, he set them down on the table and started unpacking the food bag, setting out the Styrofoam container holding Robynn's fish and chips in front of her, and putting his containing the grilled sea bass next to it, holding it carefully so as not to let any of the dark juice drip onto the snowy tablecloth.

"Isn't Mommy coming?" Robynn asked.

"Mommy's busy right now, she'll be down later. But let's you and I eat."

"Mommy's busy a lot."

"I know."

Jack scooped the fish and rice onto his plate and took a bite. It was excellent, but he was not really able to enjoy it. He had given Dani his cell and home numbers before leaving San Simeon, and gave her permission to call him if she discovered anything about the mural, but he had not expected her to do it so soon. If he hadn't been so anxious to get out of the house, he might have intercepted the call, and pretended it was Yolanda. If he hadn't been so intent on taking the time to insult the old bag at the restaurant he might have even made it back in time to catch it before Elley did. Earlier, if he hadn't been so involved in making his notes and drinking his beers, he might have given some thought to dinner ahead of time. If he had only given Dani his cell number, this would not have happened at all.

If, if, if, if, if, if.

Well, he would talk to Elley. He'd have to. The noose he had managed to tie around his neck could not be totally undone, but maybe it was possible to slacken it up a little, just enough to breathe.

He got up and went to the fridge and pulled out the one remaining Sam Adams from the six-pack. *Fucking bitch*! he thought furiously, walking back to the table, no longer certain at whom he was directing his rage.

CHAPTER SIX

God, what an idiot she had been for not simply hanging up when Jack didn't answer himself. His wife had not said anything overtly accusatory to her, but the frost level in her voice fully communicated that she did not believe for a nanosecond Dani was innocently helping Jack out with a work project. While there was no denying that his wife would be justified in feeling so had she known that Dani had climaxed more times with Jack in one day than she had with Perry in the last six months of their marriage, Dani had said nothing to indicate what they had done.

Had Jack confessed? Dani doubted it. Had he done so, his wife would have gotten screaming hysterics from his wife instead of icy condescension. From now on she would avoid calling him at home.

What she had intended to tell Jack, had she gotten him on the phone, was information she had gleaned from spending the day in Glenowen, which proved to be a charming, historic village whose local industries were arts, crafts and antiques. In the course of rambling through the town's century-old-or-better business district she had stopped into a tiny bookshop which featured locally written and published works. One of them was a book of ghost stories from the Central Coast area. The back cover had promised more in the way of local folklore than things bumping in the night, but Dani bought a copy anyway and took it back to the motel, where she started to read it while sipping a mimosa in the Pines bar.

Even though Dani had not been looking for anything in

particular, she quickly found something pertinent: a section on Wood City. It failed to provide any sources for the information, which meant it was probably a combination of old folk tales with a few newspaper articles thrown in for the illusion of veracity, but actually having visited Wood City, accepting the conclusions made by the author of the book did not take a great stretch.

CURSED GHOST TOWN IN THE PINES

Deep in the forest at the base of the Santa Lucia Mountain Range in between Glenowen and San Simeon lies the deserted ghost town of Wood City. It was originally designed and built in the 1930s by industrialist Henry J. Breen as the place where the workers of his intended lumber mill, which was to be located nearby, would live. Newspapers of the time proclaimed that Wood City would be an idyllic village, but old timers who remember the town say it looked more like a work camp. Some claimed it was the concept of a company store taken to the extremes: an entire company village.

But that isn't reason the Depression-era town has spawned a legend all its own. Even before it opened for business, Wood City was said to be cursed. Many thought it was because Breen himself collapsed and died right in the center of town just before it was completed, and that his spirit remained to haunt the place. More rational people of course simply claim that Breen's sudden death, combined with his unwise business decision to build the town before the mill that would support its residents, doomed the entire venture. Some have even said that the town was destined to fail from the very start, since Breen seems to have chosen the location for his mill more from a standpoint of nettling his neighbor, rival tycoon William Randolph

Hearst, whom Breen hated, rather than the belief that the forests of the Central Coast were prime for such a venture. Ego wars among the rich are not recent inventions.

None of that, however, can explain the reports of disappearances amongst the citizens of Wood City. Entire families were said to have simply vanished. Many have argued that these disappearances were for perfectly sound reasons. There was, after all, little reason for anyone to stay in the town once it became clear that the lumber mill would never actually be constructed. But because of its strange history, over the years the story of Wood City has taken on a legendary aspect, similar to the mysteries of the disappearances of the Virginia colonists from Roanoke Island or the abandoned "ghost ship" the Mary Celeste.

Whatever the truth of the situation, within a few years of Breen's death Wood City was nothing more than a memory. Ruins of the old town still exist, and over the decades there have been many reports from hikers and travelers through the area of having been overcome by strange, foreboding feelings.

That last part had caused Dani to shiver. Even now she could feel the uninviting aura of the place, the sense of grimness that permeated it like an old, bad memory, which could not be explained simply by way of its desolate location. It was something else, an aura that hung over the site like a cloud. And it had clung to her.

She had felt that sense of abandon, the sudden conviction that nothing else mattered except satisfying her basest urges, right before she had jumped on Jack Hayden in his truck and rode him like a mechanical bull. It was still lingering within her when they continued to make love at the motel. It did not abate until hours later, after she had actually considered picking up another man in the bar and taking him back to her room.

When the feeling had finally gone away, she had reacted not so much with a feeling of guilt, but of shock. It was not like her to be a sexual predator, or even sexually aggressive, and hard as she had tried, Dani could not explain away the feeling of being driven by some outside force to act in a way that was not natural for her as either the acknowledgement of her newfound unmarried freedom or as some kind of oncoming middle-aged itch (and actuarial statistics aside, she did not think of herself as entering middle-age). It was literally like she had just awakened from a dark dream, one that was pleasurable, certainly, but one that was also disturbing.

The Devil made me do it. That used to be the catch phrase from some old television comedian. Then the Devil went away again, leaving her with a swirling storm of contradictory emotions: a strange kind of shame for pouncing on a man she had only just met, offset by the desire to see him again, mingled with worry over having complicated his marriage and home life.

But there in Jack Hayden's pickup truck in the woods, she at once knew what it felt like to want to be a bad girl, the kind of girl so bad that at the moment of orgasm she had a sudden, horrible urge to take her two thumbs and push them as far as she could into Jack's eyes, shove them inward until her fingernails went up into his brain.

And some small part of her enjoyed the feeling.

Dani Lindstrom shuddered. She desperately wanted to talk to Jack. She desperately wanted to learn if had felt the same sort of dark shadow steal into his soul up there at Wood City.

Or was she having some kind of breakdown?

CHAPTER SEVEN

"You told him *what*?" Jack Hayden shouted, sitting in Marcus Broarty's office. Ordinarily he would not have taken such a liberty as screaming in his boss's face. But after a largely sleepless night resulting from Elley's having literally locked him out of the bedroom, followed by her leaving early this morning without so much as a word, just a good deal of slamming and thumping, he was not in a good state of mind.

"Jack, I just relayed what you told me," Broarty responded, looking like a finalist in the Mr. Guileless competition.

"What I told you, Marc, was the place was a near total loss!"

"You used the word 'encouraging,' and I'm quoting you, Jack."

"Maybe I did, Marc, but I used a lot of other words around it, and they add up to the fact that there's nothing there. Didn't you even look at those pictures I emailed you?"

"What pictures?"

"Don't tell me you didn't get the pictures."

"I believe that is what I am telling you, Jack."

"Okay, okay, fine. Even without them, how could you ignore my telling you the place was a disaster area?"

"I don't remember hearing you say that."

"Maybe not verbatim, but—"

"Oh, so now I have to interpret what you really mean instead of what you say?" There was a hint of a triumphant smile on Broarty's face.

"Oh, fuck off, you fat asshole!"

"What...did...you...say?"

Hayden looked at his boss, feeling his own face starting to redden. As with that crass old bat at the restaurant the night before, he had not intended to say what he really felt, and certainly not so vehemently, but it had come out anyway. God, he must be more tired and upset than he thought. "I'm sorry, Marc, that was way out of line. Totally. I'm a little ragged this morning. I slept on the couch last night. I apologize for my rude, unconscionable behavior."

"Accepted," Broarty said in an uncertain tone. "I just hope you know what to say to Emac, after he's gone and told his board that the project is completely doable."

Jack exhaled slowly, attempting to maintain what little control he had left. "Look, I know you got my phone call because I remember talking to you. And I remember what I said to you. So please tell me how you came to the conclusion that the place was in usable condition."

Broarty leapt up from his chair and leaned over his desk, as much as his 44-inch waist would allow. "Okay, mister, I'll tell you. You think I do nothing around here. You think I'm a total shithead, don't you? What were your words? A fat asshole?"

Jack said nothing in contradiction, just continued looking at him.

"Well my contribution to this place is keeping the goddamned doors open. Emac was about to pull the contract on us unless I saw reason. Is that what you would rather have happen? A big, juicy, lucrative contract with a deep pockets corporation just yanked out from under us, and the news spread around the industry that we had failed in our responsibility to Resort Partners, which would serve to drive other prospective customers away? Is that what you really wanted to happen, Jack?"

"Marc, our responsibility to Resort Partners, the job for which we are getting paid, is to give them an honest evaluation of a parcel of land, pure and simple. Apparently we've already failed in that."

"Goddammit, Hayden, you are not getting it! The lights in

here are still on, thanks to me. Not you, *me!* We still *have* the contract with Resort Partners. We'll *find* something to tell them. We'll *find* a way to get around this. We still have time to do that. Had I told him the truth, that would have been the end right there. Why can't you be enough of a team player to acknowledge that?"

Jack exhaled loudly again. "Okay, Marc, what do you want me to do?"

"Those pictures you took, you still have them, right?"

"The original ones, the ones I sent you, or tried to, no. I don't know what the hell happened, but they disappeared."

"Ahaaaaa," Broarty said accusingly.

"But I went back and took more. Those I still have."

"Good, that's good. The ones you sent me...tried to send me...are gone, so we're clear. And the new ones...those we'll doctor in Photoshop."

Jack stared at Broarty's fat, jowly face. "Please tell me you're joking."

"Do I look like I'm joking?"

"You're proposing we commit fraud?"

"Bullshit. This isn't fraud, just a little cosmetic surgery."

"What happens when they see the site for themselves, Marc? I mean, at some point they're going to have to visit the place in person."

"We'll worry about that later."

"I won't do it, Marc," Jack said, rising and heading for the door. "Sorry, but I draw the line here. I won't falsify the photos."

"You know, Jack," Broarty said, "even though I have personally accepted your apology for your outburst with no hard feelings, I'm afraid it will have to go into your personnel file, which will strongly reflect on your next performance review. However, a little cooperation from you might convince me to just forget the incident altogether. Now get me the goddamned pictures."

"Fine, I'll give you the pictures. That's the reason I went up there, after all. But don't make me Photoshop them."

"Since I need the job done correctly and *soberly*, I won't."

Jack Hayden said nothing. He merely stared open-mouthed at Broarty's smirking face, then left the office, walking past Yolanda without so much as a glance, and went back to his own office. He had only been there a few seconds when his phone rang. It was Yolanda.

"What happened back there?" she asked. "You looked like you were walking to the executioner."

"Good day for a hanging, don't you think?"

"Jack, Mr. B. wanted me to remind you to submit your written report along with the pictures he asked for."

"Right," Jack said, hanging up. He was halfway through typing out his report when he realized something: if Broarty was so crooked as to fake the photos for Emac's benefit, what was to stop him for altering the report to match it? Then when Resort Partners finally found out they were sinking money into a wasteland, someone was going to have to take the fall for the debacle, and Jack strongly doubted it would be Broarty. He could argue that his report had been altered, and it would be his word against Marcus's. He could refuse to file the report at all and risk termination, particularly after his stunning performance earlier this morning. He could contact Emac over Marc's head and tell him the truth about Wood City, and run the risk of exposing the company to exactly the kinds of legal action and attention that Marc viewed with terror.

No matter which direction he looked, he was screwed.

Only one direction held any appeal: the one that led from his office to The Tap House, a brewpub three blocks away which, unbeknownst to Elley, he frequented at lunch hours (always paying cash for his burgers and beers, so as not to have them appear on the Visa bills). It was only a quarter to ten, and he was not even sure the place was open yet, but he would like to find out. Maybe leaving this job and heading for the pub was the answer. Maybe telling Marcus Broarty what he could do with his fat self was exactly what he needed at this point in his life. Crane wasn't the only building inspection company in the greater L.A. area. There were others, many others, and finding another job shouldn't be too hard, even in this economy. Or maybe it was time to chuck the whole inspection game altogether and go do something else. What was stopping him from walking out on both Broarty and Elley, and restarting his life?

Robynn, that's what.

Her face popped into his mind, and even though he wanted a beer now more than ever, he knew he could not run away and get one. No matter what, he had to stay put. He had to do it for Robynn.

Jack's cell phone rang and half expected it to be Elley calling from the airport, giving him an ultimatum, but he was surprised.

"Hi, Jack," said Dani's voice. "I hope this isn't a bad time to call."

"No, no, it's fine," he said, going over to shut his office door. "In fact, given the day I've had so far, hearing from you is quite welcome. What's up?"

"I wanted to apologize if my calling your house last night got you in trouble. Your wife seemed a little annoyed."

"Annoyance is the only human emotion Elley expresses these days."

"God, I'm sorry."

"It's okay. I was already in the doghouse before you called. The worst part was that my daughter picked up that something was wrong and she fell into a snit. She was kind of a mess this morning when I dropped her off at school."

"Did you tell Elley about us?"

"No. You didn't, did you?"

"No, of course not." There was a long pause before Dani said, "Jack, how do you feel about what we did?"

"I don't know. If you're asking me did I enjoy it, hell yes. If you're asking did it make me feel like I was alive for the first time in quite a while, again yes. If you're asking am I proud of it, then no. If you're asking if I'm ashamed of myself, I really don't know."

"I guess I'm asking if it was worth it. I mean, was it worth risking losing your family."

"My daughter, no," he said quickly. "Nothing is worth risking that. As for Elley, well, I think it's only a matter of time. Maybe I've been in some kind of denial about that and meeting you was the catalyst I needed to finally accept the truth."

"Jack, what I really want to ask is...this might sound a little crazy...but when we were having sex, particularly the first time in the truck, did you feel like it was really you? Or did you feel like you were somebody else?"

"I think I'm ready to be somebody else for a while, Dani. Being me isn't exactly paying dividends."

He didn't feel it, Dani thought, *he didn't feel that sense of wrongness. Maybe there was nothing to feel.* She changed the subject then and started to tell him what she had learned from the folklore book, and Jack telling her the stunt that his boss was about to pull on their client. Then his intercom buzzed. "Uh oh, that's trouble calling. Can you hold on a second?" Jack jabbed the intercom button and said, "Yeah, Yoli, what's he want now?"

"He's still waiting for the Wood City pictures."

"Right. I'll send them right now." Hanging up on Yoli, he told Dani: "I have to go, but call me again, just make it on the cell, okay?"

"And you have my number, right?"

"It's displayed, I'll write it down. Bye, Dani." Jack hung up, and after a brief but dangerous pang of loneliness, he pulled out his laptop out of its carrying case and powered it up, then went to his picture file. He found photos of a job site from the week before, an abandoned warehouse in Torrance, and there were a few personal shots he had taken of Robynn playing in the backyard, but the photos of Wood City were nowhere to be found. "Aw, *no!*" he cried, launching a general search through his entire system, which came up empty.

How could this happen *twice*? There had to be a problem with the camera.

Jack was about to call Yolanda, but decided that news like this might have to be delivered personally. Trying to ignore the cold feeling in the pit of his stomach, he got up and walked to Broarty's office, telling Yolanda on the way that he had to see him. Jack was told to wait, a move he interpreted as one of Broarty's patented "power-pauses"—the attempt to put the other person on their guard by making them cool their heels before deigning to see or speak with them. But if it had been Broarty's intention to put him in his place, this time it had backfired, because Jack used the next four minutes to formulate an idea, one that might solve several problems all at once.

The intercom on Yolanda's desk rang, and she picked it up, then announced that Jack could go in.

"Pictures, Jack, pictures," Broarty said as he entered the large corner office.

"Marc, I don't know what in hell I did," Jack began, "but I can't find any of the second group of pictures that I took of the place, either. The first ones I emailed to you from the motel, but those didn't arrive, and then they disappeared. The new set I took have disappeared too. I don't know what the hell's wrong with my machine."

"No pictures?"

"Sorry, Marc, no pictures."

"That was money well spent, sending you up there," Broarty sneered.

"I know, and I'm sorry. But look at it this way: now you don't have to Photoshop anything, because they don't exist."

"You may have a point. But we have to tell Emac something."

"I know, so tell him the god's honest truth, that I screwed the pooch on this one. Tell him I'm going right back up there to take more pictures. Maybe the lighting will be better this time. I'll take two cameras, my digital and a camcorder, so that if anything goes wrong this time we've got a video backup."

"Great. Now tell me how I'm supposed to convince Emac to fund a return trip, because I'm not paying for it, Jack. This is not going to come out of our profit."

"I'll pay for it myself."

"You will?"

"I'm the one who screwed up here, so I'll make good on it. I'll leave as soon as I clear up a few things on my desk, and I can be up there by late afternoon. I'll pay for the gas, the motel room, everything."

"Let me think about it."

"No time, Marc. If I'm going back I have to do it now. This is the only solution, as far as I can see. Even if you want to take me off the job, you've got to send someone up there, right? If you send someone else, it will cost you or Emac. If you take another chance on me, it's at no cost to you. I'm on my own dime."

Marcus Broarty looked deep in thought, or as close as he could come, then said: "No, screw it."

Shit! "Marc, eventually we've got to show Resort Partners something, don't we?"

"Why offer proof the place is a wasteland? That is what you said, right? That there was nothing up there? By not having pictures we buy more time to figure out what to tell them later."

"Can I make a confession, Marc?" Jack asked. "I've been in kind of a bum mood lately."

"No shit."

"I don't know whether you fall into bum moods or not, but sometimes you look at things and everything on the outside looks just as bad as they do on the inside. Maybe when I was looking around Wood City, I was seeing things through my bad mood, making everything look worse than it really was. Maybe I need to go back and look at the place again with fresh eyes. I think I owe it to the project to take a second look, don't you?"

"Frankly, Jack, it sounds to me like a waste of time."

Why was Broarty being so dismissive of the idea? It would not cost Crane Commercial Building Engineering a penny, and Jack's time was not an issue, since Broarty had freed up his schedule so he could devote the entire week to Wood City. What difference could it possibly make to his boss if he went back up the coast? Surely Broarty could not detect the ulterior motive that Jack was harboring. He was not that insightful or clever. There had to be some other reason.

Jack had one card left to play. "Okay, Marc, you're in charge," Jack said. "So I guess it's up to you to call Emac and tell him that Crane is breaching its contract and that Resort Partners should find another firm."

"What the hell are you talking about?" Broarty shot back.

"Well, look, what if Emac finds out that I was willing to bend over backwards to make up for an error in judgment and some slipshod follow-through, and you wouldn't allow me to?"

"You're up to something."

Oh, if only you knew. "I just don't like making mistakes, particularly big ones. It bothers me, so I try to do whatever I can to rectify the screw-ups. God's honest truth."

After a moment of silence, Broarty said: "I'll have to think about it. Now go away."

Jack left, his mind already made up. Broarty could think about it all he wanted. Jack would not be there to hear the decision. He would be home throwing some clothes into a suitcase, clothes for both him and Robynn. Then he'd call Nola and tell her that he would be taking Robynn on a trip and she would not be needed for several days—unexpected time off that she would likely find welcome—after which he would swing by Robynn's kindergarten class and pick her up, telling the teacher that it was an emergency and they would have to be gone for the rest of the week. The teacher, who was very young and not terribly sure of herself, would of course agree and hope that there was nothing seriously wrong, and Jack would assure her that they would be back as soon as possible. Then he and Robynn would drive up the coast, stay in San Simeon, and rendezvous with Dani, and live like a happy family...until he got caught.

And worrying about getting caught was tomorrow's problem.

CHAPTER EIGHT

Even when seated in first class, Elley Gorman Hayden hated flying. Over the years she had learned effective techniques for hiding her fear, but every time the plane banked to one side or took a sudden lurch or bounce, her heart leapt up into her throat and her hands broke out in a sweat. This trip had been particularly bad, with almost non-stop turbulence from the point they had reached cruising altitude. The turbulence wasn't that violent, but it was constant and unnerving. She turned to Blaise Micelli, her boss, and said: "I feel like a martini."

Blaise Micelli looked up from his *Adweek*. "Easy enough," he said. "I'll signal the flight attendant."

"No, Blaise, I being metaphoric. I don't *want* a martini, I *feel* like one. I feel like I've been shaken for the last two-and-a-half hours."

"What a coincidence," he said, grinning. "I feel like an olive on a long swizzle stick that's pretty eager to get dunked in a martini."

Elley grimaced back at him. Normally when he made juvenile comments, accompanied by that Tom Cruise smirk, she would raise an eyebrow and cock one side of her mouth upwards, and threaten to spank him. Today she could not even muster that. "I just want to rest a bit," she said, leaning the seat further back and closing her eyes, and absently fingering the tiny silver charms on the bracelet Jack had given her representing characters from *The Wizard of Oz*, which was her favorite film, one she completely identified with as a girl, stuck in a home life from which she desperately wanted to escape, complete with her own personal Wicked Witch in the form of her mother. It was time for her to stop lying to herself. Her sick feeling had started even before airplane began bouncing. It had come on in the limo on the way to the airport, a tiny burning ache in her chest that would not go away. At first she feared that she was starting to come down with something, but the longer she had the dull ache, the more she realized that it was like nothing she had ever felt. Maybe it was worry. Maybe she was actually worried about her marriage.

She knew Jack had been fucking up at work lately. That was easy to gauge: his increasingly vehement rants against Marcus Broarty implied that he had been incurring his boss's displeasure more frequently than usual. She had little reason to doubt that Broarty was a horse's ass, but he nevertheless represented authority at Jack's office, and respect for authority was not on her husband's asset sheet. Jack's saving grace had always been how he dealt with Robynn, but the sight of all those empties on the counter last night had sent sirens through her brain. If he was drinking that much around the child, then something was deeply wrong.

And then that phone call from a woman with a sexy voice.

Sure, it could have been taken at face value. Sure, the relationship between Jack and this woman could be completely innocent. Elvis could still be alive, too, and space aliens might have shot JFK.

But Elley knew bullshit, knew it by sight, sound, touch, smell, and, yes, taste. She sold it to thousands of idiots on silver plates every day of her life. That was her job. And with that phone call her bullshit detector hit the red zone.

She knew what was going on. The man who refused to do half the things she wanted him to do with her in bed had to go somewhere else to get what little gratification he needed. That explained everything else: the drinking, the argumentativeness, the trouble at the office. Explained it nicely, neatly, color-coded and with a slogan.

Elley felt a dry, warm weight on her fingers. It was Blaise's hand, casually sliding onto hers, so casually that anyone watching would simply have assumed they were a married couple. After all, they were both wearing wedding rings. "Please don't," she said, without opening her eyes. His hand slid back off.

Actually feeling hurt by Jack's infidelity threw conflict and confusion into her status quo existence. It was not as though she was guiltless. She and Blaise had been screwing around for a couple of years now, but in her mind, it was not an affair; certainly not a love affair. Blaise was conducting a love affair with himself, with which no woman could possibly compete. Her opening up for him was a business arrangement, nothing more. For a woman, sleeping with the boss was the modern equivalent of paying union dues: you did it to keep your job. And that was imperative since Jack was not making so much that she could jeopardize her employment. And now that he was clearly antagonizing his boss, she had to be particularly vigilant.

Hell, she doubted Jack had any idea it was going on. He was too attuned to his own problems, real, imagined, or bottled.

So then, why did she feel so shitty?

Maybe because her impractical, sometimes impossible, increasingly toasted, but basically decent husband meant more to her than she had stopped to consider for a long, long time.

Maybe because getting that phone call was like a sharp slap in the face.

Maybe because she didn't want to be a forty-year-old divorcee in a couple of years.

"Fuck," Elley uttered.

"Later, later," Blaise whispered.

Elley opened her eyes and looked at him. Blaise Micelli was good looking enough. He was a well-preserved forty-nine, vigorous and wielding that kind of in-born sexiness that you either have or you don't, no matter how your facial features are arranged. But looking at him, she could only think of him in the past tense.

Somehow, she would work things out with Jack. Somehow,

she had to.

The plane suddenly bucked and Elley groaned. "Could you get me a headset, please?" she asked.

"Sure." Blaise signaled for the flight attendant and got the cheap headset. "I hope whatever you're coming down with isn't going to impact our business." She was not sure which business he was referencing. As she plugged the headset into the plane's music channel she said: "I'm sorry, Blaise, I'll try to get it together for the meetings." Slipping it on, she closed her eyes again.

And damned if Jack's smiling face wasn't the first thing she saw out of the darkness.

* * * * * * *

"But how come Mommy's not going to be there?" Robynn asked her father as they sped up the Pacific Coast Highway.

"Punkin, like I said, Mommy went on a trip," Jack replied. "We'll see her when we get back home."

Robynn frowned. "I wish she were with us."

"I know you do."

They were three hours up the coast from L.A. and traffic was good, which was a rare treat. They were zipping past miles of crop fields, beans and strawberries, mostly, punctuated by an occasional vineyard. Aside from missing her mother, which was understandable, Robynn's behavior in the car had been far, far better than Jack expected, given the black mood in which she had arisen that morning. She had remained calm while strapped into the car seat beside him in the pickup truck—something she did not always take so placidly—and she had spent most of the trip playing with a plush monkey that she had named "Mr. Booty," because its white feet made it look like it was wearing boots.

"Daddy, I have to go," she said, as they zoomed past the green highway sign promising a town called Tarelton to be the next exit.

Her timing was better than usual. Normally Robynn waited until they were just past a turn-off to declare her needs. "Okay, I'll pull off in this next town and we'll find a place, and maybe we can get a soda or some ice cream or something while we're there," Jack said.

"Okay!"

Robynn sang softly to Mr. Booty for the few miles it took to arrive in downtown Tarelton, which was three blocks long and looked like the Western street from a film studio back lot. Most of the buildings dated back to the late 1800s, though there had clearly been a concentrated effort in recent years to renovate, if not completely remodel, some of them. One old brick building that appeared to have been a fire house at one time looked freshly tuck-pointed. Jack had never thought of central California as a bastion of the Old West, but these days, old towns did whatever it took to bring in the tourists. Three men ambled out of a feed store connected to a towering grain elevator on the main drag as Jack drove by, each one in jeans and a white lacquered straw cowboy hat. Jack pulled his truck into a space in front of an old brick building whose bottom floor housed a bar and grill. Next to it, in a small, recently remodeled store front, whose design contrasted with the Victorian-era buildings around it, was an ice cream shop, and when Robynn saw it, she dropped Mr. Booty on the floor and started to try and unbuckle herself from the car seat.

"Whoa, whoa, punkin, hang on, you can't do that yourself," Jack said, reaching over and unfastening the buckle. "We'll get there in plenty of time, wait for me."

"I want p'stacio nut."

"We'll see if they have it."

The two of them were the only customers in the ice cream shop, which unlike practically every eatery in Los Angeles except the major junk food chains boasted of a public restroom. Jack got the key from the bored-looking teenaged girl behind the counter and opened the door, but Robynn went in on her own.

She was getting so big.

It turned out the place did not have pistachio nut, but it did have bubble gum, which appealed to Robynn even more. Jack ordered a bottle of water for himself and the two retired to one of the small, wobbly tables in the shop. While Robynn was happily licking her cone, Jack pulled out his cell phone and called Dani to tell her that he was coming up, but got her inbox. "Hey, it's Jack," he said into the phone. "Don't be shocked, but I'm on my way back up to San Simeon. The second set of pictures at Wood City didn't turn out either, so I'm going to take another set. I may need to get a new camera, though. I have my daughter with me. I'm going to be staying at the same place. You've got my cell number if you need it. Bye."

"Who were you calling?" Robynn asked.

"Oh, just a friend," Jack said. Putting the phone back into his shirt pocket, he started staring silently at a poster that had been taped up on the wall of the place, showing a triple-decker Neapolitan ice cream cone, with a scoop of vanilla on the bottom of the stack, strawberry in the middle, chocolate on top. The colors were somewhat off, so that the strawberry was more flesh tone than pink and the chocolate was a dark almond. It did not take much imagination to get a skin tone out of it as well, a bronzed, beach-tan skin tone. Jack kept looking at the join between the flesh and the bronze, the way they almost melted into each other, and he began to see two bodies: his and Dani's. Jack was the pink layer and she was the bronze, rubbing wetly up against him, glistening with the sweat of passion. It was the most sensual thing Jack Hayden had ever seen in print, far more erotic than any girlie magazine.

He continued to stare, transfixed, for who knew how long? Everything around him seemed to disappear except for the flesh colored images. Finally he shook his head and broke his gaze away from the poster. His lip was perspiring and he was hard. He took a drink of his water. Sneaking a look back at the poster, he now saw only a triple-decker ice cream cone. Jesus, did simply hearing Dani's recorded voice on a cell phone greeting really have that big of an effect? Even if it had, what exactly he would be able to do about it now that he had his five-year-old in tow? *You just sit there and watch Elmo, punkin, while Daddy and Dani go into the bathroom and get all bare nakedy and rub up against each other and make funny noises until they scream. Oh, and don't say anything to Mommy, okay?*

"What the hell am I doing?" he asked the poster. He knew he should call Dani back right now and tell her that he had committed a terrible lapse in judgment having rushed up here with Robin in tow. Shit, maybe Elley was right all those times she'd rail about how he was nothing more than a fifteen-year-old in the body of an adult. He turned back toward Robynn to tell her that it was time to go. But no words came out of his mouth, only a gasp.

Robynn was not there.

His daughter was gone.

"Robynn?" he called out inside the ice cream shop, but he could clearly see that she was not there.

Leaping up from the table so forcefully that he nearly knocked it over, he demanded of the girl behind the counter where his daughter had gone.

"I dunno," the girl shrugged.

"Maybe she's in the bathroom."

"Nope, key's right here."

"Well didn't you see her leave?" Jack demanded.

"It's your kid, not mine."

Jack had a sudden impulse to slap her, but he held it in check. Then he saw the girl look behind him through the window. "Hey, isn't that her out there on the sidewalk?"

Jack turned around and saw Robynn standing near a concrete-and-board bench on the street, her half-eaten scoop dripping down her fingers, chatting amiably with an old woman, who was seated on the bench. "Jesus," Jack exhaled. He ran out of the door of the shop. "Robynn!" he shouted, and the girl turned to look at him.

"Hi, Daddy," she said.

He knelt down and grabbed her arms tightly.

"Ow!" she cried, nearly dropping her cone.

"Why did you leave like that?" he demanded. "You know better than to go off on your own!"

She looked frightened now. "Sorry, Daddy, but this lady needed help."

Jack looked up into the face of the woman seated on the bus bench. She was old and had snowy hair, a lined face, and clear hazel eyes that right now looked a bit confused.

"I didn't mean to do anything bad," Robynn was saying, now near tears.

"Okay, punkin, it's okay," Jack said, loosening his grip and managing to turn it into a hug. "I just got scared because you weren't there and I couldn't find you at first. We're in a strange town so if you got lost, I wouldn't know where to look."

"I hope I haven't caused any trouble," the old woman said.

"No, no, it's just that we try to teach her not to wander off, you know."

"You and your wife?" the woman asked absently.

There was a pause before Jack answered, "Yes, and usually she's pretty good about it."

"Oh, well, you know how kids are," the woman went on, seeming to clear. "Nobody really looked after me like that when I was young. Today it's different, of course." She looked at Robynn and smiled. "I think she's the one I'm supposed to meet."

"I'm sorry?"

The woman looked at Jack. "I was told to meet a girl here. Why here, I don't know, but there she is."

Jack was now convinced he was dealing with some poor, senile woman who had wandered off from home, or perhaps from a care facility, and had gotten hopelessly lost. Robynn, in her innate sweetness, probably saw the woman walking around in circles with a puzzled look on her face through the window of the ice cream shop, and slipped out to see if she could help her when Jack was not looking.

When he was looking at pictures of ice cream and turning them into sexual fantasies.

"No harm done," Jack said to the old woman. "My name's Jack Hayden, by the way, and this is Robynn."

The woman looked at Robynn and smiled. "Oh, like the bird?"

"Actually, it's with a y and two n's," Jack said. "My wife's idea. Look, is there some way I can help you?"

"I don't know, actually. My name is Althea Kinchloe. I guess you could say I'm visiting here too. I'm really from Vancouver."

"Canada?" Jack asked, amazed he had managed to get so far away from home.

"No, Washington State, just across the line from Oregon. I grew up in California, though. Does my name mean anything to you?"

"Uh, no, not really. Were you famous?"

"Oh, heavens no, I just thought that, well, Howard is the one who told me to come down here, and I thought maybe that Howard spoke to you, too."

"I'm sorry, but I haven't spoken with anyone named Howard. Is he your son?"

"Howard? Oh, no, he and I were talking about getting married, but that was a long time ago."

"You've kept up with him, though."

"No, no, I can't say as I have, but he contacted me a couple of days ago. I *think* it was a couple of days ago. I'm a little tired from the bus ride. It was in the middle of the night, so I don't know which day to count it as."

Howard must be her husband, then, Jack thought. In the poor woman's addled mind, he must have been relegated to a suitor. "You know, if you have Howard's number we can call him," he suggested, taking out his cell phone and showing it to her.

"Oh, no," Althea replied with a knowing smile. "Howard's dead. That's why I was so surprised to see him."

"Yeeesss...I imagine that would be something of a surprise."

There was an awkward silence, filled only by the sounds

of cars driving slowly by on the street and the crunching of Robynn's wafer cone. Then Althea said: "I know what you're thinking, young man, that I'm some old biddy who's not right in the head."

Jack had to smile at her candor.

"I think you're nice," said Robynn.

"Thank you, honey. I think you're nice, too. If you like, you can call me Noni. That's what my own grandchildren call me."

"Look, Mrs. Kinchloe, I just want to make sure you're okay, because you seem far from home."

"Yes, quite a ways. I took the bus because I don't drive anymore. Maybe Howard didn't know that. I just threw a few things for the trip in this bag"—she patted an old cloth tote—"and headed out. I had to change buses in Paso Robles. Anyway, this is where Howard told me to come, and since he had never tried to talk to me before, I figured it must have been important."

"How did Howard contact you?"

"In a dream. Like I said, he's dead, has been for more than sixty years."

"So he told you to come here and meet someone."

"Yes, a little girl, like this sweet thing here." She smiled down at Robynn, who smiled back.

The conversation was starting to make Jack nervous. "Howard came to you in a dream and told you to come and meet my daughter?"

"A little girl is what he said. She's the only little girl I've seen since I've been here."

"How long have you been here?"

"The bus got in just after ten. What is it now?"

Jack looked at his watch. It was nearly two. The woman had been sitting here on this bench, in the heat of the day, for almost four hours waiting for a little girl at the request of an old dead boyfriend. Every instinct he had told him to pick up Robynn and run, run away as fast as possible, but he knew that was out of the question. He could not simply walk away and abandon a woman who was clearly confused, if not infirm, in the middle of an unfamiliar town. At the very least, he would have to find a policeman or some other city official and turn her over to them.

"Mrs. Kinchloe, do you know why Howard wanted to you come down here to meet someone you've never met?"

"Why he wanted me to come down here?" she asked, as though the question was puzzling.

"Yes, what is it he intends for you and this person you are to meet to do?"

"That's the part that doesn't make any sense. I'm supposed to fight the legion."

"What's the legion?"

"I don't know. Gracious, it's hot out here. Usually I like the heat, but today it's too much."

"Okay, maybe we should all go inside," Jack suggested. The last thing he wanted was the old woman fainting, or worse, in front of him and Robynn. "I have an idea. Let's all go into that restaurant over there and have a cup of coffee and a piece of pie, or something, and talk about this."

"Pie *and* ice cream on one day?" Robynn said excitedly. "I don't think Mommy would like that."

"Mommy isn't here," Jack replied, a bit sharply. Then: "Don't worry, punkin, lots of people eat pie and ice cream together, it's called *à la mode*. It will be all right this once. Mrs. Kinchloe, will you come?"

"Sure, sure," she said, lifting herself off the bench.

Jack picked up her small bag and the three of them made their way toward the restaurant, which was called O'Dowd's Place. The interior was done in Early American Cowtown Fantasy, a combination of oaken tables, heavy wooden beams with decorative gingerbread, hanging lights with ornate red glass shades, a long bar complete with a brass foot rail and prop spittoons, a stuffed buffalo on the back wall, and a sawdust-covered floor. Jack and Althea each got coffee, while Robynn, with some help, decided on a slice of chocolate cream pie. Her eyes grew wide when she saw the size of it and even wider when she tasted it. "I *like* this!" she declared.

"Okay, punkin, you eat your pie and color the pictures on that menu while Mrs. Kinchloe and I talk, all right?"

"Hmm-hmmm."

Althea Kinchloe stirred some cream into her coffee. "You know, when I think about what I've been saying to you, I wouldn't blame you for thinking I must be out of my mind. It sounds pretty crazy."

"It sounds like you must have been a very vivid dream."

"Real. It was very real. Usually I don't smell things in dreams, but in this one I could actually smell the wet paint around the studio." Althea laughed softly. "I'm sure that won't make a lick of sense to you, but my Howard was an artist. He worked for the WPA during the thirties on all their projects, things like those great big—"

"Murals?" Jack interrupted.

"Yes, you've seen them?"

"I've seen one just recently, or at least a small bit of one, up at the ruins of an old abandoned town in the woods."

"Daddy, can I go out and get Mr. Booty from the car?" Robynn asked. "He'd like this pie, too."

"Can he wait a little bit, punkin?"

"Okay."

"You must mean that old lumber town," Althea said.

"You know it?"

"I haven't thought about it for ages. They were building it when Howard and I were up at San Simeon."

"We're headed for San Simeon."

"That must be why Howard wanted me to come and meet you. He must have specified the little girl so I'd know who to look for."

Jack did not know what to think. Things had seemed not quite normal for the past couple of days, but now here was a woman completely out of the blue who claimed to have been directed to meet him, or at least Robynn, by a ghost who happened to be a WPA mural artist. Could it be that he was dreaming?

"Daddy, now I'm thirsty," Robynn said, and Jack flagged

down the waitress and asked her to bring a glass of water.

"Oh, what a lovely picture you're coloring, Robynn," Althea said, looking across the table at the printed menu with the broad drawings of cows in cowboy hats and bonnets on them. Robynn smiled back at her as the waitress brought three waters. After a quick sip, Robynn went back to concentrating on her crayons.

"I find all of this very strange," Jack said, "but strange or not, we have to decide what we're going to do now. What exactly were your plans, Mrs. Kinchloe?"

"Please call me Althea. I'm afraid I don't have any. I came down here like I was instructed to and I met you and the sweetie here, like I was told to do, but that's the end of my marching orders. I only bought a one-way bus ticket."

"Can Noni come with us?" Robynn asked excitedly.

"Well, one of the problems with that is that I'm driving a pickup truck with a bench seat, and I'm not sure I can fit all of us in."

"Oh, I could ride the little one on my lap," Althea offered, smiling toward Robynn, who smiled back.

How much simpler things were in Althea's generation, Jack thought. He shook his head. "Not these days, I'm afraid. She has to be in a car seat. Maybe I could leave the truck here and find a place to rent a car."

"Oh, you're going to so much trouble for this," Althea said. "Let's just give the truck a try and see if we fit, first."

Jack reluctantly agreed. The waitress brought the check on a plastic tray, topped with three root beer barrels. He scooped up the candies before Robynn saw them and glanced at the check, then fished out a ten from his wallet and placed it on the tray. "Are we ready to go, then?"

"I have to go again, Daddy."

"Okay, punkin." As he started to get up, Althea said, "You know, it wouldn't hurt me, either. I'll go back with her." With a grandmotherly smile, she took Robynn's willing hand and the two strode back to the restrooms.

The last thing Jack had anticipated was picking up an elderly, possibly unstable woman and including her in the travels. Jesus, was he in control of *anything* any more? Then again, she might definitely be a help with Robynn, and it really wasn't that far to San Simeon from here. He could take her that far and then decide what to do.

While waiting for Althea and Robynn to return from the bathroom Jack absently looked over the kid's placemat on which his daughter had been coloring so diligently. There were the usual animal drawings—puppies were a specialty of hers—and the cow pictures had been colored in mostly with green, which was her favorite color. Even more oddly, there was a crayon line that coursed diagonally across the paper, culminating in an arrow at the lower right corner. Jack studied this simple creation: the point of the arrow was surprisingly well drawn, small and fine, and looking more like the kind of mark a mechanical draftsman or architect would put alongside a measurement on a blueprint. How on earth did she manage that with the blunt end of a crayon? Perhaps she had genuine artistic talent. Since the clear implication of the arrow was that the sheet should be turned over, Jack obliged.

Then he froze.

A face stared back at him from the flipside of the menu. It was a woman's face and nothing short of a crayon masterpiece: vibrant, alive, expressive, and disturbing. The waxen eyes, the brown color of which had somehow been created by over-drawing with primary colors, were riveted on his, refusing to move no matter how he changed the angle of his head or shifted around the paper. It was as though the face on the placemat was looking at him. There was a slight, sardonic smile on the face; a knowing smile.

It was unmistakably the face from the mural.

CHAPTER NINE

Jonelle Armour's desk groaned under the weight of Marcus Broarty. "Didn't you wear that top last week?" he asked her.

Jonelle was an African-American woman of twenty-six with straight hair, large warm eyes and Caucasian features, like Halle Berry. More importantly as far as Broarty was concerned she had a bust that that stretched the front of her white button blouse to the absolute maximum. She had been working as the company receptionist for slightly less than two months, which Broarty considered enough time to decide whether or not she was happy in her job, which in turn would dictate the sort of steps she would take in order to keep it.

"I'm sure I have worn this before top, Mr. Broarty," she answered demurely. "Y'know, with a raise I could buy more tops and I wouldn't have to wear the same ones all the time."

"Oh, don't go replacing this one on my account."

He was about to deliver the preliminary question on the job security exam when Jonelle's phone board buzzed. "'Scuse me, Mr. Broarty. This is Jonelle. Oh, hi, Yolanda. Yes, he is here, should I hand the phone to him?"

Broarty rolled his eyes. "I can't go anywhere," he sighed under his breath.

"Oh, all right, I'll tell him." She hung up. "That was Yolanda."

"So I gathered."

"There's a call for you in your office from a Mr. McMenamin. He's holding."

"Christ. Okay, well, we'll continue our discussion some other time."

Once he was gone, Jonelle buzzed Yolanda. "He's on his way back, and thanks. It was getting a little uncomfortable here."

"No problem, we've all been there," Yolanda replied.

As Broarty lumbered back to Yolanda's desk, he asked: "What the hell does Emac want now?"

"I don't know, but he doesn't sound happy."

"Couldn't you have told him I was out?"

"I'm sorry, Mr. B., I thought you'd want to talk to him. Shall I tell him we can't find you?"

"No, no, I'll take it. It can't be that bad." Broarty went into his office and nudged the door almost shut. "Hey, Emac, what's up?"

"My patience with you, that's what!" McMenamin roared.

"Wait, whoa, whoa, Emac, what's the problem?"

"Those pictures of Wood City you sent!"

"Pictures, what pictures?"

Yolanda knew it was risky to pick up the phone and listen in. Instead she strained to hear her boss's voice coming from the office.

"No, I didn't, Emac, they didn't come from me. Maybe Jack Hayden sent them. He's the one who took them, after all. No, I haven't seen them. No, I have no idea. What? Emac, please, calm down!"

Yolanda could no longer stop herself. As gently as she could, she eased the receiver from the cradle and held it up to her ear and heard McMenamin's angry voice yell: "You fucking *assured* me yesterday that we could go ahead with our project! Now today I received a set of photos by email showing a ghost town in such dilapidated shape that a rat wouldn't move in!"

"I told you what you wanted to hear yesterday, Emac."

"I wanted you to tell me the goddamned truth, not some fantasy about buildings that aren't really there! Now my ass is on the line, because not only did I get these photos, but the president of Resort Partners got the fucking things! He is not happy, Mr. Broarty, not...ah, fuck, hold on, my other line is ringing.

Don't you *dare* hang up!"

The line went silent, and all Yolanda could hear was the labored breathing of Marcus Broarty. She almost felt sorry for him. Almost.

When McMenamin came back on the line, she swore she could actually feel heat radiating through the phone. "Broarty, goddammit, I'm going to hang your balls on my Christmas tree!" he screamed.

"Emac?" Broarty whimpered.

"That call was from a newspaper reporter. The local press has a set of the photos too! They're starting an investigation into the project. Do you have *any* idea how much the people I work for *hate* the fucking *press*?"

"Emac, I swear to you that I did not send any pictures to you. I did not send any pictures to the president of Resort Partners. I certainly did not send any pictures to any newspaper. Why would I?"

There was a grunting sigh, followed by McMenamin's defeated voice. "Well, somebody sure as hell did."

"I'm telling you, Emac, it had to be Hayden."

"Hayden again."

"Who else could it be? He's the one who had the goddamned things. I deleted all mine."

There was a long pause before McMenamin said: "Yesterday, Mr. Broarty, you told me you never got the pictures. How can you delete them if you never received them?"

"Well, hold on now, what I meant was I accidentally deleted them, but I never actually looked at them."

"You didn't inhale, in other words."

"I didn't do what?"

"THIS IS THE BIGGEST MOTHERFUCKING BULLSHIT MESS I EVER SAW!"

Listening in, Yolanda nearly dropped the phone from the force of McMenamin's voice.

"Emac," Broarty said desperately, "this has to be Jack Hayden's doing. Just between you and me, he's been having some personal problems lately."

"I thought you told me Hayden was the best person on your staff.

"Well, he is, or at least he was. I don't know if it's burnout or what, but lately he's kind of snapped."

"Get him on the goddamned line. Now."

"Just hold on, Emac," Broarty said, setting the phone down and running out to Yolanda's desk. She had just managed to noiselessly hang up herself when he arrived. "Yolanda, transfer Emac to Jack."

"All right," she said, picking the phone up and saying, "Mr. McMenamin? Hi, hold on please while I transfer you." Then she buzzed Jack's office, but there was no answer. She tried again, and finally turned back to Broarty. "I don't think he's in."

"What do you mean he's not in?" Broarty yelled, and sprinted down the hall toward Jack's office, providing quite a spectacle for the other workers. He got there, winded, to find the door closed and the lights off behind it. "I don't freaking believe it!" Hurrying back, he instructed Yolanda to tell McMenamin that Jack wasn't available and that he would have him call as soon as he appeared. Then he went back inside his office. He had not even had the chance to sit down when Yolanda was on the intercom again. "Mr. Broarty, he wants to talk to you again."

"Goddammit, can't anybody else handle anything around here! *You* talk to that asshole!"

Then he realized he had never replaced the phone receiver back in the cradle, he had only set it down on his desk. He could still be heard on the other end.

"*Broarty!*" McMenamin's voice roared from the phone. Picking it up gingerly, Broarty said: "I'm right here, Emac."

"Where the fuck *is* your boy Hayden if he's not in the office?"

"I, uh, don't know."

"*I, uh, don't know,*" McMenamin sneered, and all of the bullies who ever taunted and abused Marcus Broarty when he was a schoolboy resided in that voice.

"Emac, please, as soon as I find him, I'll make sure he calls you."

"I have a better idea. You meet me on the property tomorrow."

"At Wood City?"

"Yes, goddammit, at Wood City!"

"You're going to come in all the way from Vegas?"

"If that's what I have to do, yes. Get Hayden's ass there too."

"Is it really necessary that I be there?"

"I am giving you one last chance to straighten this fucking disaster out, and I'm doing it for one reason only, and that's because *I'm* the one who engaged Crane Commercial, so if *you* jump in a shit puddle, it splashes back on *me*, and *I* don't like getting wet! I expect to see you and Hayden tomorrow at noon. And don't you even think about firing that cocksucker until I'm through with him!"

The line went dead.

After a half-minute, Broarty called for Yolanda to come into his office.

"Anything wrong, Mr. Broarty?" she asked, stepping in to find him half-slumped against his desk, looking ashen and sweaty. "Sir, you don't look too good."

"Yolanda, you need to find Jack Hayden, now. If he's in the building, get him in here. If he's not in the building, find him and then get him in here. Drop whatever else your doing and work on getting Jack in here. Please find him for me, Yolanda. Please."

Staggering back into his office, Broarty closed his door and dashed around to his chair, pulling open the bottom drawer of his desk where was stashed a bottle of vodka, and drank straight from the bottle.

How was he supposed to get to Wood City? Where the hell *was* Wood City, anyway?

* * * * * * *

Jack Hayden's cell phone beeped repeatedly, and he pulled it out of his pocket, glancing at it quickly so as not to take his eyes off the road for long. *One missed call*, it read, and he recognized the number as coming from Crane. "Fine, it can stay missing," he said, putting the phone back in his pocket.

They were only about a half-hour away from San Simeon. Althea had spent the time since leaving Tarelton talking about how much the middle of California had changed since she was a girl. Jack had occasionally tuned her out to concentrate on driving, but for the most part he found her monologue interesting. The old woman had a very pleasant voice, like an aging actress, and her stories were entertaining and varied enough to belie his initial suspicion that she was senile. Still, it seemed to Jack that she deliberately avoided talking about the dreams she had alluded when they first met, or any other discussion of why she had impulsively pulled up stakes from her comfortable home and put her trust in fate. Neither did Jack try to coerce the information out of her.

Robynn was happily snuggled in between them in the truck. Jack had dug out the middle seat belt from the purgatory behind the seat so he could buckle in her car seat, and it was quite a tight fit in there. And he couldn't help noticing that she was leaning more toward Althea than him. Robynn really liked this old woman, more than she liked her own grandmothers, which was not that hard for him to understand. Elley's mother was a handful even for children, or perhaps especially for children, since only the most compassionate of young people would be able to comprehend why a grown-up was so emotionally needy. But Lois Eunie Gorman walked around as though under a perpetual spotlight, incapable of the kind of normal human conversation that required give and take, able only to hold court. It was little wonder to him why Elley's father had abandoned the marriage the moment Elley had left for college, and equally little wonder that Elley was such an overachiever; growing up in a household where attention was constantly demanded by one's parent but never given in return would turn anyone into a person with something to prove.

Robynn's other grandmother, Rebecca Hayden, had been

battling illness for the entire duration of the girl's lifetime, which made it difficult to get the two of them together. Jack's mother had seen her granddaughter as a baby, but even that had been something of an ordeal for her. She would not hold the child out of fear—real or imagined—of dropping her. Rebecca usually remembered Robynn with birthday cards and Christmas presents, but she was not a vital part of her grandchild's life. Over the last couple of years, since Jack's father's death, his mother had been so chronically depressed that even he had a hard time being around her.

As opposed to her natural grandmothers, Althea truly seemed to like Robynn. Some older people just have a talent for grandparenting, whether or not the grandkids in question are their own.

Jack's phone beeped again and this time he did not even bother taking it out of his pocket. He simply let it beep. He'd check in at the office later this afternoon or not, depending on his mood. Finally it stopped.

"Have you ever been up to the castle, Jack?" Althea asked.

"Castle?" he replied, dumbly. "Oh, you mean the Hearst place? Nope, missed it."

"I was at the castle only once, many, many years ago."

"Did a princess live there?" Robynn chimed in.

The old woman chuckled. "A woman who was treated like a princess lived there, sweetie. Her name was Marion and she had, oh, I guess you'd say boyfriend, and he liked to throw parties."

"I've heard about those parties," Jack said. "You actually went to them?"

"Just one. The theme of this particular one was the Renaissance, so everyone had to come dressed like Leonardo, or whoever. They had real painters running around in period costumes and painting portraits of the guests, and my Howard was one of them. I was there with him, and to lend atmosphere, kind of like a movie extra. I walked around in this gorgeous dress and tried not to faint if a movie star came up to chat. I think Howard got two hundred dollars for working that party, which was a fortune back then, but he earned it."

"I should think so, having to whip up paintings of people so quickly."

"They had a trick to them. They'd have already painted the background and the figure, everything except the actual face, which they were able to fill face relatively quickly. Remember, these were all movie stars, so they already knew what they looked like. The real trick, though, was covering the already-painted parts of the canvases with a light whitewash, so they looked empty. Then they'd take a big, broad brush, the kind you slop paint onto a fence with, and quickly wash down the canvas with water, revealing the part they'd already done beneath, and go on to the face. Something went wrong, though, in one instance."

"What happened?"

"You know, that was so long ago, I can't recall the details. But one of the people at the party was so upset that she had to be taken out, and it was all related to the painting of her."

Another painting, Jack thought grimly. *What the hell was it about paintings all of a sudden?*

* * * * * * *

Elley was waiting for her luggage at JFK when she remembered that she had forgotten to ask Nola to pick up her dry cleaning. Stepping away from the baggage carousel, she punched the speed dial number for home and waited for Nola to pick up, but there was no answer.

Elley glanced at her watch and frowned. It was nearly seven in the evening New York time, which meant it was four in L.A. Nola should be there. Robynn's kindergarten class let out at two-thirty, and even if they stopped somewhere on the way home, they should surely be there by now. Maybe Nola was in the bathroom.

It was taking forever for Elley's suitcase to show up on the luggage carousel. Blaise Micelli's had already bounced down and been retrieved, and he had gone out to the transportation area to hail a cab to take them to their mid-town hotel. Elley was just on the verge of going to the luggage office to complain when she saw her plain green bag sliding out of the chute. "'Bout damn time," she muttered, grabbing it.

Once she had retrieved her suitcase, Elley tried calling her house again. Surely by now Nola would be out of the bathroom. But there was still no answer.

Elley was getting worried.

She tried calling Jack at the office, but he was not there. The receptionist actually asked her if *she* knew where he was.

Now Elley was getting angry.

Blaise was at the doorway of the terminal, waving at her. "Cab's waiting, Elley," he called.

"Just a moment," she said, fishing through her purse until she found her address book. Looking up Nola's home number, she tried calling it. Nola answered on the second ring.

"Nola, where the hell are you!"

"Miz Elley, I'm right here."

"Is Robynn with you?"

"No, ma'am. Mr. Jack called me earlier and said not to come over."

"What?"

Talking slowly, Nola repeated, "Mr. Jack called me earlier today and said not to come. He was going to get Robynn."

Elley took a deep breath. "Oh, okay. Sorry." That at least made sense. Jack wasn't at work, for whatever reason, so he decided to get Robynn himself. And knowing Jack, he probably took her out to some junk food restaurant and that's why there was no one answering the phone. "There's something I'd like you to do for me. Tomorrow when you get Robynn from school, I need you to stop at the Prestige Cleaners and pick some clothes up for me. The claim ticket is magneted to the fridge."

Blaise was now shouting, "Elley, the cab's waiting for us, let's go!"

"But Robynn's not in school, Miz Elley. Mr. Jack has him.

They've gone."

Elley stopped dead, five feet from the door. "What did you say?"

"Mr. Jack said they'd be gone for days."

"Goddammit!" she screamed, silencing the noisy baggage claim area. "Son of a *bitch*!"

Blaise ran up to her and grabbed her arm. "Will you stop making a spectacle of yourself?"

Elley shook herself free of his grasp and glared him down. "You go to the hotel, Blaise. I have a problem at home I have to deal with. My goddamned husband has taken my daughter somewhere, and I don't know where."

"He's the father, right?"

"What do you think?"

"There's no law that says a father can't take his own kid."

"What if he's kidnapped her?"

Outside the terminal, the cab driver, tired of waiting, accepted another fare and took off.

"I'm missing something here," Blaise said. "If it was the babysitter, then that would be kidnapping. If you and Jack were divorced and he came and took her away, maybe that would be kidnapping. But right now, I don't see a problem."

"The problem, Blaise, is that I don't know where they are!" she screamed.

Two airport security guards were now coming their way.

"Will you put a fucking sock in it?" Blaise snarled, grabbing her.

"Let me go!" Elley lost control and slapped him so hard that her hand stung.

The guards were there in a flash, and one of them was on the walkie-talkie, stating: "Backup to United baggage terminal, we have a potential diversionary tactic in progress, repeat—potential diversionary tactic."

Another guard, a very tall, tough-looking man, said: "Folks, I'm going to have to ask you to step over here with me." He spoke quietly but in a tone of voice that conveyed there was no option for argument.

"Look, officer," Blaise began, "she's just a little distraught, is all. It's nothing. You know how it is with women."

The tall guard's faced remained chiseled out of stone. "What I know is you'd better come over here with me. Now, sir."

Elley remained silent as a guard with a dog appeared to examine their baggage, though Blaise complained, pointing out that they were trying to take the luggage out of the airport, not into it. They were then led away surrounded by uniformed security down a hallway and into a small room, where they were questioned for the better part of a half hour by a non-uniformed security expert who insisted upon being convinced that they had not staged the argument on purpose to deflect attention away from another person or persons, who might use the cover to engaging in dangerous, even potentially deadly, activities inside the airport.

Three-quarters of an hour later, after security had turned up no suspicious persons or parcels in the baggage area, he was finally convinced. Blaise and Elley were released and escorted to the exit.

"I suppose you're going to tell me that tomorrow we'll be laughing about this," Blaise spat. "Well, don't count on it."

"I'm not."

"My face is still stinging, you know."

"Good."

"Just what I fucking need. This is the most important client meeting we've had this year, and right when I need you most, you flip out. If you're like this tomorrow—"

"I'm going back home, Blaise," she said. "Whatever's going on with my daughter is more important than the client meeting."

"This is why I fucking hate married people! Listen, if you leave me in the lurch like this you're finished!"

Not long ago, Elley would have reacted with dread at the thought of losing her job. But now she only said, "Whatever."

"I mean everywhere! I'll make sure you never get hired again by anyone!"

"Sure." Elley pulled away from him and her heel and strode back into the terminal, lugging her suitcase.

"Goddammit, get your ass back here!" he shouted.

She did not look back, but raised the middle finger of her left hand to him over her shoulder, then marched to the marched up the stairs to the ticketing counter to reserve a seat on the first flight back to L.A.

* * * * * * *

Dani Lindstrom was driving south on the Pacific Coast Highway, away from her motel, away from San Simeon. On her right was the ocean, impossibly blue and imposing, glistening in the vibrant, soon to be fading, light of the afternoon. On her left were the kind of green hills that hoped to be mountains when they grew up, each one dotted with cows who stood around chewing grass so lazily that a tourist might wonder if they were on vacation too. It was a perfect kind of day, she thought; a beautiful day for a drive.

Now if only she knew why she was driving.

Dani had planned to spend the day poking around the remnants of historic San Simeon, but it turned out that did not take very long. Then she got Jack's message saying that he was coming back up, and she went back to the motel. She tried reading for a while, but grew increasingly restless, the walls of her motel room seeming to close in on her. Almost out of desperation, she had decided to go to that spot on the beach a few miles up that attracted hundreds of elephant seals each year, for reasons known only to them. But once she had gotten into her car, she turned the opposite direction on Highway One and headed south, without understanding why. Before long she was slowing down to turn onto what was left of the road that led to Wood City.

Dani did not want to go to the site. She wanted to turn around and go back, but seemed incapable of ordering her hands and feet to comply. That's when the sudden attack of gooseflesh hit her; it was like she was no longer in control of her driving.

She continued to bump over the rutted, washboard road until she saw the figure standing in woods up ahead. It was hard to make out whether it was a person or a bear standing upright until the figure raised its arms over its head and waved, like it was trying to flag her down. As she approached, though, there was no sign of anyone.

Had it been her imagination? Or had it been Jack?

Dani brought the car to a halt and put down her window. She called out Jack's name. A sound of some sort answered her from the woods, but it was too faint to understand. It might have been the cry of a person, but it might not have. If it had been Jack, she would surely see his truck soon, since she figured the point that became impassible by vehicle due to the toppled tree had to be nearby. Switching on her headlights against the darkness of the woods, she slowly crept toward the ruined town, the car bouncing with every rut in the road. *When I get to the tree trunk, if Jack's truck isn't there, I'll just maneuver around and go back*, she told herself. *I won't get out of the car.*

But the fallen tree that had prevented her and Jack from penetrating the woods any further by car only yesterday seemed not to be here this afternoon. Had somebody cleared it? Is that what the strange figure had been doing there?

Dani had only been in Wood City that once, but it had been enough to imprint the look of the ruins of the one-time village in her mind. But something was wrong; it was different now. The thicket of brush through which they'd had to fight in order to get to the site was no longer there either. There was no trace that it had ever been there.

An unfamiliar structure was looming up in front of her. It was one of the houses, but it was more or less intact. The paint had been worn away by the weather, but the building's walls remained. She knew she had not seen it before; yesterday, when it was lighter and easier to see things, there had been no signs of any wooden buildings in this complete of form. Good god, was she on the wrong road, heading into the site from another direction?

Dani stopped the car and got out. She started walking closer to the building, but halted when she heard the creaking sound. It was the sound that wood makes under some kind of strain, but it was not rhythmic, like footsteps. It was more consistent, like something being slowly stretched, or maybe like something....

"Oh my god," Dani whispered, her eyes locked on the house. *It was moving. Somehow the beams and studs were moving, growing.*

Now panicked, Dani started to run through the woods, trying in her mind to return to the car, desperately wanting to jump back inside, turn around, and get the hell out of here, but she was going the wrong way. She stopped and turned back, but could not see the car.

Dani started running again. She wanted to stop her legs from moving, but could not. She was passing more and more skeletons of buildings now, on each side of her, each one creaking and groaning, each one growing and reaching for the sunlight. No matter how fast she ran, she could not outrun the creaking wood sounds.

She was only able to stop when the city hall building came into view. Dani knelt down on the ground, breathless, then rose again and began walking toward it. *I don't want to be here!*

There were no sounds coming from the massive stone building, but there was something different about it. It was less dilapidated somehow; newer, cleaner, more alive.

At that moment, the lights inside the stone structure came on.

Dani's legs traitorously carried her to the steps of the City Hall, and then began to ascend them. There was nothing she could do to stop them.

It was like she was a puppet being controlled by strings, with no will of her own. Tears were now streaming down her face, all but blinding her as she stepped through the open doorway and went inside.

There was no one inside; no other person to see her standing there; no other presence to help her.

Nothing human heard the scream that rose up from the depth of her soul.

BOOK TWO

CHAPTER TEN
SEVENTY-FIVE YEARS AGO

Althea Dorneman had never felt more out of place, or been more fascinated, in her life. It was like she had been transported to a fantasy land of wealth and ostentation, someplace not really on the earth, or at least, not really in the United States of America. This was more the stuff of old decadent Europe than modern, progressive California. Or maybe it was simply a dream.

Althea had actually pinched herself through her stiff, beaded dress when Fredric March smiled and winked at her. A moment later, he was pulled away by his wife, Florence Eldridge, the actress who had played Mary, Queen of Scotts, who gave Althea a withering stare, as though the wink had been her fault. Althea didn't mind at all. In fact the stare was almost as exciting as the wink, because it meant that a movie star was looking at *her*.

Althea was trying not to be star struck, but it was difficult. She did not want to do anything that would embarrass Howard, but here she was, decked out like a lady-in-waiting to a Renaissance queen (to good effect, if the reaction from March was any indication), in a palatial castle, the likes of which she did not think they made in this country, surrounded not simply by film actors, but by the kings and queens of Hollywood, people who until tonight did not, could not, seem real.

In one corner of the massive assembly room of the palace that William Randolph Hearst quaintly called his "ranch" Howard was feverishly working on a canvas depicting a woman who looked like Paulette Goddard, and probably was. In the opposite corner, looking a bit on the foolish side in his badly fitting Renaissance garb, was Hearst himself. He was a huge man, more than six feet tall and weighty, but paunchy and soft looking. One of Howard's friends had called him *The Lard of the Manor*, but she could not help being awed by the sight of the man, and was startled to hear him speak in an incongruously high and squeaky voice.

Feeling warm, Althea moved further away from the enormous stone fireplace in which a blaze was raging, and carelessly bumped into a man who turned out to be Douglas Fairbanks, Jr. He flashed the smile she had often seen on the screen to her and nodded in apology, and Althea tried to smile back, but felt her breath catch. Just then a scream pierced the cavernous room. Immediately all chatter died down, and all eyes were focused on a young woman in a platinum Marie Antoinette wig, which was somewhat incongruous with the Italian Renaissance theme, who was clamping her hands over her mouth in terror. In front of her, on the floor, lay a canvas. "My god, what is this thing!" the woman cried. "It moved! The painting moved!" Althea could see Fairbanks rushing to the woman's aid, but she continued to stand, frozen, as though a statue. Then she screamed again, and kicked at the canvas.

Another man dressed as an Italian duke picked the canvas up while Fairbanks and now Marion Davies tried to calm the woman. They could not.

"Destroy it!" the woman now shrieked and, breaking away from Fairbanks and Davies, she tore the canvas out of the grip of the "duke," ran it to the massive fireplace, and flung it in. Confused silence reigned, and Hearst himself finally lumbered over to see what was going on. The "duke" intercepted him and began putting on an act that included prancing around eccentrically and pretending to laugh, hitching his shoulders as he did so. Althea was now able to see through the Renaissance costume enough to realize that it was Charlie Chaplin, unrecognizable because of his gray hair and the absence of a toothbrush moustache, but identifiable through his gestures and movements. Chaplin's antics not only drew a chuckle from Hearst, but released the tension of the room for most of the guests, who were now laughing at him. Meanwhile, Marion Davies and a servant were now leading the hysterical guest away. Within seconds, the entire incident had blown over and some of the guests treated it is though it had been part of the planned entertainment for the evening.

Althea, however, continued to stare at the hearth and the flames within it that were consuming the canvas. She was not the only one: a man stood in front of the fireplace, watching equally intently. She recognized him as the artist who had painted the picture. If he was upset about the ignominious end to his work, he was not showing it. Standing with his back to the room, hands on hips in dramatic fashion, he exuded a sense of pride as he concentrated on the flames.

Then he turned around and his gaze met Althea's. It was almost as though he had known she was watching him. The man's face, fire-lit, glowed reddish-orange, and his eyes, which appeared to have no color but black, bore into her own. He wore a moustache and goatee—probably false—and had a head of thick, bushy, dark hair. The man smiled at her seductively, licked his lips, and nodded her way, and Althea felt a chill course through her. While he was not particularly brutish or threatening looking...his wild hair was almost comical, in fact...she sensed there was something about this man that was dangerous.

No, not dangerous. *Evil.*

A collection of people walked in front of her and by the time they had passed, the man was no longer standing in front of the fireplace. Althea looked around the room, but was unable to spot him. It was as though he had disappeared.

CHAPTER ELEVEN
TODAY

Jack Hayden, Robynn and Althea Kinchloe got to the Tide Pool Inn a little before four, and he was glad to see the *Vacancy* sign lit, since he had not bothered to phone in for a reservation. As they trudged into the lobby, Jack was a little disappointed that Dani was not waiting there for him. He had no right to be disappointed, but he was.

Jack signed in for one room shared by him and Robynn, and took the one next door for Althea. Maybe once everybody had gotten to know one another the old woman might be able to move into Dani's room, which would give his MasterCard a needed break. He had yet to resolve in his mind what Althea's part in this strange adventure was, but he was convinced that she had one.

He lugged his hastily packed bags to his room, where Robynn turned on the television and immediately found the Disney Channel. Althea took her small bag to the room next door, while Jack desperately tried to think of a reason to get away from them and have the woman watch Robynn while he was gone. He could really use a cold one right now, ideally with Dani, but he knew he had to come up with a better excuse.

Finally, he got one. "Punkin," he said to Robynn, who was glued to *Phineas and Ferb*, "I'm going to go see Noni right next door. I'll leave the door open so you can hear us, okay?"

"Uh huh," she said absently.

Going out into the hall, Jack knocked on the door to 121,

waiting until the old woman answered it. "Althea, I hate to impose upon you," he began, "but would you mind watching Robynn for a bit? I noticed the truck was a bit low on gas, and I don't want to take a chance on running out up here, since I have to go into the woods tomorrow to the site that I'm inspecting, and all."

"Not at all," she said, smiling. "It will be a pleasure, in fact."

Making sure that she had her card key, Althea shut the door to her room and followed him into 119. "Punkin, Noni's going to watch you for a while, okay?"

"Cool," Robynn said, still staring at the TV.

Cool; he had never heard her say that before. It was such an un-Robynn word. Had Althea used it in conversation and he'd missed it? No, it probably came from the television. Jack jotted down his cell phone number and pulled out twenty, handing it to Althea. "That's for food, in case Robynn gets munchy, or whatever else you might need. Call me if you have any questions. I'll be back as soon as I can."

"Take your time," she said. "We'll be just fine, won't we punkin?" Hearing his pet name for his daughter coming out of the mouth of someone else gave Jack a funny twinge. Still, he trusted the woman. He was still not sure what to make of her story of being visited by a dead boyfriend, but he trusted her with his daughter. Or was it that he was just desperate to talk to Dani again and get a beer that he would have left anyone in charge of Robynn?

No, he couldn't be that far gone.

Leaving them, he went down to the front desk the front desk, back to the smiling, fleshy young man who had registered him. "Hi, do you happen to know if Dani Lindstrom in room 207 is in?"

"I'm afraid I don't," said the clerk, whose nametag identified him as Alex. "Guests can come and go without checking in or out. I can call her room if you like."

"No, that's fine, I'll just go up and knock."

"You can take the elevator to the second floor, then go down the hall."

"Thank you." Jack stepped over to the elevator, which seemed like a waste for someone not dragging luggage through the place, and punched the button, listening to the metallic hum that announced its arrival. When the elevator stopped on the second floor, he jumped out and practically ran to room 207 and knocked. There was no answer. After a few seconds he tried again, louder and more forceful this time. When nobody answered, he tried calling through the door, "Dani, it's Jack, are you there."

No reply. He tried again.

Where was she?

Standing in the hallway the motel, Jack realized he was acting like the kind of person that women often accused all men of being: unreasonable and controlling. It was not like he had any claim over Dani Lindstrom, legally, emotionally, morally or otherwise. She was her own person. But in that moment, Jack realized just how much he needed her to be there. Whether she realized it or not (and she probably did not), she had become the closest thing he had to an emotional anchor. He relied on Robynn, too, but that was different: Robynn was a five-year-old who needed a parent. As much as his daughter gave back to him on an emotional level, she would hardly be able prop him up if he got into trouble.

He reached for his wallet and pulled out a business card, on the back of which he wrote: *I'm in room 119 now, please call me when you're back*, and then slid the card under the door. It looked like his hour of freedom really would be spent seeking out a gas station.

Jack decided to go on to Glenowen instead of driving around the San Simeon loop. There had to be a gas station there someplace and maybe the price would be better than the highway-access stations. There should be a toy store, too, where he might be able to get some kind of little surprise for Robynn.

The station was right at the edge of the town and it took no time at all to tank up (though he did not get his desired price break). Heading up the street he spotted a gift and toy store that had a plush otter in the window, the sort of thing that he knew Robynn would love. Finding a parking spot on the street, he pulled in and bought the otter, despite the fact that its twenty-five dollar price was outrageous. At this rate, he'd have to find an ATM soon. He also thought about getting a loaf of bread and some bologna, just to have on hand at the motel, and a six-pack since drinks with Dani appeared to be out, and asked the shop clerk where the closest market in town was. She directed him to go two blocks up the street. Jack decided to walk instead of driving, but he stashed the otter inside the truck before heading off to find the market. It was supposed to be two blocks up, the woman had said, but after three blocks he still had not seen it. He was about to turn around and head back when he spotted the old saloon, just up ahead and across the street.

The place looked like it could have been the setting for an old Hollywood Western. It was a three-story building with a clapboard façade the color of brick—which looked to Jack to be original—and it was dotted by a half-dozen windows. The entrance was a stereotypical swinging door. It probably had originally been a hotel (though he knew enough to know what most old Western hotels with bars were *really* used for). There was a tiny balcony just above the entrance, which had probably been used for many a late night escape from the second floor. The place was called The Saddleback, which seemed to fit it perfectly.

Jack glanced at his watch: he had been gone from the motel only twenty minutes. But Althea had told him to take his time. Buildings in general interested him, which was why he did what he did for a living, but he found old buildings particularly fascinating. He liked to study the construction and finishing, outside and in. Crossing the street, he gave a cursory examination to the façade and front window before going in.

The interior of The Saddleback was very dark, which made careful study of the architectural features difficult. Portable neon signs, most advertising brands of beer, glowed from every wall, and over the bar there was an age and smoke-stained painting of a dance hall girl, barely contained in her frilly dress, seated on a saddle. In films and on television, this kind of Western bar always had a long mirror backing it, which invariably one of the cowboys would get catapulted into during the obligatory barroom brawl, yet this place did not. Maybe that was simply a Hollywood touch. A juke was playing an old Doors song (like there was another kind of Doors song) and the only other people in the bar were a couple down at the end. The man was beefy trucker type with a shaved head, moustache, goatee, and tattoos that crawled out of his sleeves. The woman was stacked like a centerfold and was packed into her tee and jeans like a sausage in its casing. They were clearly having a party of their own.

"Hi, what can I get you?" The bartender was a woman, maybe forty, or maybe only thirty but with a lot of miles, who wore a tee-shirt with the bar's logo on it, a crudely-sketched picture of a cowgirl whooping it up on a saddle.

Jack surveyed the beer taps, finding the usuals: MGD and Pabst; imports Heineken, Bass and Guinness; microbrews Alaskan and Firestone, and one that startled him to the point of eliciting a gasp. A square box at the top of the pump said: *Wood City ESB.* Some microbrewery actually named a beer after the ruined town? Maybe the place was not as forgotten as he had assumed. "What's that Wood City?" he asked the woman.

"I'm not sure, we just got that in," she said. "I think it's local. I can pull a sample for you, if you like."

"Please."

The woman took a shot glass and filled it with a dark amber brew and placed it in front of Jack. He smelled it first, and found it to have a rich, almost chocolaty aroma. Sipping it, he found it smooth and not at all hoppy; almost wine-like. No, make that ciderish. It was unlike any other kind of beer he had ever had. "Interesting," he said. "I'll take one of these." The bartender pumped a pint glass full of the ale and placed it in front of him. As he drank, Jack tried to think about things. His life; his family; Dani; what the hell he thought he was accomplishing by running off with his daughter only to leave her with a near-total stranger. He took another long swallow of the ale, and this time detected a kind of nutty flavor. That was certainly fitting; everything about this week so far had been pretty nutty.

Before he knew it his glass was empty and the bartender was asking him if he wanted another, and he sure as hell did. As he sipped his eyes were drawn down to the couple at the end of the bar. The woman was now crouched down under it, like she was hiding. Maybe she dropped a contact lens, or something, Jack thought. But a second later, registering clearly over the vocals of Morrison, he heard the sound of a zipper. Jack watched as the woman on the floor unsheathed the grinning man's cock and began blowing him.

"Christ," he uttered, strangely unable to look away.

The guy getting head took a bottle of Corona upturned it, the movement of his throat as it accepted the beer matching the woman's under the bar, pull for pull. Easy in; easy out.

Finally Jack was able to break his gaze. The bartender was standing right in front of him, a sly grin on her face. "Does, uh, this sort of thing happen often in here?" he asked.

She smiled broadly, revealing small, crooked, nicotine-stained teeth. "You'd be amazed what happens in here, Jack."

He stiffened. "How do you know my name?"

The bartender laughed. "You're really a Jack, huh? That's so funny. I just call everyone Jack, kinda like Mac or Doc or Bud. Ready for another one?"

"Sure, why not." It would have to be the last one, though, since he was starting to feel them, surprisingly so. Maybe Wood City was one of those microbrews that was crafted with a higher alcohol content than the average beer.

The woman was back up on the bar stool now, and the still-grinning man bought her a beer, which seemed like the *least* he could do. As Jack glanced over, the woman met his gaze and smiled, then winked at him and licked her lips. Christ, was she about to come onto him now? He looked away, actually embarrassed, and heard the woman laugh raucously. Jack felt like a teenager who had stumbled into a party for which he was not quite ready. Forcing himself to look somewhere, anywhere, other than the woman at the end of the bar, he glanced back up at the painting of the saloon girl.

Jack blinked. Something was wrong.

When he had first looked at the picture, he had a seen a blowsy woman who was barely contained by the low-cut bodice of her dress and was showing a lot of cleavage. But now the figure in the painting was topless. Her breasts were large and skillfully rendered, showing such realistic details as being slightly different sizes, which while not all that uncommon in real life, was virtually never displayed in art, photography or film. Or maybe it was just a perspective flaw. The figure's dark nipples stood out as though three-dimensional, and looked wet.

"Good god," Jack moaned.

The face now looked different, too. Previously, the painted woman had worn an open, happy, if slightly naughty expression. But now it was not so much naughty, as demented. Her eyes were just a little too widely open, glaring madly, while her mouth was not so much smiling as grimacing. But the biggest change was that her skimpy dancehall trunks now had a slit in them; the woman was not simply sitting on the saddle now, she was using the saddle horn for a dildo.

Jack felt hot. Dizzy. He had to go to the bathroom.

What in god's name was in that beer?

"Where's the restroom?" he asked the bartender, who directed him to the end of the building and to the right. Jack ran for it, his bladder near-bursting. He made it to the men's room just in time, and ignored the general condition of it, which was smellier and grimier than those of most of the off-ramp gas stations he'd been in. Fearing he did not have the time to pull his dick through the openings in either his pants or briefs, he just jammed both down his legs and stood there, bare-assed, flooding the reeking urinal. The feeling of relief was almost orgasmic. He was nearly done when he heard the door open, and swiftly wondered how he was going to explain to the other guy from the bar why he was standing there with his pants and shorts around his shins, like a three year old just getting used to a public urinal.

He did not have to; it wasn't the bald tattooed man from the end of the bar. It was the woman who had been with him.

"Shit!" Jack crouched and pulled his shirt tails down to cover his penis.

The woman laughed. "I love a man who knows how to curtsey. And from where I stand, you got nothing to apologize for."

"Do you mind?"

"I don't mind nobody," she laughed. "How about I get out of these?" The woman unfastened her skin tight jeans and slid them down. She wore no underwear. Once the woman had shed her jeans, she slid her top off, revealing her full heavy breasts with large brown nipples, standing erect. As she grinned hungrily at Jack, whose breathing was becoming labored, what was left of his rational mind realized that there was something vaguely familiar about her face, beyond having just seen her out in the darkened saloon, but he could not place it. The woman's face was pleasant, but not drop-dead gorgeous. But she did not need to be drop-dead gorgeous. Such an aura of animal sexiness was coming from her that her face was almost immaterial. Her full auburn hair looked clean and there was not a mark on her body anywhere, no scars, no tattoos, nothing. Unlike the bartender, she did not look like she'd had a hard life.

Jack did not know what to do. At least his brain and his voice did not. Another part of him, however, acting completely on its own, did.

Glancing at his cock, which was now poking through his shirttails, as hard and straight as a cedar, the woman smiled and then sashayed past him to the toilet stall next to the urinal. "I'll be in here when you're ready." She slowly closed the stall door behind her.

Jack felt weak, intoxicated, like he might pass out. The guy who was stepping frantically out of his pants and briefs, and ripping his shirt off seemed like someone else altogether, someone whose actions Jack was watching instead of performing. Within seconds, he had yanked open the door of the stall, so horny that he was developing chest pains. The woman was waiting for him. She wrapped her arms around him and, like a dancer, spun him around, then pushed him down on the toilet seat, while mounting herself on top of him. They began rocking and bouncing on the toilet, which gave way a little with each thrust, but right now Jack did not care of the thing tipped over. All that mattered was the redhead.

When he finally came it was an explosion. His mind went red and he moaned like an animal. For a moment Jack thought that he might pass out from its intensity. All he could do was sit there, eyes tightly shut, gasping for breath, clutching onto the woman's warm sweaty body for safety while he plummeted back down to earth.

Jesus, Jack thought absently, *nine years of absolute faithfulness to Elley, and then sex with two different women in as many days.* And both times the ground seemed to move. Maybe he'd been a goddamned fool for being so faithful all those years.

Apparently the redhead was experiencing a similar loss of physical control as him, since she now felt like dead weight on him. They had generated so much heat in the cramped stall that Jack would not have been surprised to see the paint on the walls blistered, but they were now quickly cooling. At least she was; the woman's skin felt almost cold to the touch.

"I don't know what to say," Jack panted, still inside of her.

There was no answer from the woman.

"Hey," he said, opening his eyes. He could not see her face because her head was draped over his shoulder. He smiled. "It was like that for me, too." He now had control of his breathing and was taking air in and out rhythmically. "Are you all right? Hey." Jack stopped talking. He held his breath, waiting to detect the rise and fall of her chest against his.

There wasn't any.

"Jesus," he said, pushing his left shoulder forward to force her head off. The woman's head flopped like a bag of flour, her long hair trailing along his skin wetly.

Her long *blonde* hair.

Jack opened his mouth to say something, but all words caught there. He was now able to see the woman sitting on top of him. It was no longer the voluptuous auburn-haired woman who had lured him into the stall.

It was Dani Lindstrom.

And she was dead.

Jack tried to scream but only a whimper came out. He lurched up from the toilet and the woman's body slumped to the floor like a pile of muslin rags, her flesh a ghastly, pale shade of bluish-gray, her dead eyes wide open and staring at him accusingly.

Then Jack heard the bathroom door open, and his heart nearly stopped. He was about to be found in the stall of a grungy men's room with the dead body of a friend with whom he had just been having sex! He began to pant out of terror, and felt light-headed. He was hyperventilating. He couldn't get air. Jesus, it was like he was in a vacuum!

A scent hit him, the last scent he could have expected in a place like this or at a time like this. It filled the room, overwhelmed him to the point of making him gag.

It was the scent of oil paint.

Jack reached out and tried to maintain his balance by pushing against the stall walls. He looked down again at Dani. He started to laugh. *That's why she's that color. She isn't dead. She's been painted.*

Then he stopped. However cold Dani Lindstrom's corpse was at this moment, Jack bested her. He felt ice in his gut as the face of the auburn-haired woman came back to him, and he realized why she had looked vaguely familiar.

Her face was the one he had photographed from the mural at the Wood City city hall, the same face that his daughter had drawn with unnatural skill in crayon at the restaurant. Only in here she had not been rendered in a cold, artistic, expressionless way; here she had been real. At least she had appeared real, and if not a real, living, flesh-and-blood woman, what in hell had he just been screwing so wolfishly?

A corpse. He had entered and copulated with and ejaculated his burning seed into a corpse.

That was Jack's last conscious thought before blacking out.

CHAPTER TWELVE

The right half of Jack Hayden's face was cold. There was something wrong with it. He couldn't move it. Christ, had he had a stroke or something?

He heard a voice from a distance, a woman's voice saying, "There, leaning up against the window."

Somehow Jack knew they were talking about him.

Somehow he managed to open his eyes.

He was literally pressed up against a pane of glass. That at least explained why half of his face felt cold and dead. He looked around and saw a policeman coming toward him. Maybe he could explain everything else.

"Sir, step away from the building, please," the policeman said.

"Sure," Jack muttered, taking a few shaky steps onto the sidewalk. "What's wrong?"

"Put your hands on your head, sir."

"What?"

"Put your hands on your head, now." Jack could see a small crowd beginning to form around him. Small crowds were the only kind of crowds they made in Glenowen.

"All right," Jack said, complying.

The policeman, a well-built guy of about thirty, patted him down for a weapon and, finding none, helped himself to Jack's wallet and checked his ID. "Los Angeles, huh? Kind of a long way from home, aren't you, Mr. Hayden?" he asked.

"I'm here on business."

"Okay, you can lower your arms. Having you been drinking, Mr. Hayden?"

"I had two beers, but I'm not drunk." Only when he saw his wallet in the policeman's hands and realized it had to have been taken from his pocket did Jack become cognizant of the fact that he was fully dressed. "Hey, what's going on here? Why am I—" Then the fog in Jack's mind began to part. "She was dead... my god, she was dead."

The policeman tensed. "Who is dead, Mr. Hayden?"

"Dani...back at the saloon...in the bathroom...I have to get back there." Jack looked around but could not see the Saddleback Inn. "I must have walked away." He turned and started to run clumsily down the main street of Glenowen.

"Hold it!" the policeman commanded, but Jack ignored him. He raced down the block and into the cross-street looking for the old saloon. It was nowhere to be found. He could hear the policemen yelling at him behind him, but paid no attention. Jack went another block, and eventually saw his truck up ahead. He stopped. *The other way; the Saddleback had to be in the other direction. He had to go back.*

Powerful arms grabbed Jack from behind, immobilizing him. Before he could protest or even cry out, he had been lowered to the sidewalk. The policeman held his arms fast, and while he was not particularly large, the man was strong. "You try a stunt like that again and I'll graze your calf with a bullet," the cop said. "It won't kill you, it won't even maim you for long, but it will hurt like hell. You want to try me?"

Jack shook his head.

"Then I'm going to let you go, and you better not move."

Jack nodded. He felt the rush of blood enter his arms after the policeman released his iron grip from them. It was temporary relief, though, since a second later the cop muscled his hands behind his back and cuffed his wrists. Then he pulled Jack to his feet as though he weighed nothing. "What have I done?" he asked.

"Perhaps you're a little too far gone to remember it, but more than one person saw you pull your little man out and relieve yourself on the corner of the store."

"I did *what*?" Jack looked down and saw that his zipper was half open. What's more, his shorts felt damp. "Shit!"

"We're going to walk back to my vehicle," the policeman said, "nice and easy, and as we do, you're going to tell me who was dead."

"Christ," Jack moaned. "I'm not sure I know anymore. That stuff was labeled Wood City ESB, but I think it was more LSD."

"What stuff is that?"

"The beer I had in the saloon, the Saddleback Inn."

"And where is that?"

"What do you mean, where is it? Right in the middle of town! Right where you found me."

The policeman stopped walking, so Jack stopped. "Mr. Hayden," he began, "I have lived in this village most of my life. I know every inch of it. I have to. There has never been an establishment called the Saddleback Inn, and there has never been a saloon, as you call it."

"Oh, bullshit! I was there!"

"Show me then."

They continued to walk until they had reached the place where Jack had first been approached by the cop, and then went further. One block; two. With each successive step, Jack became more agitated. "Goddamn, where *is* it?"

"It's not here. Now let's go back."

Jack said nothing as they walked back to the khaki-colored Jeep that passed for a police cruiser, and nothing as he was helped into the backseat. The Glenowen police station, which appeared to be a double-wide trailer on a concrete foundation, was a half mile away, on the north edge of the town. The inside was as austere as the outside, with simple desks and plastic chairs. There was only one other person inside, a uniformed officer considerably older than the man who had arrested Jack. Jack was told to sit in one of the chair beside the workspace of the officer, who was identified by a name plaque on his desk as

Robert Creeley, Chief of Police. He seemed awfully young to be the commanding officer. His subordinate, meanwhile, was a big, gray-haired, red-faced guy an inch or two over six feet and on the far side of fifty.

The lack of clutter on the desk implied that Glenowen was not a hotbed of criminal activity. In fact, he was probably the most exciting thing that had happened here for a very long time. Since the policeman was still holding onto Jack's wallet, he took what information he could from his driver's license and then asked for the rest, and Jack willingly gave it. He didn't see that he had much choice. "I'm going to give you a breathalyzer test, Mr. Hayden," Creeley said, holding up a small box with a digital screen on it. "It's very simple, you just breathe into this opening and it gives an instant read-out."

"I've seen things like this hanging on the wall in restaurants, but I didn't realize the police used them too."

Creeley actually smiled. "We had an eatery go out of business here last year, and we picked it up at the auction. But it's pretty accurate. Now, breathe, please."

Jack breathed into the opening and Creeley examined the results, frowned and asked him to breathe into the contraption again. Jack did, and Creeley asked: "How many beers you say you had?"

"Two. They were pints. Thirty-two ounces."

"Well, Mr. Hayden, according to the results of your test, you have absolutely no alcohol in your system."

"That can't be. I'm not faced, but I know I had three of those beers."

"Sorry, but I have to go by the facts, and the fact that you have no alcohol in your system kind of makes me wonder what it is that's really wrong with you."

"Meaning?"

"Do you take drugs, Mr. Hayden?"

"No. I do not. I went into a saloon called the Saddleback Inn. I had three pints of something called Wood City ESB. I...well, some other things happened, and then I saw the body of a friend of mine, and she was dead."

"But there is no place called the Saddleback Inn, no saloon, and for the record, I've never heard of a beer called Wood City ESB. What's ESB mean, anyway?"

"Extra special bitter, I think."

"I'll remember that, thanks. May I assume that you have no recollection of urinating in the street?"

"I have a recollection of urinating, but I was in the men's room of the Saddleback Inn."

"Which does not exist."

"So you say."

"What about that dead body? You said it was someone you knew. Somebody named Danny."

Jack's temples had begun to throb, but he could not rub them cuffed. "Creeley, if the saloon doesn't exist, then the body doesn't either. It must have been part of the same hallucination. Could get these things off my wrists? I'm getting a little numb."

"Free him up, Carl," Creeley instructed the other officer, who did so, keeping his gun in his hand.

"Thanks," Jack said, immediately starting to massage his temples.

"You need to see a doctor?" Creeley asked.

"No, no, I'm okay, I think. I've been under some stress lately. Maybe the atmosphere of the town did something to my subconscious and I blacked out."

"I can't help you there," Creeley said, setting his gun down on this desk, where it was still reachable should he need it, "and you seem to be rational enough now. I'd just prefer it if your subconscious would stop pissing on our buildings."

"Chief Creeley, I really don't know what's happening to me, but if I did indeed piss on one of your buildings, I am truly sorry."

"That's a good start. Now the question is, where do we go from here?"

"What are the options?" Jack asked, for the first time wondering how he was going to explain this to Althea once he had informed her that she was going to have to look after Robynn until further notice.

Creeley turned to his subordinate officer. "Carl, can you go get me a burger from someplace? I missed lunch today."

"Sure thing, Chief," the other man said, and he quickly exited the station. Jack was alone now with the young policeman, a fact that made him nervous. Creeley had already proven his strength, and if he decided he wanted to get physical with Jack, there would be little Jack could do to defend himself. Neither would there be any witnesses. When the policeman stood up and put his gun back in his holster, freeing up both fists, Jack was not sure whether it was a good or bad sign.

The policeman began to pace leisurely. "I asked Carl to leave because he's more of an old school law enforcement officer," he began. "He likes to do things by the book. Sometimes I like to cut to the chase a little more. That's the reason I didn't bother Mirandizing you."

Oh, Christ," Jack thought, trying to steel himself for the worst.

"You wanted options. Well, we've got a little cell back there, so I could hold you on public indecency charges until your arraignment, which would take place in San Luis Obispo. You could plead not guilty at the subsequent trial test your blacking-out excuse with the jury to see what they think of it. You like that option?"

"Not really," Jack croaked.

"Me neither. All of that would take a lot of time, and time is money, and money is something in short supply up here on a community level, as you can probably tell from our plush accommodations." Creeley stopped pacing and faced Jack. "You ever been in trouble with the law before, Mr. Hayden?"

"Parking tickets are about all."

"Yeah, you don't strike me as the criminal type. So the easier solution might be if you were just pay a fine right here and now, and then be on your way."

"A fine," Jack said. "This would be paid to you?"

"The check would be made out to the city of Glenowen."

"What kind of fine are we talking about?"

"Oh, how does three-hundred-and-forty-two dollars strike you?"

Jack sighed, relieved. He had been expecting to get clipped for a lot more. "Three-hundred-forty-two, and that's it?"

"That's it."

"Okay, though I want to make my position absolutely clear. I have absolutely no recollection of carrying out the act of which I have been accused, and therefore, it was not a conscious, premeditated act. Despite that, I plead culpability and will pay the fine as you suggest."

Jack reached into his pocket and saw Creeley tense. "I'm getting my checkbook." Withdrawing it slowly, he wrote out a check to the City of Glenowen in the amount of $342.00, signed it, and handed it over to the policeman, who looked at the signature and compared it against the one on Jack's license.

"By the way, can I have that back now?" Jack asked.

Creeley handed him his wallet. "Where are you staying?"

"The Tide Pool Inn in San Simeon."

"You going to be back in Glenowen at any point?"

"Possibly."

"Okay. The city limits are clearly marked, you can't miss them. So whenever you're between them, how about you pull out that cell phone that I felt when I was patting you down and you call me to let me know that you're here, providing you can get service. If not, use a pay phone." Rob Creeley took a business card from a ceramic holder on his desk and handed it to Jack. "Number's right there. Me or ol' Carl are either on duty or on call just about all the time, and I've got an officer on the graveyard shift named Ray Marciba, and a reserve to boot, so any time you're in the village, day or night, you check in. Got it?"

Jack nodded. "Can I go now?"

"Have a nice afternoon, Mr. Hayden."

Jack got up and headed for the door of the tiny station, but then stopped and turned back. "Mind if I ask a question?"

"Shoot."

"Why three-hundred-forty-two? Why not a round number like four hundred?"

Creeley smiled. "Well, the last time I was down in your area I saw those carpool lanes that they put in on the freeways, and there was a sign that said violators would pay a fine of three-hundred-forty-one dollars if they were in the lane illegally. Seems to me that what you did was a little more serious than not having enough people in your car when you try to get around the traffic. At least a dollar's worth more serious."

"So you got a ticket for driving in the carpool lane in L.A., and this is your way of getting even?"

"Well, like I said, my deputy probably wouldn't see the value of my system of justice, but I've found it to work."

"What's that money really going to be used for?"

"Well, ol' Carl's birthday is coming up, so maybe I'll buy him one those fancy cakes they sell down at Luntz's Bakery."

"Get a good one."

"You can count on it. So long, Mr. Hayden, and remember what I said about calling first."

While Jack had been inside the police station, dusk had begun to filter down over the village. Back in his truck, heading out of the village he passed a small liquor store, but he fought off the urge to pull in and get something to take back to the motel. As much as he wanted a drink, the memory of his hallucination, or whatever it was, was just too disturbing to actually crack open a bottle.

All things considered, he had gotten of easy. If Creeley had really wanted to stick it to him, he could have, but he chose not to. In fact, Jack was finding it very hard to try and work up a dislike for the young officer. Under different circumstances, spending time with Creeley would probably turn out to be a lot more pleasant than spending time with Marcus Broarty. Or at times even with Elley.

He arrived back at the Tide Pool much later than he had

planned, and hoped Althea was not upset by his prolonged absence. Before he chanced finding out, though, Jack stopped at the front desk. "Has Ms. Lindstrom from room 207 come back yet?"

"I don't know," the chubby young clerk answered, "let me try her room." He dialed and stood there long enough for seven or eight rings, then hung up. "No one answers."

"Okay, thanks," before heading back for his room.

As he walked in, Robynn cried out, "Hi Daddy! Noni is reading the funnies to me." The two of them were on the bed—Robynn sprawled, and Althea sitting—with the comics page of the local newspaper spread out between them.

"Great, punkin," Jack said. "Here, I got something for you when I while I was out." He held out the plush otter.

With a gasp and a squeal, Robynn ran for it and grabbed it, hugging it tightly. "I *love* him! What's his name?"

"I thought you could name him."

"How about Oyster Cracker?"

Jack laughed. "Sounds perfect."

Happily lost in her own world, Robynn then took Oyster Cracker on a tour of the room, showing him every drawer and corner, even under the bed, where she admonished the toy not to hide.

Jack smiled, watching her, and then turned to Althea. "No problems, I take it," he said.

"Oh, heavens, no," the woman answered, but the slightly worried expression on her face belied her words. "She was good as gold. Did you get everything you needed to get done?"

"Yeah, yeah, but I guess I'd better start thinking about dinner, huh? How about the motel coffee shop for tonight?"

"Fine with me," Althea said.

Jack was examining the old woman, who seemed to be working hard to put on a cheerful façade. "Althea, are you sure everything is all right?" he asked quietly.

"Yes, why?"

"I don't know, you look a little distracted is all."

"Oh, well, to be honest I think I might have nodded off for a few minutes while you were gone," she said. "I know that's not a good thing to do when you have a small child, but I'm not used to this much activity. I had a dream. Or, if I wasn't really asleep, then it was some kind of vision."

"Howard?" Jack asked.

"Only partly," Althea replied. "I was back at that party at Hearst's castle, the one I mentioned. Remember I told you that there was some kind of commotion involving one of the artist's paintings? Well, it all came back to me. One of the guests was an actress, I can't even remember her name, but she was a nice looking girl who suddenly became hysterical and screamed that her painting changed when she looked at it."

Like the painting of the woman in the Saddleback Inn, Jack thought. His body temperature felt like it instantly dropped several degrees.

"And in the midst of all this was a strange man," Althea went on. "There was something about him that was very unpleasant. Well, having had that memory come back so suddenly and vividly after all these years troubled my mind a little bit. But I'll get over it. What is it they used to say? Press on, regardless?"

Whatever was happening around them, Jack only hoped he had the strength to.

Robynn, having finished showing her new toy around, came running back up to him. "Daddy, I'm hungry." She held up Oyster Cracker in front of her and in a low voice added: "Me hungry too. Me want soup."

Jack laughed. "All right, Oyster Cracker, we'll get you some soup. You too, punkin. Let me just clean up a little, then we'll go."

Jack went into the bathroom and washed his hands, splashing a little of the water on his face. He did not close the door because he did not have to go. He had obviously taken care of that in downtown Glenowen. Grabbing one of the undersized towels, he dried his face and then checked his hair in the mirror.

And then Jack Hayden nearly cried out.

Hanging on the wall behind him, reflected in the mirror, was a framed antique photograph. He spun around to look at it and felt his heart rate triple. It was an example of the kind of decoration one usually finds in motel rooms, though not always in motel room bathrooms. The photograph was clearly old; it was sepia toned and depicted a building front with a horse tether rail to the side. A woman in an old fashioned dress was standing by the door of the building.

Jack inched closer to the photo, feeling his gooseflesh rise as he examined it.

There was no question; no mistake. It was a photo of The Saddleback Inn. And the woman in front was the one he had screwed in the men's room.

The woman from the mural.

CHAPTER THIRTEEN

"You're white as a sheet," Althea said as Jack staggered out of the bathroom. "What's wrong?"

"Could you do me a favor?" Jack said, and when she nodded, looking concerned, he asked her to go into the bathroom and look at the picture. Althea did, returning a moment later, a frown on her lined face. "Of all the framed photographs to put in a motel suite, that has to be the strangest," she said. "Why would anyone think a guest would like a picture of a hearse?"

"A what?"

"That's what that horse-drawn cart in the photograph is, an old-time hearse. It's in poor taste, if you ask me."

Forcing himself to go back into the bathroom, Jack looked at the picture and saw that Althea was right: it was a hearse, parked in front of the Saddleback Inn. There was no sign of the woman.

Had he simply imagined her? Was he imagining everything?

Taking one of the neatly folded towels from the metal rack over the toilet, Jack draped it over the frame, covering the picture up, then went back out into the room. "You know what, Althea? I'm really not very hungry. Could you take Robynn down to the restaurant while I stay here and rest?"

"Oh, sure, that's no problem, is it, punkin?" she asked Robynn. Then to Jack she added: "I hope you feel better." Her expression, however, virtually shouted: *You're experiencing something too, aren't you?*

Jack did not answer. Instead he handed over two twenties

and hoped there would be change back, and then watched as they left the room. "Bye-bye, Daddy," Robynn called from the hallway, clutching Oyster Cracker tightly to her, right before the door swung shut.

Jack sat on the bed and massaged his head. "What in god's name is happening to me?" He stretched out on the bed and pulled out his cell phone. He tried Dani again but once more he got the flat, dead-air, searching signal that mean her phone was not receiving service. Maybe he should tell her about his service the next time he saw her, whenever that would be.

He turned on the room TV and found an old Eddie Murphy movie, but did not really watch it. It was simply noise.

* * * * * * *

When Jack heard the key card lock on the door clicked and the door opened, Jack wondered why Robynn and Althea were back so soon. Could the restaurant be closed? But then he glanced at the clock and saw with surprise that nearly an hour had passed since they left. There was now a violent crime drama on the television. Had must have fallen asleep and not realized it.

Robynn leaped into the room and blurted, "Hi-daddy-guess-what?"

Jack switched off the television. "What, punkin?"

"They have popcorn chicken at the restaurant and it's really good. But how do they pop it? Is it in a bag like regular popcorn and they put it in the nuke?"

The smile on Althea's face told him that his daughter had already asked her, and the shrug that followed told him that she had not been able to come up with an answer.

"Gosh, Robynn, I don't know," Jack replied, sitting up in the bed. "Those chefs can really be tricky."

"Like in *Ratatouille*?" *Ratatouille* was one of her favorite films.

"I guess."

"Can we go back tomorrow?" Robynn asked. "I want you to

go, too."

"Sure, punkin, we'll go there tomorrow. Turning to Althea, he asked: "Was your dinner good, too?"

"Oh, yes, though not quite so exciting. Are you feeling any better?"

"Yeah, some, thanks."

"If you want to go get something, go ahead, we'll be fine."

"No, I'm still not very hungry, but thanks."

"I have to go," Robynn said, rushing into the bathroom.

"Close the door," both Jack and Althea called out, then they laughed.

Once Robynn was out of earshot, Althea said, "She's such a sweetie."

"Yeah," Jack agreed.

"Look, Jack," she said, lowering her voice, "we both know that something unusual is going on here. I don't presume to know what it is, but the fact that I somehow knew I had to go to that town and wait for someone to come along, it was like...well, I can't say what it as like. And if you don't mind my saying so, you've been a little spooky since you came back from getting gas, even before the business with the picture in the bathroom. So I have to assume something along the same lines as Howard's coming to me has happened to you."

Jack sighed and nodded.

"I won't ask what," Althea went on. "I figure if you want to tell me about it you will. But if you need to be alone some more, I'll understand. Robynn and I will be fine." She sat down on the edge of the bed, next to him, which made Jack surprisingly uncomfortable. "I've pretty much been alone myself over the last decade, so I tend to take it for granted. But for people with responsibilities, like you, some alone time can't hurt."

"What are my responsibilities?"

"Well, Robynn, for one."

"I have a wife, you know."

"Yes, but she's not here."

Jack leaned back on the pillow. "I wish I could put it into

words, but I feel like...I don't know...like something is coming that I have to be a part of. Almost like...well, this will sound strange."

"Like you're being called by a force," Althea finished for him.

Jack stared at the older woman. "Yes."

"I know. I feel it, too."

"What is it?"

"I have no idea, but I trust Howard."

"He must have been a very special person."

She smiled. "Everybody should have someone like Howard in their lives, at least once. Oh, I guess what I'm trying to say, not terribly successfully, is that as I've gotten older, I've come to believe that everything means something, things don't just happen randomly. I usually don't know what they mean at the time, but I often find out. And I think we're going to find out what all of the strangeness we've each been encountering means at some point. I just hope I'm up to it." She smiled again, and for the first time Jack realized that Althea must have been a beautiful young woman. He almost wished he had been around then.

The toilet flushed in the bathroom and soon Robynn came bounding out. "Why is there a towel stuck up on the wall?" she asked.

"Oh, that?" Jack began, groping for an explanation that would satisfy her probing five-year-old mind. "There's a picture underneath it and, uh, the glass over it is cracked, and I couldn't get it off the wall, so I put the towel over so than none of the glass would fall out onto the floor."

"Oh," the girl said, accepting it.

The rest of the evening passed uneventfully. Robynn wanted to go to the motel swimming pool, but it Jack decided it was too late, and she was tired enough to accept the decision. Once Robynn was tucked in, Althea went to her room, and Jack went into the bathroom, careful to keep the door closed so that the light did not bleed into the room. He sat on the toilet, pants on, for about a half-hour, trying to think. Every so often, he would glance up into the mirror and see the reflection of the covered picture on the wall behind him.

He had to know.

Jack rose slowly and turned, reaching out for the towel, feeling moisture spring from his upper lip. His hands stopped just as they were about to grab the towel and froze.

"This is ridiculous," he muttered, but even so, it took another minute before he could summon the courage to rip away the white terry cloth.

Jack had tried to prepare himself for just about anything, but when he pulled the towel away and stared again and the photo, he found there was no change. He had actually been expecting one. It would have fit in with all the other strange shit that was going on around him. But the photo was exactly the same as it had been the last time he saw it: the Saddleback, the hearse, the sepia tint, all the same. But still different from the first time he had seen the picture.

Jack sat back down on the toilet and put his head in his hands. What has happening to him? What could he do about it? Not much, he decided. Maybe tomorrow in the daylight things would be clearer.

* * * * * * *

"Hey, babe?" Rob Creeley called from the bathroom, "do we still have that local history book lying around somewhere?" Maria Ruiz Creeley stepped into the room, wearing nothing but panties and a tee-shirt so white it made her skin look even darker.

"You're not going to read in bed," she said, staring him down. "Not tonight. I've turned off your cell phone, too." She slid out of her panties and threw them in the corner, then disappeared through the door. The white tee came flying through a second later. "Don't be long," she called out from the other room.

Creeley looked in the mirror and, for the millionth time, thought: *You are one lucky sonuvabitch*. He and Maria had been married just under two years, were still technically newlyweds, and they acted like it. If anything, they acted more like it now then the first six months of their marriage. How had managed to land her was anybody's guess. It's not that he considered himself homely, but he sensed that in ten years his hairline was probably going to be halfway up the top of his head and his physique would start getting soft, while she was still going to look like the star of a hot Telenovela.

Why ask why? he decided (for the millionth time) stepping out of his boxers and tossing them on top of her panties, and then following her into the bedroom, switching off the lights on the way.

An hour later, Maria was asleep, softly snoring next to him. Creeley smiled. You don't think of goddesses snoring. He, on the other hand, was wide awake. Satisfied as hell, but awake. As quietly as he could he got up and snuck back into the bathroom, grabbing his lightweight robe. Then he went out into the living room, gently closing the bedroom door behind him. Turning on one light, he began to inspect the underfed bookcase near the television.

There it was, lying on its side on a top shelf, with a small onyx bear sitting on top of it, as though holding it down: *Central Coast California in the Pioneer Era*. It was a big hardcover book that he had only barely bothered to look at before this, having been given to them as a gift by someone. But now he wanted to check something out, something that was bugging him.

Carrying the book over to the chair near the light, he looked in the back, hoping to find an index. No such luck. So he began flipping through, page by page, scanning the text and the photos, which depicted the middle of the state over the last century or so. Halfway through, he found the first mention of Glenowen, but it was only in passing. It took one more chapter before anything of note about the village appeared.

Mining town...founded by Scottish immigrants...originally called 'Quiraing'...tide pools...seals...blah blah blah.

Creeley skimmed, several more pages and began to wonder if he was being a bigger fool than usual for sitting out here in the semi-darkness boning up on history, when he could be in the other room doing a little more boning with his wife. Then, turning the page, he saw it.

Rob Creeley sat and stared in the darkened silence for a full two minutes, then shook his head and muttered: "Sonuvabitch."

* * * * * * *

The house was completely dark when Elley got home.

Getting out of the Lexus, Elley realized just how exhausted she was. The flight back to L.A. had not left New York until nearly ten, East Coast time. By this point she was running on very little food but a lot of Sudafed, which she gulped for its value as an upper rather than to clear her sinuses. She had actually nodded a few times while driving back from LAX (where she annoyingly had been charged for an entire twenty-four-hour day in the long-term parking, even though the car had only been there since that morning), and more frighteningly, had had a few of those exhaustion-based hallucinations that she used to experience while driving along back and forth to college.

Stillness greeted her in the foyer. Dropping her suitcase, she switched on the lights and headed for the phone in the dining room to see if Jack had possibly left a message saying where he was. The light was flashing, which gave her a small sliver of hope. Hitting the playback button, she heard a woman's voice say: *Jack, are you there? This is Yolanda. I have to find you before MBA has a cow. Emac's not too happy either. I tried your cell but it just rings. If you get this, please call me. It's now 3:21 and I have a feeling I'll be here late tonight. Call me, Jack.*

The message ended with the recorded sound of a phone hanging up. There were three more messages from Yolanda, who Elley vaguely recalled meeting at one of Jack's office functions, the last one coming in at 6:30. She probably continued to call Jack's cell phone, too, but wherever Jack was, he was not answering.

She slammed her fist down on the portable bar so hard that

the bottles underneath rattled. Should she call the police? No, there wouldn't be anything they could do about it. He hadn't been gone long enough to be counted a missing person, and Blaise was right about pressing the kidnapping charge: it wouldn't stick.

Elley yawned heavily and scratched her head. She should at least make one last attempt to find him. It probably would not work, but she knew she should cover all the bases, just in case—

Say it, goddammit; just in case this ends up in court.

Fighting off an unexpected sense of sadness, she picked up the phone and dialed his cell. It rang three times and almost to Elley's surprise, Jack answered it.

He spoke only one word. It was not hello, or "This is Jack," or "Yeah," or any acceptable greeting. It was not a greeting at all, in fact.

"Dani?" her husband's voice said.

Elley stood there unable to reply. *Dani, short for Danica.* In spite of herself, a tear formed in the corner of her eye and journeyed down her cheek. She hung the phone up, her exhaustion instantly transubstantiated into cold numbness.

Elley Hayden made it all the way to the couch before her legs gave out, and she sunk down in a heap, cradling her head in her hands. He was not on a bender. He was not insane. He had not taken Robynn out of nuttiness.

He was leaving her.

She was not blameless, of course. Hell, the way her mother would look at it, she bore most of the blame, if not all. But she had not really expected that her professionally-oriented affair with Blaise would have resulted in this. She genuinely did not believe it would affect their marriage one way or the other, but clearly she was wrong. And while she believed that she was not wrong often, it had been proven more than once that on those rare occasions when she was wrong, she was not simply wrong, but *WRONG!*

"Fuck," she muttered, hearing the name *Dani* over and over again. It was not simply the name but the hungry desire she had detected in Jack's voice as he said it. He had wanted it to be that woman who had called him last night, wanted it desperately. It was all in his voice, how much he had wanted it to be her.

Elley felt a sharp, cold ache in her chest. She had right-halved the concept of splitting up with Jack for the last year, thinking about it, and even talking about it with a Janice from work over a Chardonnay lunch. It had seemed so casual then, such an abstract, no big deal. But now that it actually appeared to be possible, she did not know what to feel.

She went to Jack's bar and dug out a bottle of Chivas and some flat mixer from the tiny fridge underneath and made herself a piss-poor whisky sour, which did nothing to fill the cold emptiness inside her. *Where in hell are you, Jack? Where in hell is Robynn?* He had to be somewhere around her, this Danica woman. He must be back up the coast to that site he had been dispatched to last week. But where was it? She had not paid that much attention to him when he mentioned the name of the place.

She was about to pour herself another one when she remembered his receipt basket on his nightstand in the bedroom. Whenever he had an expense, out of town or otherwise, he would habitually drop the receipt in that basket and then at some point in the future—usually when it was near overflowing and she nagged him into it—he would tally them up and submit them for reimbursement. Jack had no sense of money; none. If it had not been for her, he probably would be standing out on an off ramp now with a cardboard sign that read: *Will inspect your basement for food.* Wouldn't it be just like him, though, if this is the one time he actually submitted his receipts in a timely fashion?

She headed up to the bedroom and switched on the light. Was it her imagination, or was it colder in this room than anywhere else in the house? Glancing over at Jack's nightstand, she saw that his basket was still full. Good. She took it and spread the contents out on the bed, looking for any from the last week.

There it was, right on top: The Tide Pool Inn in San Simeon, a bill for $197, complete with address and phone number.

The phone in the bedroom was on her side, so she sprawled herself over the bed to reach it, dialed in the number of the Inn, and waited for the youthful, but bored-sounding voice to answer: "Thank you for calling the Tide Pool Inn, how may I help you?"

"Hi, has Jack Hayden checked in yet?" Elley asked.

"How do you spell the last name?"

Elley spelled, and the receptionist confirmed that Jack was there. "Would you like me to connect you to his room?"

"No, thanks," Elley replied, "but do you know if he has a child with him, a little girl?"

"Oh yes, I remember them when they came in. The girl is staying with him in his room, and the woman has a separate room."

"The woman?"

"Yes, I figured it was the girl's grandmother."

"Her *grandmother*?" *How the hell old* was *this Danica Lindstrom*?

"Ma'am, can you hold on for a moment?"

"No, actually I can't, thank you for your information." Elley hung up.

At once an explanation cut through the confusion. What if the woman he was with was not Dani at all, but Jack's mother? She lived in Reno, which was close to the California border. What if Jack had contacted Rebecca Hayden, with whom Elley had an edgy relationship at best, and was arranging to meet up with her so that the two could best decide how Jack could abandon her and take Robynn with him? *Christ, have I really been* that *bad of a mother*? she wondered.

Of course she hadn't. She was the provider.

Elley raced out of the bedroom and back downstairs to the small desk they kept in the den that was the official telephone location for the house. It was there that they kept a rolodex with family addresses and numbers. Elley quickly flipped through until she found *Rebecca Hayden*, followed by a number. The last she had heard, Rebecca was on death's doorstep, but she had been at death's door since the first time Elley had met her, and she no longer bought it. Rebecca would probably outlive her. She dialed the number and held her breath through three rings. Four rings. Five rings.

At seven rings the line picked up. "What is it?" the woman's voice answered. It sounded like Jack's mother, but Elley had so little contact with her that she could not be certain. Lowering her own voice she said, "Nadine?"

"Who?"

"Is this Nadine?"

"No, this is Rebecca, there's nobody here named Nadine, and it's two in the morning."

"Sorry." She hung up.

So it was not Jack's mother who was with him. Elley did not even need to bother checking her own mother, who tried not to admit that she had a grandchild out of fear that people would think of her as old.

Whatever was going on, she was going to have to check it out for herself, and get her daughter back in the process. And maybe Jack, if he was sane enough to bother with.

Since she was still packed from the abortive New York trip, part of her wanted to get back in the car and head up to San Simeon right then and there. But she knew she couldn't. Now that she knew where Jack and Robynn were, and that they were safe, her mind was calming down enough to let the exhaustion back in. She had to get some sleep, even if only a couple of hours' worth. Then she'd head on up for the Tide Fucking Pool Fucking Inn at San Fucking Simeon.

She only hoped her husband and whoever he was shagging were prepared for what was going to happen when she got there.

CHAPTER FOURTEEN

Rob Creeley was unusually tired the next morning. He had drifted in and out of sleep for most of the night, trying to solve the puzzle inspired by that book he had perused during the night. By sunrise, it was still a puzzle. Creeley hoped he would have an easy day ahead so he could take some time to do a little more research on a subject that he thought he already knew well: the history of Glenowen.

"What's up, Carl?" Creeley asked his officer upon walking into the tiny police station. "Nothing big, I hope."

"Big, no," Carl Dorgan replied, "but unusual."

"Swell. Let me get some coffee then fill me in."

Despite Dorgan's age and greater experience, there was no friction over Creeley's being Chief. When the Glenowen Chamber of Commerce had stumped for incorporating the city and had actually managed to get it chartered four years back, part of the deal was the establishment of its own police department, created largely in response to some vandalism that had occurred in the town's historic cemetery. Creeley figured it was being done by bored kids who had seen too many horror movies, and was no real threat to anyone, but if that was what it took for the creation of his job, then that was fine with him. Even though he had been an MP during his stint in the military, Creeley knew his qualifications to run the department weighed more heavily on the fact that he was a native son who knew the village and its people. For the rest there were extension courses at the university and the experience of Carl Dorgan, who had been lured over to Glenowen after being a San Luis Obispo Sheriff's deputy for twenty-five years. But Dorgan had no desire to be in charge of things. He hated both paperwork and responsibility other than enforcing the law and protecting the citizenry. He was a good man and he had seen an awful lot in his half-century-plus, so if Deputy Carl Dorgan (whose old sheriff's department title Creeley continued to use as a measure of respect) said something was unusual, you could believe it.

Creeley poured out a cup of coffee from the stained Mr. Coffee in the corner and sat down at his desk. "Okay, Carl, let's have it."

"There's a woman in the back," Dorgan said.

"In the cell?"

"There was nowhere else to put her. She appeared to be distressed and confused, and seemed to need a place to lie down. I made it as comfortable as I could for her."

"Who is she?"

"Her ID says she's Danica Lindstrom," Dorgan answered. "Lives in San Diego."

"What was she brought in for?"

"She was reported driving erratically on the highway. Maybe booze or drugs, I don't know. A couple of motorists saw her and thought she might need help, so they called 911 and I ended up with the call"

"You check with the CHP first?" Creeley asked.

Dorgan nodded. "They said she was close enough to town that I should deal with her."

"Wasn't that nice of them? I guess I'd better talk to her."

"I think she's still out," Dorgan said. "It's been quiet anyway."

"Did she say anything when you picked her up?"

"Nothing coherent. She was kind of moaning like she was frightened or in pain. The only word she said sounded foreign. She kept repeating it over and over again, something like *jacadin*."

"Jacadin?"

"That's what it sounded like. Might be French. Maybe it's a

perfume, or something. Her car's still out on the highway, 'bout a mile down, but I brought the keys with me. What do you want to do with it?"

Creeley didn't reply. Instead he repeated the word a couple times to himself. Then he got it.

"Chief?" Dorgan tried again. "What about her car? Can't just leave it on the roadside."

"Hmm? Sorry, I was thinking. Tell you what, Carl, you just get Jessie to take you out there and then you drive it back." Jessie Lawler was the town's reserve officer.

"Not exactly regulation."

"We'll bend the regulations for a good cause, okay?"

Dorgan shrugged, and then got on the phone and called Lawler, who agreed to meet him in front of the station in ten minutes, then went outside to wait, which was fine with Creeley. "*Jackadin*," he muttered. It was not a brand of perfume, and it was not French. It was English. It was a name.

Creeley rummaged through the papers on his desk until he found the slip he was looking for, the one with the cell number of Jack Hayden. Then he went stepped back toward the small, hardly-ever-used lock-up. Carl was right; she was asleep, stretched out on a hard bunk. Attractive, too, from what he could see through the bars, tanned and fit, though he was surprised she didn't do something with that hair. You would think that someone with a face and body like hers would at least try to make a friend of Miss Clairol. When the time came, Maria sure as hell would. But it did not seem to bother the mysterious Danica Lindstrom, so what the hell. If she wanted to have the whitest hair Creeley had ever seen on anyone under eighty, that was her business.

* * * * * * *

When Jack awakened that morning he found Robynn curled up in bed with him. It was not unusual for her to walk from her bedroom to his and Elley's at home in the middle of the night, ostensibly because she was cold in her own bed, though occasionally she confessed to having had a bad dream. Jack spent the night dreamlessly, which he appreciated. He was having enough strange nightmares during waking hours, and he did not need any more of them during the night to deprive him of sleep. Someone, though, had called his cell phone at some ungodly hour of the morning, and he groped around in the dark until he found it, hoping it was Dani. But whoever it had been simply hung up, leaving him to fall back asleep. Maybe it was the sound of the ringing cell phone that had awakened Robynn and sent her over to his side of the room.

The digital clock on the nightstand said it was after nine o'clock. This was the latest he had slept in a long, long time. He crawled out of bed, careful not to awaken Robynn, and grateful for the opportunity to jump in the shower without hindrance or distraction. He showered, shaved and dressed as quickly as he could, while forcing himself to ignore the covered-up picture on the wall, and then went back out into the room.

Robynn was not even stirring. Cradling Oyster Cracker against her, she breathed deeply and rhythmically. Jack could not help but smile.

Jack desperately wanted to sneak out to the lobby and a get a cup of coffee and a roll, or whatever they had to offer by way of a continental breakfast, but he was hesitant to risk having Robynn wake up in an empty room. Still, she seemed down so deeply. This was usually the time she was at school, but clearly she needed her sleep. She had had a pretty active day yesterday. Surely he could dash out and be back before she stirred awake. How long could it possibly take to run out and grab a Styrofoam cup of coffee and a stale donut?

Just to be safe, he turned on the room's television, muted the sound, and flipped until he found the local PBS station. *Sesame Street* was on, which was good. Then he took a sheet of motel stationery and wrote in very large, block letters: *PUNKIN, I'M RIGHT OUTSIDE. DADDY.* She was an early reader and he knew she would be able to get the gist of it. Then he drew a couple of hearts on the paper, folded it, and stood it tented on top of the TV. Then as quietly as he could, he opened the door and stepped out into the hallway.

Jack stopped at the front desk and asked yet again if Dani had come in. "Do you want me to try the room, sir?" asked the clerk, now a managerial-looking woman.

"No, that's okay," Jack said. "I'll sneak up there in a bit and see for myself."

"I'll just bet you will," said a voice behind him. It was a voice he recognized, but could not believe he actually heard. It had to be his imagination, just like hallucinating the damned Western bar and the strange illusions in the picture.

Slowly Jack turned around. If this was a hallucination, it was a damned good one, for standing right in front of him was Elley.

Jack Hayden was rendered speechless.

"Maybe we should both go up together and knock on her door," she said, her eyes turning to hard, red agate. "Where is she, anyway?"

Jack's cell phone rang and he shut it off. He didn't need the distraction right now. He was still attempting to think of something to say to his wife. All he could muster was: "Asleep in the room."

"*Alone?*"

"Aren't you supposed to be in New York?"

"I flew back when I found out you'd snatched Robynn and run away. I've been on the road since four this morning, I'm tired, and I'm not in a good mood."

"Look, Elley—"

"Jack, I swear to Christ, if you say, 'I can explain everything,' I'll tear your balls off right here and now!" The woman behind the counter considered hiding under the desk for cover.

"Don't worry. There's not much of this I can explain. Robynn's down this way."

Jack led her to the room and opened the door quietly. Robynn was still blissfully asleep on the bed. Elley hovered over her for a moment, uncertain as to what to do. Finally she decided to let her sleep. "Just what the hell's going on, Jack?" she asked softly.

"I wish I knew. Come into the bathroom, I don't want to risk waking her."

The two stepped into the motel bathroom and shut the door. Jack turned on the overhead fan in hopes of covering the sounds of what he feared would turn into a screaming match. "I'm not going to give you a bunch of bullshit excuses for my behavior, okay? It's true that I've met someone."

"Thank you for not insulting my intelligence," Elley said. "Though I would like to know why you picked someone old enough to be your mother."

"My mother? Are you talking about Althea Kinchloe?"

"I'm talking about this Dani bitch."

A wave of latent defensive anger suddenly rushed up to the surface and nearly overwhelmed Jack. "You want to bust my chops over Dani? Fine. But first you look me in the eye and tell me you aren't screwing Blaise Micelli."

Elley stared him in the eye, and then blinked. "That's over."

"Really. Well, then, if it's over, I guess it's the same as never having happened in the first place. Just wipe the slate clean. I wish I could use that one, but it's the kind of rationalization that only applies to women."

"I'll tell you what only applies to women, Jack," she spat back. "Office sexual abuse only applies to women. Do you really think I'd be in my position with the company if I hadn't put out? Do you know how many women have come and gone through the office because they told Blaise to go take a fucking hike? *That's* the difference, Jack. I slept with Blaise because I *had* to, but if you slept with that Danica bitch it's because you *wanted* to."

"Had to?"

"Somebody in this family has to make the money, goddammit! Somebody has to maintain stability! Who's that person going to be, Jack, *you*? You think we could live where we're living on what you make? What about Robynn? You know she can't go to public school, where every malicious little monster is going to make fun of her scar. But will your salary pay for private school? Will it? And will you turn that fucking fan off!"

Jack switched it off and then slumped down onto the toilet, a submissive, seated position that signaled he was forfeiting the argument. "You make it sound like I'm on welfare."

"You've been living off of me for so long, you might as well be."

Jack's mouth moved open and closed, but no sound came out.

"Well, say something," Elley demanded.

"What is there to say? It sounds like it's over between us."

From the sudden flash of shock that played across her face, Jack sensed that she just got it too. "What do we do now?" she asked.

"Whatever's best for Robynn, I guess."

"All right, she's going back home with me. Today. Right now."

"Can't it wait a little bit? You must be exhausted."

"A little, but I'll manage."

"Oh, right. You have to get to work this afternoon."

"That's not a problem anymore, thanks to you and your impromptu road trip. I think it's fair to say that I resigned by flying back to L.A."

So everything was his fault. Jack desperately wanted to put up an argument, but he had no ammunition left. There was nothing he could say. Going home with Elley, where she would return to school and be cared for by Nola, was undoubtedly the best thing for Robynn at the moment. Jack sighed and nodded. "At least let Robynn say goodbye to Althea."

"Who the fuck is this Althea?"

"A woman we met on the way here. She's great with Robynn."

"So of course you just brought her with you. I suppose you're paying for her to be here, too." A light clicked on in Elley's eyes. "I get it. You needed someone to look after Robynn while you were banging your Swedish angel, so you just picked up a hitch-hiker, right? My god, what my lawyer is going to do to you."

"Whatever," Jack sighed. He had never felt so tired in his life.

From outside the bathroom door came a small, plaintive voice, calling: "Daddy? Are you here?"

"I'm in the bathroom, punkin," Jack called back. Then he opened the door and said, "And guess what, so is Mommy!"

Robynn looked up sleepily from the bed, and her face broke into a broad grin. Leaping down she ran toward Elley, crying: "Hi, Mommeeeeeeeee!"

"Hi, honey," Elley said, picking her up and kissing her. "I'm going to be taking you home while Daddy finishes his...business up here, okay?"

"Is Noni coming with us?" the girl asked.

"That's her name for Althea," Jack said.

"No, but...." Elley shot a look toward Jack. "We'll make sure we say goodbye before we go, okay?"

"Will I get to see her again?"

"Noni must really be special."

"Hmm-hmmm," Robynn said, smiling.

"Where is she?"

"Next room," Jack said.

"Let's go see her now, okay?" Elley carried Robynn out of the room and Jack could hear the sound of knocking on the door of the next room, followed by a soft conversation. Within two minutes, Elley was back, and alone. "That old bat has some kind of power over Robynn. I've never seen anything like it."

"She loves her," Jack said.

"Goddammit, I love her too! She's my daughter! I'm sick of these little comments about what a crappy mother I am!"

Jack did not recall making one, but it did not matter. He simply shrugged.

"Christ, Jack, yesterday morning I got up and drove to the airport and parked my car and got on a plane, and once we were airborne my entire existence suddenly fell to shit. I want it to be normal again. Is that too much to ask?"

"It might be."

After glaring at him, Elley Gorman Hayden spun around and marched to the door, opened it and left the room. Through the walls, Jack could hear the faint voices of Elley, Robynn and Althea. A few moments later, Robynn slunk into the Jack's room alone and looked at him with Keane painting eyes. "How come you're not going home with us, Daddy?" she asked with all the hurt one can fit into five years of experience.

Jack knelt down and hugged here. "There are a few things I have to do here, punkin. Then I'll come home." *Whether I'll be allowed inside or not is another matter.*

"How come Noni can't go?"

"She has to help me. But you'll be fine with mommy."

"Yeah, but I miss you, Daddy."

"I'm still here, punkin."

Elley exhaled impatiently. "I'll be in the lobby. Bring her out when the two of you are finished."

"Elley—"

"Clearly you're the one she wants, so just finish your business then come out." She spun on her heel and stormed out of the room.

"What's wrong with Mommy?"

"She's tired," Jack said. "Grown-ups get tired, too."

"Are you and mommy going to get 'vorced, like Molly's parents?" Molly was a classmate from kindergarten.

Jack opened his mouth to say something, but no sound came out. Finally, he said: "Robynn, listen to me. I'm not going anywhere. Right now I have to stay here because it's part of my job, but I'll be home soon."

Robynn did not look convinced. In fact, she began to tear up. "I don't want anything to happen to you."

He took her in his arms and her hug was surprisingly forceful, almost desperate. "Punkin, is there something bothering you that you're not saying?"

Robynn pulled away and looked at him. "It was that man. He was in my dreams."

"Who was he?"

Robynn shrugged. "I don't know. I couldn't even see his face. He was like a shadow, but he scared me. He had a special name for me, like when you call me punkin."

"Oh?"

"Yeah. His was 'Harelip.'"

Jack froze, but he tried to cover it.

"That's wrong, though. I don't have a moustache."

"I know you don't, Robynn. It was probably some kind of bad joke."

"Yeah, prob'ly," the girl agreed. "But this man was talking about you, too."

"What did he say about me?"

"He said if you didn't stop what you were doing you were going to be one dead muverfucker. What's a muverfucker?"

Impossible as it seemed, Jack became even colder. He heard a hollow parody of his own voice say from a hundred miles away, "It's a kind of bird," not having a clue where that had come from.

"Why a dead one?"

"That's just an expression, like, you know, when you're really in trouble you say, 'I'm a dead duck now,' or 'I'm dead tired,' something like that."

"Is Mommy a dead muverfucker?"

Christ. "Do me a favor, okay, punkin? Don't tell mommy about these dreams. They're just between us. And don't say anything about her being a muverfucker, dead or otherwise, okay?"

"Okay."

"It's time for you to go now."

"Bye, daddy," she whimpered as she hugged him.

"Bye, punkin. I'll be home as soon as I can."

Jack walked her out to the lobby, where Elley was actually pacing, and handed his daughter over to her. He felt a horrible pang as he watched the two of them leave. What in god's name *was* he involved in? He only hoped that getting Robynn away from here would keep her safe; save, even, from her dreams.

Jack found himself wandering around the lobby of the motel, absently looking at the continental breakfast spread that had been laid out for the guests. He got himself a cup of coffee and a roll, and headed back to his room. The door to Althea's room was propped open, so he stuck his head in. She was reading a newspaper and looked up. "I guess they've gone."

"Yeah," Jack said, "and that's probably for the best."

"I'm certainly going to miss her."

"I already do."

The two of them made small talk for a while, though Jack deliberately tried to change the subject whenever Elley came up. After some time he heard a familiar sound, faintly and through the wall. It was his cell phone ringing in the next room. If it was Dani, he could finally talk freely now. "I'll be back in a minute," he told Althea, and dashed into his room, holding precariously the coffee and roll while he slid the key card through the lock. Once inside, Jack grabbed the phone and clicked it alive. "Yeah, this is Jack," he said.

"Thank god!" a woman's voice said. At first he didn't recognize it, but it went on: "Jeez, Jack, where have you been hiding, the Moon? MBA's fit to be tied!"

Jack sighed. "Hi, Yolanda. What's the crisis now?"

"Emac's freaking out for some reason, and Marc can't bluff his way out of it this time, so he's a total spaz."

"Yolanda, is Marc there?"

"No, he's on his way up to the site, Jack."

"The site? You mean Wood City?"

"He should be there by noon. He left in the early hours and was not a happy camper."

"Why the hell is Marc going to Wood City? What's going on, Yoli?"

"I can't tell, but it doesn't sound good. I've been trying to get hold of you since yesterday, but I could never get an answer."

"Sorry. I've been dealing with some other matters. Christ. I guess I'd better try to contact him."

"You may want to pretend you were killed in a car accident instead."

"That bad?"

"He was on and off the phone to Emac practically all after-noon yesterday, and in between he'd storm out of the office and rage against you for either doing or not doing something. From the sounds of it, the whole project might get flushed."

"Well, if it does, it's Marc's hand on the chain, not mine. He's the one that refused to believe my report."

"I've no doubt that you're right, but the point is, Jack, what-ever is happening sounds serious and MBA has been already started to make you the scapegoat for it. I don't want to see anything happen to you, Jack. I'm talking to you now as a friend, not as your inferior in the company."

"I don't think of you as an inferior, Yoli."

"That's my point. You're about the only guy around here who doesn't. If something happens to you, I'll be stuck here with a lot of creeps who think I'm nothing but a life support system for set of chi-chis."

Jack laughed in spite of himself, and then apologized for it. "Okay, Yoli, here's what we'll do. Call Marc up and tell him that you finally got a hold of me, and that I've been up here since last night at my own expense in order to take more pictures of Wood City, which is exactly what I offered to do, so he can't claim he didn't know. Tell him that the reason you couldn't reach me because my cell phone service went out. Tell him I will meet him at the site around noon. I'm only about twenty minutes away. Make it sound like I'm painfully sorry for being unavail-able. Can you do that?"

"I'll try."

"I have faith in you, Yoli. Call me back if you need me." Jack rang off and then dashed back into Althea's room. "I'm really sorry, but I have to go out for a while. Believe it or not, I actually have to go do some work. But I'll be back later."

"No problem," she replied. "I may just go outside and enjoy the sunshine."

"Althea, I really want to thank you for being so good with Robynn."

"How could anyone not be?"

"Yeah," Jack nodded, and then he left. After stopping for a quick cup of coffee in the lobby, he went out to his truck and headed out for Wood City. It looked like the beginnings of a beautiful day, with a clear blue sky and white clouds, with no marine layer anywhere to be seen. At least it would be a good day to take pictures.

He was only five minutes down the highway when his cell rang. "What it is, Yoli," he said into the phone.

"Is this Jack Hayden?" a man's voice replied.

"Who is this?"

"This is Chief Creeley from the Glenowen PD."

"Now what have I done?"

"Nothing, but I need to talk to you on a separate matter."

"I'm on a job right now. Can I come by this afternoon?"

"All right. Shouldn't have a problem keeping the woman here, given her condition."

"Woman? What woman? What are you talking about?"

"There's a woman here who's had some sort of lapse in memory. The only thing she's said is your name, over and over again. Her name's Danica Lindstrom."

"Jesus," Jack moaned. "I'll be right there."

"Thank you, Mr. Hayden." The phone line went dead.

Now what? Jack stomped on the gas and tossed any further consideration of Marcus Broarty out the window.

* * * * * * *

"You're awfully quiet, Robynn," Elley said to her daughter, strapped into the car seat behind her. "Is something bothering you?"

They were already thirty miles down the highway because Elley was not being particularly watchful of her speed. It was not so much that she felt she had to get back home in a hurry; rather she felt an overpowering compulsion to get the hell out of *here*. And she was not even certain where *here* was.

"I just wish Daddy were with us," Robynn said. "And Noni."

"You like Noni, don't you?" Elley asked.

"Mmm-hmm. She read to me."

"That was nice of her."

"When was the last time you read to me, mommy? You selfish cunt."

Elley Gorman Hayden nearly lost control of the car, causing it to drift across the centerline and come dangerously close to an oncoming SUV before she managed to swerve back into her own lane and then onto the shoulder of the highway, where she slammed to a screeching stop.

"*Mommy!*" her frightened daughter called, but Elley ignored it. Snapping her head around to the back seat, she demanded: "What did you say to me?"

"I didn't—"

"*What did you say?*"

Robynn was now in tears. "I said I liked Noni."

"After that."

"I said she read to me."

"After *that!*"

"Nothing." The girl could barely get the word out.

"That's not what I heard!"

Now the waterworks and racking sobs were in full force. "I didn't say anything!"

"You didn't call me a bad name?"

Robynn looked shocked. "No!"

But Elley had heard it. She heard it clear as day. And it was Robynn's voice that had spoken. But looking at the girl melting into terrified emotion before her, she could easily believe that Robynn was telling the truth.

Christ. Jack had been right: she was exhausted to the point of hearing things.

Elley exhaled and a big-rig tore past on the highway, the force of which shook her car. "Mommy's sorry, honey. I guess I'm more tired than I thought."

"You're not mad?" Robynn's voice was the size of an amoeba.

"Well, to be truthful, I'm mad at myself for reacting so badly that I scared you, but I'm not mad at you. Okay?"

"Okay."

"Let's go, then."

Elley put the car back into gear and carefully watched for traffic as she eased back onto the highway. "Look out the window at the ocean, Robynn. Maybe you can see some whales."

"Whales?" Robynn said, recovering from her spell and adjusting her position in the car seat to see out of the rear passenger window. Elley thought about trying to tune in Radio Disney as they headed down the coast, but decided to leave the radio off until Robynn asked for it. At the moment, she needed the quiet.

Twenty more miles later, the quiet was still there, and becoming somewhat oppressive, so she went ahead and switched on the radio and started fiddling with the dial, turning on both the music and the fragile normalcy.

But she had heard it, those horrible words coming from her daughter's lips. She wasn't crazy. *She had heard it.*

CHAPTER FIFTEEN

It had taken Marcus Broarty fifteen minutes just to baby his Jaguar up this washed-out wreck of a road and he cringed every time the bottom of the expensive car scraped the trail. Broarty had his car washed every week and detailed once a month, and driving through the middle of the goddamned forest, where millions of tree branches just ached to scrape against the sides and mar the ironic forest green paint, was the worst thing he could imagine putting his Jag through.

Just up ahead he saw the statue-like figure of Egon McMenamin, anger radiating off of him in waves and pointedly looking at his wrist watch. Pasting a big phony smile on his face, Broarty got out of the car. "Hey, Emac, great to see you." He approached the other man hand outstretched, but Egon McMenamin kept his gaze on his watch and his hand where it was.

"I've been waiting here for thirty-seven minutes. Did you get lost, or something?"

The last thing Broarty wanted to tell the bastard was that yeah, he did get lost. It took him for ever to find this godforsaken Davy Crockett trail, and then he had to jeopardize his car to get into the middle of the frigging woods. Instead he said: "Someone on the freeway was driving like an Asian woman, slowing everybody down like it was a funeral procession."

McMenamin looked at him. "My sister-in-law is Japanese."

Fuck! "Well, you know what I mean, Emac. I'm not saying it's *true*, but that's the stereotype."

Another long glare from Emac caused perspiration to break out on Broarty's forehead, despite the coolness of the forest. "Any word yet from your boy Hayden?" he asked.

"My assistant was supposed to be contacting him, but she's probably screwed up again. You know how it is with the staff."

"If somebody at Resort Partners screws up, they're shown the door. It's called professionalism."

"Absolutely, and this will be Ms. Valdera's last screw-up, I can promise you that."

"This still does not tell me where Hayden is."

"But isn't it beautiful out here?" Broarty said in desperation. It was beautiful; streaming rays of sunlight shone down through the tall trees, creating a patched quilt of light on the forest floor. The air was still crisp and moist and smelled of pine.

"That's what we at Resort Partners offer, beauty," McMenamin said, seeming to accept the subject change. "If we can't find it, we make it, and if we can't make it, we convince people it's been there all along. How far is it up to the site?"

The first words of *How the fuck should I know?* nearly escaped Marcus Broarty's mouth, but he managed to bite them back, saying instead: "Not far."

"Ever informative, aren't you? If Mr. Hayden is not going to show up, then that puts you in charge. I'll leave my car here. We'll take yours up."

"Fine." *Yeah, let my car get beat all to hell while yours stays safe!*

McMenamin got in the passenger seat of the Jag and Broarty took his place behind the wheel. The extra weight of Emac's body was going to make the Jag bottom-out on every bump. He started the car up and very gingerly pulled onto the road.

After a few minutes McMenamin said: "There's an outline on the left. It looks like the first building."

Broarty saw it, too. He picked up speed (at least as much as he dared), until they got to it. It was a wooden cabin built on a concrete foundation, with a plain shingle roof, on one side of which stood a sturdy stone chimney. The front door, while a bit weather-beaten, was still straight and strong on its hinges and perfectly centered within the jamb. "Jesus, look at that," McMenamin said, whirring down the window. "It looks damn near new! I feel better about this already. Let's go further."

As they went deeper into the woods, the buildings became more plentiful.

McMenamin looked at the structures and shook his head. "Why weren't there any photos showing these? Is your boy Hayden just a moron or is he deliberately trying to queer the deal?"

Of course he's trying to queer the deal, a voice suddenly said in Broarty's head; *and he should be dealt with accordingly.*

"I think you mean my *ex*-boy Hayden, Emac," Broarty said. "It's a good thing we came up here."

"My bosses will certainly be relieved."

Because of our diligence, the voice whispered.

"Marc, go up to those buildings," Emac said.

Go ahead; I'll be with you.

Just up ahead of them was the main part of the town, which they could both see appearing bit by bit through the trees. Then the pines appeared to recede, giving them a clear, unblocked view of the heart of Wood City.

"My god," McMenamin muttered, as he gazed on the town. "It's like the fucking place was built yesterday!"

All of your problems are over now, the voice told Marcus.

Broarty said nothing. He simply nodded to acknowledge he understood the voice that had spoken, and fully comprehended what he was being asked to do. He was no longer listening to McMenamin at all; only the other voice, the supportive one inside his head.

* * * * * * *

Jack Hayden roared into a parking spot right in front of the Glenowen police station and opened the door to leap out even before he had gotten the key out of the ignition. Dashing inside the trailer-cum-official building, he was greeted by Rob Creeley. "That was fast," the policeman said. "Should I be writing you a ticket?"

"I wasn't very far away when I got the message," Jack replied. "Can I see her?"

"Sure, c'mon in." He led Jack to the tiny barred cell, the door of which was hanging open. As soon as Jack saw her, he called out: "Dani?"

She was sprawled out on the cot that was anchored to the wall, her face toward the bricks. She did not move. Jack called her name a couple more times, and Creeley added: "Miss Lindstrom, are you all right?" There was a slight twitch of her head this time, and slowly she rolled over to face them.

Jack turned pale as he saw her snow white hair.

She stared at him for a moment as though unable to focus, then whispered, "Jack?"

"It's me, Dani,"

"Jack, oh Jack, *oh my god, Jack*!"

Her scream reverberated throughout the brick building, shaking both Jack and the policeman. Dani leapt off the cot and ran to Jack, and without a thought he took her up in his arms as he might have Elley, had she been so distressed. But Elley never got so distressed.

Dani clutched him back as though for her very life.

"Dani, what happened?"

Instead of answering, she dissolved into a series of wracking sobs.

"Talk to me, honey." The word slipped out as easily as if it had been his wife; maybe easier.

She regained her composure just enough to blurt out: "I went to Wood City. I didn't want to, but I couldn't stop. Jack, it's alive. Wood City is alive."

"I don't understand you."

"The whole place, it's alive! The woods, the buildings, and that damned mural. They're all alive." She buried her face in Jack's shoulder to cry. He looked helplessly at the policeman.

"Miss Lindstrom," Creeley said, as gently as possible, "could you be a bit more specific as to what happened to you?"

Dani looked up at him, her face calm. "I was raped."

The policeman and Jack looked at each other. "Miss Lindstrom, rape is a serious charge," Creeley said. "Can you identify the man?"

"No, I wasn't physically violated, I was *psychically* raped."

Creeley exhaled loudly.

"Can I speak with you privately?" Jack asked the policeman.

"Jack, for god's sake, don't leave me!" Dani cried.

"You'll be okay as long as you're here, I promise. You're safe. I'm just going to talk with the chief a few steps away, okay?"

"Don't abandon me."

"I won't, Dani."

Jack and Creeley stepped into the main room of the station, out of her earshot. "What have you got?" the policeman asked.

"I wish I knew precisely, but something strange is going on around here, even you have to acknowledge that."

Creeley said nothing.

"Is she being charged with anything?"

"No. She was brought in for her own safety and well being."

"Could she leave with me?"

"Where do you plan on taking her?"

"I have a friend waiting back at our motel who might be able to help her. She's an old woman who seems to have the facility to accept this bizarre shit."

"By bizarre shit, I assume you mean spending time in a bar that doesn't exist and being raped by the pine trees."

"And more. The woman's name is Althea Kinchloe and she's been getting visited by an old dead boyfriend."

"Okay," Creeley said slowly.

"This is what I'm talking about. You aren't accepting any of this for a second, and god knows, I don't blame you, but Althea does accept it. I don't know if you've ever found yourself in the situation of watching everything around you turn upside-down, or be surrounded by people who tell you that you can't possibly have seen what you've seen or experienced what you've experienced, but it's not a lot of fun. You start to wonder if they're right, even though you know they're not. When someone comes along who accepts it, and who doesn't look at you like you should be straight-jacketed, it's rather comforting."

Creeley studied Jack and came up with the picture of a man who was not quite at the end of his rope yet, but was working on the last yard or so. "I'll try to keep that in mind, though you have to understand, dead boyfriends, psychic rape and ghost saloons aren't subjects they teach at UCSBO extension, so it might take me a while."

"Are you still there, Jack?" Dani called from the cell.

"Right here, Dani."

"Do you know what happened to my car?"

"If she's worried about her car, she's at least starting to think straight again," Creeley said. "It was left by the roadside when she was brought in. I sent Dorgan out to fetch it and bring it back."

"Could he take it straight to the Tide Pool Inn?"

"I'll radio him and tell him to leave it there. Don't worry about the car."

"Jack?" Dani called again.

"Coming."

"Look, before you go, take this," Creeley said, pulling out his ticket pad and beginning to write.

"You're going to ticket her car?"

"No, I'm giving you my private phone numbers, home and cell." He ripped the ticket off and handed it to Jack. "If something happens that you think you need help for, go ahead and call, even if it's at night."

"Thank you." At least the policeman was not totally blowing him off. Maybe he even believed that something strange was going on, just a little. Maybe something had happened to him that he wasn't telling. He didn't bother to ask. Instead he went back to where Dani was waiting, sitting on the edge of the cot, shivering silently. "Let's go, Dani."

"What about my car?"

"It's fine. They're taking it to the hotel."

"There's so much I don't remember."

"It's okay. There's someone back at the motel I want you to meet, someone who might be able to help us

She rose slowly and said: "Can we eat first? I'm hungry. Isn't that funny? After everything that's happened, I'm hungry. It seems so dumb to be hungry."

"Your body still needs to keep going, no matter what. We'll stop at the first place we see."

That proved to be a restaurant called McGillicuddy's. As they approached the door, Jack stopped and knocked on the rough-hewn timber exterior, just to make sure it was real.

Dani ordered breakfast and the waitress, a fortyish woman with dusty brown/blonde hair whose nametag read *Trish*, soon arrived with a near-overflowing plate of eggs, bacon, hash browns and fruit garnish, and a second, smaller one stacked high with toasted homemade bread, which she set down in front of her. *There's no way Dani's going to eat all that*, Jack thought. But amazingly, eating slowly, almost mechanically, Dani Lindstrom cleaned up every bit of food from her plate. Jack wondered when her last meal had been.

When his cell phone rang, he thought about ignoring it again, but then thought it might be Elley. "I should probably take this," said, putting the phone to his ear. "Hayden."

"Jack, where are you?" Yolanda's voice demanded. The concern, nearing panic, in her voice was tangible.

"Yoli, I'm sorry. I know I was supposed to meet Marc, but I got delayed. What's wrong now?"

"I got this frantic call from Marcus. He was babbling like an idiot."

"That's unusual?"

"Something is seriously wrong up at Wood City. You need to get there."

"I was actually on my way there when something came up. But tell me what's happening?"

Yolanda was not someone given to hysteria, or even hyperbole, which made her intense agitation even more concerning to him. "Take a deep breath, Yoli, and give me the details."

A deep, hollow, despairing sigh came over the phone line. "Marcus called and kept saying over and over that he had done something 'righteous.' That was his word"

"Like what?"

A pause, then: "He said he killed Emac."

CHAPTER SIXTEEN

Jack said nothing.

"Are you still there? Jack, please, you have to do something!"

"Christ. Okay, I'll do something."

Yolanda hung up and Jack put the phone back in his pocket. "This just keeps getting better and better. There's an emergency at Wood City and it sounds like I have to check it out. I'm going to drop you off with Althea back at the motel and then head on up." Without bothering to wait for the check Jack took out his wallet and set down a twenty and a couple of ones, and then got up to go.

"I need to use the bathroom," Dani said.

"Take the mirror slow, all right?"

"Did I wake up green, or something?"

Jack shook his head. "White."

She looked at him uncomprehendingly.

"Your hair, Dani."

With a look of alarm, Dani grabbed a strand and pulled it as far as she could into her sight line. "I don't understand."

"It's not unattractive," Jack said quickly. "Besides, if you don't like it I'm sure it's something you can color, it's not like a scar—" Robynn's face immediately jumped into his mind, and he felt momentary shame for not even giving a thought to her since going to rescue Dani from the Glenowen police station.

He watched her as she made her way through the tables to the marked restroom door, and smiled at the thought that, even with snowy white hair, she was still causing men's heads to turn and watch her walk. Dani remained in the bathroom for what seemed like an hour, during which time Trish reappeared to collect the money and chirp over the size of the tip, which Jack realized was about seven dollars. He was just about to ask her, or someone from the restaurant, to go check on Dani when she finally emerged. She looked pale, stunned, but she was still functioning. She had tied her hair behind her in a ponytail. "I don't understand any of this," she said as they left the restaurant.

"I know, but you still look fine, Dani."

"I look like something from *Star Trek*."

Neither said anything more until they got to the motel. Dani's car was already in the parking lot; Dorgan was nothing if not efficient. Jack took her to Althea's room, hoping that she was in, and was happy to find that she was. He introduced the two women and was happy to see a faint smile on Dani's face when Althea said: "Oh, what lovely platinum hair!" As soon as he felt comfortable leaving them, he went back to his truck and headed for Wood City.

As he drove, Jack insanely found himself hoping that Marcus *had* killed Emac. With McMenamin dead and Broarty in prison for it, maybe this whole crappy Wood City fiasco would just go away. That would hardly solve all of Jack's problems, but it would be a start.

The sunny day was beginning to cloud over. Or maybe he was just getting closer to Wood City.

It was only early afternoon, but he was already getting thirsty.

At the turnoff from the highway, Jack felt a drop in temperature, and he was uncertain as to whether it came from the outside or inside of him. As he got closer, he started to shiver. It was not simply the temperature, real or imagined, but something more fundamental; a shedding of life, almost, as though little by little he were dying. Not dying himself, but entering something dead. If being born was entering the realm of the living, then Jack was doing the opposite. He was driving his truck into the womb of something dead.

Instinctively he pulled out his microcassette recorder.

Switching it on, he spoke: "Today is May seventeenth and I'm driving into Wood City, completely unaware of what I am going to find here. I have been told that my boss, Marcus Broarty, has experienced some kind of breakdown, possibly one involving our client, Egon McMenamin, of Resort Partners. I do not know what awaits me at the sight, I only know what I am feeling, and that is extreme discomfort—" He stopped talking when he saw the car. It was a Chrysler luxury job with Nevada plates—it had to be Emac's—and it was parked off to the side, leaving barely enough room for him to squeeze his truck past. Why would he have left it out here? Jack wondered. But that thought was driven away a second later when he recognized the spot in which he was stopped. It was the place that only days before had been impossible to pass because of a felled tree, but now it was perfectly clear. What's more, the road ahead was completely free of tangle and brush. Raising the recorder to his lips he said: "Someone has apparently been doing some brush work out here." *But if someone had, they took all the chopped debris away with them, because there are no piles of brush and branches lying around anywhere.*

Jack drove past the car and deeper into the woods, until he came to another car, and this one had to be Dani's, the one that the police were supposed to pick up for her. But that wasn't what worried him. It was the forest itself. Something was not right. It was all different. In only a couple of days, something had happened to the entire woods.

"What the *fuck!*" he shouted when he saw the first building.

Jack pulled the truck up in front of it, jumped out and ran to the porch of the cabin. It was built of clapboard, a technique no longer in use, but fairly common in the early part of the last century, and it had a stone chimney and glazed windows. Touching the glass, the putty holding in the pane felt supple. "This is nuts," Jack uttered, then remembering that he had brought his camcorder with him this time, he ran back to the truck and retrieved it, fumbling to the small video device free of its zippered fabric case. Switching it on, he lined up the cabin in the viewfinder and began talking, knowing that the condenser mike would pick his voice up clearly.

"I am standing on the porch of a complete cabin, which appears to be inhabitable," he said. "Its walls are made of bevel siding, and I would estimate its floor space to be about six-hundred square feet. The structure appears new, and either I am insane now, or I was insane the last time I was here, but I would swear on every Bible in America that this building was nothing but a ruined foundation just a few days ago."

Could Resort Partners have already started their reconstruction? That was possible, but if so, where were the construction vehicles? Where was the scrap dumpster? Where was any sign that anyone except him had been here within the last month?

"I'm getting back into my truck and continuing to drive into Wood City," Jack said, holding the camcorder lens up to the windshield and trying to keep it steady as he slid back behind the wheel. "And while I'm not a religious man, may God go with me."

Driving and taping at the same time was not easy, but he did the best he could. He passed cabin after cabin, slowing down to get a good video shot of each one, muttering over and over, "I don't fucking believe this." When he finally came to "down-town" Wood City, he saw Marcus Broarty's Jaguar parked in front of the City hall building. So Marc was still here, some-where. Jack made his way to the city hall building, stopping only to mutter, "Goddamn."

The structure was not simply newer than the last time he had seen it, it was *new*. Its marble walls shone, and there were now doors at the entrance, which hung open like the arms of a preacher waiting to re-welcome him into the fold. A freshly-mown lawn sat in front of the building and the windows had glass in brass frames. There was a dedication plate on the cornerstone to the right, which Jack did not take the time to read.

Holding the video recorder in front of him almost like a shield, Jack started up the stairs toward the building. "Marcus?

You here? It's Jack Hayden. Hello! Emac? Anyone?"

No sound came back to him. If Broarty was here, he was keeping silent.

Jack was at the doorway now, looking in.

The inside of the City hall was as pristine as though the ribbon had not yet been cut. Marble facing tiles gleamed and brass fixtures on the walls shone. The place seemed filled with light and looking up Jack saw a huge chandelier, its many bulbs blazing.

"There's electricity," he uttered, feeling cold. "The juice has been turned on."

Almost reluctantly, he looked over to the far wall, the one that contained the mural.

The painting was completely revealed now. There was no trace of gray covering paint anywhere. In fact, it smelled like the pigment was fresh.

"Marcus, are you in here?"

No answer.

In a shaky voice, Jack said into the camera: "I'm inside the City hall building now. The last time I was here, only days ago, it was in ruins. Now it is new, brand new. I can't begin to explain this. I'm not even going to try. But the mural, the WPA mural that was complete covered up on the back wall is now totally exposed in all its original glory." Jack stopped talking as he examined the mural more closely.

Among the dozens of figures it portrayed was one that particularly drew his attention. The setting was a slaughterhouse— not a particularly popular subject for a piece of artwork, but one, he knew, that did occasionally surface in the pop culture of the Progressive movement, nowhere more obvious than in Sinclair Lewis's *The Jungle*. But here it showed innocent looking pigs being led into an abattoir, not by white-jacketed workers, but instead by evil-looking men in three piece suits. These were no doubt intended to represent Capitalists, and the symbolism was not all that hard to decipher. But what really caught his eye was the first "pig" in line: it was not a pig at all. It was not even an animal.

It was Egon McMenamin. Emac's severed head was lying on the ground in front of his kneeling body, his face twisted in a scream of agonized horror.

Jack was unable to tell if he had any feeling left in his body.

Lifting his gaze upwards from the painting of Emac, Jack focused more clearly on the suited capitalists in the painting, particularly the one leering gleefully over the slaughtered body of McMenamin.

It was the image of Marcus Broarty.

Jack suddenly felt ill. He made it outside just in time and vomited all over the City hall steps, then dizzily sat down, oblivious to the smell beside him and to the fact he had captured his losing his breakfast on tape.

Confronting the impossible was not Jack Hayden's strong suit. Looking at real existing walls, floors, ceilings and corners and searching for any clues that would indicate whether they were all working together or acting like a '70s rock group on the verge of splitting up—harmonious on the outside to the casual observer, but dangerously weakened on the inside—that was his job. But he could not ignore what was happening around him. Whatever the hell it was wouldn't *let* him ignore it.

He had to go back in. He had to examine that damned painting.

Steeling himself, Jack rose up off the marble steps on shaky legs and pushed himself back inside the city hall. Focusing the camera lens on the slaughterhouse scene, Jack saw that the painted body of Emac was now beginning to decompose. So, for that matter, was the figure of Marcus Broarty.

The goddamned thing is repainting itself! Just like the whole fucking town is rebuilding, renewing! It was insane, but there it was. Maybe he was insane too, but he did not believe so. For one thing, it was too easy an explanation for what was happening around him. For another, Jack had read somewhere that truly insane people don't spend a lot of time worrying about whether they're insane or not.

The painted figures glistened wetly and Jack held out a finger to them, when a strong, loud male voice commanded: *Don't touch it!* Startled, he spun around to see who had come inside the building with him.

There was no one there.

"Marcus?" he called out, but got silence in return. "Okay, that was in my mind, right?" he asked aloud, almost hoping for a reply, which did not come.

Turning back toward the wall, Jack pulled his pen out of his shirt pocket and gingerly pushed it toward the painting. Upon contact, he rubbed it back and forth and saw the paint smear. Sure enough, it was wet, as wet as though the artist had just left for lunch a moment ago.

Then another sound was heard: that of a motor starting up. It didn't sound like his truck, which left only one possibility. "Marcus!" he screamed, turning and bolting for the door of the City hall building. He made it to the steps in time to see the rear end of the Jaguar bouncing down the road, kicking up dirt and stones in its wake. Where had the bastard been hiding? After half a minute, it disappeared completely, having been swallowed up by the woods.

Shit. Should he have taped Broarty's car roaring out of wood city? Would that have been valuable evidence, or just another bizarre image capping a home-made film of a living nightmare? Even if he had recorded Marcus's getaway, Jack seriously doubted he had the courage to ever rewind the tape and watch the playback. He powered down the camera and set it on the marble step, then took out his wallet to get the slip of paper with Creeley's numbers written on it. Stuffing his pen back in his pocket, he pulled out his cell phone and dial the policeman's number, but then cancelled the call before the policeman answer it.

What would he tell Creeley? He had not actually *seen* Marcus, only his car. As for Marc's claim that he had killed Emac, he had only the word of the rattled secretary, which he believed would qualify in court of law as hearsay.

Maybe if he could bring himself to genuinely believe that Marcus Broarty was capable of taking the life of another he would have felt more responsible to pass on the information he'd received. But Jack doubted the fat fuck had it in him. If anything, his confession was a hallucination brought on by Broarty's looking at the mural.

Jack tried to figure out what to do next, but nothing came to him, nothing except get the hell out of the woods. Racing to his truck, he got behind the wheel and started it up, maneuvering it around so that it pointed the way out, then took the mysteriously smooth road as fast as he dared, dreading the thought that he would ever have to come back to this place again.

Jack distinctly heard a voice somewhere in the truck say: *Don't worry; you'll be back soon enough.* That was when he floored it.

CHAPTER SEVENTEEN

By the time Carl Dorgan made his way back to the point where he had watched Jack Hayden turn off the highway and into the woods, he figured he was a hound who had lost the scent. Earlier, he had followed Hayden out here from the Tide Pool Inn, where he and Jessie had delivered the Lindstrom's woman's car. He had radioed the chief to tell him they were coming back, but Creeley surprised him by asking him to keep an eye on Hayden, just in case. Since he had to stay put, he left Jessie to sweet-talk the motel into shuttling her back to the station (though he knew ol' Jess could talk just about anyone into just about anything).

After twenty boring minutes in the parking lot, Dorgan had radioed back in. "Chief, Hayden's truck is still in the lot, though there's no sign of him," he'd said. "You want me to go inside?" Before he could receive an answer, though, Jack Hayden had rushed out of the hotel like he was on fire, jumped in his truck, and tore out. Dorgan followed at a safe distance, trailing him all the way to the woods. But then what sounded like an emergency call came in that pulled him away from his stakeout—a call that proved to be bogus. Dorgan could not figure out how someone could have circumvented dispatch and hack into the official channel to deliver a crank call! Whoever had done it, though, had sent him on a thirty-minute wild damn goose chase, and now that he was back, he seriously doubted that Hayden was anywhere in the area.

Still, he was here, so he might as well look for him.

Carl Dorgan turned the police vehicle onto the nearly-hidden turn-off and headed into the woods. He had only driven a couple of minutes when he spotted the car parked up ahead. It wasn't Hayden's, that was for sure. It was big and expensive, a Chrysler with Nevada plates. What was it doing out here?

Once he had gotten up to it, Dorgan pulled the police car over and got out to investigate. He could see through the windows that there was no one inside. Raising his head, he took a deep breath and called into the woods: "Police!" then waited for an answer. None came. "Is anyone here?" he called again. "Yoooooo!"

Nothing.

Okay, so maybe Hayden had come up this road because he knew the owner of this car, and maybe the car had broken down, so Hayden had shown up to give him a ride back to town. That made sense. It didn't explain a helluva lot, but it made sense.

Circling the Chrysler, pretty well satisfied that the owner was not anywhere near, Dorgan tried opening the passenger door, and to his surprise, found it unlocked. He went around to the driver's side and slid in behind the wheel. Nothing looked fishy, just a big expensive car sitting for some inexplicable reason out in the middle of the woods. He got back out and circled it again, taking one last look just for the record, before getting back in his own vehicle and heading for the station.

It was on that final inspection that he saw something.

A small puddle of liquid had collected under the rear license plate. Even though it had mostly soaked into the ground, there was enough on the surface to discolor the earth. Carl Dorgan carefully touched a finger to it and then examined it. "Aw, hell," he said.

It was red. Blood-rust red. It appeared to be dripping down from the trunk.

"Sweet Jesus," Dorgan muttered as he went back to the driver's seat and popped the trunk open. Moving back to the rear of the car slowly and carefully, drawing his gun as he went, he lifted the trunk lid up and peeked inside.

Carl Dorgan was not a man who frightened easily, but this

came the closest of anything in recent memory.

* * * * * * *

Jack Hayden was still shaking when he got back to the Tide Pool Inn. He hoped it would stop by bedtime. He hoped a lot of things.

To his annoyance, he discovered that his room had not yet been made up by housekeeping. They were late today. He didn't really care much either way, it was just that while he was in the bathroom washing his face with cold water, a knock came to his door and he assumed it was the cleaning staff. "Just a minute," he called, toweling off, and then answered the door.

It was Dani Lindstrom. She had tucked her hair up under a baseball cap. "You look awful," she said.

"I'd say that it's been one of those days, but so far it's been unlike any day I've ever experienced," he replied.

"Can I come in?"

"Sure."

She seated herself one of the cheap stuffed chairs at the tiny dining table. "I looked out the window and saw you drive in. I need to talk to you, Jack."

"Okay."

"You know what it's like when you have a stuffed up nose, and then suddenly your sinuses clear and you can breathe again? That's happened to my mind just a short while ago, while you were gone. Just like that it opened up."

"Isn't that good?" Jack asked, sitting up on the couch.

"Yes, except that I now remember what happened out there at Wood City. I remember what I saw in the damned mural. Jack, am I going insane?"

"If you are, then so am I, and somehow I think insanity is too simple an answer for what's happening. What did the mural show you?"

She flinched. "God. When I went there it was like I was being drawn into the City hall building. I couldn't stop my own legs, just like in a dream. When I got inside, the mural was completely revealed. I stared at it for a moment, and then I noticed that one corner of the painting showed a row of women. It looked like they were coming out of a whorehouse."

That was a new one on Jack. When he had been there that afternoon, there was nothing that even remotely resembled a whorehouse. "Go on, Dani."

"One of the women was familiar. Uncomfortably familiar. It was *me*, Jack. I was in the painting. That was bad, but it wasn't the worst. My picture...god, this is so crazy...my painted image began to *move*. Then a line of men in the painting all began to move, too. They lined up and they—"

She quietly began to sob. Jack leapt up and went to her, gently lifting her from the chair and walking her over to the sofa, where he sat her down beside him, holding her. "It's all right," he said, knowing it wasn't really.

Hot tears fell from her eyes onto his hand. "I couldn't move, Jack. My picture could, but I couldn't! I was frozen, standing there watching as man after man after man raped me."

"Dani, it was just in the painting."

"*No*," she cried. "I *felt* it, I felt *them*, each one of them, every painful thrust."

Jack winced.

"It took nearly two hours for all of them to finish. Then I blacked out. I don't even know how long I was there. I don't know what might have happened to me while I was unconscious."

"Dani, listen to me. Whatever we are suffering through, it's in our minds. Whatever this force is, it's attacking our heads. You weren't really violated back there, not physically."

Dani rose up and reached into her jeans pocket, pulling something out and holding up to Jack. It was a pair of white panties, but there was something on them. "I was wearing these the whole time," she said.

"Is that blood I see on them?"

"Look closely. Smell them."

Jack grimaced. He was not really into sniffing panties, particularly those that looked like they were stained with menstrual blood. But he did. Then he recoiled like he had been shot. "Oh, Christ!"

It was not blood on the panties. It was paint. Her underwear was smeared with paint.

"There were also traces of it on me," she said, weakly. "Want to tell me now that nothing physical happened in there?"

There was nothing Jack could say. Dani carried the panties over to the trashcan and dropped them in. "I'd flush them if I didn't think it would wreck the plumbing. There's something else, Jack: I don't want my own room anymore. I want to be with you. I'd like to check out and come down here."

He hesitated.

"Please, Jack. You have two beds. I'll pay for my half of the room. I'm not asking for sex. I don't think I'm capable of sex right now, or any time soon. I just don't want to be alone."

"Okay, let's go up front and take care of it."

"I have to get my stuff out first."

Jack helped her move her travel belongings to his room, and then went with her as she checked out of room 207. After she had finished, he told her he wanted to go into the coffee shop and grab a sandwich to take back to the room. Dani went with him and got a large cup of hot chocolate. "It's my traditional comfort drink," she said. By the time they got back to room, Althea was waiting for them.

"Oh, there you two are," the old woman said. "I've been knocking on the door of an empty room."

"Sorry," Jack said, holding his ham and cheese sandwich with one hand while slipping in the key card with the other. He opened the door and let them both in. "What have you been doing, Althea?"

"I ended up falling asleep in my room," she replied. "Again."

Jack unwrapped his sandwich. "The rest probably did you good," he said. "Do you want something to eat?"

"Oh, no, dear, I'm fine, thank you. You go ahead. I wish I

could say the nap did me good, but I had a dream."

"About Howard?"

"No, not this time. There was another man and he was wearing an artist's smock, and he was tormenting me."

"Tormenting how?" Jack asked though a full mouth.

Althea took in a deep breath, closed her eyes and then said: "By telling me exactly when and where my death would occur."

Jack and Dani looked at each other.

"He told me the day, the date, even the time," Althea went on. "That horrible, mocking voice...'*From the enchanted hill to the entombing hole*,' it kept saying, whatever that means."

Dani set down her chocolate cup and rummaged through the tourist magazines that came with the room until she found what she was seeking. "See here? '*La Cuesta Encantada*, the Enchanted Hill.' That's what William Randolph Hearst called his castle."

The old woman took a deep breath and her eyes got a faraway look. "Oh, Lord," she uttered.

"Althea, are you all right?" Jack asked.

"I've just now realized where I'd seen that horrible man before. Remember, I told you about that party that old Hearst gave where everyone was dressed in Renaissance regalia? The one where Howard was hired as a painter? One of the other painters, he was the one from my dream. In fact, he was the one who had painted the picture of that poor actress who had the breakdown."

"The one who claimed the painting changed?" Jack said.

Althea nodded. "Perhaps he's also the one that Howard was trying to warn me about."

"Could he be the one who painted the mural?" Dani asked.

They each looked from one to the other in silence, which was suddenly shattered by the ringing of Jack's cell phone, which startled all three of them. With a sense of apprehension, Jack answered it. "Hayden.... Oh, hello, Chief. What? Of course I know about the ghost town out in the middle of the woods, that's the project I've been working on. You're out there now? Why?

Yes, I was there earlier today, how did you know? You had me followed? Jesus, Creeley!" Jack raised a hand to his forehead. "Yes, I saw a car when I was out there, two cars in fact. One was a parked Chrysler that I'm pretty sure belongs to my client, and one was a Jaguar. That one belongs to my boss, but—" Jack stopped talking and listened for a minute, and then his face blanched. "My god."

Jack sunk down onto the floor of the room and started to shake again. "Okay," he said, "the owner of the Jaguar is named Marcus Broarty. No, I didn't see him, just the car, but I know the car and I saw it drive away, so I assume that Marc was behind the wheel. Yes, I think I know who the man you found is. His name is Egon McMenamin. Yes, I can come right down. You have my word I'm coming right down. Okay." Jack clicked the phone off. "I don't know how much worse this can get."

"Now what?" Dani asked.

"They found the body of my client stuffed in the trunk of a car out at Wood City."

* * * * * * *

Twenty minutes later Jack bumped his pickup into Wood City, pulling up behind the Glenowen police car. There was also a state trooper's car nearby, and in the center of the scene he saw Egon McMenamin's Chrysler. The trunk was open, though facing the other way, which Jack was grateful for. Getting out of his truck, he walked toward it. At other times he would have relished the clean piney scent of the woods, but today the aroma of nature was being intruded upon by another odor, one that hung like a thick cloud just above his head. Real or imagined, Jack Hayden smelled death.

A uniformed trooper started to approach him, but Creeley appeared from behind a tree and shouted, "He's okay, I've called him here." Walking up to him, Creeley did not bother to shake hands, then Jack saw that he was wearing rubber gloves.

"How are you, Mr. Hayden?"

"If I were capable of laughing right now, I'd laugh at that, question," Jack answered.

"Want to a peek at what we found?"

"No."

"Too bad. Follow me."

It was not the first body Jack had encountered. Years ago, not long after he had started working as a building inspector, he had been hired to go into an old abandoned warehouse in Skid Row that was then in line for gentrification. It had been vacant for a while and there were ample signs of squatting, including piles of trash, graffiti, ashes, even old feces. But there was a smell on the second floor of the place that could not be attributed to human waste. Checking it out, Jack had found his first body. It had been an old man and based on the state of decomposition he had been there for quite some time. Jack had managed to keep both his head and his last meal and run out to find a phone and call for the police (this had been before the era of cell phone dominance). Only later that evening did he begin to feel sick. It was the mental image of the maggots that did it.

So Jack figured he would probably have no trouble handling a much fresher body now, even if it was someone he knew. Still, his heart began pounding as he walked around to the open trunk with Creeley.

"Do you recognize this man?" Creeley asked.

Jack winced when he saw the face. "Good god, what happened to him?"

"What do you mean?"

"His face."

The body of Egon McMenamin had been shoved into the trunk at such an unnatural angle that he had to have been dead before going on. His head was at a near right angle from his neck and one arm was wrenched behind him, probably dislocated from its socket. But what disturbed Jack was Emac's expression. It was one of abject horror, like he had seen the devil himself at the moment of death.

"Mr. Hayden, can you verify this is Mr. McMenamin?"

Creeley repeated.

"Yes, it's him. He works...worked...for a company called Resort Partners. They're the ones that are trying to turn this area into a vacation complex. My god, I can't believe Marc did this."

"You seem pretty certain your boss is the killer."

"Who else could it be?"

"You were out here this morning, too, Mr. Hayden."

"Sure, but—" Jack stopped and stared at the policeman. "Are you saying you suspect me?"

Robert Creeley studied him for a moment, then said, "Your boss was driving a Jaguar, right?"

"A dark green one."

"I don't suppose you happen to know the plates, do you?"

"Actually I do: MBA-500."

"Vanity plates, huh?"

"Everything about Marc Broarty is rooted in vanity."

Creeley called over a uniformed officer and relayed the information about Broarty's car, then sent him away again. When the trooper was out of earshot, Jack said: "You don't seriously think I had anything to do with Emac's murder, do you?"

"I thought it was Egon."

"Emac is...was his nickname."

Creeley exhaled heavily. "I'm not supposed to judge suspects, or anyone for that matter. That's not my job, that's the judge's job. But I'm going to level with you, Mr. Hayden. No, I do not think you had anything to do with this. But I do need to talk to you privately. Come on with me." Creeley started to walk away from the hubbub with the state police, but Jack remained where he was. "Come on, Hayden, I'm not going to take you in the woods and murder you. I just don't want the others to hear this, or else they'd threaten to put me away."

"So something strange has happened to you, too."

The policeman just motioned for Jack to follow, and this time he did. The two walked through the woods until they were out of earshot of the remaining state policemen. "The first time I talked to you, when we pulled you in for public urination, I thought you were probably just another drunk or druggie or maybe a crazy person," Creeley began. "But I stopped thinking that pretty quickly. Same with your friend, Ms. Lindstrom. On top of that I've got my wife who believes in angels and devils and ghosts and she's been sensing something. She's spent the last two days lighting candles all over the house to protect us. If I were to say this to anyone else, they'd think I was just as substanced-out as I first suspected you of being. But I kind of feel it myself. There's a big dark nasty cloud that just dropped down on this whole area. I just don't know what the root of it is."

"That I think I can show you," Jack said. "It's up this way."

"First let me go tell the staties I'm stepping out," Creeley said, jogging back to the troopers to explain his disappearance. Then he and Jack walked up the road through the forest to the heart of Wood City. "These places are kind of nice," Creeley said, looking at the houses that dotted both sides of the path. "I've spent nearly all my life here and I never knew this place existed."

"They weren't nice a few days ago," Jack replied. "They were nothing but foundations, some of them." Coming to the City hall, whose walls now gleamed, he added: "And up until recently, this place was a mess."

"Who fixed it up?" Creeley asked. "I don't see any work crews or service trucks."

"There aren't any, Creeley." Stopping in front of the City hall, Jack turned to the policeman and said: "You know all about 1930's WPA murals, right?"

"That a kind of cigarette?"

Jack smiled. "They're decorative paintings that were done in buildings during the Depression, when the government hired artists to keep them from starving."

"Like up in Coit Tower in San Fran?"

"Exactly. Well, this building has a mural of its own. And as crazy as it sounds, I think that it is the source of this evil cloud you're looking for. You want to come in and look?"

"I made you come out and look at a body. I suppose I can go look at a painting."

"The body might end up being the more pleasant of the two," Jack said as they slowly walked to the steps. Creeley pulled a small flashlight from the holder in his belt. "You won't need that, the lights are on inside."

"Who's paying for the juice?"

"Damn good question." The two walked into the City hall, which was indeed alight, but dimly so, the chandelier only operating on half power. Still, it was enough to see the mural.

The figures were vibrant and colorful, almost alive. Jack and the policeman stood and looked at it, examining every image, every scene, every figure, every corner of the large work. "Fucking son of a *bitch*!" Jack cried.

"What's wrong?"

Nothing was wrong with the painting. It was a perfectly legitimate period mural showing characters going about their business in a perfectly ordinary way. "Son of a bitch," Jack said again. "I'll bet I can tell you something else, too." He walked over to the painting and smacked the palm of his hand on it, then pulled it away and examined it. Jack smacked his hand on the painting three more times in different places, then held his palm up to Creeley. "It's dry," he said. "Bone dry." Turning back to the mural, he went on: "It was wet when I was here before. The paint was *wet*. The goddamn thing's toying with us. It's tricking us. Or maybe it's just tricking you, Creeley."

"Why would it want to trick me?"

"Because I've seen the way it works. It's evil, for lack of a better word. If it could convince you that I'm just a whack job who's making all this up, it will."

"Mr. Hayden, I'm giving you every benefit of the doubt I can, but I have to tell you, if you start talking to any of those other officers out there like this, claiming that a painting on a wall has a consciousness, well, I don't know how they'd take it."

Jack wiped his tired eyes. "You think I don't know that?"

"Okay, let's get out of here." They went back outside and

Creeley sat down on the steps, motioning for Jack to sit as well, which he did. Jack grimly noticed that the spot where he had thrown up was now cleaned up and spotless. "Here's the point I'm making," the policeman began. "Everything you say is based on asking someone to believe you, and that goes against everything I was every taught in police training."

"But you still believe me, right, Creeley?"

"I'd prefer it if you didn't call me Creeley, Mr. Hayden."

"Sorry, chief."

Creeley smiled. "The day I haul your raggedy ass into jail, you can call me chief. But friends call me Cree, like the Indian tribe."

"All right, Cree. And I'm Jack, not Mr. Hayden."

"Fair enough, Jack. To answer your question, I do still believe you. Even though it may cost me my career."

"Because of your wife?"

Again, Creeley breathed in and out heavily. "Well, there's certainly that. But there's something else, too. The day I brought you into the station, I had a hard time getting to sleep that night, so I got up and prowled around, and finally pulled out this big book on the history of this area and started flipping through it. I don't even know why, just seemed like the thing to do. Guess what I found?" Jack shook his head. "An old picture taken a hundred or so years ago of a saloon called The Saddleback."

"And in the photo was a woman standing out in front of the place, right by the door," Jack said.

Creeley frowned. "So I guess you've seen that book," he said.

"No," Jack said, "but there's an identical photo hanging on the bathroom wall in my motel room, or at least there was. It's changed, too. Cree, there's no question it's the place I spent that demented afternoon, and for the record, that woman in the picture was there. I saw her. I talked to her. And I know the next thing you're going to say, that if I've seen the picture, I could just be describing the building and making up the story about being in the saloon to cover my little peccadillo out on the street. I feel bad about asking you to take my word for it, but—"

"Here's the thing, Jack. After I found the reference to the Saddleback in the book, I poked around for some more information. I called a friend of mine who works in the local historical society and asked him to check it out.

"What I learned was that there had been such a place, but it burned down some seventy-odd years ago. Where it stood is now Linder's Gallery."

"Is that good?"

"For you it is, because Linder's was the building we found you leaning against that day. So you were in exactly the right place to be coming out of the saloon that doesn't exist anymore."

Jack let that sink in. "Your fellow policemen would say that I called this historian just like you did and got the information."

"I know they would, and that's why I asked my friend Nicky if anyone else had contacted him and asked for the information. He said no, and I trust him. So, unless you're one godamighty good guesser, there's no way you could have known you were standing on the site of the old Saddleback saloon."

"And this is what's convinced you I'm on the level?" Jack asked.

"It helped. But last nights ago, my wife Maria woke me up, talking in her sleep, which is something I've not known her to do before. This is after filling the house with candles. I couldn't understand what she was saying at first, but once I became fully awake and started listening hard, I was able to catch the words. She said, 'legion is rising.' Does that mean anything to you?"

Jack felt cold. "My friend Althea mentioned something called the legion," he said. "What it means, I don't know."

"Althea?" Creeley said sharply. "Damn. Maria mentioned that name, too. Also someone named Howard."

"Howard was Althea's boyfriend. He's dead, though."

"Damn," the policeman said, wiping his upper lip. "What I was able to get from my wife's talking in her sleep is that you, me, Althea, Howard, and another person have to team up to fight this legion thing, and apparently the last person is the most important player in all this. That one's name is Robin. You know anyone named Robin?"

Jack had to force himself to remain conscious.

CHAPTER EIGHTEEN

Elley knew she was probably in for a rough evening when Robynn fell asleep in the car somewhere around the city of Ventura and stayed asleep for the rest of the trip home. She was not a kid who took naps during the day—at least that's what Nola always told her—so to sleep this early meant Elley would probably never get her in bed. And after this drive on top of last night's drive, plus all the other shit going on in her life, Elley desperately wanted some *me time* that evening.

They had not gotten in until after three. Thanks to the heaving traffic that started around Oxnard, made even worse by a three car pile up, it took almost seven grueling hours to get back. She tried to wake Robynn up, but ended up unbuckling her and carrying her inside, taking her to her room and laying her down. *I won't get her down until midnight at this rate*, she thought. Then again, it wasn't like she had to get up and go to work the next morning.

After pouring herself a Bailey's on the rocks, Elley noticed that the phone machine light was blinking, signifying that a call had come in, so Elley went to check it. It was from Chelsea Lackteen, one of the junior account execs from the office. *Elley, we've all been told that you're no longer working here*, Chelsea's recorded voice began. *Mr. Micelli called en route from New York and told Shakira to clean out your office for you. He isn't even letting you do it. The stuff's already packed up in boxes. My god, what did you do? Call me.* There was a beep and the message stopped.

"Honey, if you stay there long enough, you'll find out exactly what I did," Elley told the now-silent machine. Fine, so they packed up her office. Whatever. Fuck Blaise Micelli and the assistant he rode in on. He'd get his someday.

Picking up the phone, she dialed the office and asked for Chelsea.

"My god, Elley, what *happened*?" the young woman asked in a voice that sounded more eager for gossip than illumination.

"We had a difference of opinion at JFK," Elley said. "A five-finger difference of opinion."

"What's that mean?"

"It means I slapped his sexist pig face across the river into New Jersey."

Chelsea whooped on the other end of the line, and Elley knew that all the juniors would be dining on that tidbit for the rest of the week. Fine. Let them.

From upstairs, a cry of "Mommeeee!" was sounded. "Hey, Chelsea, I'm home with my kid and I have to go now. I'll come in tomorrow to pick up my stuff, okay?"

"It'll be here."

Robynn called again and Elley hung up the phone and went upstairs to her room. She had awakened disoriented, but Elley assured her that everything was all right.

If only.

As it turned out, the rest of the afternoon with her daughter went very smoothly. Robynn watched all her favorite shows on television, leaving Elley largely alone, and when dinnertime came Elley found some Boboli pizza shells in the pantry (how they got there she had no idea; she hadn't bought them; maybe Nola had) along with packets of sauce and a bag of shredded mozzarella in the fridge. Together she and Robynn made their own pizzas for dinner, and both of them had a great time. *I've missed all of this*, Elley thought absently as she pulled the bubbling, aromatic pizzas from the oven, and saw the eager smile break out on her daughter's face.

After dinner, Robynn colored in her coloring books, and

despite her earlier nap, showed signs of sleepiness by eight-thirty. After a quick bath and brushing her teeth, she was more than willing to crawl into bed, though she insisted that she take Oyster Cracker with her. At first Elley thought she meant the actual crackers and told the girl no, because she did not want to start the habit of her eating in bed. But she learned that it was a new toy Jack had bought for her, which had been left in the car.

Despite her weariness, Robynn asked for a book to be read to her. "Oh, honey, you can read almost as well as I can," Elley said, but Robynn wouldn't take no for an answer. So Elley pulled out *Goodnight, Moon*, which had always been one of Robynn's favorites, even though she was getting a little old for it. Robynn laid there and smiled through it and when Elley was finished, she said: "I like it when you read to me, Mommy."

After tucking her in and turning off the light, Elley went downstairs and poured herself a large Baileys over ice, then sat down on the couch in the den. *Okay, so my career is over and my marriage is on the rocks; at least I might be able to try and salvage my relationship with my daughter. Five years from now I'll look back and see this as the best thing that ever happened to me. It's a wake-up call.*

Right.

She went back to Jack's bar and refilling her glass. She felt like tidal wave had hit her with no warning whatsoever, and wiped out her life as she knew it. All her stuff was still there—the house, her car, her clothes, the gadgets, the things that tidal waves usually target—but her *life* was being snuffed out.

And she still couldn't get over what she had heard in the car, what Robynn has seemed to say, but apparently hadn't. Even assuming that it had all been in her imagination, why was she punishing herself so severely?

I like it when you read to me, Mommy.

Elley Gorman Hayden began to weep silently.

CHAPTER NINETEEN

Dani Lindstrom peeked through the motel window shades and squinted in the sunlight. She did not have a restful night. It was now a little after eight in the morning, but she had already been up for a while, trying to stay as quiet as possible so as not to awaken Jack in the other bed. She stood in the bathroom of the motel room, staring into the mirror, still trying to get used to her new hair shade—or lack thereof—vacillating over whether or not she liked it, whether she could even tolerate it. Everyone who had commented on it had assured her that the platinum somehow suited her, but always in the tone of voice that someone uses to say: *No, really, that glass eye is hardly noticeable in this light*. But it was distinctive and Jack didn't seem to mind, though it would probably be wise to stop arriving at decisions based on what Jack Hayden thought. Even though such things remained unspoken, she was beginning to sound like someone who was envisioning having Jack a key player in her life from now on, and she knew that was not to be. Jack had a wife and a daughter, and the fact that the two of them had jumped on each other and had sex multiple times was an aberration. He was not going to jettison his entire life just to be with her. Maybe some men did that, but not Jack. Everything she had seen of him indicated that he was too devoted to his sweet, sadly scarred little girl.

Besides, Jack snored like a lumberjack.

She was rearranging her hair to see if perhaps a new style would be more accommodating to the new color when she heard her cell phone ring in the other room. Dashing out, hoping the ringing didn't disturb Jack, she grabbed it up off the small bedside table and ran back into the bathroom to answer it.

It was her agent, Lillian DeLaRosa, the person responsible for booking her into her radio gigs. She was based in Reno, of all places, though staying non-coastal gave her the ability to stay in touch with smaller regional markets, and long ago Dani came to conclusion that she never slept, since she would call her at any hour of the day or night. "How's it going, sweetie?" Lillian asked.

"It's been a little strange."

"Breaking up is hard to do, kiddo."

"No, it's not about Perry. I can't really explain it over the phone."

"Well, whatever. I've got a rush job for you."

"How rush?"

"It starts tonight—"

"*Tonight?*"

"Yes, tonight," Lillian said with a touch of annoyance. "It runs through the weekend. It's in Bakersfield, a station called KSOG, it's FM and they do religious programming."

"Oh, not a K-God," Dani moaned.

"You've done Radio Free Jesus before. You just show up and stick in a few CD's and say 'Praise the Lord' at the top of the hour, and everybody's happy. It's not like they're asking you to be baptized."

"Look, Lillian, its not just that, it's simply that right now is not the best time for a gig."

There was a silence on the other end of the line. "Well, that's too bad, sweetie, because I've already booked it."

"Don't I even get a chance to say yes or no anymore?"

"Not while you still owe me money."

Dani ran her hand through her long white hair. As a result of her split-up with Perry she had borrowed three-thousand dollars from Lillian four months ago on the assumption that she would be able to pay it off quickly, but that had not been the case. She had never figured her agent for a usurer, though.

"Okay, fine," Dani sighed. She had to earn a living, now more so than ever, so turning down work of any kind was not really part of the equation, no matter how galling.

"Look on the bright side, kiddo," Lillian said, "you're getting the emergency rate. I made sure of that. Eighteen hundred for the weekend. Here's the address."

"Hold on, Lillian, I have to get something to write this with." She ran out of the bathroom and went to the nightstand in between the two beds. Jack's pen was sitting on top, as was a small pad of paper provided by the motel. Grabbing both, she dashed back to bathroom, closing the door behind her, then picked up the phone and jotted down the information. "Okay, I'll be there," she said.

"That's 'cause you're a pro, sweetie. Ciao."

Dani clicked off the cell phone. She did not want to leave Jack right now, but what choice did she have? Dani did not want to wake him up to tell him that she was leaving, either. He might try to talk her out of it, and he might be successful. Maybe the best way would be to just leave a note. It seemed cold, but it also seemed easier than looking into his eyes and telling him that she had to run off immediately.

As quietly as possible, she went back out into the room and started gathering up her things, putting them into her suitcase. Jack never stirred. She took everything with her back into the bathroom, and began to collect her toiletries. Once she had everything packed, except for the clothes she would wear that day, she took up the pad, ripped off the top page which contained the information about her gig, and then began to write. *Dear Jack*, she wrote, *I'm sorry but I've been called away for an emergency job. It's one I can't really refuse. I'll be gone the weekend, but I will come back. I will try to call in a day or so. Thanks.*

Dani was on the verge of writing *I love you*, but she held it back and simply jotted *Take care,* then signed her name. She carried the pad back to the nightstand and set it down. She set the pen down next to it, but then noticed something on her hand. "Damn," she whispered, thinking it had leaked. Going back into the bathroom where she could turn on the light, Dani examined the wet smudge on her hand. It was green, not the blue of the pen's ink. Studying it more closely, she detected the faint odor of paint.

There was wet paint on the tip of Jack's pen, the sight and smell of which made Dani Lindstrom feel colder than she ever had before in her life.

CHAPTER TWENTY

The moment Elley Hayden got back to her car after dropping Robynn off at school, she started to wonder if she was making the right decision leaving her there. There was no reason to feel apprehensive about it; it was what Robynn had wanted that day, and Elley certainly didn't want to take her daughter with her into the office if there was a chance that things were going to get ugly. Even though Blaise was still in New York, he had plenty of underlings to whom he could delegate ugliness. Yet for some reason, she felt like it was a mistake not having her daughter with her. Well, it would pass. There were other things she had to take care of that day.

Elley planned to march inside the offices of Orbit Marketing, head held high, pick up the boxes of her stuff that Shakira had packed, and then march back out, head still held high. If she had to be escorted by a guard each time, then fine. She was not going to play the victim; not for Blaise Micelli, not for one of his toadies, not for anybody.

The headquarters of Orbit Marketing was on a high floor in one of Santa Monica's few towers, and Elley had a corner office, which offered her a nice view of the ocean. She turned into the parking garage and shoved her card key into the employees only slot in the gate machine, probably for the last time, and drove to the parking spot that had been exclusively hers for the past three years.

Her name on the sign had already been covered up.

That was when the enormity of her situation fully sank in,

and Elley could not keep a small, dry sob from escaping. She sat in the Lexus for a few more moments. If she was really going to cry, she was going to do it in private. But the tears did not come. So after a quick glance in the rearview to see if her make-up was smudged, she got out of the car and headed for the elevator.

After a thankfully solitary ride up to the tenth floor, Elley stepped out of the elevator car and strode into her office as though nothing was wrong, stopping conversations with every footfall. "Morning, Jim; morning Andrea; morning Luis." In a strange sort of way, she was enjoying this. The discomfort was palpable only on the others in her office, not Elley.

Coming to Chelsea's desk, she crisply announced, "I'm here to get my stuff."

"Elley," the junior AE said, looking startled. "Oh, god, I tried to call you to tell you not to come in. Something's come up and—"

Just then Blaise Micelli walked out of his office. He froze when he saw Elley. "What the bloody hell are you doing here?"

"I've come to get my personal belongings before you sell them on eBay," she shot back. "How come you're back from New York?"

"How come?" Blaise screamed. "Because Metrolife not only cancelled the party when you disappeared, they cancelled the whole goddamned account! A twenty-five-million dollar account down the crapper because of *you*!"

"So what are you going to do, Blaise?" Elley said quietly. "Fire me?"

Micelli was starting to turn purple. "I'm going to fucking sue you for every penny you've ever seen, that's what I'm going to do!" he shouted. "By the time I'm through with you you're going to be pushing a shopping cart on the street! You'll be working as a whore in Tijuana!"

The room suddenly turned into a vacuum; no air was present.

My god, Elley though, *he must be hopped up on something.* She knew Blaise occasionally took recreational drugs—the usual ones, pot, poppers, coke, sometimes Ecstasy—but she had never seen him out of control like this. The rational side of her knew she should back down for the benefit of everybody, particularly herself, but that side was soon overwhelmed by a tsunami of anger that she was unable to stop. "I hope you do sue me, Blaise," she said in a calm voice. "I want to be in court when you say, 'You see, your honor, she was so important to the company that without her, we went out of business, and so that's why I underpaid her, refused to make her a full partner, and forced her to have sex with me as a condition of employment'."

Elley never saw his fist coming. It connected with her left temple and her vision exploded into a wash of silver and red. She fell backwards, her head colliding with a desk on the way down. Landing on the floor, she felt like she cried out but could not hear herself. Every sound was drowned out by a high-pitched whine. She could feel someone taking hold of her, but could not yet see them. Hands were moving her, helping her to lie down. The whine started to ebb and she began to hear Blaise's voice screaming, "*Let go of me! She had that coming! Take your fucking hands off me or I'll fire every one of you motherfuckers!*"

When Elley's vision returned and cleared, the first thing she saw was Chelsea's face. "Honey, are you all right?"

Elley put her fingers on the side of her head and felt the lump rising. It was sore and hot to the touch. "I think so," she said, thickly. Chelsea helped her up and the two watched as Barney, one of the other AE's, and Amid from personnel fought to keep Blaise restrained in a chair, despite his hoarse threats, which now covered not simply firing and suing, but killing.

"Do you need a doctor?" Amid called to Elley while he struggled with Blaise. "An ambulance?"

"No," she said, rising with help, "I just need to get my stuff and get out of here." It hurt to talk.

"I want to you know that if you decide to file suit or press charges, I will be there to testify on your behalf," Amid said.

"*Fuck you!*" Blaise shrieked.

"And fuck you back, boss," Amid said. "I quit."

Elley did not know what Amid did to Blaise next, but her ex boss suddenly screamed in pain.

Chelsea helped her into her now-stripped office and put her in her chair, then examined the lump on her temple. "That ain't good, baby. I think you'd better get it looked at, or at least have some pictures taken in case you do decide to sue the bastard."

"I want to thank you for sticking up for me, Chelse," Elley said. "You and Amid."

"Shit, honey, you would've done the same for us."

"I just hope this doesn't put you in jeopardy you. He really could fire everybody if he wanted."

"On what grounds?" Chelsea said. "Just like you said, I'd like to be there in court when he comes up to the judge and says, 'Yeah, I shitcanned my entire staff because they should have been at their desks working instead of looking at me go after a woman like Oscar de la Hoya!' Shit, girl, Johnnie Cochran's ghost couldn't save him from that one."

Elley smiled, which hurt. "I suppose not. But maybe this is all my fault. Maybe I should have shut up and stayed in New York and not panicked and put out like usual."

Chelsea took her shoulders firmly, but not roughly. Her eyes bored into Elley's. "No, *no*, you hear me? You are *not* the victim in this one, Elley. Don't you even *go* there. You kept your cool like a hostage negotiator while he went postal, and damn near everyone on the floor was a witness to it. So you don't worry about what's going to happen to us, you just get yourself to the damn hospital to get checked out, and then get a picture of that damn bump. It might be your retirement fund."

"Okay. I guess I'd better do it before they turn off my insurance."

"I'm coming with you," Chelsea said. "I'll drive. Give me your keys."

Elley didn't argue with her. Feeling woozy, she let Chelsea lead her down the elevator and back into the garage. Sliding into the driver's seat of the Lexus, Chelsea said, "You know, I always wanted to drive one of these. It's just a damn shame this had to be the reason."

As they pulled out onto Arizona Boulevard, they could see the police cruiser heading toward the building. "I hope they take him out in cuffs," Chelsea said.

"Wait, maybe I should stay and talk to the police," Elley said.

"Nope. They'll come to you if they need you. Trust me."

"You almost sound like you have experience at this sort of thing." Chelsea did not answer. Elley closed her eyes and rode to the hospital in silence.

Chelsea had been right; while Elley was waiting for x-rays a policewoman arrived at the emergency room to take a statement, which Elley gave honestly. But when the woman asked if Elley wanted to press charges, she was unable to decide. Even with Chelsea encouraging her to, she could not make that step. Maybe tomorrow she would be able to see things with more decisiveness. Right now her head hurt like the devil, and she just wanted to get through the emergency room and then go home.

The x-rays revealed no serious damage, so both sides of Elley's head, where Blaise had hit her and where she struck the desk on the way down, were treated, bandaged and she was released. Chelsea drove her home and offered to stay with her, but Elley politely refused, saying she simply wanted to lie down for a while. She offered to pay for the cab that Chelsea was going to have to take to get back to the office, but her co-worker refused, equally politely. "I'm gonna expense that mother," she said, making Elley laugh. Hugging her gingerly, Chelsea left.

Had Elley Gorman Hayden kept a diary, the entry for today would have become a book. It was the worst day of her life. At least the worst day of her professional life. *One* of the worst days of her life, certainly. So why did she feel so strangely triumphant?

Elley wetted a wash cloth with cold water and placed it over her forehead as she lay down on the sofa. If she did not wake up until Nola (whom she had called and "reactivated," after Jack's little escapade) arrived that afternoon with Robynn, then that would be just fine.

Inside the surprisingly quiet house, Elley was asleep within ten minutes, which meant she slept through the sound of the phone ringing. She awoke about a little less than an hour later because of a dark, disturbing dream, the details of which she was unable to remember, other than that it left a lingering feeling of unease. She glanced at the clock. It would be another hour and a half before Robynn was home, so she still had time to pull herself together.

It was another twenty minutes before Elley noticed the phone machine's blinking red light. "You'd better not be Blaise," she cautioned the machine as she hit the playback button.

"Hi, Mrs. Hayden?" a woman's recorded voice greeted her, and Elley immediately thought, *fucking telemarketer.* "This is Jennifer from Sera Elementary, and we're just checking to make sure everything is fine with Robynn."

Why wouldn't everything be fine with Robynn?

"I'm assuming we'll see her back tomorrow," the voice went on, "but if she needs to be out again, please let us know." The woman left a number and then hung up.

Back tomorrow? Jesus, now what? Had Nola and Robynn come home while she was asleep? There was no noise in the house that would identify them, but she called their names anyway. There were no answers. She jabbed the number of the school into the phone, screwed it up, swore, and punched it in again. "Yes, hello, this is Elley Gorman Hayden, I need to talk to Jennifer immediately," she said. A few seconds later, the voice came on, live this time.

"Oh, hello, Mrs. Hayden, thank you for getting back to—"

"Where's my daughter?" Elley demanded.

"Um, I'm sorry, but—"

"Where is she, dammit! You said you want to see her back tomorrow, what do you mean 'back'? Why isn't she there now? I dropped her off this morning. What's going on?"

"Please, Mrs. Hayden, calm down," Jennifer said. "Mr. Hayden came to pick her up earlier. He said she had a doctor's appointment."

Goddammit, Jack! "I know of no doctor's appointment. When did he come?"

"Umm, it was right around lunch time, say 11:30."

"I'm going to hang up, I will call you right back," Elley said, disconnecting the line. She then hit number five on speed dial, which was Robynn's doctor's office. "Westside Pediatric," a voice said after the second ring.

"This is Elley Gorman Hayden, the mother of Robynn Hayden. Apparently my husband brought my daughter in to the office today."

"Let me check," the receptionist said, and Elley could hear paper ruffling in the background. "I'm sorry, Mrs. Hayden, but we don't see any record of Robynn's having been here."

Elley hung up again, and this time dialed Jack's office. If the asshole was in town and he wasn't here at home, and he wasn't at the doctor, he had to be at work. "Yes, hello, I need to speak to Jack Hayden. Are you sure he's out of town? Christ." She slammed the phone down. Elley could always call his cell phone, of course, but that wasn't going to tell her where he was unless he told her where he was, and if he was pulling this kind of shit, she doubted she would get any kind of straight answer from him.

Phones were no longer going to handle this situation. She was going to have to go down to the school in person to see what the hell was going on. Her head throbbed horribly as she roared out of the driveway and sped to Robynn's school, rolling through every stop sign she could. She got there in record time and sloppily parked against the curb. Leaping out, she ran into the office, demanding to see someone named Jennifer.

Jennifer Vater proved to be the school nurse. She was a youngish African-American woman with a ready smile, but Elley was not in the mood for smiles. "I want to know what you did with my daughter!"

"Good heavens, are you all right, Mrs. Hayden?" Jennifer asked, sizing up the bandages on her temples.

"Never mind me, where's my daughter?"

"I'm sensing something is wrong here."

"Aren't you the perceptive one!"

"Please come into my office," Jennifer said, leading her to a room more the size of a closet and closing the door. "Now then, Mrs. Hayden—"

"Cut the crap. I know you probably can't deny a parent if they show up wanting to take their child, but this has happened *twice* now this week, and I don't know where my husband and daughter are. They didn't go the doctor, I checked. Did Jack say anything to you before he left with her?"

"Actually, I didn't see them at all, I just got a note on her absence," Jennifer said. "Let's go talk to Miss Kacirk, who runs the kindergarten." The two got up and walked to the kindergarten classroom. It looked to Elley like free play time, with twenty or so kids split up into groups covering the entire room. A very young Latina was officiating. "I thought Lainie Kacirk would be here," Jennifer said.

"I'm subbing," the Latina responded. "Gloria Menéndez."

"Were you here when Robynn left?" Jennifer asked.

"Robynn? Oh, the little one with the scar. Yes, she was here this morning and then left. Doctor's appointment, right?"

"Doctor's appointment wrong," Elley said.

Gloria did not appear to understand. "All I know is that she seemed frightened of the doctor," she said.

"Nonsense, she likes her doctor. Why would you say that?"

"Because she seemed really reluctant to leave. The man had to keep telling her that it was all right, that her daddy was waiting in the car and that—"

"*What did you say?*" Elley shouted, and instantly, twenty-two four-, five-, and six-year-olds froze like statues and stopped talking. Three of them started to cry from fright.

Gloria Menéndez blanched. "Robynn's uncle said that her daddy was in the car."

"Robynn doesn't have an uncle! Oh, Jesus Fucking Christ! You gave my daughter to somebody you didn't even *know*?"

"I'm a sub, okay? I don't know *any* of the parents!"

Jennifer Vater got between them. "Look, let's just all try to calm down."

"*Calm down?*" Elley screamed. "You gave my daughter to someone you don't even know and now you tell me to *chill?*" More kids started to cry.

"Mrs. Hayden, please," Jennifer begged. "They had to check out at the front desk, if something was wrong they wouldn't have let Robynn go."

"The only way out of this building is through the front?"

"Well, not exactly, but—"

"So someone could have come in and snatched my daughter and gone out a side door and nobody would ever know!"

"I think we'd better go talk to the principal," Jennifer said.

"No, I think we'd better go talk to the goddamn LAPD!" Elley screamed.

"Mrs. Hayden, please, there are other children here."

"Yes, other children who are going to go home to their mothers tonight." Elley broke down and began to sob. Her head felt like it was splitting open. Her legs gave out and she sank to the floor. "I don't believe it," she moaned.

Turning to Gloria, Jennifer said, "Go take those kids onto the playground. Get them out of here."

"But they've already had recess."

"Just do it!"

Gloria nervously assembled all the children, including the crying ones in a line, and announced they were going to have an extra recess, and then led them past Elley and out of the room. One boy on the way out asked, "What's wrong with her?" As gently as she could, Jennifer picked Elley up off the floor and set her in a chair. "Can I get you something?" she asked.

"A new life, maybe," Elley mumbled.

Another teacher, a more motherly-looking one, then poked her head into the room and said, "I heard some yelling, is everything all right in here? Where are the kids?"

"They're out on the playground, Maggie," Jennifer said. "Are you on break?"

"Yes."

"Could you ask Lucy to come down here ASAP?"

A minute later Lucy Marshall, the principal, came into the room, asking: "What kind of situation have we got?" The nurse gave her a brief summation, which was punctuated by Elley's sniffling. Lucy Marshall's eyes got huge. "You've got to be kidding," she said. "Where's Gloria?"

"Playground."

Lucy Marshall stuck her head out the classroom door and shouted for Gloria to come, which she did, seconds later. "Ms. Menéndez, don't you know enough not to let a child go with someone not authorized?"

"I'm sorry, okay?" Gloria whined. "The guy recognized her by sight, so I figured he really was her uncle."

"You say he recognized her?" Elley said, wiping her nose.

"He pointed her out, he said that her father was waiting out front but that he didn't want to come back to where the kids were because he had a bad cold and didn't want to spread it, so he was going to take her up there."

"Did he give a name?"

"He did, but I can't remember it."

"Jesus Christ!" Elley wailed.

"Stop yelling at me!" Gloria screamed. "It's not my fault! He said he was Uncle somebody. I remember it was a Gospel name."

"There are only four," Jennifer prompted.

"Mark," Gloria said. "He said he was Robynn's Uncle Mark."

"My god," Elley said. "What did this man look like?"

"He was heavy and he had on an expensive suit."

Marcus Broarty. For some insane reason, Jack's boss had taken her daughter. Jack was forever showing the latest pictures of Robynn to everyone. Marcus had to have seen them by the dozen. He could easily have recognized Robynn from a crowd.

But why? Why in Christ's name would he want Robynn?

Ask your husband, a voice said in her head. Elley did not

recognize the voice, but it was so clear as to be audible. *Jack knows.*

CHAPTER TWENTY-ONE

Two of the women seated at the Pines bar of the Tide Pool Inn looked nervous when Chief Rob Creeley strode in, but Creeley ignored them. Instead he looked around until he spotted Jack Hayden seated at a dark corner table, nursing a beer. Creeley walked over and said: "Had a feeling I might find you in here. I tried your room."

"Sit down, Cree," Jack Hayden said. "Want to order something?"

"No, even if I weren't on duty it would be too early for me."

"What a coincidence. It seems to be too late for me."

"Where's your lady friend?"

"She left before I got up this morning."

"Trouble in the Paradise Motel?"

"Come off it, Cree. She got an emergency work call and had to leave. She left me a note." The truth was, even though there was no way they could become a couple—at least not at the moment—Jack felt a little bruised by her abrupt departure.

Creeley pulled a chair out from under the small round table and sat down. "I came by to tell you that we've got a statewide APB out on Mr. Broarty, so hopefully he'll do something stupid and get caught."

"If that's the criterion for capture, Marc's already in custody." Jack took a long swig of his beer.

"How many of those have you had?"

"Not enough." The policeman did not appear to be amused. "Okay, Cree, this is pint number three. Believe me, it takes a helluva lot more than this to get me wasted."

"Is that your goal today, Jack?"

He shook his head. "My goal today, were it within the realm of possibility, would be to return my life to the way it used to be, warts and all. Even normally stressed out would be better than this. If whatever is tormenting me can change a pernicious mural back into a harmless painting, then why can't some floating cloud of good drop down and change my life back to normal?" He started to take another drink then stopped. "Hey, I just realized something. When I dragged you in there to see, it was perfectly normal, like it was wearing a mask because it wanted you to think I was nuts, or behind the strangeness, or in some way responsible. But I have the proof, Cree. I have it on my camcorder. I videotaped the mural before we went in there! I'll show you the tape and then you'll see!"

"You don't have to prove anything to me, not any more. I'm already convinced that there's something unnatural is going on and it somehow involves a painting."

Jack's eyes narrowed. "Has it done something to you?"

"No. But your friend McMenamin? When we got him out of the car trunk we found traces of blood all over him, which isn't too surprising. But the coroner found something else: paint."

"Christ. Emac had paint on him?"

The policeman rubbed his forehead and leaned in closer. "Not on him, Jack, *in* him. There was a trace of it on his buttocks, but more of it inside his anal cavity. Deep inside. Like it had been ejaculated in there."

Jack thought he might be sick right there on top of the table in the Pines Lounge of the Tide Pool Inn. *Raped*, Dani had said. She felt she had been *raped* out there in the woods, and she had traces of paint on her goddamned panties! At that moment his cell phone rang and Jack jumped so violently he shook the table and knocked over the beer glass, spilling the reddish liquid onto the table top. "Damn!" he said, dropping a napkin on the puddle while clumsily fishing out the phone to answer it. "Yeah, this is Hayden."

"Jack, where are you?" he heard, and was only barely able to recognize his wife's voice through the tone of desperation.

"Up at San Simeon. Elley, what is it?"

"Robynn's been kidnapped."

"*What*? When? How?"

"That asshole boss of yours took her, Jack! Marcus Broarty took my daughter!"

"Marc?"

At the sound of that name, Creeley sat up at attention.

"I need to know why, Jack. Why did he take her?"

"Elley, I don't know! But I'm sitting across from a policeman right now. They have an APB out on Broarty for another reason. They'll find him. We'll get Robynn back."

Creeley had overheard enough. He gestured for the phone and Jack handed it to him. "This is Robert Creeley, Chief of the Glenowen, California, P.D. I'd appreciate it if you'd give me whatever information you have on the whereabouts of Marcus Broarty. Where was he last seen?" Creeley knit his brows as he listened. "This was today?" he asked. "Have you called the police locally? Good. I'll call them from up here, too, just to make sure they take this seriously. Thank you, ma'am, and I promise you that we will do everything to get your girl back. Here's your husband." He leapt up from the table and ran out to the radio in his police car.

Jack meanwhile was saying: "Elley, look, they'll find her. Why don't you lie down for a while, try to rest. Everybody has everybody's phone number. Someone will call once they know something."

"I need you to come home."

"I think I need to stay here."

"Why? Oh, of course. *She's* up there."

"No, she's not up here! She's gone, so don't worry."

"Then why can't you come home?"

"What if Marc's heading back up this way? Shouldn't I be here just in case this is where he's taking Robynn?"

"Why on earth would he be coming back up there? Dammit,

what do you know that I don't?"

"Nothing, it's just a hunch. I think it's safer for me to stay on this end."

There was a pause, after which Elley said: "Oh my god, I get it now. You're in on this, aren't you? Broarty's coming up there to deliver her to you!"

"What? No! Elley, listen to me—"

"You're behind the whole thing! You weren't able to keep hold of her on your own so you got your ratfucking bastard of a boss to kidnap Robynn, just to get back at me!"

"Oh, grow a goddamned brain, would you?" Jack screamed back. "If I wanted to take her, I could have done it and you'd never even know! That's how fucking attentive *you* are! She was snatched on *your* watch, not *mine*! Who's the worthless parent now?"

Without another word, the line went dead.

"Elley! Elley!" Jack cried into the phone, but she was gone.

Way to go, fuckhead. Of all the times to finally lose it and start flinging his built-up resentment at his wife like a chimp throwing shit at zoo visitors, this had to be the worst possible, right after she had learned of her daughter's abduction. He imagined that there might be a combination of words that could have been more hurtful to a woman in her vulnerable state, but he could not imagine what they were. Jack tried calling her back, but the phone only rang. Jack gave up and buried his face in his hands.

That was the way Creeley found him when he returned to the bar. "You all right, Jack?" he asked.

"I'm great, Cree. I've just taken the gold in screwing up." The policeman sat back down and Jack described the phone call from Elley. When he was finished, Creeley leaned back and started clicking his tongue on the roof of his mouth.

"You're upset over the argument, right?" Creeley asked.

"You've no idea."

"If I'd said something like that to Maria, I'd be walking funny for a month. But how come you're not upset that your little girl's been kidnapped?"

Jack looked at his friend. "So you think I'm in on it, too?"

"I'm just asking. It's my job."

The young barmaid appeared at the table with a rag to wipe up the remainder of the spilled beer. "Will there be anything else?" she asked in the tone of voice that implied *if not, then get out*.

"No, I'm fine, thanks," Jack said, and she retreated with his empty glass. Once she was out of earshot, Jack went on. "I guess I'm not more upset because I have a strong feeling that they're headed back up here, Broarty and Robynn. And I don't think he's going to hurt her, Cree. Marcus is too big of a pussy for that."

"He seems to have hurt McMenamin."

"Yeah, I know. But only after the mural told him too. I don't think the mural has told him to hurt Robynn. Not yet, anyway. I think he's bringing her back here so he can do whatever the mural wants him to in front of me, because here's the thing, Cree: the mural on its own hasn't been able to break me. It's given me visions, or teleported me, or whatever the hell it is that I've been going through, and it's done the same for Dani. It's given us temptations like you wouldn't believe, and frankly, we succumbed to them early on. But it hasn't been able to break either of us. So it's now using Marcus to help it."

"There you go again, talking like this painting has a consciousness."

Jack nodded. "Don't ask me to explain how or even why it works, but yeah, I'm talking like it has a consciousness. Or else some kind of consciousness is controlling it. Honest to god, Cree, sitting here listening back to some of the shit I'm saying, I don't know why you don't lock me up."

Creeley turned around and called out to the barmaid. "Ma'am? Turns out we'd like another round after all. Another one for my friend here and I'll have the same, whatever he's having. Thanks."

"Just got off duty, huh?" Jack asked.

"Something like that. You're not driving, you're staying here, so you don't have to worry it, and to paraphrase a friend of mine, it takes more than one to get me wasted. But I'm going to show you the reason why I don't lock you up, and I figure we both might need the extra fortification before I do." Creeley pulled a folded piece of heavy paper from his back pocket. "You remember my telling you about my friend Nicky at the historical society? He called me this morning and said he'd found another old photo of the Saddleback Inn. Prepare yourself."

Creeley handed Jack the paper and at first Jack hesitated taking it. He finally did, unfolding it and looking at the image. He had tried to steel himself for anything, but what he saw in the old brown photograph almost made him lose control of his bladder. "Oh no, Creeley, c'mon. This is a fake, right? You've got one of those souvenir photo shops in town and you had this made, right?"

"It's a color copy, Jack, but I saw the original, which was absolutely genuine. My friend Nick authenticated it. It even had a date written on the back. May 1918. More than ninety years ago."

"But...this can't be."

"I know. But this is why I'm not writing you off."

Jack continued to stare at the copy of the photograph, which showed the Saddleback Inn on a dirt street. There were no other buildings immediately around it. A man was standing in front of the place, a man Jack recognized.

It was *him*. *Jack Hayden* was standing in front of the Saddleback Inn in a nearly hundred-year-old photograph.

* * * * * * *

Elley Gorman Hayden's hands were shaking so badly that she could barely catch hold of the items in the bedroom closet she was tearing apart. Her distress, combined with the fact that she had just emptied an entire bottle of wine like it was water, was having a serious affect on her ability to move. She came across a box containing shoes that she had not seen in a good five years and lobbed them across the room. She was not looking for shoes, or outfits, or gloves, or even old photo albums. "Where did you stick it, you fucker?" she spat, yanking things off the closet shelves and pitching them onto the floor of the bedroom with such carelessness that she was scraping and bashing her fingers red.

Then she found it.

It was in the original box, and buried under a pile of sweaters. Elley remembered when Jack had bought it; it was while she was pregnant. Jack had come home late one night and spotted someone snooping around the house, peering in a window. The lights from his car scared the would-be burglar away, but it gave him a lingering sense of nervousness about being gone and leaving her home, in his words, defenseless. Elley had never considered herself defenseless but she went along with him that time, in part because it was easier than arguing with him during pregnancy.

Bringing a gun into a house that would shortly be inhabited by a child; who was the lousy parent now, you fuckhead?

Lifting the lid of the box, she stared down at the .38 caliber handgun, which was small enough to fit comfortably in her hand. Elley had never actually fired it, and to her knowledge, Jack never had either. Like ninety percent of suburban gun-owners, he believed the very act of possessing it was protection enough. The bullets were in a small box inside the larger one, and Elley tried to remember how to open the barrel and load it, and then tried to get her fingers to comply. Christ, her head hurt. Her heart, too. She wanted more to drink, but had brought up only one bottle of wine. She'd had pain medication at the emergency room, too. Would that mix with the alcohol? Elley stopped and gave a racking, sobbing laugh. At this point, what difference did it make if she mixed wine with medication?

Grow a goddamned brain, Elley. Make it a big one, too, so that it splatters well against the wall.

Stumbling over the piles of stuff she had torn out of the closet to get to the bed, she sat down on the edge, in her nightgown, holding the loaded gun in her right hand. It was heavy, but oddly pleasurable to hold. She held onto the gun, weighing it, for some time. Since her call to Jack and her realization of what was going on, time had become an abstract anyway.

Her husband was gone.

Her daughter was gone.

Her job was gone.

Her lover was gone, the rat bastard.

There was nothing left.

Who was the worthless wife/mother/worker/lover now?

She put the barrel of the gun in her mouth. It didn't taste good, but she wasn't doing this for the flavor. Elley squinted her eyes shut and put pressure on the trigger. She heard a strange whine coming from somewhere in the room, but did not realize it was coming from her.

Presently, the telephone rang.

Elley opened her eyes and lowered the gun. Maybe it was news about Robynn. Dropping the gun, she ran to the phone and picked it up. "Hello," she said, her voice hoarse from sobbing.

"Elley, don't be a fool," a man's voice said. She had heard it before, only then it had been on the inside of her head. It was the voice that had suggested to her that Jack knew why Marcus had taken her child.

"Who is this?" she demanded.

"Your savior," the voice said. "I know what you were about to do."

"Can you see me in here?"

"Only the weak sacrifice themselves. You are not weak. You are not a worthless parent."

"What should I do then?" she begged.

"You know as well as I," the voice purred. "Trust your instincts."

At once, she did know. It was so obvious. It was as though she had always known.

Elley pushed the button to cut off the call and laughed. Then she released the button and dialed a private number. When it picked up at the other end, an irritable voice said, "What?"

"Blaise, don't hang up. It's me."

"What the fuck do you want now? The fucking cops were here, you know. What more do you want from me?"

"Look, this isn't easy for me, but I want to apologize."

"*Apologize*?"

"You were right, it was all my fault, everything, and I feel like such a shit. I shouldn't have walked out on you in New York. And I certainly should not have slapped you."

"Well, I kind of lost my head today, too. I said some things I probably shouldn't have. Did some things, too. Are you all right, by the way?"

"I'll heal."

"Look, I've been hammered on all day by the fucking cops and my own personnel department, and my goddamned lawyer, but maybe we just need to work this out between the two of us. You think?"

"I'm home alone. No husband, no kid. Come on over, and we'll talk. I need to see you, Blaise."

After a pause, he said: "If that's what you want, I'll be over within the hour."

"Be discreet," she said. "Park a few blocks away and walk. Try not to be seen. I'll leave the back door unlocked for you. Come straight upstairs to the bedroom." She hung up the phone.

Padding down the stairs, she went into the kitchen and made sure the door was unlocked, then returned to the bedroom where she slid out of her nightgown, picked up the gun and stretched herself out on the bed, her head squarely on one pillow, and her right hand, clutching the .38 tightly, hidden under the other one.

Elley smiled to herself as she wondered how long it was going to take Blaise to arrive.

* * * * * * *

It wasn't even five yet, but it seemed to Marcus Broarty

like they had been driving for days. For the last twenty miles the brat had sat there and whimpered. Marcus had offered the hatchet faced little cramp candy, treats and ice cream—which the girl finally accepted—but she would not stop that damned sniveling. He couldn't take much more of this. Marcus had never been more convinced that his early vow to conduct his life without children was a stroke of brilliance. Or that the all-expense-paid night at the Coat-hanger Hilton he had treated the one girl at U.C. Davis that he'd managed to knock-up had been more than worth it.

"Okay, kid, I give up," Marcus said, more to himself than to the girl. "I'm going to pull off and we'll have to spend the night somewhere."

"Is my daddy going to be there?" Robynn asked.

"No, your daddy's not going to be there."

"I want to see my daddy."

"You will. You will tomorrow. But we have to get some rest first. I'm tired."

"I'm tired too," Robynn said. "And this car smells funny."

It was a smoker's car, but that was all they had available back at the car rental place in L.A. Broarty had ditched his own car and taken out the rental, knowing that would buy him several days of unencumbered travel. It was a safety precaution, just in case Emac's body was discovered sooner than he was counting on. The faint stale odor of cigarettes that had become impregnated into the upholstery didn't bother Marcus, but it seemed to bother the brat.

Tough shit. At least she was tired.

They had only gotten as far as Santa Maria, but it was far enough. Broarty exited the freeway and pulled into the first motel whose sign boasted of HBO. As he had done with the rental car, he paid cash for the room, which had two beds, and left a false name and address on the registration. No one could accuse him of being stupid; not now. Never again.

Inside the room, Robynn immediately gravitated toward one bed in particular, which made no difference to Broarty. He looked over the room service menu for dinner options, while she clicked on the television and discovered a half-dozen or kids channels. That might keep her from whimpering for a while.

When Robynn got up and went into the bathroom, Marcus Broarty got his first moment of peace that day. Oh, what he wouldn't give to have the whiny little she-demon fall into the crapper and get sucked out to the ocean! But he knew that was not part of the plan. He needed to have her intact, all the way back up to Wood City.

Those were his instructions.

He was going to have to provide food for the brat, too, before she began whining about how hungry she was. Maybe he could find a bag of potato chips for her. Most kids would think that a fantastic treat. Surprisingly, Marcus himself was not hungry at all, only tired. He hoped the girl would fall asleep early so he could get some shuteye. Even though it would be a shorter, tomorrow's drive would probably be an ordeal, too. Marcus was not used to driving long distances, and particularly not with gnats in little girl costumes. He had put more miles in over the last two days than he normally would in two months. Cars for him were status symbols, not transport.

When Robynn came out of the bathroom, she looked over at Marcus and almost smiled, prompting him to almost smile back. It was a good thing she didn't know the details of the plan that the God of Wood City—his new deity—had devised.

Marcus Broarty almost felt sorry for Robynn Hayden and what was going to happen to her.

But not really.

BOOK THREE

CHAPTER TWENTY-TWO
SEVENTY-FIVE YEARS AGO

Howard Kearney opened his eyes inside the tent and wondered if his head was still attached to his body. It was eleven in the morning and the sun was breaking through the treetops enough to heat up the heavy canvas roof, making the inside warm and humid. The spot between his eyebrows felt like he had used it to challenge John Henry to a steel driving contest.

Despite his Irish heritage, Howard had never been a drinking man, which cast him as the junior partner in the previous night's escapade, in which he and three of the other artists from the Castle party had gone into the village just south of San Simeon and tried to relieve themselves of some of the money old Hearst had paid them. It was to help the local economy, the agreed. A couple of the guys were spending pretty freely, but not Howard, who still had more than a hundred and eighty left, not including the ten-spot he always carried in his right pocket, insurance against being picked up as a vagrant in the course of his travels. That sawbuck would stay well and truly hidden. He was not even sure if WPA rules allowed them to earn money from any other source, but only he worried about such things. His mentor Fergus, for instance, would have laughed at him had he voiced such a worry.

Fergus had been the leader of the group's efforts to drink the town of Glenowen dry, emerging as the most valuable player, though some of the other guys kept up with him pretty well. Only one of the artists at the Castle, Louis Norman Igee had not been invited to join the party, which was fine with Howard. Igee was a talented artist, maybe even a genius, but Howard did not like him, and he did not know anyone else in the Northern California arts community who did. Most had a hard time even looking directly at the man. Igee's eyes were black, the blackest Howard had ever seen in a human, so black that they seemed to act like a light vacuum.

Managing the daunting task of sitting upright, Howard Kearney tried to remember how many drinks he'd had last night. He started with a couple of beers, and then was coerced into something stronger. After that, he did not have much memory of the evening. Thank heavens Althea had not been along, just in case he embarrassed himself at the dingy saloon.

He managed to muster enough strength and focus to look over to the other side of the tent to see if Fergus was there. All he saw was an empty sleeping bag. Fergus Randall was about twenty five years older than Howard Kearney but had a century's more worth of experience. He had the kind of carrot-colored hair that often accompanied a knack for mischief. Over the past few months Fergus had taken Howard under his wing, first as an artist, teaching him some of the perspective tricks necessary to creating murals on a wide variety of surfaces, and then as a man. He liked Fergus a lot, and Fergus liked him, but had to be careful not to get drawn too deeply into the older man's lifestyle, since he doubted his liver could take it.

Outside of the tent Howard could hear footsteps leading up to the flap, which quickly opened, revealing a rumpled looking Fergus Randall, holding a section of newspaper. "Hallelujah, the sleeper wakes," the older man said. "If you're in need of a jakes, lad, there's a nice short bushy one about fifty yards that way. Just watch where you step." He tossed him the newspaper, and Howard knew what it was to be used for.

"Man," Howard groaned, remaining in his sleeping bag, "remind me not to go carousing any time soon."

Fergus cackled and stepped back outside. It had been the older man's idea to live in a tent while they were on the

Central Coast rather than take a room somewhere, even at an auto camp, and while Howard at first thought the notion a bit strange (fortunately, he knew Fergus well enough not to waste any time worrying about possible ulterior motives), he was for the most part glad that he had come along. They built a campfire to do their cooking, lugged skins of water from a brook and tiny waterfall about a mile away from the campsite, and whenever they wanted to go somewhere, they hiked out of the woods to the highway and hitched a ride into Glenowen. That was how they ended up at the bar last evening—now, if only Howard could remember how they had gotten back.

"This is how the real people of this country are living, close to the land," Fergus had told him. "You can't know them or understand what they want, or like, or need unless you try living like them." Fergus Randall had a penchant for categorizing the underclass or working class of America as "real people," while disdaining, if not outright hating, the wealthy. Before spending that night in the Castle, Howard had only paid lip service to Leftist dogma. But after Miss Davies (or Marion, as she instructed everyone to call her, and whom Howard decided he liked) had put the artists up in rooms at the hilltop monument to one man's galactic ego, the outrageous, scattershot opulence of the place left him literally speechless. How many hungry people could have been fed on the price of *just one* of those medieval tapestries? How many yearly incomes would it take to equal the value of the disparate artifacts in just one of the Castle's rooms? Hell, how many of the artists and artisans who had actually created the pieces in that collection had enjoyed one iota of one percent of the wealth and comfort that the master of the Prodigal Palace was tacitly taking credit for through the act of assemblage? It almost made Howard Kearney embarrassed to be there, but Althea, who was along for the ride, seemed to enjoy it. He wished he could have shared the cold California night with her instead of with a man who could have used a few more showers and a few less cabbage-and-horseradish sandwiches. But she had taken a room in the village, which was much safer, and undoubtedly more comfortable.

Howard fished through his knapsack for his journal, in which he had been recording his thoughts and activities since joining the WPA program, with an eye to possibly writing a book someday about the experience. He felt that waking up for the first time in his life with a head that felt like it was going to explode was an experience worth capturing in words. Taking up the pencil that was wedged in between the journal pages, he tried to write, but the horizontal lines on the glowing white page would not stay still or straight, an effect that provoked a sudden wave of nausea. Howard made it out of the tent just in time.

Fergus was sitting on a camp stool near the fire ring, fishing through his own pack. "Ah, the sound of a successful evening out," he called upon hearing Howard losing a meal against a tree. "Got some dried pork in my pack if you want breakfast."

"Oh, shit," Howard moaned, his stomach lurching dryly. "You're a sadist, you know that, Fergus? I may never eat anything again."

"Oh, sure you will, and you'll drink again, too. And you'll be hung over again. It's called living, lad, and you'll never be any kind of a man if you're afraid of it." As it to prove his point, Fergus took a swig from a flask that he carried in his back pocket. Then he lifted his head like a dog hearing a far off siren and narrowed his eyes. "We're about to have company."

Five minutes later three men arrived at the campsite. The one in front was a ranger who had a state shield affixed to his crisply pressed shirt and a campaign hat balanced on his head. The other two trudging up behind him were clad incongruously in suits and ties, hardly hiking gear. One of them was a middle-aged guy with a bald head and a roly-poly body which his vest was only barely able to contain. He was flushed from the exertion. Behind him was a much younger man, who bore a fresh-minted look, and who was toting an armful of blueprint rolls. When the bald man saw Fergus and Howard, he shouted in a harsh voice: "What the hell are you doing on our land, you hoboes?"

"Your land?" Fergus called back.

The man dragged himself up to him. "I asked you a question, and I expect to be answered!"

"Let me take care of it, Mr. Elgin," the ranger said, walking up to Fergus with a less than threatening gait, despite the uniform. "Sir, I'm afraid you can't camp out here. This is private property."

"It is?" Fergus said. "Well, okay. We didn't see any signs posted, so we just assumed it was public land."

"It's always like that with you bums," the fat man snapped. "Everything in the world's free and ready to be taken. Well, not here. You two have exactly five minutes to clear out of here if you know what's good for you!"

"Mr. Elgin, I believe we can settle this without threats," the young ranger said. Howard was now standing behind Fergus, silently hoping he could absorb some of his friend's coolness under fire. "Fellas," the ranger went on, "I'm afraid I'm going to have to ask you to pack up and move along."

"Since you're asking politely, it would be ungracious of us not to comply," Fergus said. "Just give us a few minutes to get everything together and break down the tent, and we'll be out of your hair."

"I think we can be on our way, now, Mr. Elgin," the ranger said.

"I don't know," Elgin growled. "I think I should stay here and make sure these bums really leave."

"I'll do it," said the younger man. "You go on up ahead, I'll stay here and keep and eye on them."

Elgin looked uncertain about the offer, but he didn't say anything.

"I'll be fine, Mr. Elgin," the young man said. "I'll catch up with all of you later."

"All right, but don't dawdle," the fat man said, and then he and the ranger proceeded deeper into the woods, turning back every so often to check on the progress of the camp breakdown, until they disappeared from sight.

"Sorry about him," the young man told Fergus and Howard. "Mr. Elgin's a bear at the best of times, but we seem to be lost out here, and that's made him even worse."

"Lost, huh?" Fergus said. "If he's looking for the way out of the forest, he's headed the wrong way."

"What we're looking for is Wood City. Somehow we got off track."

Fergus and Howard looked at each other. "What's Wood City?" Fergus asked.

"Have you ever heard of Colonel Henry Jackson Breen?" the young man asked.

"The industrialist, right?"

"He's bought up this land and he's going to establish a town to support the lumber mill he's planning on building."

Fergus Randall stopped loosening the damp ropes of the tent and glared at the young suit. "*Lumber* mill?" he cried. "Kid, only a cretin would sink money into a lumber mill in an economic depression. They've been shutting down lumber mills all over the country because nobody's building anything. What's Breen think he's going to do with the lumber?"

"Given my level in the company I'm not party to all his plans, but I hear that the Colonel has opened up a pipeline out of the country. I think he's made some kind of deal with the Chancellor of Germany to supply wood."

Fergus shot another look at Howard, this one expressing disbelief. Then turning back to the young man, he asked: "What's your name, son?"

"Barnes, sir. Talbot Barnes." This kid was probably not yet twenty, perhaps even younger than Howard, whom Fergus had started to think was the youngest living creature on earth. "I'm Fergus Randall and the lad here is Howard Kearney. I figure you should know who you're throwing out of the woods."

"I'm sorry about that, Mr. Randall." Talbot Barnes stuck out his hand in greeting and friendship to both men, while maintaining a precarious hold on the rolls of blueprints with the other. "No hard feelings, I hope."

Fergus took his hand. Despite his youth, the kid was showing far more class than grouchy, bald-headed Elgin. Given enough time, Fergus believed he might come to like him. "Mind if I ask you a personal question, son? Does it ever bother you to be working for a bastard like your Colonel Breen?"

"I beg your pardon?"

"Robber barons like Breen and old man Hearst up the hill want nothing more out of life than to get even richer than they are, and they don't care how they do it, who they have to stomp over, or who they have to crawl into bed with to accomplish it, including the Chancellor of Germany. Don't you feel even a little bit twitchy about hitching your wagon to a guy like that?"

Talbot Barnes suddenly deflated. "Mr. Randall, all I know is I have a job. I'm earning money working for the Colonel. Not a lot, but enough to stay alive and send some back to my family. My father hasn't had a regular job since the crash. If I can keep working and earn enough to support my folks, I figure I'll have time when I'm older to worry about the guilt."

Howard Kearney looked long and hard at the young man and saw someone resembling himself. Howard had taken Hearst's money and had literally crawled into bed with wealth when he was put up in one of the Castle's bedrooms. If Talbot Barnes was guilty of some crime against society, he was too. "You know, Fergus, he does have a point."

"He does at that," Fergus muttered. "I meant no offense, son."

Barnes smiled ruefully. "None taken. You're not the first one to express that opinion, Mr. Randall. My older brother, who's never held a job in his life, gives me the same line of talk. I'm supporting him, but he doesn't see it that way. He plays his guitar and tries to sing away all the problems in the world, and tells me I'm a sell-out, all the while eating the food I provide."

"Well, if there is such a thing as a good and honest reason for selling out, my young friend, you just might have found it," Fergus said, stomping the folded canvas tent flat, "though I'd probably be expelled from the Party if anyone heard me say that."

Barnes' eyes grew wide. "Party? Are you a Communist, Mr. Randall?"

"Card-carrying, son, but that doesn't mean I'm the devil, no matter what *they* say." By now the tent had now been reduced to a two-foot square of canvas about a foot high. Fergus sat on it while breaking down the wooden poles that had held it up. "All Communism means is that you care about your fellow man and want to do something to help him. Just the way you care about your family and are trying to help them."

"I never thought of it that way," Barnes said.

"Communism is the way of the future for this country," Fergus went on. "I've been trying to sign up the lad here, but he's resistant, too. As far as I'm concerned, no self-respecting artist in this day and age should be without a card."

"You two are artists?"

"Painters," Howard said, glad to see the subject was changing.

"Do you know an artist named Igee? He's with the Works Progress Administration."

Fergus studied the dismantled tent poles in his hands, and then said: "Sure we know him. How is it that you know Mr. Louis Norman Igee?"

"He's going to be painting a mural for the city hall building here at Wood City."

"Is that a fact?"

Howard knew what his friend was thinking: *how had Igee cadged this plum*? Louis Norman Igee was rumored to have come from a wealthy family, which meant he didn't really need the government support at all. The fact that he was part of the WPA meant that he was taking food out of the mouth of a genuinely struggling artist—*if* the rumors were true. Since nobody liked Igee enough to ask him about his background, nobody could confirm or deny the stories. Conversely, the fact that so many people actively disliked him meant that some might be more than willing to start spreading unfounded rumors about him. Whatever the truth may have been, there was an aura about Igee, and attitude that he was carrying some kind of great secret that he was not prepared to tell anyone.

For Howard's part, he didn't care how Igee had gotten the job. It was not like he would have wanted it. Howard did not particularly like doing murals. Sure, the worst day of painting was better than the best day spent squatted down on the dirt picking string beans, but given the option he would rather do single-subject canvases. Fergus, on the other hand, reveled in creating the oversized, multi-themed, many-character frescoes because it was yet another chance to spread his personal gospel. In Fergus's murals, every figure holding a book was reading Karl Marx and the predominant color palette was in the red range. Fergus was nothing if not blatant.

"Is our friend Mr. Igee going to be the principal painter?" Randall was asking.

"As far as I know he's going to be the only painter," Barnes answered. Reacting to the expressions of both Fergus and Howard, he added: "Is that unusual?"

"Usually a group of artists work on a mural," Howard said. "But Igee's going on his own for this one?"

"That's what I hear. He apparently insisted on it."

Fergus Randall shrugged and began to lash the tent onto a small sledge, which he was prepared to drag through the woods out to the highway. "That's just about it for me. You finished, lad?"

"I didn't have much anyway," Howard replied, rolling a cigarette and sticking it in his mouth, then lighting it.

"So long, then, Mr. Barnes," Fergus said. "It has been a pleasure conversing with you, and you can tell Daddy Warbucks that you chased us off good and proper. Embellish it, if you like. Throw in a mob and a rail. He'd like that."

"Take care, fellows," the young man said, then turned and started slogging through the brush to catch up with his compatriots.

"To hell with the hitching a ride," Fergus said. "Feel like a hike, lad?"

"Not really," Howard said, but that did not deter the older

man, who started leading him off in a different direction through the woods, away from the path to the highway. It took ninety minutes of trudging to get back to civilization, such as it was in Glenowen, which compared to San Francisco seemed like one of the last outposts of the frontier, and when they got there Howard was exhausted. "You'd better save up some energy for your lady friend," needled Fergus, who looked energized by the hike. "Where is she, by the way?"

"She checked into the hotel here in town right after the party at the Castle," Howard replied, dropping his gear and sitting down to rest for a moment. Fergus sat next to him and uncorked his canteen, took a swig, then offered it to Howard.

"This is water, right?" Howard asked, putting the canteen to his lips. Fortunately for him, it was water. Once rested, they made their way up into town.

"I'm assuming, Howard, my boy, that I will be seeing much less of you as the evening progresses," Fergus said. "I will have to find something to do with my time."

They continued on through the village until they came to the Saddleback Inn, where Althea was rooming, and went inside. Discovering a long bar instead of a lobby, Fergus cried: "How'd we miss this place last night?" Flagging down the bartender, a fortyish, handsome, but formidable looking woman with *Lil* monogrammed on her white blouse, Fergus ordered a whisky. Even Howard had to admit the place had an inviting atmosphere, unlike the dives they had discovered the night before, though its décor appeared so old that he half expected to see Gary Cooper saunter in and start a gunfight with somebody. *What a painting this would make*, he thought.

"Can I get something for you?" the bartender asked Howard.

"Just a beer, thanks."

"Sure you're old enough?"

Fergus laughed out loud. "I'll vouch for him, Lil."

"The name's Charity," the woman said as she walked to the tap and drew a long golden draft.

"Oh. I saw the name on your blouse, and assumed."

"S'allright," she said, coming back with Howard's foamy mug. "Charity's a terrible name for a barkeep 'cause the regulars start to think you possess it. Besides, it cost too much to stitch onto the shirt."

"I do admire practicality," Fergus said, bowing to her theatrically. The woman, in turn, accepted the bow with a genuine smile and a wink.

After taking a sip of his beer, just to see if it was going to stay down after last night, Howard inquired after Althea.

"Young, slim, and brown-haired, right?" Lil asked. "Went out, left her room key up here. I think she was going investigate some of the shops in town. She should be back soon, since there's not much here to see."

After getting Fergus to agree to look after his pack, Howard went out to try and find her. The bartender was right, there wasn't much to Glenowen: a two-block main street dotted with the odd shop. If his hunt proved futile, he would simply come back and wait for her at the bar.

As it turned out, Althea was in the third place he visited, which was a small general store that smelled of liniment and horehound drops, hundreds of which were heaped in an open bucket on the counter. "Howard," she declared, surprised at seeing him, "what happened to the camping trip?"

"We got evicted," he said. "It seems we weren't on public land like we thought."

The man behind the store's counter snorted. "I'll bet it was someone from that Breen outfit," he said, his salt-and-pepper beard seeming to stand on end. "They've been comin' up here for the last year tryin' to buy up land for a sawmill, or some such."

"That's the story we got, too," Howard said, pulling out one of those new comic magazines from a small rack and flipping through it. He couldn't say much for the level of artwork in them, and figured their novelty was quickly going to wear off. Sticking it back in the rack, he added: "What's that going to mean for the village here?"

"It's gonna big lumber trucks roarin' up and down the highway all hours of the night and day, that's what," said the bearded proprietor. "There's no river anywhere's around here to float the logs, so they're gonna have to use the highway. Don't make no sense, if you ask me. But they're gonna cut down the forest and chase all the critters up this way, so we're gonna have everything from deer to cougar walkin' through the streets here till it ain't safe. Then once the forest gets all chewed up, they'll leave and move onto another patch o' woods somewhere and start razin' it to the ground."

"But won't it bring extra money and jobs into the village?" Althea asked the man.

"The workers ain't comin' from here," the man said. "They'll ship 'em in from who knows where, anyone they can find to pay slave wages. We ain't gonna see a penny, 'cause Breen's buildin' his own town with all his own stores." The proprietor shook his head disgustedly. "See, that's the way it works: you move people in and pay 'em to work for you, but then you put up shops and services that they have to patronize, so you're gettin' all the same money back again, so you're really not payin' anybody. My grandpap fought in the war to end slavery and now it's comin' back, only now they call it industry. Back then, the country was fightin' itself, and it was a pretty even fight. Ain't no more. Ain't nobody can fight those with the money, 'cept someone with even more money."

Another customer came into the store, a man who knew the proprietor well enough to call him by his name, and while the two of them talked, Howard led Althea over to a corner, near the canned goods, and stole a kiss. "What were you planning on doing for the rest of the day?" he whispered.

"Just walking around the town," she said. "What were you thinking?"

"I can't say out loud what I'm thinking."

"Stop it," she said, play-slapping his arm.

"Let's just go back to the inn, what do you say?"

"Howard, do you think they're just going to let me walk you

up to my room without saying anything?"

"No, but I can walk up to Fergus's room like I'm supposed to, and then sneak over to yours."

"And what's Fergus going to think about that?"

"If I don't make a move like that, Fergus is going to conclude that he's been wasting his precious wisdom on the wrong artist."

"You men," she said, trying desperately to look scandalized. Secretly, this sort of talk was arousing her. Althea pulled her wool sweater closed in hopes Howard wouldn't see just how much so.

"Okay, fine, we'll do things your way," Howard said. "Let's go down to the water. Moonstone Beach is only a couple of miles up the coast."

"I don't really fancy a two-mile walk," she told him.

Howard, who was getting his second wind after his earlier hike, said: "We'll take bicycles, then. There's a place in town we can rent them."

"But the expense."

"Honey," Howard admonished, pulling a wad of Hearst money from his pocket.

Althea gave up pretending she did not want to go off with him. Before the left the store, they bought a small supply of pemmican and apples and a couple of cold bottles of Pepsi-Cola to take with them.

Biking out of the village, they followed the path to the beach. The ocean announced its presence through its salt-and-fish smell and the rhythmic rushing of its waves even before the vast blue expanse of water came into view. They walked the bikes past the craggy rock jetties of Moonstone Beach, against which the waves crashed dramatically, until they found a calmer patch of sand. The sun was high in the sky and casting warming beams down on them as the walked across the beach, side-stepping the piles of green, slimy kelp that had washed up. The place was surprisingly deserted. Althea took her shoes off and felt the cool damp sand squish between her toes. She began to examine some of the shells and rocks that were randomly scattered by the tides. Howard took his shoes off too, and then his shirt. Althea removed her sweater. They were alone on the beach without another soul in sight in any direction, and not even the shape of a boat dotting the horizon. Howard removed his trousers, and now wore only his shorts. With some coercion, he got Althea to take off her blouse, and then everything else.

"What if somebody sees us!" she cried, almost panting with fright and excitement.

"We'll hide in the water," Howard said, taking her arm and running her headlong into the surf. "Ahhhhh! Good lord, that's cold!" Althea was cold too, but she was laughing too hard to scream. They dashed out of the water until they were chilled by the breeze blowing on their wet naked bodies, and then ran back in. This time the water felt warmer and more inviting. They did their best to warm each other up as well, clutching onto each other in the brine, only their heads sticking up above the tide, like seals.

Howard and Althea made weightless love upright in the water. When they finally climaxed, it was with such intensity that they both let go of each other and fell under the surface, floating in baptismal ecstasy. Althea surfaced first, and shouted out in surprise and glee, as an otter popped its head up and snorted spray not ten yards away from her. When Howard's head emerged from the water, the creature looked at him quizzically, and then dove down and sped away.

"You'd better get gone if you know what's good for you," Howard called to the otter. Then to Althea, he said: "From now on, Pookie, this is our beach. Only ours." They laughed and held each other until the sun noticeably moved lower in the sky, then, after looking around carefully to make sure no one else had shown up, charged out of the water and raced back on the sand to the spot on which they had dropped their clothes, and quickly dressed, which was not easy, given their wetness and salt-stickiness. Then they walked slowly, combing the beach for treasures, munching on the pemmican and fruit they'd bought in town, talking of futures, until the warming sun began to weaken and cool, and then decided to retrieve the bicycles and head back to the village.

Howard and Althea were in no hurry to get back—at least not until they heard the fire engine bell and siren and became curious. Peddling hard back toward the town, they could now see a plume of black smoke rising from the business district. "What could be burning?" Althea wondered, stepping up the pace. As they approached the main street, they saw more and more of the townspeople poring out to see the conflagration as well. Up ahead was an ancient fire truck, doing its best to pump enough water to douse the raging fire.

"My heavens," Althea said, "it looks like the hotel!"

It was the hotel. A plume of black smoke rose up from its top floor, and flames jetted out from every window. They pedaled up the main street, which was increasingly filling up with people and smoke. Leaping off his bike, Howard shoved his way through the crowd and ran up to the front of the building, where he was stopped by a fireman. "You can't go any closer, mac," he told him. "Get a move on, let the men work."

"My friend was in there," Howard said. "I want to make sure he's all right."

"Either he got out or he's beyond help, now move along," the fireman said, this time shoving him back as the fire hoses futilely sprayed against the roaring flames.

Of course Fergus got out, Howard thought. *Fergus is the kind of guy who always gets out.*

Althea now joined him. "It's a good thing we were gone," she said.

"But all your stuff is probably going up."

"I really didn't have that much anyway." All she had brought with her was a change of clothing and a few personal items, which could easily be replaced.

To the side of the building, Howard spotted Charity, who was looking up at the burning top floors with an expression of resigned horror. Her hands covered her mouth, perhaps an effort to keep from breathing the smoke that was beginning to become oppressive. Seated on the ground beside her was Fergus Randall. "There is he," Howard said, "come on." The two of them fought their way over to them.

"Christ, lad, where the hell have you been?" Fergus cried when he saw Howard, and pulled himself to his feet, coughing mightily. "I managed to save all our gear."

"I wasn't as worried about the gear as I was about you," Howard said, clapping his hands on the man's shoulders.

"I'll tell you, this might convince me to give up smoking," Fergus said, coughing again.

"What the hell happened?"

"It started in one of the second-floor rooms."

"That's the floor I was on," Althea said, afraid that the blaze had somehow broken out in her room. It didn't make any sense; she had not left anything behind that might have started a fire, not a lit candle or burning lamp. Althea knew none of this was her fault, but for some reason she could not shake the feeling of dread that had suddenly blanketed her.

"Charity was leading me up there to look at a room and while we were there the first sign of smoke appeared from down the hall," Fergus said. "Then...hell, I don't know what happened after that."

Howard saw his friend shudder, which was not like Fergus at all. Something was upsetting him beyond having to flee from a burning building. "I need to get away from this smoke."

Howard picked up as much of his and Fergus' gear as he could carry and with the two of them fought his way through the ever-growing crowd. They made their way down the street to a tiny diner with an outside table.

"I need a drink," Fergus said, but all the place had were soft drinks. He settled on water.

"Okay, Fergus, what's the rest of the story?" Howard asked, once they were seated and somewhat settled at the canopied table.

"What are you talking about?"

"There's something you haven't said, something you don't

seem to want to say."

Fergus Randall took a deep breath and coughed again, then drained his glass of water. "As soon as we smelled the smoke Charity and I went running from door to door, pounding on each one and rousing whoever was in there. She ran up to the third floor and I stayed on the second."

"Then you helped save everybody," Althea said.

"I suppose so. The thing is, when I got to the room that appeared to be the source of the smoke I pounded on the door for half-a-minute, but no one seemed to be inside. I was about to leave when the door cracked open and there he was: Louis Norman goddamned Igee—pardon my language—standing there in a bathrobe like he didn't have a care in the world. There was a woman behind him to, and she *wasn't* wearing a bathrobe, if you know what I mean. The two of them acted like I was interrupting something important by trying to save them from a fire. I started shouting for them to get the hell out of there, but Igee only laughed. 'We'll get out our own way,' he said, and then slammed the door in my face."

"That's crazy," Althea said.

"It gets better," Fergus said. "Through the door I heard a sound I couldn't quite identify, almost like a small explosion, and then more smoke came out from under the door. I started kicking the door and it finally gave way." Fergus Randall stopped as though trying to collect his thoughts and then started shaking his head.

"Come on, Fergus, you can't stop now," Howard said. "What happened? Did you get them out?"

Fergus looked up at his friend with reddened, smoky eyes. "They weren't there, lad. The room was empty."

"Maybe they went through the window," Althea suggested.

"It would have been a two-storey drop, straight down."

"Maybe there was some kind of secret exit," Howard said.

"Believe me, lad, I've gone over and over it in my mind. The hotel room had four walls. I was standing in front of one. The wall opposite me had a window that led to a ten-foot fall. You can survive a ten-foot drop, surely, but why would you risk it when you could just run through the door to safety? The two walls on the sides were adjoined by other rooms. Even if there had been a door in one of those walls, I would have seen them emerge from the next room. But they didn't."

"A trap door doesn't make sense either," Howard said, "not on an upper floor."

"Nothing makes sense, lad. Least of all the odor I caught."

"What kind of odor?" Althea asked.

Fergus forced a tiny smile. "Today it would be called sulfur," he said. "But old-timers would have another name for it." He spoke the word and Howard and Althea looked at him with shocked expressions.

"You asked, and I told you," Fergus went on, grimly amused by their reactions. "The last thing I experienced before fleeing for my life out of burning building was the smell of fire and brimstone."

CHAPTER TWENTY-THREE
TODAY

"When're we gonna get to my Daddy?" Robynn cried. "I want my Daddy."

Marcus Broarty wanted to deliver a karate chop to the brat's throat. The night's sleep had done absolutely nothing to dim her whine function. She'd been at it ever since they woke up this morning at the motel. He would have given anything to be able to pull the car over to the shoulder and shove the scarfaced little monkey out the door, and then drive away. But that was not part of the plan. Still, going through another entire day of this might just be the deal breaker.

"I want my Daddy," she said again, this time in a pouty voice.

"Would you just shut up?" Marcus growled.

"Daddy says saying 'shut up' is not nice."

"Yeah, well, Daddy's a frigging asshole, isn't he?"

Robynn frowned. "Frigging assle? Is that anything like a muverfucker?"

Marcus Broarty was at first shocked and then started laughing in that high-pitched girlish way that he normally tried to keep others from hearing. "Kid, maybe you're all right after all," he said. Maybe that's why the God of Wood City, who had first revealed Himself to Marcus in the Holy Painting and then had returned to him last night more clearly in a dream, wanted the girl so badly. The kid could be annoying as hell, but it any five year old who could toss off the word *motherfucker* in casual conversation was likely someone even a god would want to know. Beyond that, it really wasn't any of his business why the God of Wood City wanted the girl, no more than it was why He had demanded the life of Emac. Having at long last found a spiritual center to his life, Marcus Broarty was only too happy to comply with the wishes of his new Lord and Master.

There was a ding coming from somewhere in the rental car's dashboard, and Broarty muttered, "What the hell is that?" A quick inspection proved that he was nearly out of gas. Jesus, this rental drank like a goddamned Indian, and at nearly four frigging bucks a gallon, it as probably going to bankrupt him before they get to Wood City! "Look, kid, I'm going to have to pull off at the next exit and get gas, so if you have to go to the bathroom, let me know."

"I'm okay," Robynn answered.

"You sure?"

"Mm-hmmm."

"'Cause if you pee in Uncle Marc's car, he's going to be mad."

"Gina Shaloob wets the bed, but I don't."

"Yeah, well, that's great."

An exit was coming up and Broarty pulled off and headed into the first station he saw, a Chevron. He slid up to a pump and stopped the car, rolled down the window and shut the ignition off, and waited. After about two minutes, he swore and got out of the car. "Doesn't anybody work here?" he demanded of no one.

"Gotta go inside if you want something, mister," said another customer, a black man who was cleaning his windshield on the other side of the pump island.

"Don't tell me this is self-serve?"

"Don't know any other kind."

"I don't pump my own gas back in Beverly Hills!"

"Must be nice, brother," the other customer commented.

"Hey, tell you what, you fill me up and I'll give you a buck."

The man stopped what he was doing and looked at Broarty. Then he spat on the ground. "You need assistance, you go inside and get someone there to help you."

"Look, help me out and I'll put in a good word for you with the True God, the God of Wood City, who's going to kill everybody he doesn't like."

Now the man's eyes narrowed. "Yeah, that's fine, brother, you do that." He wasted no time getting into his car with its sparkling windows and pulling away.

Must be nice, brother. Sure. What did that doomed boofer know anyway? Broarty had a condo in Beverly Hills, as he deserved to, and he didn't have to pump his own gas, but what about all the other shit in his former life? Having to go into the office every day, where he was disrespected by everyone including the janitorial staff; having to deal with the Egon McMenamins of the world; having to constantly prove to everyone that he really was capable of managing a company. Well, they'd learn their mistakes, and soon. They'd all learn that messing with Marcus Broarty now was a real bad idea. He had friends in High places.

But for the time being, he had to get the goddamned gasoline in the goddamned rental car. Sticking his head back in the car to tell Robynn not to go anywhere, he walked into the station office, which was manned by a dikey looking woman with short-cropped blonde hair. "Hey, miss, I need some help out here," he said.

"Sorry, got no one to spare today," the clerk said. "Half my crew called in sick."

"Well how am I supposed to get gas, then?"

The clerk sized him up and down. "You either pay me here or swipe your credit card out at the pump, and then you take the pump and stick it in your gas tank, then you squeeze the handle until it shuts off automatically. It ain't rocket science."

"Where's the opening to the gas tank?"

"It's not my car, fella, I don't know. Gotta be on one side or the other, or maybe in the back under the license plate."

"You've been a great help, thank you," Broarty said sarcastically and walked back out.

The gas opening turned out to be on the driver's side, which was good, since that was the side facing the pump. He knew he really should be paying cash, but time was of the essence, so he pulled out his Visa and slipped into the slot, took it back, and then for the first time since college eased the metal pump nozzle into the gas pipe and squeezed. Broarty's attention remained fixed on the pump, which was just about to top fifty dollars (*Christ almighty!*) when a voice behind him said, "Excuse me, sir." Turning he saw a young dark-haired woman standing by the side of the car, smiling at him. "Hi, I couldn't help but notice that your little girl isn't in a car seat," she said.

"She's not my little girl," Broarty told her.

"Well, it's still not safe to have her buckled straight into the seat like that, and it's really not safe to have her in the front seat, where the air bags are."

The pump shut off and Broarty quickly pulled it out and wrestled it back into its place. "The only air bag around here is you, lady," he said. "Mind your own frigging business."

Broarty got back into the car, fired up the ignition and roared away from the pump island, leaving the woman standing there, her mouth agape. Now his hands smelled like gasoline. Jesus. The things he had to endure for his spiritual awakening.

They were less than five miles down the road when Robynn said: "I have to go to the bathroom."

"Aw, shoot me, kid! We were just at a gas station! Why didn't you go then?"

"I didn't have to then."

"Well there aren't any more exits for miles. Can you hold it?"

"No."

"Shit!"

"I really gotta go." Her voice was hesitant and whimpery, like she was trying hard not to make him mad.

Broarty emitted a low growl of frustration, then said, "Okay, look: I'll find a spot with a lot of bushes along the highway and you get out and pee there."

"Outside?"

"Yes, outside! People do it all the time. It's either that or hold it, because if you piss in this car, I'll kill you."

"Okay." Now Robynn's voice was the size of a baby mouse.

After driving another mile on the highway, Broarty found a spot that looked suitable and pulled over onto the shoulder. "Get out and go over behind that tree and piss!"

"By myself?"

"Oh, good god, you don't need help going at home, do you?"

"Sometimes."

"I don't believe it," he muttered as he got out of the car and slammed the door behind him, then stormed his way over the gravel to the passenger side and yanked Robynn's door open. Fumbling off her seat belt, he pulled her out and marched her down to the tree. "Now hurry up!"

She was whimpering. "I...don't know if...I can...."

"Do you want me to squeeze it out of you?"

"No. But don't look."

"Fine." Broarty turned away while Robynn fumbled with her elastic-topped pants. As soon as he heard the sound of running liquid, he was alternately relieved and annoyed; relieved because the frigging little she-demon was finally getting to it, and annoyed because now *he* had the sudden urge to go. Without looking back he said, "I'm going to go over here for a moment. When you're done, stay right where you are." When he got no response, he barked: "You hear me?"

"Yes."

"Good." Broarty walked a few yards to a waist-high bush. It wasn't a great screen, but it would partially cloak him from the cars that were zooming past on the highway. Unzipping his fly, he pulled his tool out and let go. This was the first time he had peed outside since that disastrous camping trip he had been convinced to go on by an old college friend about fifteen years ago. The strange thing was, he was actually enjoying it, until a voice called out from the other side of the bush: "Hey, watch that shit, will you?"

Startled, Broarty tried to stop peeing but discovered that he couldn't. Then a face appeared over the top of the bush, a striking face enveloped in long, lush, slightly wild red hair. The woman was not classically beautiful—certainly not like Janelle back at the office—but there was something about her, a sexual magnetism that Broarty breathed in like oxygen. "I'm, uh...I... sorry, but I didn't know you were there," he stammered, unable to stop peeing. "I didn't see you."

The woman stood up and stepped around the side of the bush, and Broarty's mouth dropped. She was wearing a 1970s style halter top that just barely concealed her enormous breasts, whose nipples were popping through the yellow satiny cloth like olives, and matching low-riding hip-huggers that looked painted on. What in hell was she doing out here?

The woman put one hand on her hip and cocked her head as she stared at his exposed penis. "Gonna pee me a river, big boy?" she asked, grinning.

Broarty could not stop peeing, but Jesus, what a pee! Even before he was finished, he was getting hard.

"Better 'n' better," the woman said, wetting her lips.

My god, Broarty thought, *she actually wants me*. He could hardly breathe.

The woman was breathing heavy, too. Reaching behind her neck, she pulled the string of a knot and her halter top fell down, revealing large, smooth, perfect breasts. Broarty thought he might faint. Then she unzipped her pants and shed them in one fluid move. She was not wearing underwear. The now naked woman sashayed towards Broarty and grabbed his joint. "Come with me, big boy," he said, leading him to a sandy spot and laying him down. Hungrily, almost viciously, she tore off his pants and ripped his shirt open, sending the buttons flying in all directions. Then she jumped on top of him.

This could not have been a dream. It did not feel like a dream. It felt like he was ramming his pole into a real woman whose body would make a strong man weep...*and she wanted him, too*! He could hear the cars continuing to soar past on the highway, but he didn't care if anyone spotted him. There was nothing that was going to make him give this up. There were pebbles under his back that hurt as he thrust up and down, but he didn't care about them either. He thought he was moaning, but it was hard to tell because of the animal noises that the woman was making. Lying across his chest while she still rode him, her monumental breasts damp and slippery with warm sweat, she panted in his ear: "C'mon big boy, c'mon, c'mon, more, more, more, more!"

He was on the verge of coming, but he couldn't quite get there yet. Not that he was complaining. The build-up was phenomenal. He closed his eyes and just let his sense of touch govern him. *Oh god, it's coming, it's coming, it's coming...here she blows!*

Marcus Broarty exploded in ecstasy. His head was filled with color, and sound went away. Then, all at once, it came back.

"*Freeze!*" a voice shouted. "Don't move a muscle!"

Marcus Broarty heard it, but the command was redundant. He was drained, unable to move a muscle if he'd wanted to. He cracked open his eyes, and was surprised not to see the salacious-faced redhead smiling at him, but rather the barrel of a gun about a foot away, held by a state trooper. Then he heard was the whimpering of a little girl. He started to get up but was stopped by the sound of the gun cocking.

"What are you doing?"

"I said don't move a muscle!" the officer ordered.

"Don't shoot, I'm not moving." Something was in his right hand, a cloth of some kind that was wet, like a handkerchief during cold season. Slowly turning his head over, he saw that it was not a handkerchief but rather a pair of undies.

"Oh my god," he moaned. "Where is she? Where's the woman?"

"You call her a woman, do you?" the trooper asked. "She's where you can't reach her," the trooper said. "Now slowly, very slowly, you sit up and work your way onto your knees. Drop the evidence and then put your hands in the air and keep them there."

"I don't understand."

"Then I'll speak clearly. You have the right to remain silent.

Anything you say can and will be used against you—"

"Oh, shit!" Broarty cried, having just realized that he was still buck naked. He started to jump up, but the trooper pushed the gun so close to him that it nearly touched his flesh. "Move very slowly," the officer ordered.

"Okay, okay," Broarty said, rising with effort to his feet. "But believe me, if you'd just take one look at the woman, you'll understand everything. Don't look at her as a cop, just as a man, and everything will be clear."

"Drop those panties," the trooper demanded, and Broarty did, but even after they'd hit the ground, his hand still felt wet. He looked at it and saw the remnants of his own ejaculation. The panties on the ground were sodden with his come. He'd had a real gusher.

It was then that Marcus Broarty remembered something: the redhead he had banged the daylights out of had not been wearing panties. So whose were these?

Broarty suddenly paled. "Oh my god," he moaned as he looked up and saw the huddled figure of Robynn being comforted by a female state trooper. The girl was looking down at the ground as though she had done something wrong. "What's happening?" Broarty uttered.

The policeman did not respond directly, but instead collected his strewn clothing and threw them in a pile in front of Broarty. "Slowly, *really* slowly, pick those up and cover yourself," he ordered.

As Broarty was doing so, the female trooper walked over. "The girl doesn't seem to be traumatized, just confused," she said. "I got her pants on her, though I can't find any underwear."

"Over there," the male trooper said, pointing at the wet clump of cotton that Marcus Broarty had just dropped.

"I'll talk to her again."

Now Broarty had his shorts and pants on, and was working his way into his shirt, which only had two buttons left. He leveled his gaze at the trooper, who was still holding his gun on him. "Something's not right here," he said.

"I'd kinda picked up on that already."

The female trooper came back and in a low voice said, "The girl swears the man never actually touched her, just pulled her pants and underwear off of her while she was urinating. Then she says he suddenly pulled off all his own clothes and started rubbing himself until he fell down and started rolling around on the ground and crying out. Clearly she has no idea what he was up to. She thought he had suddenly been taken ill, but her description doesn't leave much doubt. He brought a child out here so he could masturbate in front of her."

"*No!*" Broarty shouted. "She had to piss! I swear! Find the redheaded woman! She'll tell you what happened."

"There is no one else here, sir," the trooper with the gun said, forcing out the word *sir* as though saying it under protest. "Just you and the girl, and when we got here, the girl was naked from the waist down and you were having a grand old time with her panties."

"That can't be."

"You believe the girl about not being touched?" the male trooper asked the female one.

"I think so," she replied. "Though I don't know what might have happened had we not come along and interrupted."

"You've got it wrong," Broarty protested.

"Keep those hands in the air," the trooper barked. "Get his ID, Staley."

Trooper Staley looked back at Robynn, smiled and called, "I'll be right back, honey," then she drew her own gun and held it on the panting figure of Broarty while she stepped around behind him and fished his wallet out of his back pocket. She carried it back to the cruiser and radioed in the information, while Robynn stood in the door of the car and watched her.

"Look, officer," Broarty began, "there's some kind of terrible mistake here. That girl is my...my niece, and her father works for me, and—"

"Sir," the trooper interrupted, "I've read you your rights once, but I feel duty bound to warn you again that your best course of action might be to clam up. Otherwise you stand to incriminate yourself." Personally, Trooper Jerry Fitzhugh hoped the bastard incriminated himself straight into Chino, but he also knew that the biggest sleazebags tended to have the best lawyers, so he felt that he needed to make absolutely sure the prick understood that he was being Mirandized.

"You know, I have the power to make it worth your while to just let me and the girl go," Broarty told him.

Trooper Fitzhugh wanted to smile, but he merely looked back at him. *Keep going, asshole, keep going*, he thought.

Trooper Staley returned less than a minute later. "Seems like we hit the jackpot, Jerry," she said. "I radioed in his name and it bounced back immediately. You're just going to *love* what this one's been up to." She pulled the handcuffs from her belt and walked behind Broarty. "Hands behind your back, sir," she said. "Now."

Marcus Broarty lowered his hands, and dropped his head until his chin rested on his head. As he felt the cold steel of the cuffs bite into his left wrist, he smiled to himself. He knew he was protected. If this was the way his newfound God wanted to play it, then so be it. He must work in strange and mysterious ways. All he had to do was go along with what the God wanted and offer whatever help he could. And once he had been released, these asshole troopers would be sorry.

Every asshole in his life would be sorry.

CHAPTER TWENTY-FOUR

"Where did you say you went to church?" Missy LeFavre asked Dani Lindstrom. Missy, the wife of Dr. William T. LeFavre, the general manager of KSOG-FM, Bakersfield Christian Radio, was not officially on staff, though her word was accepted as rule around the station. She was a well-preserved fifty-two with shellacked Laura Petrie hair and a dress that reached all the way to the floor, while the top lifted and separated her impressive bust to a degree that could not be ignored, like the figurehead of a ship.

"Since I travel around so much, I don't have a home church," Dani said. That much was true. But the part that followed about seeking out a different church in each community she visited was painting the lily. The truth was that she had not stepped inside a church since her wedding...and look how that had turned out. But she knew that the fastest way to be shown the door was to say: "Look, I'm just here to do a job, okay?" So the lilies enjoyed a second coat.

"Well, we'd be more than happy to have you at the First Evangelical Baptist Church," Missy said.

"Thank you," Dani replied, but in a tone of voice that implied that she was flattered by the offer. It was what you had to do sometimes.

As the two women walked down the hallway of a surprisingly high tech station, they passed an open office in which a man was seated behind a glass desk, topped with both a stationery computer and a laptop. When he glanced up at Dani, a broad grin came over his flat face. "Is this our replacement DJ?" he asked, practically leaping over his desk to get to her.

"This is Dani Lindstrom," Missy said, stopping on the other side of the door so the man could catch up. "She'll be filling in this weekend. Miss Lindstrom, this is Randy Mount, our programming director."

"How do you do, Miss Lindstrom," Mount said, taking her hand and squeezing it tightly and wetly. "We're so happy you're here to help us spread the Word."

Dani forced a smile. *This man was going to be trouble.* She knew the look, all too well. She finally retrieved her hand from him and followed Missy LeFavre down to the studio itself, which was outfitted with the kind of computerized gadgetry that Dani rarely saw in regional stations. She only hoped she knew how to operate all of it. "This is quite a set-up," she said.

"Praise the Lord," Missy said, and then, peculiarly, knocked on the wooden control panel. "Now, you did hear the part about breaking for news headlines every twenty minutes?"

"I've got that. Do you use a news service or do you have your own news team?"

"Our news comes straight from the world headquarters of the FEBC."

"FEBC?" Dani asked.

Missy LeFavre looked at her like she was slow. "First Evangelical Baptist Church."

"Oh yes, of course."

The studio tutorial took another ten minutes, after which Dani did an air-check. Missy LeFavre seemed pleased with Dani's voice and delivery, so pleased she actually smiled. Dani, meanwhile, was happy that she was able to navigate the complicated control board. As they were leaving the studio they encountered another young woman who was introduced as Laurie, the station intern.

Laurie had a sweet, guileless demeanor, but also exuded the kind of poise and confidence and poise that could not be learned. Dani shook her hand and the girl smiled back revealing perfectly aligned, startlingly white teeth.

Missy took Dani back to the office that she treated as her own, even though the name plaque on the desk bore her husband's name. There Dani received her final instructions, including where to park in the station lot and how to clock in when she arrived back that evening for her actual gig. "And here's the good part," Missy said, pulling a pad of coupons out of her husband's desk. "We have a reciprocity deal with a local restaurant here in town. We give them advertising time and they provide meals." She handed two of the coupons to Dani, who saw that they were for Bailey's Sandwich Shoppe. At each corner of the coupons were tiny *Praise the Lord*'s.

"Thank you," Dani said. "This is very nice."

Less than an hour later, Dani was sitting in Bailey's Sandwich Shoppe, nibbling at a turkey and Swiss sandwich that was big enough to feed three people. She was going to have to take at least half of it with her. She had begun to wrap the remainder of the sandwich up when a voice behind her said: "Well, hi again." Dani turned to see Laurie, the intern.

"Oh, hi," Dani said.

"Mind if I sit with you?"

Even though she had been planning on leaving, Dani said: "Please do."

"Thanks," Laurie said, setting down a tray holding an enormous salad with a double scoop of tuna salad in the middle.

"Missy was talking a little about you after you left," Laurie said sweetly.

"Oh?"

"Oh, nothing bad, she just explained how you went from station to station and filled in for people. That must be exciting."

"It's definitely interesting. You find yourself working with all sorts of people." She sized the young woman up. Laurie—she didn't even know her last name—had the kind of looks more applicable for television than radio.

"Are all the stations you work for religious ones?" the young woman asked, drizzling ranch dressing over her lettuce.

"No, I work for every kind of station. I just change the delivery slightly each time to fit the music and the demographics."

Laurie nodded while she chewed on a bite of tuna salad. When her mouth was clear again, she said: "So you're not really a born-again Christian?"

Dani sighed. "Laurie, can you keep a secret? I'm working a job. I will give the best performance I possibly can and serve the listeners to the best of my ability, because that's what I'm paid for. But no, I'm not a member of the First Evangelical Baptist Church, or any other church. I hope you're not offended."

The girl shook her head, still chewing. "Oh, hell no. I'm an atheist myself."

Dani laughed. "Then why are you here?"

"Same reason as you, I guess. I'm studying broadcasting and I need some hands-on experience, and this station was one of the few who posted an opening for a paid intern. Most places want you to work free."

"I take it the LeFavres don't know?"

"Oh, shit no. I say all the right things, and I've had enough religion courses to bluff my way through if someone starts questioning me about dogma. I don't bother them, and so far they haven't bothered me. I do my job." She paused to munch on a tomato slice. "I've done a fair amount of theatre in school too, so the way I look at it is, I can work at a religious station without really being religious the same way I could play Lady Macbeth without really being insane."

"Good philosophy," Dani said. "By the way, what is your last name again?"

"Mosgionne, spelled M-o-s-g-i-o-n-n-e. It's kind of a problem for me because nobody can pronounce it on the first try. What I usually get is 'moase-guy-on' or 'moss-guy-onnie,' but hardly ever 'moss-gee-ownie.' I'm thinking of saying the hell with it and going by Laurie Moss."

"Do you mind if I ask you about somebody at the station?"

Laurie Mosgionne smiled. "You don't even have to name him. I already know who you're going to ask about. Randy

Mount, right?"

"Right. I kind of got some predatory vibes from him."

"Well, his name says it all. He's randy all the time, and if you drop your guard for a second he'll try to mount you."

Dani chuckled at that. "How do you deal with him?"

"My method is to blush whenever he tries to use a pickup line on me."

"You can blush on cue?" Dani asked, and a second later Laurie Mosgionne affected the most horrified expression she had ever seen, so convincing that Dani actually looked behind her to see if something was happening over her shoulder. When she turned back the young woman's face was a shade of bright crimson. "Oh, Mr. Mount, does your wife know you talk like that?" she declared, giggling nervously. Then in a flash, the blushing girl was gone and the savvy young woman was back. "It's worked so far."

"You should be in Hollywood," Dani said.

"I'd like to be, but I don't photograph that well."

"You've got to be kidding."

"I wish I were. The camera loves some people, and it hates others. For whatever reason, I learned in school that I fall into the latter category. That's why I'm in radio."

"Well, for what it's worth, I don't think you're going to have much of a problem getting to the top in radio."

"I don't think so either," Laurie said, forking another mouthful of tuna, savoring it, and swallowing with exquisite timing.

* * * * * * *

When the phone on Rob Creeley's desk in the tiny Glenowen police station rang, Creeley hesitated a second, thinking it might be his wife. Maria had been none too happy about his coming into work on Saturday, after he had promised her a shopping trip to Paso Robles. But there was too much stuff going on to walk away and hand it all over to Dorgan. Grabbing the phone, he said: "Glenowen PD, Creeley speaking. Yeah, Fitzhugh, what have you got? Oh, man, that's great. Good work. The girl's okay? Good. Great. And you're holding the bastard? He claimed *what*?"

That vague sense of unease now intensified within Creeley. It was not fear, not quite, but rather a perpetual sensation of being thrown off balance, like trying to walk on board a ship, only coming from inside the gut.

"Right, the father's up here," he told the state trooper. "We're, uh, not sure where the mother is right now, but you can bring girl up here, okay? Right. Bye." Creeley hung up the phone and exhaled with relief. Hayden had been right; Broarty appeared to be coming back up to the San Simeon with the girl. Fishing out Jack's cell number, he jabbed it in. Jack Hayden answered it on the second ring. "Jack, everything's okay," Creeley told him. "Robynn's fine and they got Broarty."

"Are they bringing her to you?"

"She'll be in here shortly."

"How about Marc? Where are they taking him?"

"We're the closest jail, so he's coming here, too, at least for the time being."

"Good. There are a few things I'd like to express to him, with a ball bat."

"Come on, Jack, you know I'm not going to sit back and let you do something stupid. I know you probably want to murder him by this point, and part of me doesn't blame you, but why put yourself in jail along with him? It's not worth it. From here on out you can control things, so why not use that option?"

That made sense to Jack. No matter how much he wanted to punch Marcus Broarty's face into pork sausage, he had to acknowledge that Creeley was right. He couldn't help what had happened to Robynn. He couldn't even control Elley. And god knew he couldn't control whatever it was that was floating around making people crazy. But he could at least control his own actions. "Can I at least swear at him a little?" he asked.

Creeley laughed. "Sure."

"Did they say how Robynn was taking all this?"

"She's a little freaked out, but when they told her they were bringing her to you, that made her feel a lot better. But you should know the circumstances, Jack. When the staties found them, they were both beside the highway and Broarty was in a complete state of undress."

"Oh, *Christ*, that miserable piece of shit! What about Robynn?"

"Robynn was okay, Jack. Patrolwoman Staley did a preliminary examination and questioned her and Robynn said that Broarty never so much as touched her. She had her panties down because she had to pee."

"So then why did Marcus have his panties down?"

"That's still unclear. According to the troopers, he seemed confused. I'll have the chance to get his story when he comes in."

"Okay, I'm coming right down," Jack said. "Thanks, Cree." As soon as he had hung up, Jack went over to Althea's room and informed her of the situation. He didn't really want Althea to come with him to the station, but he offered to take her anyway, just so she didn't feel abandoned. But the old woman begged off, explaining that she was engrossed was in a black-and-white Joan Crawford movie on the television, and would be fine. "I haven't seen this picture in sixty years, and I'm afraid I've gotten hooked," she said with a smile. "But I'm so glad Robynn is all right. I'll see her later, I imagine."

Jack was tempted to speed down to Glenowen, but restrained himself. The last thing he needed now was a ticket. When he got into the station, the state troopers had not yet arrived with his daughter. Over the next twenty minutes the only conversation taking place in the police station was over the telephone or radio. When the highway patrol car finally pulled up in front of the small building, both Creeley and Jack went out to greet it. Robynn practically flew out of the passenger side door, hollering: "Dadeeeeeeeeeee!" Jack knelt down to receive her and hugged her tightly. In his ear, she whispered, "I'm not wearing any underwear."

"How come?" Jack whispered back.

"'Cause that man took them from me."

Jack held her in front of him. "Robynn, did he do anything else to you?"

"No. I guess he needed some underwear 'cause he lost his so he took mine. But I got to ride in the front of the p'lice car on a lady's lap 'cause they didn't have a car seat. They were real careful."

By now Troopers Fitzhugh and Staley were out of the cruiser and pulling Marcus Broarty out as well. His hands were cuffed behind him and he walked toward Creeley without seeming to see him. His gaze was leveled at Jack and he was smiling. It was a smile that Jack did not like, the expression of a man who knew a big juicy secret.

"Daddy, that man scares me," Robynn said.

"He's starting to scare me too, punkin," Jack answered.

Creeley came up to them and said, "Look, Jack, how about you take the girl away for a bit, while we interrogate the sonuv...I mean, Mr. Broarty. If you want to come back later you can. But take a little time, all right? We have him and that's the important thing."

"Fine. It sounds like we have to do a little shopping anyway. Who around here sells kids clothing?"

While Robynn and Jack were off shopping in Glenowen, Marcus Broarty was being placed in a cramped holding tank in the police station and the two state troopers filled Creeley in on what had transpired. "He hasn't really said anything since we cuffed him," Fitzhugh said. "He might be waiting for an attorney."

"He's going to need a damned good one," Creeley said. After showing Troopers Fitzhugh and Staley out of the station and thanking them, the he returned to Marcus Broarty, who was sitting in the furthest corner of the stark holding cell like a child in a closet who's hiding from a parent. Except that he was smirking.

"As I'm sure the state police have already told you, Mr.

Broarty, you do have the right to remain silent," Creeley said. "However, if you want to talk, I'll listen to what you have to say."

"Eat my shorts," Broarty replied, grinning.

"Okay, good, that's a good start, because you've just waived your right. Want to add anything else?"

"Suck on my skid marks."

"Always a pleasure to talk to someone so articulate," Creeley said, pulling up a chair directly in front of the bars. "Since you're on a roll, why don't you tell me why you took the girl?"

"Give me one good reason why I should tell you anything."

"You're going to have to tell somebody at some point, so it might as well be me."

"You have no authority over me."

"No? Well, I think that's open for debate, Mr. Broarty. But putting that aside for the moment, I've gotten to know Jack Hayden and I've come to kind of like the guy."

"He's a drunken asshole."

"Well, that's your opinion. Mine's that he's an okay guy. But the point is, if I thought he was a drunken asshole, I'd tell him so, right out. I wouldn't try to get to him through his defenseless daughter, unless I was a big, fat cowardly pig."

"Better a pig than a faggot."

"What's that supposed to mean?"

"You know what it means. 'I've come to kind of like the guy,'" Broarty mimicked. "You sucking his cock or what? I always had Hayden figured for a queer. We've got an office filled with so much prime meat it looks like a butcher shop window, but Hayden's never given anyone so much as a second glance, not even the new girl, the black babe."

"The only reason I bring Hayden up—"

"I'll just *bet* you bring Hayden up!" Broarty interrupted, and then started giggling like a girl.

Creeley sighed heavily. "See, here's the thing, jackoff. The only thing stopping Hayden from coming in here with a ball bat and turning your head into a shit casserole is me. Now, if you want to know a secret, I think he's a little bit entitled to do that, and if he were to do it, I might be encouraged to look the other way. But I talked him out of it, so he's not here." The policeman approached the barred door of the cell. "There's nothing to stop me from doing it on his behalf, though."

The smug grin dropped from Marcus Broarty's lips. "You can't do that and you know it."

"The hell I can't, fat boy. See, you're confusing what I can *do*, and what I can do *legally*. That's a mistake, Mr. Broarty, because I most certainly could open this cell door and go in there and beat the living shit out of you and leave you bleeding and broken on the floor of that cell. Maybe at some point in the future somebody would try to bring a charge against me, but in the meantime, you'd be a pile of hamburger meat."

"You wouldn't," Broarty muttered.

"Who's going to stop me?" Creeley replied. "No one in here but you and me. My word against yours. You resisted arrest, I had to subdue you. Frankly, Mr. Broarty, I could probably do it with one hand. How many fights have you been in in your life? My guess is none past junior high. Know what it feels like to take a fist in the nose? That cold numbness? Are you familiar with that crunching sound as your cheekbone collapses?" Broarty's eyes were very wide, very frightened now. *Good!* Creeley thought. *I hope you're just as scared as that little girl must have been throughout her abduction.* "You're not saying anything, Mr. Broarty. Copping a silent act now? A little too late for that. Okay, maybe you need some incentive." Creeley pulled out his keys and started to unlock the cell door.

"No!" Broarty cried. "What do you want to know?"

Creeley backed off. "Just tell me why you took the girl."

"I was told to."

Creeley frowned. "You were told to by who?"

"The God of Wood City told me to get her and bring her back to him."

"The God of Wood City."

"The true God."

"He tell you to do anything else?"

Broarty nodded. "Get rid of Emac."

"That's the fellow we found in the car trunk, right?"

"Right. I had to get rid of Emac because he was in the way. The God of Wood City showed me how to do it."

"How'd he show you?"

"In the painting."

"The painting," Creeley repeated. "We're talking about that old mural painting in the city hall building out at the ruins of Wood City, right?"

The veneer of smugness had now returned to Marcus Broarty. "What a bright Boy Scout you are," he sneered. "The God of Wood City told me to waste Emac, and good riddance. His real name is Egon, you know. You can use the same letters to spell *gone*. Kind of fitting, don't you think? Egon...gone... Egon...gone...."

"Okay, so Egon's gone," Creeley said. "You still haven't told me about the girl."

"The God of Wood City also told me to fetch the little brat and use her to get to Jack Hayden, but I'm not going to tell you anything about that, because that's the part of the plan I still have to accomplish."

"Well, I'm afraid that your plans have been preempted. You see, Mr. Broarty, you're here temporarily until we can transfer you to a state facility for booking and arraignment and all those dirty little details that we have to follow when dealing with people like you. So you're not going to get the chance to do anything to anybody."

As Creeley watched, Broarty's face turned to the side, like he was listening to someone who wasn't in the room. Then he smiled again; that annoying, smug smile. "Don't be so sure, Texas Ranger," he said, turning back.

"You seem to have regained your confidence, Mr. Broarty. Just a few moments ago you were cowering in the corner. Why the change?"

"Because I know something you don't."

"Is that a fact?"

"Mm-hmm. I know that I'm going to be out of here very shortly. The God of Wood City is not going to let me get transferred anywhere else. He's going to take care of me. He sent me that woman, that gorgeous redhead that I was screwing when those highway patrol pigs arrested me."

Creeley said nothing.

"You look troubled, officer," Broarty said. "You should, you know."

"Oh? Why is that, Mr. Broarty?"

"Because you can't win against us. The God of Wood City is going to be ruling the world very, very soon, and I'm going to be helping him. And you'll be dead." Now he was laughing out loud gleefully, childishly.

This man is bugshit crazy, Creeley thought. "It's a good thing you like telling stories so much, Mr. Broarty. That way you'll be able to keep yourself occupied until the transfer officers arrive." He smiled back at the man and that seemed to throw a bucket or two of cold water on Broarty's manic laughter. It was because he wasn't showing fear, Creeley decided.

"You can't intimidate me," Broarty said.

"What I can or can't do isn't really your concern any more, only what I've done. And what I've done is lock your ass up in jail, where you'll stay until the staties come back. No intimidation about it. I have to go back out front now. I'd like to say it's been fun, Mr. Broarty, but that would make me as big a storyteller as you." Creeley spun around and went back to the main room of the station, leaving Broarty in the cell. After a couple of kicks on the bars and one pounding by hand, followed by a whimper of pain, it got quiet. Perhaps reality was finally sinking in, in some small way, on Marcus Broarty, Creeley thought.

He went to his desk and sat down, resting his tired head in his hands. What he wouldn't give to know just what was happening to his previously quiet-to-the-point-of-boring little village.

He needed some coffee. He was about to get up and see if the pot was still on and had any liquid in it when he heard the station door open. Good. That would be Carl coming back. He could leave him with the lunatic in the cell and slip out into the fresh air for a few minutes. Without even bothering to look behind him, Creeley said, "Hey, Carl, could you—"

He was interrupted by a sudden sharp blow to the back of his head that clouded all his senses. Creeley slumped over the edge of the desk and fell heavily to the floor, and a second later was enveloped by swirling blackness.

* * * * * * *

After Joan Crawford had walked off to happiness with Zachary Scott, Althea Kinchloe switched off the television. But after half-an-hour the stillness of the hotel room began to enfold around her like black funeral drapes. She was actively fighting off sleep because of the dreams she had been having lately, which were hateful and disturbing.

Switching the TV back on, she saw that the channel that had shown Joan was now airing one of those old Technicolor south sea island romance epics featuring a starlet in a sarong, a muscular young sea captain who falls in love with her, and comic relief provided by a teenaged Sabu. She had not particularly liked this kind of film back when they were making them—they were too goofy and juvenile for her taste—and she saw no reason to invest any time in it now.

Althea flipped through the other channels, hoping to find something remotely interesting, finally stopping on what looked like a World War II movie. There was a battle scene going on, with things exploding on every side; maybe it would generate enough noise to prevent her from drifting off and having another horrible dream. She was unable to make out any recognizable stars in the film, but the acting was certainly good. When the characters were hit by bullets they died realistically. The scene seemed to be going on for quite a long time, with the bodies beginning to pile up. Althea was about to move on to another channel, when one soldier in particular stepped into the center of the frame. He was tall and lanky, and walked with a slight stoop that Althea recognized.

She shook her head, trying to rattle out the strange thought that had come to her, but could not, particularly after the lanky soldier stopped and stared directly into the camera.

Althea gasped. The soldier walked closer to the lens, and halfway there, an enormous smile of joy burst out on his tired, soiled face.

It was Howard!

"Hi, Pookie," Howard Kearney said, now in full close up, ignoring the running and screaming men on every side around him and the loud explosions going on behind him.

"Howard?" Althea whispered. "It can't be you."

"It's me, Pookie. I don't have much time," he said. "This is what you need to do. Remember the journal I left you? You have to find it. The journal will help explain everything."

"Howard, I don't understand."

"The journal will convince you. If you get the journal, you'll know this is real, and not just a dream. You have to read it and trust me."

"Of course I trust you! But can't you tell me—"

At that moment, Howard Kearney was beyond telling anybody anything. A bullet tore through his head, removing part of it, and sending his helmet flying off in a way that would have been funny had it not been so horrific. The same went for his eyes, which crossed so extremely upon taking the bullet that he looked like a silent comedian. Howard fell forward out of camera range, and Althea tried to scream, but only a high pitched, childish whine emerged from her throat. There was a sickening thud as Howard's body hit the ground. Althea covered her mouth, but kept her eyes on the television.

Another soldier was running into the frame, this one wearing a uniform unlike any she'd ever seen. He dashed in holding a sword, and thrust it down into what would have been Howard's body, again and again and again. Spittle began forming on his lips as he did so. Then he looked up into the camera and grinned.

Then he winked at her.

It was the figure who had been coming to her in her dreams, the one who was helping her count down the days until her death.

The grinning man bent down, disappearing under the television frame, and when he reappeared a second later he was holding something. When Althea fully realized what it was, she did scream, long and terribly.

The horrible dream soldier was holding up Howard's bloody, severed, cross-eyed head for her to see, and lasciviously kissing it.

CHAPTER TWENTY-FIVE

"Do you want some ice cream?" Jack asked Robynn, as they were leaving the small clothing store where he had purchased a new set of underwear and a Dora the Explorer sweater for her. There was an old-fashioned looking ice cream parlor right across the street.

"I don't think I like ice cream anymore," she replied softly, looking almost fearful.

"Punkin, did that man who brought you up here give you ice cream?"

"He tried. He kept saying he would. I didn't want it and he got mad."

Goddamn Marcus Broarty! Was there nothing his touch couldn't ruin? Even among the roster of Great American Assholes, it took one of supreme talent to rob a child of her taste for ice cream. What Jack wouldn't give to wrap his hands around the fat miserable fuck's throat and choke the life out of him, watching him turn the colors of the spectrum as he fought painfully for each breath, relish the sight of his tongue sticking out like a calf's and his eyes bugging until they burst like pink Bazooka Joe bubbles. If he ever had the chance to kill that rat bastard, it just might be worth going to prison for.

"Ow, Daddy, you're hurting me," Robynn said.

Jack looked down and saw that his grip on his daughter's hand had gone white-knuckle. Immediately he let go and knelt down to face her. "Oh, punkin, I'm so sorry," he said, hugging her. "I didn't mean to. I guess I'm just so worried that you're going to get away from me again, I'm keeping too tight a hold on you."

Robynn smiled. "That's okay," she said. "I don't want to get away from you, not ever again."

Jack hugged her again and fought back tears. "I'll be more careful. Sometimes it's possible to want something too much, and that's not good." After another hug the two were on their way again.

They were only a block away from the Glenowen police station when Jack saw a woman rush out of the front door frantically, a cell phone glued to her ear. She was waving and gesticulating like a windmill. Jack did not recognize the woman, but clearly something there was wrong. Had he been alone, he would have run up to her to see what the problem was, but Robynn had already been through enough without exposing her to yet another crisis. They walked slowly and steadily, and eventually the woman, a young, drop-dead gorgeous Latina, ran back inside the station. As they approached the building, Jack said, "We need to stop in here for a minute, okay?"

"Okay."

Jack opened the door of the station and knocked on the jamb. "Hello," he called. "Cree, you here?"

The woman he had seen outside rushed towards him with panic in her eyes, demanding: "Who are you?"

"My name's Jack Hayden. I'm here to see Chief Creeley."

"You're the father of the girl who was abducted?"

"May I ask who you are?" Jack asked.

"I'm Robert's wife, Maria. Robert needs help, please help him!"

God, *now* what? "Can you watch Robynn?" Jack asked.

"Of course."

Maria Creeley smiled at Robynn and knelt down to her, but the girl's hand tightened around Jack's. "Daddy, don't leave me again," she whimpered.

"Punkin, you'll be fine," Jack said. "I'll be right back out." Squeezing his hand out of his daughter's grip, he stepped into the police station. "Cree? It's Jack, where are you?" There was no answer. Going back to where the tiny cells were, Jack peered through the bars and swore as he recognized the figure sprawled out on the cot: it was not Marcus Broarty; it was Rob Creeley, unmoving, his head bleeding from a wound at the crown.

The cell door was unlocked so Jack rushed in and slowly rolled the policeman over. "Cree, it's Jack, can you hear me? Damnit, Creeley, give some kind of sign that you're alive!"

"Your boss is an asshole," the policeman muttered weakly.

"I told you that days ago. You didn't have to put yourself in danger to verify it. Can you sit up?"

"Yeah, I think so." With effort, the policeman pulled himself to a sitting position. "Man, that smarts."

"What the hell happened? And where's Marc?"

"I don't know. He was locked up right here last I saw. I came back out to my desk and the door opened, and I thought it was Carl but then I got clubbed on the back of the head. Next thing I remember I was under my desk bleeding like a stuck pig. I managed to get up and stagger in here, and that's when I found the cell open and Broarty gone. I guess I collapsed on the bed."

"Mr. Hayden?" Maria Creeley called out from entry way.

"He's okay," Jack called back, "just sore."

"Is that Maria?"

"Yes, I think she's the one who found you. Does Glenowen have 911?"

"It goes to the county. But there's a small clinic on the edge of town that passes for a hospital for non-serious matters." He gingerly touched the back of his head and pulled his hand away, showing the still oozing blood. "God, whoever did this must have hit me with a damned pine tree. Hey, is your girl okay?"

"She's fine, and thanks for asking. She's out with Maria."

"I can see where that's going to lead," Creeley said, with a wry smile. "She's wants kids something fierce. This'll put her over the top."

Maria Creeley and Robynn now rushed into the cell, and the woman practically threw herself on her husband.

"Ow, hey, jeez, I'm still a little sore, honey."

Jack, meanwhile, took Robynn out into the office area and started to dial 911, but the stopped when he heard the sirens on their way, figuring Maria had called already. In less than a minute two young EMT's, burst into the small station house. Deputy Carl Dorgan joined them moments later. Jack got out of the way while the medical techs examined Creeley's head. "You'll need a few stitches," one pronounced, "but I don't think there's any serious damage. Your vision is all right, isn't it?"

"Yeah, I can see fine," Creeley said.

"Good thing your head is so hard," Dorgan commented.

"We'll take you in for an x-ray, just to make sure," the tech said. "Can you walk?"

"My feet are hard, too," Creeley said, slowly rising. "Yikes, that still hurts. Deputy, it looks like you're going to be in charge for a while."

"Hurry back," Dorgan replied.

"While I'm gone, Carl, Mr. Hayden and his girl here are to be offered every consideration. Even if he says something you might not understand, just go with it, okay?"

"Check," Dorgan replied, though his expression showed his puzzlement over the order.

The technicians, one on each side, helped Creeley through the door of the station, anxiously hovered over by Maria Creeley.

"Bye, Maria," Robynn said, as they were leaving.

"Bye-bye, baby," she called back.

When they were gone, Robynn said: "Daddy, I gotta go pee-pee."

"Okay, punkin. Officer Dorgan, where's the restroom?"

"Through that door," he said, pointing to what Jack had assumed was a small closet besides a row of file cabinets.

Robynn dashed over to the door and opened it up, reached up to turn on the light, and then closed the door behind her, like a big girl.

"Your only one?" Dorgan asked Jack.

"Yeah," Jack answered. "We got a good one, so I guess we

decided not to push our luck."

"Can they do anything about her, well, her thing?" He brushed his upper lip with his finger.

"There's a possibility of her having cosmetic surgery when she's older," Jack said, talking to this man about it with surprisingly comfort. "But there are no guarantees. Right now I'm just trying to protect her from comments from other kids, and even some adults. You'd be amazed how insensitive people who should no better can be."

"Oh, no I wouldn't." Carl Dorgan pulled out his wallet and flipped the thick photo holder open to a particular picture, then held it up for Jack to see. It showed a boy of indeterminate age who was clearly afflicted with Down's Syndrome, but who was smiling happily for the camera. "This is my youngest," Dorgan said. "He's twenty-two now and he just moved out of the house to live in a place of his own. It was his own idea."

"He looks like a fine boy, officer."

"When he said he wanted to move out and get a job and take charge of his life, no matter what, I was so danged proud I wanted to rope off the street and throw a parade for him. But that would've embarrassed the heck out of him. His mom's still crying, though. And you can call me Carl, by the way."

"I will, and I'm Jack." He stuck his hand out, which the beefy policeman took and squeezed, and Jack suddenly knew how Robynn had felt earlier, when he was inadvertently crushing her hand.

From the closet-sized bathroom (*and how the hell did someone the size of Dorgan fit in there anyway?*), the sound of the toilet flushing could be heard. Jack knew from experience there would be at least a minute of diligent hand washing yet to come.

Dorgan was tucking his wallet back into his pocket. "I gotta hand it to ol' Chief," he said, rather obviously changing the subject. "He'll go to any lengths to get out of work. What I wonder is what the transfer guards who were supposed to pick Tubby up and take him to county are going to think when they arrive and find out he's not here."

"Cree said he heard the door open and thought it was you coming back right before he got hit," Jack said. "Who could it have been?"

"Who knows? But whoever it was took the keys and unlocked the cell, and then the two of them high-tailed out. You know the prisoner better'n anyone around here. Who would be helping him like that?"

"Honestly, I don't know anybody who would go to such lengths to help Marcus Broarty." He looked at the policeman, who was staring back with a steely gaze. "Oh, good god, Carl, I hope you're not thinking *I* did it!"

"Naw." Dorgan looked away.

The bathroom door opened and Robynn came out.

"Everything all right, punkin?" Jack called out.

"Mm-hmmm," the girl answered. Then she stopped and looked at the floor for a moment, before reaching down and picking something up. "But Mommy dropped something."

"Robynn, Mommy wasn't here."

"Yes she was," the girl said, taking a couple of steps and then picking something else up.

Jack went over to her and started examining the floor. "Holy shit," he muttered.

"Daddy, that's a bad word," Robynn admonished him.

"You're right, punkin, and I'm sorry. I'm just surprised that Mommy was here. Can I see those?" He held his opened palm down and Robynn dropped in the four tiny charms, and then went back to hunting. "Here's another one!" she cried, gleefully.

"What're you two up to?" Dorgan asked.

Jack looked at the small silver charms in his hand. One was in the shape of a scarecrow, and another was a witch. A third looked like a cairn terrier, which a fourth was a monkey with wings. He knew them well. He had had them made special for Elley by a jewelry shop on their second anniversary. The charms were all figures from *The Wizard of Oz*, and Elley wore it so much that even Robynn had memorized the tiny shapes.

And now she was finding them on the floor of a police station where Elley should not have been, and where even the intimation of her presence—let alone the proof—carried implications that Jack simply did not want to consider. Swallowing hard, he told Dorgan: "These are my wife's. I had a charm bracelet made for her, and these are the charms on it. She was here. God knows why, but she was here and she left these. Oh, good god, you don't think...no, that just doesn't make any sense."

Then again, what did?

"Here's the thing, Jack," Dorgan began. "Somebody had to come in here and club Chief Creeley over the head, and then spring the prisoner. That's a given. I've been looking around the office here, and I don't see any heavy object out of place, which indicates whoever it was brought it in with them. I'm leaning toward the theory that Chief was pistol-whipped. I'm taking your word that your wife was here, based on those little charms. So here's the sixty-four-thousand-dollar question: does she by any chance have access to a gun?"

"Oh, good god," Jack muttered. "Yes, we have one at home."

"Does she know how to use it?" Dorgan said.

The butt end, obviously, Jack thought. *Did* Elley know how to fire the gun? How hard was it really? You point it and squeeze the trigger, and the only real need for skill is when you *don't* want to seriously hurt someone. God, could Elley have sprung Broarty in order to take him somewhere and kill him for abducting Robynn?

"Daddy, is Mommy going to shoot somebody?" Robynn asked.

"Punkin, I...I don't know. I don't know anything right now."

That wasn't quite true; Jack Hayden knew something. He knew he wanted a drink more right now than at any other time in his life.

CHAPTER TWENTY-SIX

"Hello," Hortensia Abrego called upon entering the Hayden residence. Hortensia had been cleaning the house every two weeks for the past five years, not long after the little one had been born. Her usual day was Monday, but this coming Monday she had promised to help her oldest daughter move to a new apartment. "Hello...hola," she called again, and received no reply.

Shrugging, she set about going to work. Back in her native Salvador, Hortensia Abrego had been had been trained as a hairdresser and worked in a salon, but here she was a house cleaner, which was the only kind of work she could get.

So much for the better life.

Hortensia's first stop was the nursery, where she stripped off the sheets and pillow cases and tossed them in a pile to throw into the washer. By the time she was finished vacuuming, mopping and wiping every other room, the laundry would be done. She replaced the bedding with fresh sheets from the closet and then made her way to the master bedroom.

As soon as she entered the room, Hortensia could tell something was wrong. There was a smell, and since she knew the Haydens did not have pets, the odor could not be explained away as the result of a dog or a cat becoming careless. Hortensia tried to ignore the odor and went about her business, pulling the blanket down and peeling off the layers until the mattress was revealed. She threw the powder blue sheets into a pile on the floor and started to pull the pillows out of their cases, but the smell would not go away. In fact, it was stronger than before.

Was something under the bed? That did not make much sense, but the smell had to be coming from somewhere. After throwing the pillow cases onto the stack, Hortensia knelt down to take a peek under the bed.

A face had stared back at her; a white, dead face with a look of horror etched into it.

Horrified, she launched herself backwards, trying to get away from it. The pile of bedding broke her fall. Hortensia clasped her mouth, trying desperately to keep her breakfast down, because if she were to vomit, she would only have to clean it up herself.

What should she do?

Anyone else would have called the police by now, but Hortensia was not about to do that. The police walked hand-in-hand with the INS, and calling them would open her up to scrutiny which she could not withstand. She ran downstairs to the kitchen and splashed water from the sink, hoping it would help her think.

The house was empty.

Nobody had seen her let herself in.

Nobody knew she was here.

Since this was not her regular day, nobody would know that she had ever been here at all.

Hortensia went back upstairs to the master bedroom and, forcing herself to ignore the stink, put the sheets back on the Haydens' bed. Coming back down, she considered stopping the load of sheets in the washer, but decided to let it run. There would be no way anyone would be able to tell that she, as opposed to Nola, the girl's *niñera*, or Mrs. Hayden, who had loaded the stuff in there.

Once she had replaced everything, Hortensia ran into the kitchen, picked up her purse from the counter, and dashed out the front door, making sure there was no on the block to see her. Quickly locking the door behind her, she ran to her car and sped away. She would decide later whether or not she would ever return.

* * * * * * *

Elley Gorman Hayden had never fully appreciated the size of the trunk in her Lexus before.

It had always been roomy enough to hold all of the groceries for a big weekend shopping, and it certainly held all the stuff from her office without any problem at all. But who knew that it could contain an entire body, and a lard-assed one at that? As to whether or not Marcus Broarty was in discomfort or pain back there, Elley didn't really give a rat's ass. The incessant screaming and kicking had ceased. Maybe the prick passed out. Hell, maybe he died. Either way was no skin off her nose.

She turned the car radio back on. Elley had switched it off earlier that day after receiving her instructions from the Voice, which had suddenly appeared to her on the way to Glenowen, while she was doing a search of stations in the hopes of finding something other than the religious and Mexican music stations that monopolized the airwaves up here. It had drawn her attention first by signing *Over the Rainbow*, and then by addressing Elley by name. She recognized it immediately: it was the same low and seductive, seemingly all-knowing voice that had recommended she shoot Blaise back in L.A.

There had been a time when Elley Gorman Hayden would have become totally freaked out by a voice speaking directly to her, first inside her head, and then over a car radio; a voice that seemed to know everything about her, what she had done, even what she was thinking. But her life stopped being ordinary days ago. There was a new reality now, and a new Elley. Her entire life had been spent doing for other people, first her mother, then her teachers, then Orbit Marketing, then Jack, then Robynn, then Blaise...the list went on and on. But now, right now, was *her* time. She was doing for Elley, and part of that new reality had been dictated by the voice on the radio. It was the Voice that told her exactly where to find Marcus Broarty, languishing in the slammer of that little toy village on the coast. It was the Voice that informed her exactly where on the head to hit the policeman with the butt of a gun in order to knock him unconscious. It was the Voice that instructed her to lift the unconscious policeman's keys and handcuffs, release Marcus Broarty from his cell, and then take him hostage again.

He is proving to be too stupid for my purposes, the Voice had said, and from what she knew of Marcus Broarty, Elley could understand that. Right after she opened the door of the cell, the shitbag had actually attempted to hit on her. *I've always thought you were wasted on Jack*, he'd said, and then winked heavily. She winked back, licked her lips seductively, and then clubbed him on the left temple with the gun, cuffed him, and when he was able to once again walk well enough, guided him outside to the Lexus, keeping the pistol jabbed in his side to keep him from calling out. She pushed him in the back seat, where he began babbling about how some god would not let any harm come to him. When that didn't work, he turned on the bullshit macho bravado, warning her that he was a dangerous man, that he had already killed someone and stuffed the body inside his car trunk.

"What a great idea," Elley had commented, screeching the car to a lurching halt just outside of the village. With no one around to see them, she had pulled Broarty out of the car, keeping the gun jammed in his gut, opened the trunk, and then shoved him inside, bringing the lid down hard on his legs so that he would pull them in. Once he was safely locked in, she'd jumped back behind the wheel and took off. "Kinda sucks being kidnapped, doesn't it?" she had shouted in the direction of the trunk.

The thumping and screaming from the trunk that had ceased for quite a few miles now started up again, if anything, heavier than before, as though Broarty was making an all-out effort to escape. There were no cars behind Elley for at least a quarter mile, so she sped up and then stomped on the brake, throwing the Lexus into a screeching, smoking sideways stop on the freeway. The satisfying thud of a body slamming helplessly against the call of the trunk told her she had produced the desired effect. She then stomped on the accelerator and listened to him slam back the other way. Elley laughed out loud and she pulled the stunt another couple times, after which the pounding stopped.

They were heading north, just as the Voice had instructed, though her ultimate destination was as yet unknown to her. The answer to that came quite a few more miles up the road, when the Voice once more came over the car radio. *Hello, my dear*, it seduced. *Are you ready to continue?*

"Yes," Elley answered.

The voice dictated a series of detailed instructions, and Elley nodded quietly as she took them in. Then the radio went silent, and she turned it off.

Another twenty-five miles, he had said, and then that would be that. For the second time in as many days she was about to commit murder, and that made Elley Gorman Hayden strangely happy.

BOOK FOUR

CHAPTER TWENTY-SEVEN

Even though Althea did not carry much in her purse, it took her a while to find the tiny leatherette-bound address book hiding in one the corners. This was shaping up to be one of those days when her brain and her hands were working as well together as a Democratic president and a Republican congress. When she finally got hold of it, she turned to the *Kinchloe* page and scanned down until she found *Tim—work*, followed by a Portland phone number. She punched it in on the motel phone and when the man's voice answered the phone, Althea Kinchloe said: "Hi, Tim, it's Noni."

"Noni!" her grandson practically screamed. "Where on earth are you? Don't you know everybody's been searching for you for days? Are you all right?"

"I'm fine, dear."

"*Where* are you?"

"I'm staying at a nice motel in San Simeon."

"*San Simeon?* California? How did you get there?"

"I took a bus part of the way, and then a nice man and his little girl drove me the rest of the way."

"So you just decided to take a little vacation?"

"It's really much more complicated than that."

"Dad's called the police, you know. By now he might even have the FBI out looking for you. He's a wreck."

"Your father always was prone to rile easily. That's why I called you instead of him. I need your help, Timmy."

"You want me to come get you?"

"No, I'm not finished down here yet, but I need you to find something and send it to me." Althea described for him an old trunk that was stashed in a corner in her garage. At least that was where it was the last time she saw it. She hadn't moved it, and she doubted anyone else had, so chances were good it was still there, if the spiders hadn't carried it off. "It's not locked," she went on. "Please go inside and look for a small journal."

"A journal," Tim repeated. "Is it yours?"

"No, it was given to me by a friend a very long time ago. Honestly, I can't remember what color the cover is, but some-where on the inside it will have the name Howard Kearney."

"Is that Carney like Jay Carney?"

"K-e-a-r-n-e-y," Althea spelled out. "If you could find that and take it to one of those overnight mail places and send it up here, you'd be helping me enormously. Here's the address." Picking up the complimentary pad of note paper on the nightstand by the phone, Althea read off the address and phone number of the Tide Pool Inn.

"Okay," Tim said. "When do you need it?"

"Now, actually, though I doubt it could get here before tomorrow morning."

"That's kind of a rush, Noni."

"Yes, and I'm sorry."

"See, the thing is, the deadline for overnight pickup is usually five o'clock. So in order to get from Portland to Vancouver, go over to your house, get in the garage, hunt down the trunk and then get this journal, and take it to the nearest FedEx, I'd have to leave right now."

"You know the traffic better than I do, dear."

"But I'm at work. I'd just have to drop everything and walk out."

"I know, but...how many times have I ever asked for anything from you kids?" Althea said, suddenly feeling every day, every hour of her ninety-three years. "Oh, maybe to help me move a sofa around if you were there, but that's all. I'm not used to begging, Timmy. I don't like the idea of it. But if that's what I have to do to get you to help me, I will. I need to see that journal. It's very, very important, and time is running out. Please, dear. Please help me."

There was a pause, then Tim asked: "Noni, are you sure you're okay?"

Althea simply couldn't lie to him. Not to Tim who, even though she knew better than to ever say it loud, was her favorite grandchild. "I don't know, dear. I really don't know."

"That's it. I'm calling Dad and we're coming down—"

"*No!*" she shouted, her vehemence surprising both of them. "I'm sorry, Tim, but no, not your father. Please, dear, just trust me. Find the journal, send it to me. And if it's not too much trouble, go up into my bedroom and get a few underthings out of the second drawer of my dresser, the one with the lamp on it, and throw those into the package as well. I didn't pack for a long trip."

"Noni, I...."

"I have to go now."

Tim Kinchloe tried to say something to keep her on the line, but the words would not form. "I love you, Noni," was all he could say.

"I love you too, dear," she said softly. "Goodbye, Timmy."

Althea hung up the phone. A tear escaped her eye as she lay back down on the bed, now afraid to turn on the television, afraid of what else she might see on it.

* * * * * * *

Tim Kinchloe hung the phone up, shaking his head. He knew he should leave right now and get in his car and drive straight to the airport and take the first plane down to wherever the closest airport was to San Simeon—probably San Luis Obispo County—and pick her up, and to hell with this journal buried in a trunk somewhere in her garage. But he also knew that he was not going to do that. There had been something in his grandmother's voice that compelled him to do exactly as she had asked. The finality, the conviction with which she had said goodbye convinced him of her sincerity. She had not been irrational in any way, simply mysterious and insistent.

Fortunately, his job as a newspaper reporter made absences somewhat explainable, if not necessarily easy. He was still on a deadline of sorts, having to file the story about the councilman's alleged use of a call girl (at least as alleged as something can be when there's a traceable debit card charge involved). But there was time. There was always time. And really, it wouldn't take long to dash over to Noni's tear the garage apart, get the book, and dash to FedEx.

Logging off his computer, Tim ran across the newsroom and into the office of Crazy Madonna, the manager of the paper's city section. Purely in terms of sanity, Donna DeCreasy-Adler probably had more marbles than most who worked at the paper, but her insistence on using her full hyphenated married name, which could be phonetically twisted into "Donna the Crazy Editor," was fodder for the staff. Then someone took it a step further, singing "Crazy Madonna" to the tune of the Beatles' *Lady Madonna*, and her nickname was assured. Tim knocked on the jamb of her open door and said: "Hey, Donna, I just got a tip I have to check out. I might be gone all afternoon."

"What is it?" she asked, looking up from her desk, peering over her narrow glasses.

"I'd rather not say, just in case it's nothing. But if it pans out, believe me, it will be worth it."

"Come on, Kinchloe, can't you give me a hint?"

"If the tip's good, it could mean a whole expansion of the Councilman Felber story."

"A series expansion?"

"If it pans out, yeah, possibly."

Donna DeCreasy-Adler's eyes got wide and the corners of her mouth turned up in a smile. "Then why are you still standing here?" she asked. She made a shooing gesture and Tim dashed away, grateful.

Of course, there was no lead, but once his mission had been

accomplished, all he had to say was that the lead was bogus, dammit, and then write the story as he planned to anyway.

In his car, heading toward Vancouver, Tim wondered if he should notify his dad that Noni had called. As much as he hated to see the old man running in circles like he'd been doing (and he was the easiest guy in the world to rile, especially now that he was retired and bored as hell), he thought that informing him of Noni's whereabouts would only make things worse. Besides, she had been absolutely right: she had never asked anybody for anything. Never. So the fact that she was doing so now meant it was important to her, even if Tim didn't understand completely.

Traffic was good this time of day, and he made it to Noni's neighborhood in near record time. But as he drove up to the house, he realized that he had never even stopped to consider this possibility, though he should have: standing out in the middle of Noni's front lawn, talking to a policeman, was his father.

Pulling his car over and crouching down, Tim watched from down the block as his father started arguing with the cop, who was remaining cool. Finally the officer started to edge Geoffrey Kinchloe toward his car. He seemed to be convincing his father to leave the premises. It took several more minutes, but he finally did. Tim watched as his dad got into the beaten old Nissan he claimed he was restoring and drove away. Then policeman took stock of the house, went up to the front door and checked it to make sure it was locked, crossed the street and got into a car that was parked there and drove away.

Tim glanced at the car clock: it was 3:43. He kept watch for another ten minutes before making his move. Deciding it best to leave his car where it was, he got out and walked to Noni's house, then as nonchalantly as he could (just in case someone was watching), he went straight for the flower pot out front under which everyone in the family knew she kept an emergency key. *What if it's not here?* he momentarily fretted, but moving the pot, he saw that it was.

He let himself inside and went straight up to Noni's bedroom, and grabbed a handful of her underwear out of her dresser (rifling through your ninety-year-old grandmother's panties... how creepy was *that*?) Then he went down into the garage. Noni still kept a car in there, though she hadn't driven it in at least a year. It was covered with cobwebs and dirt. The garage was filled with decades worth of stuff, but Noni was nothing if not neat, so it was neatly stacked stuff, box after box tucked into a honeycomb of wooden shelves that he imagined Grandpa had built at some point. It did not take long before he spotted a weathered old trunk that matched her description. Finding a small step ladder, he climbed up so that he could reach the trunk. It was not particularly heavy, but it was filthy. No one had been inside this box in a very long time.

Taking it down, he opened it up and looked through the contents. There was an ancient cardboard box with *Wedding Dress* written on it, and other artifacts from nearly a century of life. He handled each one carefully as he took them out, digging down for the journal.

It was on the very bottom. The book had pasteboard covers and age had turned the pages past yellow and straight to light brown. Opening it, he looked inside the cover and read: *The Journal of Howard E. Kearney, begun May 19, 1937.*

This was it.

Setting it down, Tim carefully picked up all of the other items and set them back inside the trunk, then closed it and returned it to its spot. Taking the journal up again, he began perusing the brittle pages. Most of it consisted of Howard Kearney's impressions of the places he visited and the people he met. Every now and then there would be a reference to painting, and a couple of the pages were decorated with pencil sketches—some of them pretty good—so Tim presumed that he was also an artist.

Wait...hadn't Noni one time talked about an old boyfriend who had been a painter for the public art administration in the thirties? Was this him? That would make sense, even if the urgency with which she wanted the journal from a few hundred miles away did not. He fanned the rest of the book, finding that not all of the pages were filled with writing. The final quarter of the pages were empty, at least until the very last page in the journal, on which something was written. After Tim read the words, only one sentence, he dropped the book and slumped against the abandoned car behind him, his breath suddenly thick.

He couldn't possibly have read that right. He couldn't have.

Tim, it had read, *stop dawdling and get this to your grandmother.*

Picking up the journal, Tim slowly opened once more to the last page and read again. Then he started hyperventilating, they way he used to when he was in high school; the way he had not done since his college senior finals. Tim gasped vainly for air as all of his limbs began to numb. The attack was so strong that he had to rush back into Noni's house, race upstairs, and pull a plastic Glad Bag out of her kitchen cabinet to breathe into, before he passed out altogether.

While breathing into a plastic bag, he had managed to convince himself that it was some sort of elaborate joke. Even though Noni had a sense of humor, he had never known her to be a practical joker, but that was the only explanation for what he had read. Once he had regained his wind, Tim went back to the garage and picked up the book, chuckling to himself as he opened it to the last page and read the words again.

And once again he dropped it; only this time he cried out as well.

There were now two additional lines that he had not read before, because they had not been there before: *Maybe you should keep one of those bags in your pocket, just in case you need it again.*

Holding his breath, Tim Kinchloe staggered back to the kitchen, grabbed a handful of Glad Bags, and shoved them in his pocket. Just in case he needed one again.

CHAPTER TWENTY-EIGHT

The Voice had been precise in its description of Elley's ultimate destination, though in the deepening twilight it was not easy to spot. It was roughly in the middle of the stretch of rustic, scenic coastline called Big Sur, which snaked the coast high over sea level while tightly hugging the mountains out from which the highway had been blasted into existence. Elley smiled at the thought of the name *Big Sur*. She had lived in California her entire life and had heard it for most of that time, but she had no idea what, if anything, it meant. The reason for the smile was because that was the name she had given to the seductive Voice on the radio: *Big Sir*.

Finding the prescribed spot was easier than locating a place to turn the Lexus around on the narrow, shoulderless road. She had to go two miles beyond her destination before seeing a half-moon shoulder carved into the mountain, which was just large enough to muscle the damned car around so that it was now heading south on the highway.

When she got back to the place where the cliff overlooking the ocean was at its steepest, her oil light went on, just as Big Sir said it would. Elley carefully pulled the car as far off the road as she dared. There was not really a shoulder, only a tiny wide patch. At one point it might have been a vista spot, but if so, it had been eroded by decades of salt wind and rain. There was a three foot guard rail running along side the patch of ground, but that was unlikely to pose a problem. Leaving the engine on and the car in drive, she got out. There were no cars coming in either direction, just as Big Sir had told her would be the case. She could only presume that he had managed dueling road obstacles a mile or so down in each direction in order to cut this stretch of Highway 1 off from traffic; maybe even a rockslide. Even so, the obstacles would not hold forever, so she had to hurry. The car inched toward the guard rail until it nudged it. A hoarse, muffled voice came from inside the trunk: "What's going on out there?"

Instead of answering, Elley scanned the side of the road for a suitably large rock, and finally found one.

"Hey," Marcus Broarty called again. "Why have we stopped?"

"I'd buckle your seat belt if I were you," she replied. "It's going to be a bumpy ride." Then she took the rock and stepped to the open driver's side door. As forcefully as she could she pitched the rock down on the accelerator. The Lexus spun gravel wildly and pushed heavily against the guard rail, which was starting to give way. It only took a few seconds for the rail to collapse under the weight and power of the car, which then plummeted over the side of the cliff, rolling and smashing against the craggy surface all the way down until it struck the rocky beach far below. Marcus Broarty's screams drowned out whatever engine sound there was until the impact at the bottom, at which point all sound stopped.

Elley took a deep breath and wiped the sweat off of her brow. She hated sacrificing her Lexus, which was not yet paid for, but that was part of the plan. There was nothing she could do about it. Big Sir would make up for it, she was certain of that. Elley now had to wait for someone to stop and give her a lift and take her back down the coast.

Elley tried to imagine what must have run through Broarty's mind on the way down, and then she started laughing when she remembered the old joke: *What's the last thing to go through a bug's mind when it hits a windshield? It's ass.* Elley smiled.

Blaise Micelli was dead.

Marcus Broarty was dead.

Two down, just one more to go.

CHAPTER TWENTY-NINE

As Dani Lindstrom was preparing for her first evening gig inside the control booth, familiarizing herself with the board, Randy Mount was circling around her like a vulture. She could have sworn Mount had been wearing a wedding ring when she first met him that afternoon, but all traces of it were now gone from his left hand. She was having a hard time not laughing in the man's face. It wasn't so much due to outrage that his family value convictions ended at his zipper as amusement over his misplaced ego, since Randy Mount resembled Alfred E. Neumann in a suit. Yet here he was acting like God's proverbial gift to women.

"Hope you don't mind my sticking around," Mount said, grinning like an idiot. "I just thought I'd see if you needed any help with anything. It's the Christian thing to do."

Remembering Laurie Mosgionne's special talent for guilelessness, Dani tried to smile back at him as sincerely as she could. "I'm sure I'll be fine, but thank you for offering."

"My pleasure," Randy Mount said. "You wear glasses all the time?"

"Um, no," she said, suddenly self-conscious about the oversized lenses she always wore when working. "These aren't even prescription, they're just slightly tinted. Different places have different lighting systems, and these make it easier on my eyes."

"Hey, that's clever," Mount replied. "Always be prepared, huh? Just like the Boy Scouts?"

"I suppose so, though I was never a Boy Scout."

Mount laughed too loudly. "I'll bet you weren't! Say, are you a married gal, Dani?"

Randy Mount certainly worked fast, even if it was with the finesse of a pile driver. "I was married, but I'm afraid that ended recently."

"*Really?*" Now he was Mr. Concerned. "I can't say as I understand why someone would leave a gal like you, but I'm sure sorry to hear it."

I left him*, jackass*, Dani thought, but said: "These things happen, I suppose."

Mount nodded with the weight of the world on his head, and his eyes became moist. "Despite the Lord's best efforts, sometimes we drift apart," he said. "My wife, for instance—" *Oh, here it comes....*

"—doesn't understand me. Some days I wonder if Satan hasn't entered her heart. Was that the way it was with your ex-husband?"

Dani was starting to feel uncomfortable. "Not exactly," she said. "I'm the one who left." Then, looking up and staring Mount straight in the eye, she added: "Truth is, I was outraged over his giving me herpes."

Randy Mount's eyes widened into fear-filled moons, while Dani nearly gasped upon hearing the words come back to her. *Where had that come from?* Perry had not had herpes, and that certainly was not why she kicked him out of her life. But given Mount's reaction, the lie appeared to be working, so why ask why? In fact, she felt a strange compulsion to keep going. "But I'm sure for the right person, that wouldn't make any difference," she said, seductively. "I mean, didn't Jesus cure the lepers? So why couldn't someone who was really righteous cure my herpes?"

"Have faith, sister," Randy Mount stammered, retreating. "I have to get back to my office now, but have a great show."

"Thank you, Randy. God bless you."

"Right," he called back, practically running out of the control booth.

Dani doubted she would see much more of Randy Mount tonight, and after tomorrow night's gig she would be away from KSOG and would make it a special point not to return, no matter what Lillian planned for her. Though before she left, she might pass on the herpes excuse to Laurie Mosgionne.

Dani put her headset on and tried a sound check, listening to her voice bounce back at her, and finessing the sound on the vast control board. The feed going out on air was that of a canned preaching show that the DJ on shift before her, an affable nineteen-year-old guy with a surprisingly good air presence, had started before he left to go to a group sing. It only had a few minutes to go, and then Dani was on. She had listened to a stack of CD's during the afternoon and picked out some tracks to play, and was relying on the sheets left to her as to the schedule: music until twenty-five after the hour, then the Prayer-of-the-Day, then more music until fifty-five after the hour, and so on until midnight.

Dani popped her first CD in and cued it up to the desired track, and waited for the canned show to end. Then she switched on her microphone and launched into her spiel.

"Praise the Lord, and God bless all of you out there listening to KSOG-FM, Son-of-God radio, spreading the Word through Central California. My name is Danica Lindstrom and I'm sitting in this evening for Marybeth Klaidy, who is at home fighting a little bug this evening. We all wish her godspeed. You get better, Marybeth, hear? I'll be taking you through to the midnight hour, the dawn of a new, perfect day, praise the Lord. So let the spirit fill your heart as we start our shared journey with the sounds of Amanda Raines singing her hit song, 'He's All I Need.'" Dani cut off her mike and hit the button for the CD, and heard the first twangs of the countryish open to the track play, then jotted down the title and time on the log. When the song was nearing the end she cued up her next one and waited for the proper moment to break back in with a hearty "Praise the Lord!" and then pop the next tune.

About twenty minutes into her set, Randy Mount poked head

into the booth again. "Uh, hi, I just had a question," he said. Dani shot a quick glance at his left hand and noted with amusement that his prodigal wedding ring had returned home. "Are you Irish?"

If this was another pick-up line, it was an original one. "Actually, I'm a hundred percent Swedish. Why do you ask?"

"Oh, well, it was just the accent, it sounded kind of Irish."

"Accent?" Dani continued to work very, very hard to make sure that she had no natural accent of her own, while practicing slight lilts and inflections for professional purposes. But here, in the middle of California, she had opted not to use any of her stock regional ones and speak in her natural voice.

"Every time you say, 'the Lord,'" Mount went on, "it kind of sounds like, 'the Lard.' You know, sort of Irish."

"I said 'Praise the Lard?'"

Mount cleared his throat. "Well, that's how it came over through the feed."

"Oh. Sorry, I guess I'll have to watch it. Thanks for pointing it out."

"No problem." He slipped back through the door as the song was coming to a close. *Like hell I said 'lard'* she thought, but it probably wouldn't hurt to take care just the same. Switching her mike back on, she announced: "That was Brain Deadman...uh, I mean, *Brian Redman*...sorry about that, Brian, with 'Jesus is the Reason.' I'd like to thank all of you for spending your evening right here with me on KSOB...I mean *G*!" Dani hit the cough button and cut her mike before the gasp emerged. Recovering instantly, she went back on air and said: "I'm sorry folks, I'm new around here and like everyone I make mistakes. We all know there was only one person in history that didn't, and he's not here tonight. I mean, he's not physically here, running the board. Sure, of course, he's here in spirit, Praise the Load."

She hit her cough button again.

What was wrong with her tonight?

Dani decided not even to try coming back on the air. She simply put in another song, took off her headset, leaned back and took a few deep breaths. She closed her eyes, but heard the door open. "I know, I know, and I'm so sorry," she said. "That time I said 'Load.'"

"Uh, Miss Lindstrom," Randy Mount said, "I don't want to falsely accuse anyone of anything, but, uh, you're not doing this on purpose, are you?"

"On purpose? Of course not. Why would I say that shit on purpose?"

Randy Mount's mouth fell open and his eyes widened again as he backed out of the studio. Through the glass she could see him going to the nearest desk in the office area and picking up a telephone. She had a pretty good idea who he was calling.

"Get a grip, Lindstrom!" she demanded of herself.

Putting the headset back on, she waited for the music to end and hit the pause, then came back on and said: "I just love the message of that song, don't you? You're listening to KS-hole-G, and—"

Had she really just said *K-asshole-G*? No, she couldn't have. She was just getting paranoid.

"—and my name is Danica Lindstrom, filling in tonight for Marybeth Klaidy, the blessed person who normally takes this time slot. Marybeth is a little under the weather this evening, and I'm so glad she is because now I can be here in her place."

Dammit!

"No, wait, that didn't come out right. I don't mean I'm glad she's sick, I mean I'm glad that I have the opportunity to share the word of the...of *God* with you while Marybeth's in the sack...I mean, slick in bed...licked in bed...oh, shit!"

This time Dani clapped her hand over her mouth, the sound of which went out over the airwaves. Immediately every line of every phone in KSOG started to light up. Through the glass she could see Randy Mount staring at her, horrified, a phone in his hand. Then she started laughing.

"I wish you could all see what I'm seeing," Dani heard herself saying. "A behind-the-scenes employee of this fine establishment, Mr. Randy Mount, is glaring at me through the window like I've just grown horns. But you want to talk horny, I'll fill you in on Mr. Mount. Jesus ain't the only one he's tried to jump tonight, folks. Before I went on the air he did his goddamnedest to maketh me lie down so he could comfort me with his rod and his staff, you know what I'm saying?"

Dani heard more words coming out of her mouth, but she had no more control over them than if they had been prerecorded on tape. Neither could she lift her hand to either bring it down on the cough button or cut her microphone off all together. She heard herself using words that she never used, even in private conversation. She wanted to desperately but her hand would not move when commanded.

It was like she was possessed.

Now through the glass she could see two security guards rush into the outer office. "Uh oh, looks like the barbarians are about to storm the gate," she said. "The Nazis have landed and they don't look happy. Well, fucks, I mean *folks*, oh, fuck it, I meant the first one, I hope you had as much fun here tonight as I did. Thanks for listening to K-SUCK, and remember: there is no God. There is no Jesus. And Mary did it with everyone. You're all nothing but a flock of sheep, being had by the biggest con organization in the history of the human race...."

Led by Randy Mount, the two burly male security guards now burst into the studio and ran to either side of Dani, taking her by the arms and stood her up. "Woo hooo, it's a gang rape!" she screamed into the microphone. Mount reached over the control panel and grabbed the headset off of her head, taking several strands of platinum hair with it, but Dani seemed oblivious to that. He tried to switch off the microphone himself, but found he could not. The red light over the door remained lit. He pounded on the cough button as the guards literally carried Dani, who was screaming and moaning as though having multiple orgasms, out of the booth, but it too had no effect. Sweat was pouring down his face and his blood was coming from his fingers and he ripped at the cord for the mike. The red light remained on.

"Mother jumpin' whore!" Mount screamed in frustration to the microphone. "What do I have to do to kill you?"

Instantly, all control panel lights went out, as did the red On Air light above the door.

"Thank God," Mount muttered, taking out a handkerchief and mopping his face.

He could hear the phones still ringing off the hooks outside, and he went back through the door and into the office. There he saw the figure of Dani Lindstrom sprawled out on the floor, while the two security guards hovered over her, nervously.

"What happened?" Mount asked. "What did you do to her?"

"We didn't do anything," one of the guards said. "We got her out here and she just fainted, smack dead on the floor."

"She's not dead, though, right?"

"No, there's still a pulse," the other guard said. "You ask me, she must be sick."

"I think she demonstrated that well enough on the air, the dirty little harlot."

"What should we do now?" the first guard asked, and after working at the station for four years, Mount still did not know the names of the building staff.

"Well...I suppose we should call paramedics to see if they can revive her," Mount said.

"You want us to do that?"

"No, no, you fellows go on with your rounds, I'll call from here. And thanks for coming up and helping. I probably don't have to tell you that I've never had an experience like this."

"Sure you don't need us to stick around till the EMTs show?" the first guard asked.

"No, no, you go on, I'll stay here with her and make sure she's okay. G'night."

Once the guards left the station was totally quiet. Even the phones had stopped ringing. Maybe everybody gave up, or maybe they jammed a circuit somewhere. Mount looked over at Dani, prone on the floor, with her arms splayed out above her head and her legs slightly apart.

"I don't know what your problem is, gal," he whispered, "but even now you're one fine-looking filly."

He stepped to her and checked her pulse for himself. He could feel the beat, and it was even and steady, if a bit faint. He touched her forehead and neck, to see if she would move. She did not. He opened her eyelid. Mount wasn't sure why people did that, but he always saw it in movies. Dani's left eye stared sightlessly.

She was gone. Far gone.

Mount had a decision to make. This woman had made a horrible mess of things, and had probably gotten him in trouble with his wife by ratting him out on the air. He'd better not get in any deeper. But as he thought, his breathing became heavier, harder. He felt his entire face and chest flush with each intake of air.

Lord, was she a babe! Even with the white hair, which he ran his fingers through. *Who would ever believe her*? he thought. *After her performance on air, who would believe anything she said*?

Panting, Randy Mount carefully slid his hand down the neck of Dani's blouse until he had her right breast cupped in his hand. She made no move. Taking his hand away, he unbuttoned the blouse and laid it open, revealing a plain white brassiere, the clasp for which was in the front—proof that she was a whore.

He unhooked her bra and pulled the sides apart, revealing her breasts. Mount gingerly fondled them.

Dani did not move.

Emboldened now, he dashed over to the light switch for the office and turned off all lights, casting the large room in darkness. There was just enough illumination coming in from the hallway outside to see Dani's sleek body. Randy Mount stuck his fingers in the top of her skirt and pulled it down, all the way past her feet, and then set it aside. He did the same with her panties.

Danged if her hair wasn't white everywhere.

Mount was less careful taking off all of his clothes, which he threw in a heap. He stood totally naked over her body, hard as a hammer. He lowered himself down on top of her, reveling in her warmth. He started kissing her chin and neck, and slowly slid down until he got to her nipples, and when he was done there he moved down her belly, and then to her snowy public hair. He kissed the insides of her thighs, but refused to enter her, either with his tongue or his dick. She had confessed to having herpes. But Dear Lord, he was about to explode!

Mount crawled back up and lay down on her again, positioning his throbbing cock flat against her abdomen, then began moving up and down, stroking his member in between their warm bellies. Mount could feel his seed rising. He pumped harder, grunting with every thrust. He was on the verge of climax, and sensed it was going to be spectacular.

Just then the lights of the radio station suddenly switched on, blinding him, as a rush of his hot semen shot all over Dani's front.

Mount heard a woman scream and looked up, squinting in the sudden light.

"*What in the name of Our Lord Jesus are you doing?*" a man's voice thundered, and didn't need clear vision to know that the shouter was Dr. William T. LeFavre. Jumping off of Dani, he made a leap for his clothes.

"Dear Lord in Heaven," groaned Missy LeFavre, who was standing behind her husband.

Randy Mount cowered nakedly in a corner, holding his pants in front of him, shivering both from the sudden cold and the sheer terror he was feeling.

"He killed her," Missy squeaked through her hands, which were now covering her mouth.

"No!" Mount shouted. "I didn't touch her!"

"Didn't *touch* her?" LeFavre roared. "My God, man, you were lying on top of her! I think that qualifies as touching."

"What I mean is—"

"I heard what you said right before the station cut out," Missy cried. "You said, 'What do I have to do to kill you!'"

"I meant that whore of a microphone!" Mount blubbered. "She's not dead, she's...she's warm."

In spite of himself, Randy Mount's little man was stiffening again, rising like that flagpole on Iwo Jima.

Dr. William T. LeFavre turned away. "I'm going to be ill," he groaned.

"It was *her*!" Mount cried, pointing a finger at the prone figure of Dani. "It's all her fault! She brought Satan into this station, and he...he...pray with me, pastor."

"Get out of my sight," LeFavre said, his face ashen.

Randy Mount thought it best not to press the issue. He threw his clothes back on as quickly as he could and ran toward the door, trying to maintain as much distance between him and his former boss as he could. Once Mount was gone, Missy LeFavre asked, "What should we do about her, Bill?"

"Get her cleaned up and throw her clothes over top of her," he replied, weakly. "I'll call for an ambulance and...oh...oh... God...I'm going to...." Dr. William T. LeFavre rushed for the studio bathroom and made it inside just in time to vomit. After rinsing his mouth in the sink, he lurched back out, sweating profusely.

"My heavens, Bill, you look terrible," Missy said. "Sit down."

"Lord, save me," LeFavre moaned, clutching his chest and falling to the floor of the radio station.

"Bill!" Missy cried, rushing to him.

Dani Lindstrom, meanwhile, opened her eyes and found herself lying on the floor of KSOG, feeling chilled. She quickly realized why: she was naked. "What the hell!" she cried.

"You!" Missy screamed. "You witch! Look what you've done to Bill!"

Dani felt something slimily sticky on her belly, and for a terrible moment, she thought it was paint. But touching it, she realized what it was, and moaned, "Oh, god, *no*!" Desperately pulling her clothes on, she said, "What happened to me?"

"Don't try to be cute," Missy replied with hatred. "We came in and found you and Randy on the floor."

"Oh, Jesus...."

"*Stop it*! Don't you *dare* take His name in vain now, after everything else!" Turning back to her husband, Missy LeFavre moaned, "Oh, God, oh Bill, honey, oh...*look what you've done to him, you whore!*" She raced to the telephone and dialed 911.

Dani ran into the bathroom and began to sob. What had she done? What in god's name had she done? What was wrong with her? Memories—scattered, dreamlike memories—of her on air performance flitted through her mind, and she prayed it was a nightmare, that it had never really happened.

But it did happen, a voice, not her own, said inside her mind. Just like the fact that she was drenched with semen meant that *something* had happened between her and Mount, though she could not remember any details. The fact that it was her midriff that had been come on, and not her crotch or legs, indicated the sick bastard had masturbated on her. She cleaned herself as best she could with paper towels.

When she finally summoned up the courage to leave the bathroom, Dani saw a team of paramedics arrive with a gurney, onto which they hoisted the still, gray form of Dr. William T. LeFavre. "Is he...?" she managed to utter.

"He's had a coronary," Missy replied, her voice hard, her face streaked with runs of mascara. "He's alive, but only barely. No thanks to you."

"Missy, I...I don't...."

The paramedics began wheeling LaFevre away. "I have to go with my husband," Missy told Dani.

"I know saying I'm truly sorry is nowhere near adequate—"

"You're right, it isn't. I never want to see you again, Miss Lindstrom. May God forgive me for saying this, but I don't care if you die in the streets." Then, along with the paramedics wheeling the prone figure of William T. LeFavre, Missy LeFavre left the building, leaving Dani alone in the offices.

How had her life become so thoroughly ruined in less than a week? Walking numbly to where her purse was, Dani picked it up and staggered out of the building. All she wanted now was to get out of this city and back to safety; relative safety, at any rate. No, that was bullshit. What she wanted was to get back to Jack Hayden, who was the only remotely sane element of her existence at present. And if anything happened to Jack...Dani did not want to consider anything happening to Jack. She just needed to get back to him.

Her car was the only one remaining in the station parking lot, and she took small satisfaction in seeing that no one had slashed her tires. She got in and started to drive away from this catastrophe, but had not even made it to the I-5 on ramp before her cell phone started to ring.

Please let it be Jack, she thought, pulling it from her purse, on the passenger seat. "Hello, this is Dani," she said into the phone.

"Well this is Lillian!" her agent shouted. "What the *fuck* did you think you were *doing* back there?"

"You certainly found out quickly."

"A listener called me. But don't change the subject! I want to know what you thought you were doing, and I want to know *now*!"

Dani sighed. "Lillian, I have no idea what happened. It was like it wasn't me talking, like I was listening to someone else, but the words were coming out of my mouth. I can't explain it." *The Devil made me do it*, she thought grimly.

"That's it?"

"I just don't know what happened to me back there. Look, Lillian, a lot of strange things have been happening to me. Maybe it's the divorce, I don't know, but I think I need some time off. No more gigs for a while, all right?"

"You're kidding, right? You're joking me."

"I'm serious, Lillian. I need some time to figure things out."

"Honey, from now on, you've got nothing *but* time! After what you did to me tonight, do you really think I'd line up another gig for you, *ever*?"

Dani Lindstrom had never been fired before, and the realization that it was happening now was like swallowing ice whole.

"Lillian, what are you going to do if I'm gone?"

"Not your problem."

"But who are you going to replace me on such short—" Dani stopped speaking, because one ray of understanding had suddenly filtered through the darkness. "Lillian, you said that a listener called you about my set, right?"

"So what?"

"How did they know that you were the right person to call? How did they even find you?"

"Who cares? She knew, that's all."

She. Dani felt dead, unable to believe how completely she had been set up. "Her name was Laurie Mosgionne, wasn't it?"

"Laurie Moss," Lillian confirmed. "Since she's already got an in with the station she thinks she can clean up your little Titanic voyage to the point where they won't sue me."

"Why would they sue you? This was my fault, not yours."

"Because you don't have any fucking *money* and I do! That's the way lawsuits work, sweetie. And speaking of money, you still owe me twenty-one hundred."

"I'll pay you back, Lillian," Dani said. "I don't know how, but I will."

"Yeah, well I'm not holding my breath. Goddamn, sweetie, after everything I've done for you, you ratfuck me like this."

Dani could not hold back the sob. "I'm so sorry."

"Yeah, yeah, yeah. Goodbye and good luck."

"Don't hang up, Lillian, there's something else I want to tell you. Watch your back."

"Now you're threatening me?"

"No, I'm trying to warn you about Laurie Mosgionne. Just watch your back."

The line went dead.

Dani held onto the phone for a mile or two before dropping it back in her purse. Her urge to cry had gone away, and it was not being replaced by a wave of indignation; not at Lillian, not even at Laurie Mosgionne, but at herself. What a total idiot she had been! She had not merely helped her replacement push her down and stomp all over her, she had fitted her with the proper cleats. Dani tried to imagine how Laurie had played it. Had the girl run to Randy Mount after Dani had confessed to her in the sandwich shop that she was anticipating problems with him, and told him that Dani was waiting for a move? God, had she gone so far as to somehow *drug* her at lunch so that she would later lose her mind on the air?

If the Devil really had been in that radio station, making both her and Mount destroy themselves, he was wearing a dress and blushing on cue.

* * * * * * *

Robynn Hayden knew enough about dreams to know when she was having one, and she was having one now. She was with a group of her friends in her school, playing out on the playground, and that man suddenly appeared, the bad man who had taken her for a long car ride, promising to take her to Daddy but never doing it. In the dream she was scared, maybe even more scared than she had really been on the car ride. But then somebody else appeared. It was man who smiled a lot. He came to Robin, who was now alone, all her friends having disappeared, knelt down and said: "Hi, honey, my name's Howard."

"I'm Robynn."

"I know."

"How do you know?"

"I just do."

Robynn looked over at the bad man, who was still glaring at her. "He scares me."

"I know, honey. There are some people who can really be scary sometimes. But he can't hurt you any more, okay."

"Okay."

"In fact, I'll make him gone." The man named Howard pointed to the bad man, and he vanished. "There, he can't bother you any more. You know, Noni tells me that people call you punkin. Can I do that?"

"You know Noni?" Robynn said.

"I knew her very well, a long, long time ago."

"I love Noni."

"So do I, punkin. That's why I'm here. There are a few things I need to tell Noni. Can I tell them to you?"

"I guess so. But why don't you tell them to her?"

"Well, punkin, it's because she's not asleep right now, and I need to tell someone in a hurry."

"Ohhh. Okay."

"And you're such a big girl," Howard went on, "that I know if I tell you, you'll give her the message."

* * * * * * *

Dani Lindstrom awoke in the motel room, having only vaguely remembered getting back to the Tide Pool Inn in the middle of the night and checking in. She remembered even less about the drive. It was all like a faded dream. It was now a little after eight in the morning and she felt shockingly refreshed, despite getting only a few hours' sleep. She thought she still had one change of clothes in her bag, which was still in her car. Hunting down her car keys, she left the room and headed out to the parking lot. She was nearly to the front door when a young voice behind her squealed: "Hi, Dani!" She turned around to see Robynn Hayden.

"Hi, Robynn," she said, kneeling down to greet the girl. Robynn did not throw her arms around Dani, but she looked like she might want to. "How have you been."

"Well, I'm kinda getting a little bored," the girl said. "Daddy won't even let me go to the swimming pool."

"Really? Well, I'm sure he has a good reason for that."

"He does," Jack said, coming down the hallway toward the lobby with Althea, who smiled warmly to her. Dani didn't rush up to him and take him in a desperate embrace, but she wanted to. "In fact, punkin," Jack went on, to Robynn, "I really don't want you coming out here in the hallway unless I'm with you."

"I'm not a baby anymore, you know," the girl protested.

Jack ruffled her hair as he passed, and then walked up to Dani. "I got your note. But I didn't expect to see you back here so soon."

"Plans changed," she said. "I got in early this morning. I just got up."

"What time did you get in?" Jack asked with sudden intensity.

"It was three o'clock or so. I'm not a hundred percent sure, to be honest. Last night is a little blurry."

Jack turned to the old woman. "Althea, would you mind taking Robynn into the restaurant? I'll be in soon. I need to talk to Dani first."

Once they had gone, Dani asked Jack what was wrong.

"Come with me," Jack said, leading her back to his room. Inside, Jack sat her down on the bed. "You didn't by any chance come into this room last night, did you?" he asked.

"No, of course not," she responded. "How could I? I don't have a key. Oh, wait, I do still have one, don't I? You know, if I had remembered that at three this morning I would probably would have just let myself in and saved a few bucks. But I didn't. Why?"

Jack went and got his laptop from the nightstand drawer and turned it on. He fumbled with the buttons until one particular picture came up. As Dani looked at it her mouth fell open. It was a shot of the motel room's bathroom mirror. She could see Jack holding the camera and its flash reflected in the glass. But the primary subject of the picture was the writing on the mirror's surface. It appeared to be done in a thick red substance, maybe lipstick. It read: *Your ded and you dont know it you muverfuckers.*

"My god," Dani uttered. "I don't understand."

"This was written on the bathroom mirror this morning," he said. "I went to clean it off, but then thought maybe I'd better take a picture of it, which loaded onto my laptop. I probably should have taped it on the camcorder, but it's still in the truck and I didn't want to leave Robynn to run out and get it. The reason I asked if you had come in the room last night is because I wanted to believe that *somebody* had come into the room and done this. That at least would be a natural explanation, unlike the others."

"What are the others, Jack?"

He sighed and brushed his hair back with his hand. "That word *muverfucker*, the way it's spelled, I've heard Robynn pronounce it that way before. The mistakes in the spelling and punctuation are those even a very bright five-year-old would make."

"You think Robynn wrote that?"

"No. No I don't. And least I don't think I do."

"Did you ask her about it?"

"She was still asleep when I discovered it, and I'd rubbed it off by the time she got up. I didn't say anything to her about it, and at first I was waiting to see if she made any kind of reference to it."

"Would she admit it?"

"I know my kid," Jack said. "She's the kind who's terrible at lying and at keeping secrets. If she breaks something at home, you can read it on her face. If she's done something that bothers her, she comes right out with it. So yes, if she had done this, more importantly, if she realized she had done it, she would have said something."

Realized she had done it, Dani thought. Just like she had not realized what she was saying on the air last night. Chills formed on her arms.

"But there's a bigger problem," Jack continued. "The letters on the mirror were written in paint, wet red paint. When I wiped them away, I searched all through the bathroom, looking for any trace of either paint or a paintbrush. There were none. After Robynn got up, while she was in the bathroom, I searched the rest of this room, top to bottom. There was nothing. No paint, no paint-covered rag, no brush, nothing. Robynn's hands were perfectly clean."

"So...."

"So, if Robynn did it, she first had to figure out how to get the paint and the paintbrush, and then afterwards had to figure out how to get rid of it."

"Flush them down the toilet?" Dani suggested.

"Okay, but where did they come from? I don't think she pulled them out of the toilet."

"So if Robynn didn't write the words, who did?"

"That's the question that's given me a crashing headache," Jack said. "Who could have come through a locked door, unseen, unheard, gone in there and painted words on the mirror, managing to use a word that I've only heard Robynn say? Who else knows my child so well that they could possibly do that? There's only one other possibility, and I don't even want to think about that one."

"You have to tell me, Jack."

He looked at her with ancient, tired eyes. "I wrote it myself. I got the paint and painted the letters on the mirror, then threw the evidence away and forgot all about it."

"Why would you do that?"

"Because I'm losing my mind." *Or maybe I go so drunk I blacked out*, Jack thought, though he did not remember getting drunk, either.

"Or maybe something made you do it," Dani said, softly. "Jack, the reason I'm back today instead of tomorrow was because I got fired for saying things on the air, things I could not control, things that horrified me as I heard them coming back from the feed, but I couldn't help saying them any more than I can help breathing. It was like I was being controlled by something else." She rushed to him and threw her arms around him. "What's happening?" she asked.

He hugged her tightly. "I don't know, Dani, I don't know."

"I came back hoping that you would be able to prop me up, but now you've got your own problems. At least now I understand why you didn't want to let Robynn out of your sight, though she really does want to go swimming. She told me."

"I know," he said. "It's hard on her and she doesn't understand the situation. It's worse than you could imagine."

Dani broke the embrace and studied Jack. "What aren't you telling me?" she asked.

"The real reason I'm keeping Robynn in sight at all times, either my sight, or Althea's, and now that you're back, yours, is because of her mother. Elley is out there somewhere. I'm afraid that she's going to come after Robynn."

"You're afraid of your own wife?"

"She hasn't been acting very rationally lately." Jack picked up his laptop and started to power it down. "Speaking of Robynn, I'd better get to the restaurant. Coming?"

"Let me get my bag out of the car, and I'll be there." Dani started out of the room and then stopped. "Jack," she said, turning back, "do you think Elley would have heard Robynn use that word? Muverfucker?"

"Maybe. Why?"

"Could it have been she who came in here last night and wrote on the mirror?"

Jack suddenly tensed. *God, could it?* Could she be here, at the motel? "I have to get to Robynn now," he said, rushing out of the room.

This just gets better and better, Dani thought, closing Jack's door behind her as she heading back out to the parking lot to retrieve her garment bag. She hurried back to her room, where she peeled of her clothes, which were still from yesterday, and put on the fresh ones. Then she went into the bathroom to try and do something with her now-white hair.

Then she screamed.

On the mirror, directly across from the shower, were words written in bright red block lettering. She shoved the corner of the towel into her mouth to keep from screaming any more as she read: *Gonna die, you white-haired dogfucker!*

She was also sure that she did not have to touch them to know that they were written in paint.

CHAPTER THIRTY

The sun streaming through the dirty windshield of the old station wagon awakened Elley even more than her sudden need to go to the bathroom. She had spent the entire night in the station wagon, which was surprisingly comfortable. No wonder so many children had been conceived in old vehicles like this one. You could damn near have a threesome in it.

Glancing at her watch, she saw that it was almost nine. She had slept far later than usual, but it wasn't like she had to go into the office anymore. With her gone and Blaise dead, there might not even be an office anymore. She opened the door of the truck and found the morning a bit more bracing than she had been expecting, and dashed to the outhouse she knew was fifty yards or so behind the double-wide trailer. It was a reeking, fly-infested one-seater located past the apple trees, the strawberry plants and the thriving marijuana crop. Directly behind it was a rusted wire fence, which at one time probably protected the outhouse and the pot garden both, but now seemed redundant. It looked like nobody had been back here in years. That was fine with her; that way it would be a long time before the body was found. If it was ever found at all.

She stepped into the dark outhouse and seated herself, replaying the events of the night before in her mind like a film. After ditching the Lexus with the spare idiot in the trunk, Elley stood out on the shoulder of the highway until dark, trying to hitch a ride. She gave up counting the vehicles that zipped past her, some dangerously closely, before the old Buick Sport wagon squealed to a halt. The driver, a skinny one-time hippie with a white Z.Z. Top beard and a pony-tail held in place with a tie-dyed headband, which almost matched his threadbare vest, leaned over and rolled down the passenger side window. "Need a lift, ma'am?" he asked her.

Smiling, Elley got in and pulled the door closed, which took both hands.

The guy introduced himself as Zephyr and said he was the last local member of an old commune that had been tucked away in the woods of Big Sur since the Summer of Love. "You might not know it now, but I was quite something back then," he told her. The way the guy was talking about sex to a virtual stranger, Elley figured he probably hadn't actually had any of the two-person variety since Reagan was president. In between descriptions of his earlier love life, Elley had asked the guy what his profession was, to which Zephyr reacted as though it were the funniest question he had ever heard. "I guess you could say I'm a master herbalist," he replied, still giggling.

Right.

It had taken very little suggestiveness to get the guy to take her to his disgustingly filthy trailer stashed back in the woods. The place was illuminated by lanterns; in fact, there was no evidence of any electricity. The kitchen area had a small oven and fridge, but the presence of a battered ice cooler and a greasy hibachi strongly indicated the appliances were not being used. "Facility's outside, if you need it," the guy had told her, which is how she learned about the outhouse.

After pouring her a glass of cheap white wine, Zephyr pulled out the biggest bong Elley had ever seen and stuffed with about a pound of home-grown shag, and proceeded to get so stoned that his eyes began to move independently of each other, like a chameleon's. "You're fiiiiine," he drawled, appreciatively. Elley responded by smiling at him and slipping off her blouse, then her bra, which brought the old hippie's eyes back into focus. When he finally made a wobbly lunge for her, it took no effort at all to knock him to the floor, then take the wine bottle and bring it down hard on the back of his head.

He was still alive but unconscious. Skinny as he was, Elley had little difficulty dragging Zephyr outside, where she dumped him on the dirt and shot him in twice in the head. She didn't want to leave blood stains on the inside of the trailer. Out here in the dirt, there was a good chance they would be absorbed by the forgiving earth.

It was the automatic release of his bowls at the moment of death that had given her the idea of where to deposit the body. Taking her slacks off so she wouldn't get anything nasty on them, she laboriously dragged him to the outhouse, her path illuminated by a couple of dim solar-powered lawn lights, threw open the door, and hoisted Zephyr's torso up, wrestling his head into the hole. Then she went around and picked up his legs, and shoved. His thin body disappeared through the seat of outhouse with no trouble and splashed satisfyingly into the filth pit below. There was just enough residual light to see a half-full sack of quicklime, which she poured in on top of the old hippie. Reclaiming her slacks, she went back inside where she washed her hands and her legs, for good measure, as thoroughly as his ridiculous hand-pump sink would allow. She started to dress again, then thought, screw it; there was no one here, no one to see her. She decided to slide off her panties, too. Now stark naked and feeling freer than she had in decades, Elley went through the dump and carefully wiped her prints off of everything she had touched inside, taking special care with the wine bottle. Looking around at the dump of a trailer, she decided it was probably better to spend the night in the station wagon. Picking up her clothes and shaking them violently, so as to force out any bugs that might have settled in, she got dressed again and then headed out for the vehicle.

That was last night. It was now a chill morning, even colder inside the outhouse. When she was finished she reached for the roll of toilet paper, which was the ultra-soft, cottony kind. For some reason that made her laugh.

Elley picked a handful of apples on her way back to the station wagon, and then started the old wreck up and headed down the washboard road the stretched from the secluded encampment to the road that in turn led to the highway. She had tried to turn on the radio, but nothing came out. It appeared to be dead as a Zephyr. Glancing down, she saw some bare wires hanging down loosely. That was probably why the radio didn't work. Instinctively, she grabbed the ends of the wires, forcing them together, and felt the zap of a minor electric charge. Even so, she held on, and a moment later was rewarded.

I see you have arranged for your transportation, Big Sur purred over the radio. *You are remarkable resourceful.*

"You ain't seen nothin' yet," she replied with a laugh.

* * * * * * *

As soon as Dani Lindstrom came into the restaurant, Jack knew that something was wrong. Her face was almost as white as her hair. "You okay?" he asked as she slid into the booth where Althea was finishing off a poached egg, Robynn was pouring more syrup on what was left of her pancakes, and Jack still had one half of a ham, egg and cheese breakfast croissant.

"Something strange happened to me in my room," Dani replied.

"Strange things have been happening to all of us, dear," Althea said, taking a dainty sip of coffee.

"What happened?" Robynn asked, innocently.

"Oh, uh, it was kind of funny, really," Dani said, brightening her voice for the benefit of the child. "I, uh, set the remote on the edge of the bed, and while I was in the bathroom it fell off, hitting the 'On' button and the TV came on. I thought the TV came on by itself, and it scared me a little."

Robynn seemed satisfied with the answer, but Jack knew she was covering for something else. "That show that was on the television when it came on," he said, "was it anything like that thing I showed you on my laptop?"

Dani nodded.

"Did you leave it? I mean, leave it on, the TV."

Dani nodded. "I put the Do Not Disturb sign on the doorknob so none of the staff would come in."

A waitress reappeared at the table, refilled Althea's coffee cup and took Dani's order for a cheese and avocado omelet, then went away again. After it came, the only conversation at the table was between Jack, Althea and Robynn, and it centered on Robynn's recitations of cartoon shows that she had seen over the last couple of days. If being abducted by Marcus Broarty had affected her young psyche, she wasn't showing it. Even being separated from her mother did not seem to be bothering Robynn. The girl's only complaint was that Jack was not allowing her to use the motel pool.

"You know," Althea said, "I feel like I've been cooped up inside the room too long. Instead of the pool, maybe we should all go to the beach."

"Oooohh, can I, Daddy?" Robynn squealed.

"Well—"

"With three of us watching her, I'm sure nothing could happen," Althea said.

"What's gonna happen?" Robynn asked.

"Oh, you know, punkin, if you go into water that's too deep or something."

"I won't," she replied.

"Okay, that works for me," Jack said. As Dani was finishing eating he placed his credit card down on the table for the waitress and waved off efforts by both women to contribute. Once the bill was paid the group got up and left the restaurant, but only made it to the front desk before they were stopped. "Mrs. Kinchloe?" said the young male clerk, "something came for you FedEx."

"Oh, thank you," Althea said, picking up the large envelope. "Do I have to sign for it or anything?"

"Nope."

"What's that?" Jack asked.

"I called my grandson and asked him to find something for

me and send it down. I need to change before we go to the beach, I'll just be a minute."

"You brought a swimsuit with you?" Jack asked.

"Oh, heavens no, I'm not going into the water, but I still need to change," the old woman responded. "I've been wearing the same things for days now." She headed toward her room.

Dani followed Jack and Robynn into their room while Jack cut the tags out of the brand-new blue and yellow swimsuit he had bought for Robynn at the Tide Pool's expensive mini-boutique. She rushed to the bathroom to change, but Jack stopped her. "Hold on just a second, punkin," he said, going into the bathroom himself and coming out a moment later. "Okay, go ahead and change. If you need any help, punkin, just let us know."

"'Kay," the call came back.

Dani handed Jack her room key. "Would you please check out my bathroom now?" she asked. "I don't know if I can face it again." Jack nodded. He knew from experience it would take several minutes for Robynn to get changed, so he went over to Dani's room and let himself in. Stepping into the bathroom, he glanced at the mirror and felt chilled. Quickly leaving the room, he went back to his own, finding Dani sitting tensely on the corner of the bed, and Robynn still in the bathroom, humming happily. "Are the words still there?" Dani asked

"There were words, yes," Jack said. "I wiped them off."

"You look shaken."

"Dani, what did the words say to you?"

"Something like, 'You will die, you...you white-haired dogfucker.' Isn't that what you wiped away?"

Jack shook his head.

"Are you going to tell me what they said?"

"Not right now." Jack did not want to explain that the message on the glass had read, *You know, Romeo, she's got herpes, right*? That wasn't even the worst part: it had been written in Elley's handwriting.

Neither spoke until the ringing of Jack's cell phone broke the silence. Answering it, Jack heard: "Hey, Jack, it's Cree. We got something. Your wife drives a silver 2010 Lexus, right?"

"That's right, why? Did you find her?"

"No, just the car. It was at the bottom of a cliff about forty-five miles up the highway from here. It apparently crashed through a guard rail at the highway level and plummeted down to sea level, about two-hundred feet below."

"Good god! Was she inside?"

"There doesn't seem to be a trace of her anywhere, only her name on the registration. Your other friend wasn't so lucky though."

"You mean Marc?"

"He was down at the crash site, too, at least what was left of him," Creeley said. "Seems he rode the car all the way down and then was thrown about forty feet on impact. He landed on the rocks. His wrists were cuffed together, but, well, only one arm was still attached to his body. The staties think he was locked in the trunk when it went over."

"Jesus Christ!"

"According to Carl, you found evidence that she was at the police station, indicating that she was the one who pistol whipped me, and implying that she sprung Broarty. That, at least theoretically, puts the two of them together. But there's a bigger problem up on the coast highway, right where the Lexus went through the rail. It was to do with the skid marks."

"What about the skid marks?"

"There aren't any. The car didn't brake before it hit the rail, there's no trail of lain-down rubber. It was sent over deliberately."

"And you think Elley...."

"We need to find your wife, Jack. We need her for questioning if nothing else. If you see her or hear from her, you contact Carl or me immediately. Understood?"

He wanted to tell Creeley about the messages painted in the bathrooms, but could not bring himself to. He had absolutely no proof it was actually Elley's doing.

But if not hers, then whose?

"Believe me, Cree, I will." Jack cut off the call and dropped the cell phone on the bed, just as Robynn burst through the bathroom door, resplendent in her new swimsuit.

"I love it, Daddy!" she said, holding her arms out and posing. "I just wish Mommy could come to the beach with us."

"Yeah...that'd be great, all right," Jack said, fighting back nausea.

CHAPTER THIRTY-ONE

They was no way they could all fit into Jack's truck, so Dani offered to drive to the beach. "Any idea where we're going?" she asked, pulling out of the motel parking lot.

"There's a place called Moonstone Beach," Althea said. "I used to go there when I was young."

"Where is it?"

"Not far from here," she said, vaguely.

"I think I recall seeing an exit sign for it on the highway," Jack offered. "Just get onto the One, and we'll find it."

"Okay," Dani said.

A couple of miles up Highway 1, the sign for Moonstone Beach appeared. From the back seat, Althea Kinchloe started to sob.

"Althea, are you all right?" Jack said, turning back.

"Oh, yes, good heavens, I'm just a foolish old woman, is all," she said, wiping her eyes. "I've been reading this journal and it's bringing back so many memories. So many happy ones."

"That's what you got in the mail from your grandson?"

"Yes, the one Howard wrote when we were young. I never realized it at the time, but he wrote like a poet."

"He must have been a special man," Dani said.

"I'm realizing now that he wasn't really a man at all," Althea said softly. "He was a boy, a child. We both were. He was all of twenty-five-years old when he was killed in the war. That's no age at all. My grandson Tim, who sent me this, is thirty-three, eight years older than Howard was, and yet I still think of Tim as a boy." She closed her eyes and leaned her head back. "He was impetuous, Howard was. But then, so was I. We were two impetuous children."

"I like Howard," Robynn said.

"What, dear?" Althea said.

"Howard. He's nice. He loves you, Noni."

"Well, he loved me, a long time ago."

"He still loves you. He told me so."

Jack turned back and exchanged glances with Althea, who looked shaken. "Punkin," he said, "what do you mean he told you so?"

"I saw him last night, when I was asleep."

"Oh...oh dear," Althea muttered.

"He said he would have talked to you, Noni, but you weren't asleep."

The old woman put her face in her hands to hide her tears.

"Robynn, did Howard say anything in particular?" Jack asked.

"Mm-hmm," she said, keeping her eyes focused on Oyster Cracker, whom she was making dance. "He said to tell Noni that eye-dine will make the words come out."

"Do you know what that means?" Jack asked the old woman.

"Oh, lord," Althea said, looking up. "It refers to invisible ink. Howard sent me a letter once in invisible ink, so my father wouldn't find it and read it. Running the pages through an iodine solution makes the letters appear."

"Mm-hmm," Robynn said. "Howard told me that he wrote part of a book in invis'ble ink 'cause he was afraid people would think he was loony if they read it. What's loony, Daddy?"

"It means crazy."

"Howard didn't act crazy. He was real nice."

"The last part of this journal has empty pages," Althea said. "They must contain the invisible writing."

"Mm-hmm," Robynn answered.

"Good heavens," the old woman uttered. "I knew Howard always carried some sort of secret around with him, something that had happened to him in his past that he never divulged to anyone, even me. He was quite sensitive about it, so I stopped trying to find out what it was. Maybe that is what he wants me know. Where can we get iodine?"

"Any pharmacy should have it," Dani said.

"There's at least one in Glenowen," Jack said. "Let's turn around."

"Daddy, you promised we'd go to the beach!"

"I know, honey, but—"

"You promised!"

"Jack, look there," Dani said. She had taken the Moonstone Beach exit, which led to an outer beach road that ran past a string of hotels and beachwear shops...and one drug store.

"Pull in," Jack said, and Dani did. Jack ran inside and came back a few minutes later with a large bottle of iodine, a bottle of drinking water, and a plastic party bowl. "We may need something to develop the pages in," he said. "Okay, punkin, now we're going to the beach."

"Yay!" Robin cried.

Following the signs, Dani pulled into a large parking lot for Moonstone Beach, and everyone got out. Looking around, Althea said, "I can't believe how everything has been built up. Even this road was not here back then."

It was the warmest day so far that week. The sun was nearing its apex over the water, radiating heat and comfort down on the sandy patch of coastline, and the rhythmic, comforting pattern of the tide waving in and out almost made Jack forget about the way his life had turned into a bizarre waking nightmare over the past week or so. Whatever instincts had prompted Althea to choose this location were sound, for the place felt not only peaceful, but safe and protected.

There were a few other people out on the beach, which increased the feeling of safety for Jack. Robynn, naturally, rushed to the surf, but came running back a second later. "It's cold!" she cried.

"Just stick your toes in until you get used to it," Jack said, walking down with her to make sure she didn't get in over her comfort level.

Althea and Dani stayed back a ways from the water, settling in near a rock outcrop that was dotted with a mysterious honeycomb pattern, the delicately elaborate product of wind and water. There Althea took a handful of blank pages from the journal and ripped them out of the binding.

"What are you doing?" Dani asked.

"It's the only way, dear," the old woman said, putting the first page in the bowl Jack had bought, and smearing iodine over it. Immediately, rust colored words began to appear. "Could you do the rest of them, one at a time?" Althea asked. "Use the iodine sparingly, and if you need to, dilute it with the water." Dani took over the developing process, while Jack was totally focused on watching Robynn, who was now in the water up to her knees. Dani smiled as she watched the two of them having fun.

"Please give me the next one, dear," Althea said.

"Oh, sorry," Dani replied, handing the next developed page over.

"They're special, those two," Althea commented, looking at Jack and Dani.

"Yes they are," Dani agreed. "Althea, do you really believe that Howard came to Robynn in her sleep?"

"Of course he did. She's too innocent to lie."

"But why her?"

"Well, he came to me, too, remember."

"But you knew him in...well...."

"Go ahead and say it. In *life*. It's not like I don't know he's dead." The old woman took another page and held it up in a futile attempt to dry it in the sun. "What you're really asking me is why a ghost is appearing to an old woman and a little girl, instead of you or Jack, isn't that it?"

"I suppose it is."

Althea turned to Dani and smiled. "I'm ninety-three years old, Dani, and soon I'll be dead too."

"Althea—"

"No, let me finish. When you get to be very old, something happens to you. You start believing again. Howard came to me and I believed it was him. I didn't look for an explanation. It's the same with the very young. Their minds are open, they believe. If Howard had appeared to you or Jack, you would have wracked your brains trying to figure out what had caused such a strange dream, and then dismissed the whole thing. But the old and the young, we believe." She put a withered hand on Dani's sun-warmed arm. "You'll understand someday."

Dani continued handing Althea damp page after damp page; so many that the old woman started to carefully lay them down on the sand in the sun. "I hope that won't make them fade again," Dani said.

"So far, so good," Althea said.

When the last page had been developed and slightly dried, she picked them all up and began to read. For the next fifteen minutes, the only sound any of them heard were the waves lapping up onto the sand, and Robynn's delighted squeals. When Althea finally looked up, having finished the last page, all the color in her face had drained away. "Dear god in heaven," she uttered.

"What is it?" Dani asked. "Are you all right?"

Althea shook her head, and then slumped over onto her side.

"Jack," Dani called.

Jack and Robynn were at the surf line, with the girl happily building a sand palace. Jack turned back to see Althea, seemingly stricken. "Punkin, stay right here, okay? Don't go back in the water on your own."

"Okay."

Jack ran back to the old woman and knelt down beside her. "Althea, what's the problem. Do you need us to call a doctor?"

"No," the old woman responded. "It's not me. I'm fine. It's us. All of us."

"What do you mean?"

She looked up at him. "I've just read everything Howard wrote to me. Everything he wanted me to read."

"And?"
"And we are in more danger than you can possibly imagine."

BOOK FIVE

CHAPTER THIRTY-TWO
THE JOURNAL OF
HOWARD E. KEARNEY

Dearest Sweet Althea:

I have done something that is horrible. I am hoping that in confessing this I might be able to clear my soul, if indeed a black mark has been imprinted upon it. I imagine that you will find it funny to hear me speak about a soul, but the hard truth is that I have never acquired the glib rejection of all things spiritual that some of my colleagues have. Without a soul, could a man truly be an artist? Or even a good man? Or—

Howard Kearney stopped and took a deep breath before dipping his pen back into the chipped shot glass containing the lemon squeezings and writing: *an evil one?*

A few short months ago, had anyone asked him to describe his concept of evil, he would not have given it any particular supernatural connotation. Howard believed that evil, like good, existed within everyone, like white blood cells and red, and the same with Heaven and Hell. He had certainly known men, along with a few women, who had taken up residence in both places long before they left the living world. But now, knowing what he knew, having done what he had done, he could only pray that his own soul was safe. Fergus's as well; his friend and mentor, and the man he had murdered. Or maybe it wasn't murder at all, given the circumstances. If only he could know for certain.

In the week since the killing had taken place, Howard kept hoping that it had only been a nightmare. He had dreams sometimes that were so realistic he would later become confused as to whether the incidents in question had really happened or whether they were night fantasies. But the murder did not feel like that. It seemed too real, no matter how fantastical it had been.

After the fire that destroyed the inn in Glenowen, he and Althea returned to the Bay Area, where her family had been waiting for them. To say that her father had not been pleased about her jaunt down the coast with a struggling artist was like saying the Bolsheviks of Russia had not been pleased with the Tsar. Mr. Dorneman became almost apoplectic when he heard about the fire that had, in his mind, threatened their lives. Howard could hardly defend himself by saying, *No sir, she was never in any danger because when the fire took place, I was having sex with her in the Pacific Ocean.* For everyone's sake, Howard decided that maybe he and Althea needed to be sneakier in their trysts.

As for Fergus Randall, he went off in some other direction after the fire, and the only thing Howard had heard from him over the next three months was a scrawled note, partially obscured by a blotch of liquid (and he could well imagine what kind of liquid it was), that had come from Mexico.

Then in early September, Fergus had showed up unannounced at the door of Howard's tiny artist's flat in San Francisco, near Chinatown. At first Howard thought he was in the midst of a bender, because he looked terrible and smelled even worse, but the older man assured him he was stone cold sober as he all but pushed his way inside. Stopping to examine a canvas Howard was working on, Fergus muttered: "You're getting damn good, lad." Then he sat down on Howard's sole spare chair. From inside his worn, workman's shirt, he pulled out a stack of folded papers, some of which were newspaper clippings. "Got anything to drink around here?" Fergus asked.

"I think there's some wine in the other room," Howard replied.

Fergus Randall winced, but then shrugged and nodded, and Howard left his living room-studio to find a glass. He returned with jelly glass filled with red wine and handed it to his friend. Fergus took a sip, shivered, and then took another before setting the glass down on the bare wood floor.

"So, are you here on a job?" Howard asked, seating himself on a short stool.

"Not a paying one, no. Though it might be the most important thing I've ever done. Take a look at me, lad." Howard did, and saw a man who appeared to be much older than the friend he last saw in Glenowen. Fergus's red eyes were ringed with worry, like he had not been sleeping, and his unruly hair showed streaks of gray that had not been there before. His stubble was almost thick enough to qualify as an early beard. "Do I look insane to you?" Fergus asked.

"What a question. You look awfully fatigued, maybe even ill, but no, you don't look insane."

"So if I tell you an insane story, you won't throw me out of here?"

"Of course not. What's wrong, Fergus?"

"I'm scared, lad, that's what wrong." Fergus picked up his jelly glass and drained the wine in one gulp. When Howard offered more, the older man shook his head. "You remember this, of course," Fergus said, handing Howard a clipping from his stack of papers. It was a newspaper write up of the burning of the Saddleback Inn in Glenowen."

"How could I not?"

Fergus passed over another clipping. "How about this?"

Howard took it and read: *Artist falls to his death from Coit Tower.* "This was a couple of months ago, right? I remember hearing something about it. He was drunk, wasn't he? Wasn't he standing on the ledge at the top, and that's why he fell?"

"That's what the one and only eye witness told the police," Fergus said. "It's all there."

Howard scanned the article and found testimony attributed to an Italian tourist who was watching from the bottom and saw the victim, a man named George Behlmer—whose name meant nothing to Howard—appear to dance and scream at the top of the tower before launching over the side. He was killed immediately. "This is pretty horrible, Fergus, but I don't see what it has to do with the fire at Glenowen. Did you know this Behlmer guy?"

"No. He wasn't really an artist."

"So the paper got it wrong?" Howard had absolutely no idea where Fergus was going with any of this.

"The paper printed what they were told, lad. Behlmer was only pretending to be an artist. He was really an undercover Pinkerton's operative on the tail of someone. I did some investigating on my own when I heard about this. That's about all I've been doing for the last few months." He pulled a half-crushed package of Camels from his pocket and lit one, and then wiped his left eye with the heel of his palm.

"Fergus, I'm not really following any of this."

"Okay, here's what got me into it. Read that story again, and pay close attention to the name of that Italian tourist who was the witness, and who, not so coincidentally, disappeared as soon as he gave his story to the cops."

"All right," Howard sighed. Scanning the article again, he got to the part about the eyewitness and read, "'Giulianno Morese, a visitor to the city from Sicily.' I don't know if I'm pronouncing it right."

"Pronunciation doesn't matter," Fergus said, blowing out a gust of cigarette smoke. "You got a piece of paper lying around? Go get it and write that name down."

Shaking his head in puzzlement, Howard got up and went to get his sketchbook from the kitchen, where he had been sketching a bowl of fruit, and brought it in. Turning it to the first empty page, he grabbed a pencil from his pocket and wrote the name down. "Now what?"

"Give it to me," Fergus said.

Taking the pad, he began crossing off letters and then rewriting them. When he was finished, he handed it back to Howard, who glanced at the page and felt a sudden strange cold spot in the bottom of his stomach. "Oh, wow," was all he could say as he read:

GIULIANNO MORESE
LOUIS NORMAN IGEE

"It's an anagram," Fergus said. "A perfect goddamned anagram."

"Okay, it's an anagram," Howard said. "How much did you have to drink before you discovered this?"

"Not enough. The whole anagram thing came to me in the middle of a dream that I had in the course of my last good night's sleep."

Howard dropped the pad. "So you're saying that Igee was the witness and he pretended to be an Italian tourist to hide from the police?"

"It wasn't Igee. Igee wasn't anywhere near Coit Tower that night. He was at a fine tavern in Monterey, near Cannery Row, miles away from Knob Hill and San Francisco, and I know that for a fact because I saw him there. A group of us were there to discuss a possible project coming up, and Igee strolled in. He scowled at us as he went past our table, but one of the boys tried to flag him down, bring him over. Another one had just gotten a Brownie camera and wanted to get a group shot of the artists. Igee refused outright, and when the guy forced a picture with him, he became nearly violent, so after that we just left him alone, and he went off to drink by himself. The point is, he was there until closing. There is no way he could have been at Coit Tower that night. None. Not only did I recognize him, but so did four of the others."

"Okay, then, I guess it's just a coincidence, the names and all," Howard said, "or am I missing something?"

"Missing," Fergus Randall said, showing a parody of a

smile. "That's pretty funny, considering." Before Howard could ask for explanation, Fergus rifled back through his stack of papers and pulled out a photograph, then handed it to Howard. The photo was of a bunch of men in a tavern, posing rather raucously, several of them clearly feeling no pain, all of them summoning up a scene of hilarity and camaraderie the likes of which Howard would have enjoyed being a part. Smack in the middle of the group was Fergus.

"Looks like a fun night," the younger man said.

"It was," Fergus confirmed, "at least I thought so at the time. But something is missing. Look directly to my right and slightly over my shoulder. What do you see?"

Howard looked more closely and described what he saw: a black, faintly humanoid smudge, more solid than a shadow, but not defined in any way. "What is that?"

"That, lad, is Louis Norman Igee."

"What?" Howard looked again. "Was he moving too fast for the camera and just created a blur?"

"No. He was not."

"I'm not getting it, Fergus."

The older man reached into the stack and pulled out yet another picture, this one appearing to be of the same shot, but enlarged. Instead of full body shots, there were now a row of faces. The photo was awkwardly cropped, leaving a lot of head-room over top of the men. Howard's eyes instinctively went to the dark smudge, which was only marginally more defined now. It almost looked like a face, but a face at night, or maybe a face covered with a caul of dark material. But it had definition. "My god," Howard muttered.

Studying the blurry, shadowy image, he could make out the faint visage of an enraged demon, with abnormally large teeth bared in a snarl, and huge, hate-filled eyes. Or maybe it was just the power of suggestion. Either way, he felt goose pimples rising on his arms.

"Here's the capper," Fergus said. "The reason there's so much white space in that shot is I wanted to zero in on the background.

See that mirror against the wall behind the bar? See how if you look closely, you can make out the backs of our heads reflected in it? Count the heads."

Howard did. One was missing.

Where the reflection of the back of the blurry dark smudge in the foreground should have been, there was a gap in the mirror's image. "Couldn't this be some kind of camera malfunction?" Howard asked.

Fergus sighed heavily. "I'm going to ask you to do something, lad, and after you do it, ask me again if it's a camera malfunction. Pick up your pad and draw a picture of Louis Norman Igee."

"A picture of him?"

"You know him, you know what he looks like, and you're a talented artist, so it should be no problem for you. Just make me a sketch of him from memory."

With a shrug, Howard got up and went for a rust-colored Conté crayon, then returned and took up his sketchpad. "Okay, Fergus, here goes." He sketched quickly for about two minutes, and then frowned. Flipping the page over, he stared again, but this time interrupted his work by muttering, "What the hell is this?"

Fergus looked at him with exhausted eyes. "You can't do it, can you?" he said. "Neither can I. I tried drawing the bastard twenty times, and every line I put down was the wrong one. I'd try drawing someone else, and they'd come out fine, but not Igee. He can't be drawn."

"This is insane!" Howard said, going to a third page and scratching frantically on the thick paper. When he stopped, Fergus asked to see the result.

"Looks like W. C. Fields," the older man said, dropping the pad on the floor. "In one of my attempts, I came up with Teddy Roosevelt. Like it or not, Howard, the truth is Louis Norman Igee cannot be photographed, cannot be drawn, and does not cast a reflection in a mirror."

Howard tried to speak but it took a couple of tries before the words came out without a squeak. "Fergus, you're not going to try and tell me that Igee is a vampire, are you?"

"In the Dracula sense? No, I don't think so. But he isn't entirely human, either."

Howard remembered what Fergus Randall had said when the Saddleback Inn was burning to the ground, about detecting the smell of brimstone around Igee's room. "You think Louis Norman Igee is the devil?"

Fergus shook his head. "Again, no. There can only be one devil."

"What does that mean?"

Fergus dropped the unfiltered butt of his Camel into the jelly glass, where it sizzled when it hit the dregs of red wine. He flipped through his stack and pulled out another clipping and handed it to Howard. That one described a tragedy at a synagogue in Milwaukee, which had caught fire during a temple service, trapping about two dozen people inside and killing them. There seemed to be no connection to either the Saddleback fire or the death fall of the detective-cum-artist, until Howard got to the name of a man who was questioned by the police: Raoul Moeisening, the leader of the local German American Bund chapter, who was on-record opposing the presence of the synagogue.

Fergus had another clipping ready, which Howard took. That one was about a film made in France had been banned from exhibition by the government after it was claimed that a disproportionate number of people who had viewed it had either committed suicide or gone on to kill someone else. None of the authorities could offer any kind of logically explain it, and the press seemed to treat the entire matter as some kind of bizarre joke, particularly after the film's writer, producer and director Simon LeGironeau, had ridiculed the decision as insanity.

Another clipping involved a child prostitution ring in Mexico organized by a man named Luis Ramón Gieno. Still another one described the actions of a woman named Sienna Gourelimo, a high school teacher in Alabama, who encouraged her white students to harass, torture and even kill the black ones.

Howard upper lip was moist as he handed the articles back. He didn't need to sit down with a sheet of paper to see what Fergus was showing him, that every name was also made from the same letters that spelled Louis Norman Igee.

"There's more," Fergus went on. "A woman named Imogene Noraulis started a book burning campaign in Topeka. It spread to other American cities. In Havana a man named Romeo Alinguines tried to overthrow the government. In Britain, Sir Noel Augimone—"

"Okay, Fergus, I get it," Howard said, weakly. "They're all anagrams. But *why?*"

"I think I've figured that out. See, once I caught onto the recurring anagram, I started seeing it everywhere. It's almost hard to read a stack of papers and *not* to come with at least one example. There's a lot of them. A lot." Reaching down, Fergus Randall picked up same sheet of paper from the floor and quickly wrote something out. "This is who he...they...really are," he said. "It's the ultimate anagram." He turned the sheet around and Howard read:

OUR NAME IS LEGION

"I've read that before, some place," Howard said.

"It's a reference to a passage in the Bible," Fergus said. "The Book of Mark, chapter five, verse nine: 'My name is Legion, for we are many.' It is the name by which a demon identifies himself to Jesus. In the Bible it's singular, but I find the plural version even more frightening because that implies there are more of them than ever before." Fergus lit another cigarette then stood up and started pacing back and forth in the room. "You ever read Edgar Allan Poe, Howard?"

"Some. I've always found him a little gloomy."

"Perhaps he had reason to be. He wrote of something he called 'The Imp of the Perverse.' That's an inner force that causes you to do something you know is blatantly wrong. Even though you know in your mind and heart that it's the worst thing you could possibly do, you can't resist doing it because of this imp, or spirit, or gremlin, or force, or however the hell you want to characterize it. That, I think, is Legion, and it's been around for a long time. I wonder if people haven't been encountering creatures like Igee for thousands of years and have interpreted them as vampires or demons. Hell, maybe Bram Stoker met one and that's what caused him to write *Dracula*. Maybe every horror cliché that's ever been recorded draws its source from Legion."

"So what is this Legion up to?"

"It's here to stir up trouble, pure and simple. And I think it's attracted to power. Association with power creates power. Just look at our friend Igee. He spent the night inside the palace of one of the most powerful people on the planet, William Randolph Hearst."

"But so did we, Fergus, and we aren't part of Legion."

"Maybe it's because we rejected the power. Maybe the will still counts for something. But when we were up at that party, did you find yourself tempted at any point?"

"I don't understand."

Fergus sighed. "Tempted, kid. By anything. I was."

"Tempted by what?"

"Do you remember seeing a Giotto Madonna hanging in the hallway right before you went into that massive dining room? That whole goddamned night, I fought off the urge to go and pull that painting down from the wall, march back in and throw it on the fire, just for the sheer destructive hell of it. I'm telling you, lad, I had to fight that urge like nothing I've fought before in my life. It's crazy, wanting to senselessly destroy priceless art like that, but the desire was there. I finally did fight it down, but it was tough. That's what I mean by tempted."

"Okay, Fergus, I'm going to tell you something in strictest confidence. I don't want you to get the wrong idea, but in the middle of that party, I had the strongest urge to...oh, hell. Why am I even talking about this?"

"Tell it, lad. No matter what it is, I won't hold it against you."

"It's stupid, really, but I can't tell you how much I wanted so much to yank down the Renaissance tights I was forced to wear and let my dick hang out for all to see. I almost did it, too! Jesus, I almost exposed little Howard to everybody in the room...Hearst, Marion Davies, movie stars, Althea, everyone!"

Randall chuckled wetly.

"I didn't think it was funny, Fergus. At one point I had to leave the room so I wouldn't start playing with myself."

"Oh, I believe you, lad," Fergus Randall said, "and I'm not laughing at you. I'm laughing because I know that's just about the last thing you would ever do in a public place. But I think that's my point. We were both tempted by crazy thoughts and we both resisted."

"And you think Igee doesn't resist?"

"I think its Igee who does the tempting. How, I don't know. Maybe he plants thoughts in your head."

"And all these other anagram people, they're also planting thoughts in people's heads?"

"Yeah, for lack of a better explanation. But even at that, I think Igee's different. I don't think he's simply a foot soldier in this outfit. I think he's a general. All armies need a leader, and I think he's this one's. And you know why I think that?"

Howard shook his head.

"Because the bastard is drawn to wealth like a moth to a lantern and he ends up all the more powerful for it. As soon as Igee left Hearst's employ he dove right into the welcoming arms of another rich so-and-so, the late Henry J. Breen."

"Breen's dead?" Howard said.

Fergus handed another clipping to Howard. The one was from a newspaper printed only last week and it reported the discovery of the body of Colonel Henry Jackson Breen, who had succumbed at the site of his proposed new city built to accommodate his lumber mill. A county official who had gone out to the site to inspect the construction work had found Breen, or at least what was left of him. He appeared to have been partially eaten by animals that had gotten inside the city hall building.

"Good god," Howard muttered. "So Igee killed Breen?"

"We both know that Igee was out there at that building site," Fergus said. "Breen's own people told us that. Officially, the old sucker died of a stroke, but I think Igee caused it."

"Christ, Fergus, this is nuts."

Fergus Randall ran his hands through his hair. "You think I haven't tried to convince myself of that? You think I haven't come close to having myself committed on a number of occasions? Each time I get to that point, the dreams come back even stronger, assuring me that I'm on the right track. Are you religious, Howard?"

"Not really. I was raised Methodist, but not much of it stuck."

"What's your opinion of holy water? Is it real?"

"It's real water, yeah."

"You know what I mean. Does it really have special qualities?"

"I don't know, Fergus. I've never tried throwing it at a vampire, if that's what you're thinking."

Fergus nodded. "That's what I'm thinking."

"You're going to walk up to Louis Norman Igee, hold up a cross, throw some holy water in his face, and what? Hope he dissolves?"

"Lad, look at the whole picture for a moment. Let's say I walk up to the bastard and splatter him water that's been blessed by a priest, and it does absolutely nothing but dampen his collar and make him mad as hell. What have I done? I've made gigantic horse's ass of myself. Well, guess what, Howard: I've done that before and I'm sure I'll do it again. The sun will continue to rise. But what if I'm *right*? What if I'm not crazy and I really have tapped into knowledge about a worldwide army of evil, and I've got some inkling of how to fight it, but I don't do it? I can live with being a horse's ass, but I don't think I could live very long knowing that maybe I was able to make a difference in the speed with which the human race marches toward the abyss, but I didn't even bother to try, because I was afraid someone might think I was cracked."

Now it was Howard Kearney's turn to get up and pace the room. After a few seconds, he turned to his friend. "By your coming here, I'm assuming that you are planning on asking me to help you confront Igee."

"That's right."

"And if I say no?"

"Then you say no. Maybe you're the type who could continue to live knowing you might have helped, but didn't. Are you saying no, lad?"

Howard shook his head. "No," he said, softly. "I mean, no, I'm not saying no. I'll probably be sorry, Fergus, but I'm in."

"Thank you. Now I'm about to drop, so is there anywhere in here I can bunk for a while?"

Over the next two days they plotted and prepared, two days in which Howard went out of his way to avoid contact and even communication with Althea, which he hated, but he knew that she could not become involved in this. Fergus tasked himself to track Igee, while Howard's assignment was to procure the holy water. Taking an empty bottle to the nearest Catholic church, he dipped four times in the font to get the desired amount, and if anyone objected to his filling it, they never presented themselves.

On Sunday the two re-met in Howard's flat.

"He's out at that city in the woods," Fergus said. "He checked out of his boarding house a week ago and apparently hasn't been seen in town since. I guess we'll have to go confront him at Wood City."

"Do you know where this place is, outside of somewhere in the woods?"

"I found the road that leads to it."

Howard sighed. "Okay, when do we need to go?"

"Tonight might be good."

"Fergus, what are we about to get ourselves into?"

Fergus Randall's tired face barely managed to muster up a smile. "Lad, I've known men who faced the devil every day in a coal mine. Others faced him in a whisky bottle. Seems like at some point, every man faces the devil in his own personal way. What we're going to do is face the devil, or at least one of his most trusted employees, where he's least expecting it, right where he works."

Howard Kearney wished he could feel reassured.

CHAPTER THIRTY-THREE
SEVENTY-FIVE YEARS AGO

Howard picked up his pen again and once more started to write.

> *I hope I'm not boring you with all the details*, he wrote in lemon juice, *but please know that both Fergus and I had reason to believe that Mr. Igee was up to something not quite right. That is why we went to look for him on that night that was to transform my entire life....*

Howard had no idea where Fergus had acquired the old gray Packard, but it ran well enough so he did not complain. It was nearly nine before they found the road through the forest that would lead them to the so-called Wood City. They drove in as far as they dared, the Packard's bottom scraping dangerously along the rough, narrow road, and then they got out. The middle of the woods was the darkest place Howard had ever been in his life. They had flashlights, but they were so overwhelmed by the dark that they might as well have tried to make their way through without any illumination. "Turn the headlights on," Fergus Randall suggested. "It might help a little. You've got the sauce, right?"

"Got it here," Howard said, clutching the bottle. Then the two set out deeper into the woods. It did not take long until Howard had decided that this might be the single stupidest thing he had ever done. With the sound of every footfall crunching into the gravel and dirt road, he felt a little more childish. How much power did Fergus Randall really have over him to get him to blindly, or nearly so, follow him out into the middle of forest at night to take a stand against someone who may or may not be some kind of earthly demi-devil? How he wished he were back home, or with Althea, or anywhere other than here!

As they got deeper into the woods they began to see signs of the new city: cabins dotting the sides of the road, cracker-boxes with tall, pointed roofs, all standing empty and dark. "Guess no one's moved in yet," Howard commented.

"People were here, lad," Fergus replied. "Those in the village confirmed that. But now they're gone."

"Gone where?"

Instead of answering, the older man pointed toward a strange green glow that was penetrating the darkness up ahead. "Look," he said.

"What the hell is that, Fergus?" Howard whispered.

"I don't know, but we came here to find Louis Norman Igee, so I have to assume it's him. Let's go." With Fergus in the lead, they trudged through the woods toward the glow. It only took another five or six minutes to arrive at the center of the burgeoning city, a large hollowing in the forest where stood a row of city buildings, the centerpiece of which was the city hall, imposing in his stone façade, if out of place in the middle of the woods. The green glow was coming from inside the building.

As they approached the building, the glow from within, seen through the windows of the stone building, seemed to pulsate. "I don't like this much," Howard confessed.

"I'd rather be inside a tavern myself," Fergus replied.

As they crept up the stone steps toward the door, it opened, as though on its own. The light inside was now insanely bright, though it did not take Howard long to figure out why. "It's a road flare!" he cried. "A goddamned road flare!"

"Still, it serves the purpose," said a voice from somewhere inside. Howard and Fergus spun around into the direction from which they thought the voice was coming, and ended up twirling in circles, which drew a lusty laugh from the voice.

"Igee?" Fergus called. "Louis Norman Igee? Where the hell are you?"

"Right here," the voice said, much more softly, and again the two startled friends spun around to find the strange painter standing directly behind them.

Howard had never really studied the man up close, and the fact that he was now seeing him in the eerie light of a flare did not present an accurate picture of his face, which appeared a sallowish green. His hair, unkempt at the best of times, now looked like it had been charged with electricity. He was dressed like someone who was not struggling with money; a white silk shirt with an open collar, a pair of gray pinstriped trousers and matching vest, buttoned all the way. And those eyes...those damned slag-black eyes that seemed to repel light and heat. They were disturbing enough from a distance, but up close, Howard now realized why so many people refused to meet the man's gaze.

Igee smiled. "Come to admire my work?" he asked.

"Not really," Fergus replied.

Igee studied him. "You're the tosspot with the idiotic name. Fungus, isn't it?"

"At least my name can't be made into an anagram," Fergus countered, and for a second, just a fleeting moment, Howard thought he saw Igee's smirk weaken a little and his eye twitch. "My name isn't important, really. Let's just say I'm a guy who's curious as to why you murdered your benefactor, Breen."

Good old Fergus, Howard thought; *always one for approaching a subject carefully.*

"I did not kill Breen," Igee said, casually. "His own corruption killed him. His inner rot killed him."

"But you helped, I'm sure." Calling back to Howard, he added: "Stay on your guard, lad. The last time I saw this bastard he had a woman with him. She might be around here somewhere."

"I assure you that you will find no one here but me," Louis Norman Igee said. Then he noticed the bottle in Howard Kearney's hand. "You have come to toast my success, perhaps?"

"That's not champagne in there."

Igee looked at Fergus like he was an imbecile. "Unbelievable," he said, smiling. "You've got priest water in there, don't you? Kindly do me the honor of not attempting to play me for a fool. I do not fit that role."

That was when it came to Howard Kearney, the epiphany he had been seeking. *Holy water, silver bullets, none of that was going to do anything at all; it's the effrontery of ridicule that this man cannot tolerate.* Howard held up the wine bottle filled with the holy water and uncorked it. Before Igee could react, Howard flung the contents at him, but not at Igee's face; rather his crotch, creating a large, dark stain. "Look, Fergus, Igee had an accident! The great one pissed his pants!"

Fergus Randall gasped, and then doubled over with long-pent-up laughter.

As Howard looked on, Igee's cool demeanor shattered into an expression of inhuman rage, and green glow or not, Howard swore his eyes turned red. Igee lunged toward him and grabbed the bottle from his hand, then murderously swung it at his head. With a cry, Howard threw himself back onto the marble floor, narrowly missing having his temple bashed in. Fergus, handling his flashlight like a club, swung as hard as he could at Igee's right shin. It did not stop the man, or even cause him to cry out in pain, but it threw his balance off enough to allow Howard to roll out of the way before the bottle crashed down on the floor and shattered into a thousand shards.

Neither Howard nor Fergus were laughing now, which caused Louis Norman Igee to reclaim his smug demeanor. "That's better," he said. "I suggest we call a halt to this foolishness. The two of you came out here to see something, so why don't I show it to you?" Igee walked over to the back wall of the building which was covered by a ceiling to floor drape, hung with hooks and wires. Yanking on one corner of the drape caused drape to fall to the ground, revealing his mural.

The first thing that struck Howard was the work's power. The figures on the crowded mural were so real they seemed almost to breathe. In fact, in the flickering light, he almost convinced himself he saw one move. His attention was then drawn to the bottom center of the mural, where there was the image of a covered truck. What struck him was that the truck looked like one he used to drive.

"Sweet Jesus," Howard muttered, looking closely enough now to see that the painted figure of the driver also looked familiar... *it was him*! The painted version of Howard wore a demonic expression, as though filled with diabolical glee. While one hand was kept on the steering wheel, the other was thumbing behind him, where several arms and a head were sticking out from under the canvas cover over the bed of the truck...no, not arms as such, *bones*. There were three skeletal arms and hands, and one rotted face peering out at him. "How? How?" Howard muttered.

How in god's name had Igee known about this? Howard's own family, his parents, had no idea what had happened when he had taken that job to transport a payload of what he thought was produce from Mexico to California three years ago, only to find out that his main cargo was children packed in the crates, some of whom had died in the back of the truck before they reached their destination.

Even though Howard had not been a willing accomplice in their deaths and had fled from that job as soon as he had learned what had happened—the Depression be damned—it continued to haunt him in his private moments, in large part because he had never done anything to report the incident to the authorities. *How many more foreigners had died because he had stayed silent?* It was the secret that he alone had carried like a millstone and now here it was, depicted in paint! Howard heard a gasp coming from his friend, who was now staring at the mural with a childlike look of terror. "What's the damned thing showing you, Fergus?" he asked.

"I didn't mean to drown him," Randall spoke in a hoarse, sick whisper. "I was only a kid myself."

Howard spun around toward Louis Norman Igee. "How are you doing this?"

"I'm not *doing* anything," Igee answered. "What my masterpiece is revealing to you has already been done, and by you, not I."

Fergus Randall was breathing heavily, and even in the waning green glow, Howard could see that his color was not a natural healthy one. "I get it now," he panted. "We're here for the wrong reason. We came here to get him, but what we really have to do is get rid of this monstrosity." He gestured towards the mural. "This must be his magnum opus, the one work of art he really put his heart and soul into, particularly his soul. Even if Igee dies this thing and its evil keeps soldiering on, forever, unless we destroy it."

"You're a raving fool," Igee said smoothly.

"Yeah, you may be right," Fergus mumbled, staggering back. "I guess I hit the bottle a little too much tonight."

That surprised Howard, who knew that Fergus had not consumed anything that evening. But a second later he realized it was simply a distraction; Fergus suddenly transformed himself from a middle-aged man about to black out from drink to an Olympic athlete, diving through the air to grab the road flare off of the floor. Crying out as the sparks burnt his flesh, Fergus chucked it as hard as he could toward the mural.

With an unnatural howl, Louis Norman Igee threw himself in front of the flare and took it full force. The flare bounced off of his chest and hit the floor, but not before a small spark from it lodged into Igee's vest began to smolder. Within seconds, the spark developed into a flame. Seeming to ignore it, Igee leapt through the air toward Fergus, but Howard pulled his friend out of the way, watching as Igee, his shirt now aflame as well, spun around in the air and landed flatfooted, facing them both. The smell of charring flesh was beginning to permeate the inside of the building. The fire had reached Igee's head, burning his bushy hair to nothing and blackening his scalp. Only the lower parts of his legs were not ablaze, and even now Igee seemed not to notice. He ran toward the two artists.

"Step up to the mural, it's the only safe place!" Fergus instructed Howard. "He can't get too close to it or he'll blister the paint."

As Fergus and Howard hugged the mural with their backs, Igee remained several helpless paces away, engulfed in fire.

"Fergus, something's touching me!" Howard shouted. "Something in this damned painting is moving!"

"Ignore it!" Fergus shouted back. "Just don't move. The bastard can't last much longer, he's got to die soon!"

"We *cannot* die, you fools!" Igee cried, forming the words with difficulty since his lips had burnt away. "You can kill our host bodies, but you cannot kill us...we can always find others." The sound that followed was a harsh, guttural laugh.

It took another minute, but finally the burnt corpse that had once been known as Louis Norman Igee collapsed into a smoking, stinking heap on the floor of the building. At that instant, Fergus Randall pulled away from the painting and began leaping, twirling and dancing around like a marionette. "Jesus!" he shouted. "He's trying to get inside me!"

"Fergus!" Howard screamed. "Fight him! You have to fight him!"

"I can't...not strong enough...you have to...have to...."

"Have to what, Fergus?"

"*Kill me!*"

"No, no, *no!*"

"Only way. For god's sake, *do it!*"

Without even thinking, without even wanting to think, only cognizant of the living, writhing hell that his friend now appeared to be going through, Howard Kearney looked around for any kind of a weapon. The flashlight was too impotent to do the job and he did not carry a knife. Then he spotted a chunk of broken bottle lying on the floor, the handle still attached to it. With his own howl of anguish Howard dove out and grabbed it, managing to deeply cut the palm of his hand in the process, and then tackled Fergus, knocking him to the floor. With another howl, he brought the broken bottle as hard as he could down on the side of Fergus's throat, where the carotid artery resided.

Hot blood shot all over him as though from a geyser, and Fergus's shaking and twitching stopped, but he did not complete cease moving. He heard a gurgling sound, and realized Fergus was trying to talk. "I...got...him...," he said wetly. "Holding... on...tight."

Tears fell from Howard's eyes. "Fergus."

"No...other...way."

"If I can get a doctor out here...."

"Too...late." With a show of Herculean strength the likes of which Howard could not even imagine, Fergus lifted his head up off the floor. "It's...all right," he whispered, grimacing. Then the shaggy, blood-drenched head of Fergus Randall fell back limply onto the stone floor."

"*Nooooooo,*" Howard wailed.

Only a dim glow remained in the building now, the flare that had ignited the body of Louis Igee having nearly burnt itself out. Howard stood up and tried desperately to figure out what to do. He had just killed a man; not simply a man, but his mentor. No; his *friend*. What he should do is what he should have done after that driving job to Mexico: go straight to the police. But what would he tell them?

And there was still the mural to take care of.

Howard turned toward the mural, which was now cast in shadowy darkness. Retrieving his flashlight, he shined it on the surface. Even though he was not completely surprised, having all but expected it, he was still shocked by what he saw.

In painted form, he was shoving a broken bottle through the neck of Fergus Randall. All the other characters in the painting, meanwhile, looked on with approving smiles. Standing in the middle of the mural, looking happiest of all, was the figure of Louis Norman Igee.

It waved to him.

Howard Kearney slumped to the floor, unconscious.

* * * * * * *

At dawn's first light, Howard awoke. He had spent the entire night in the city hall building, a few yards away from the pile of ashen bones that had been the earthly form of Louis Norman Igee and the body of his friend. Zealously avoiding looking at the mural (despite the sounds of movement that were coming from it) he left the building, squinting under the brightness of the morning sun, and relieved himself in the woods, using his own urine to wash the dried blood off his hands. He sought out large, dew-covered leaves and used them to clean his hands and face as best he could.

Now Howard had to think about getting rid of the bodies. He had no tools with which to dig graves in the woods. He would have to go into town for supplies. Howard made his way back to the Packard. Getting in, he tried to start it up, but it was dead.

"Oh, *shit!*" he cried, pounding on the steering wheel as he remembered that they had left the headlights on so they could see in the pitch black woods the night before. The battery had gone dead, rendering the car useless. He had no choice but to hitchhike back into town.

After ditching his bloodiest pieces of clothing, he made it to the highway on foot and was ready to stand there for however long it took and exercise his thumb.

As luck would have it, it did not take long.

Luck?

A Ford Woody Wagon pulled over right in front of him, and even before the driver could brake the car and leap out, Howard could see it was Talbot Barnes, the young Breen intern he had met several months ago. "Heya, Howard," Barnes said.

"Uh, hi, Talbot," Howard answered. "Quite a coincidence running into you."

Barnes shook his head. "It's no coincidence. Where do you need to go?"

"Glenowen." *What did he mean it was no coincidence?*

"Hop in."

The two got into the Woody and Barnes pulled back onto the highway. For several miles, neither young man said anything. Then Barnes started. "Mr. Randall was in my bedroom last night," he said quietly.

"Oh?"

"He said he was dead."

Howard cleared his throat. "Yes, Talbot, Fergus is dead."

"But he told me you'd be needing help. He asked me to come here and pick you up."

"Thank you for doing it."

"You must have been painting. You've got red on your clothes."

"Yes...painting."

A mile or so down the highway Barnes asked: "Am I going to get visited by Mr. Randall's ghost every night?"

"No, I don't think so."

"Good, because it's a little unnerving, you know?"

"I can imagine."

Looking over at the young man, seeing how calmly and casually he spoke about things that were simply not natural or rational, Howard realized with great empathy that the guy must be in shock. Once his role in the drama was over, he probably snap out of it and would not remember any of this. At least Howard hoped he would not.

When they had reached Glenowen, Howard asked Barnes to take him to the closest hardware or supply store. Finding one, Howard went in to buy a good sturdy shovel and a length of canvas. After the order was rung up, though, he realized he did not have enough money to pay for it.

Barnes stepped in and asked: "Does the Breen Corporation have an account here?"

The store clerk checked his records and said, "Yes, as a matter of fact it does."

"All this is for the corporation, so could you please charge it to that account?"

"Yes sir," the clerk said, writing down the order on an invoice. When he was finished, the two men took the shovel and canvas, and were almost out of the store when Howard had a sudden inspiration. "Oh, you know what? I forgot something," he said, and turning to the clerk, asked: "Do you have any paint with a lead base?"

"Yeah, but only in gray."

"That's fine. I'll take ten gallons, and some brushes. Oh, and how about a step ladder?"

It took a while to load all of the stuff into the Woody, and before leaving the village, Howard made one more purchase: two fifths of whisky. Then they were on their way back to Wood City. Once there—or at least as far as they could drive in before being hindered by Fergus's dead Packard—Barnes helped Howard drag all the stuff up to the City hall building. "Something burning?" Barnes asked calmly, sniffing the air.

"There was a small fire last night," Howard said, "nothing to worry about. Thanks for everything. I really appreciate it. Fergus does, too."

Barnes nodded. "I liked Mr. Randall, even if he was a Commie. I'm sorry he's dead. Goodbye, Howard." He shook Howard's grimy hand with youthful formality and hiked back to his car and drove away. *Definitely in shock*, Howard thought. *Lucky him.*

Digging the graves for Igee and Fergus was more work than he anticipated. It always looked so easy in horror films. Even a hunchback could do it. When the holes were finally dug, he loaded each body onto a length of canvas and dragged them out to it. He left Fergus in the canvas, but dumped Igee's charred remains in naked. If the animals wanted to dig him up and pick at his bones, let them.

Howard Kearney opened the first fifth and drained a quarter of it. It did not take long to have an affect. He poured some into his hands and washed them. Then he went into city hall and got to work on the mural. He had to force himself to not look closely at it as he painted, but when the peripheral movement of the characters and the whispers, which before long devolved into angry and profane shouts, threatened to become too much for him, he took another drink. A hand shot out of the painting and reached for him and Howard fell backwards. Lurching upright, he threw paint on the hand and it withdrew.

It took coat after coat after coat before he could no longer see the leering, evil faces glaring back at him. He was so exhausted, drunk and half-sick by the first evening that he actually fell asleep on the ladder. He went back to work the next morning with a crashing hangover, but greeted the new day with another shot anyway.

By the end of the second day, the damned thing was covered, which was good, because he was also out of paint. And whisky. Howard dragged the empty cans and wet brushes around to the back of the building and simply dumped them, then went back inside and folded up the ladder, leaving it leaning against the wall. Howard took one more look at the gray wall that had once been a skillfully rendered, if horrifically evil, mural, and nodded his head. Then he sat down and cried until he thought his lungs would come up through his throat. Afterwards he went back up the road, painfully hungry and thirsty, exhausted, morally and physically drained, and made his way to the highway. Somehow, he found the strength to hike back to Glenowen.

...and since then I have lain awake at night worrying about whether I might still be worthy of you, my darling.

It is my intent, Pookie, that you shall not read this in my lifetime, that you will never know of that terrible time as long as you know me. It is also my intent that I will never again turn away from the opportunity to combat evil of any kind. I leave it to your judgment and God's as to whether I deserve the fires of Hell, or whether I might have helped to save humanity from the same.

Your loving,

H

P.S.: For what it is worth, Fergus in his dying moments believed that the malignant spirit of Louis Norman Igee had entered his body. Having done what I have done and seen what I have seen, however, I do not believe it remained there. I believe that when I killed Fergus, Igee's spirit escaped. I pray that when Fergus took in his last breath, it was with a sense of relative peace.

I believe I know where Igee's hateful spirit ultimately went.
It entered the mural.
I believe it resides there still.
Pray God the mural never becomes revealed again.
Pray God.

CHAPTER THIRTY-FOUR
TODAY

Nobody spoke during the walk back to the cars from the beach. Nobody dared to. They had all, except for Robynn, read the journal.

Back at the Tide Pool Inn, Dani and Althea checked out of their individual rooms and moved into one with two beds. Jack, of course, paid the balance. "I really wish I could help pay for this, Jack," Dani said, as she carried her bag to the new room, "but I don't know how I'm going to pay for much of anything now."

"Don't worry about it," he said.

"Daddy, can Noni and I watch TV?" Robynn asked.

"Punkin, we can't wear Noni out," Jack said.

"Jack, I'm worn out already," Althea told him. "Spending time with Robynn helps me forget...well, you know."

"Okay, punkin. You can go to Noni's room. I guess Dani and I will stay in here." That brought a slight smile to Althea's face, which actually embarrassed Jack. Then his daughter and her surrogate grandmother disappeared into the new room Althea was meant to share with Dani, closing the door behind them.

"She thinks we're going to have sex," Jack muttered, leading Dani into his room, which was several numbers down the hall.

"Well...do you want to?" Dani asked, sitting on the edge of the bed.

Jack sighed. Hell yes, he wanted to have sex with her! Who wouldn't? But was that really the best use of their time, or was it a way—a remarkably exciting way—of avoiding figuring out a way to fight...what? *What*? An old painting?

"I guess that means no," Dani said.

"No, it means yes, but would it be a good idea?"

"What's bothering you?"

"It's stupid, but...you remember when you sent me into your room to look at the message on the mirror? It didn't say anything about white hair or your history with German Shepherds. Dani, forgive me, but do you have anything sexually transmittable?"

"Have I *what*? Oh, good lord! Good *lord*! The message you wouldn't tell me about, it claimed I had herpes, right?"

"Yes, and I know it's all lies, but—"

Looking like she wanted to laugh but could not manage it, Dani related the story of how she rejected the advances of Randy Mount at the radio station but claiming she had the disease. "For the record, Jack, no, I do not have herpes, or any other venereal disease, though god only knows how far that rumor has spread by now. Radio is a surprisingly small world. I'm sure Laurie Mosgionne herself is dining on it wherever possible."

"Who?"

"Laurie Mosgionne, this little backstabber from the K-God station, the one who set me up for the fall."

Jack regarded her with an odd expression. Then he grabbed the tiny pad of paper on the motel nightstand, and pulled a pen from his pocket. "Could you write down her name?"

"Why?"

"Do you remember what it said in that journal?"

"Oh, god, you don't think...." Dani took the pen and pad and quickly wrote Laurie's name, and then handed it back to Jack, who took only a few seconds to perfectly anagram it into *Our Name Is Legion*.

Dani shuddered.

The remained silent (and fully clothed) for a few moments, and then Dani said: "Jack, I've just had an idea. Your talking about herpes gave me the thought. What if this...this whatever... is some kind of virus, a brain virus, or maybe a spirit or soul virus, that's spread by the mural?"

"How?"

"By touching the paint. I remember getting a smudge of paint on my finger from your pen, right before I left to go do my gig. You told me you touched the paint, too. So far Robynn and Althea have been spared—"

"Because they haven't touched the paint," Jack finished for her.

As Jack was attempting to wrap that idea around his head, his thoughts were shattered by the cry of "Daddeee!" Leaping up from the bed, he saw Robynn running into the room from the hallway. "What's wrong, punkin?" he asked.

"I can't find Nick'lodeon on the TV!"

Althea came in right behind her. "The reception on that television is pretty poor for any of the channels," she added.

Jack sighed. How blessed it must be to have the biggest problem in your life not being able to watch SpongeBob. "Well, punkin, we'll check this TV and if it works better, we'll just trade rooms, okay?"

"'Kay."

While Robynn was checking out the television (which worked perfectly fine, Nickelodeon and all), Jack's cell phone rang and he grabbed it immediately. It was Rob Creeley, who told him to brace himself. "Has Elley been found?" he asked.

"Not yet," the policeman said, "but she left a problem for you at home." Creeley related how a gas company employee had detected a rank smell coming from their Westwood home when he had gone by to check the meter. The man tried to get in to check it out but received no answer at the door. Knowing the methane odor was not simply a gas leak, he got the police involved. The cops broke in to find the body of Blaise Micelli.

Jack decided then and there that he had to put Robynn somewhere safe. He thought about asking Creeley and his wife to watch her, but Creeley was already involved too deeply in all of this; in fact, Elley had already assaulted him once. Elley was either mad or had somehow been overtaken by the evil of

Legion, or both. Either way she was lethal.

Even though he had kept his voice low while talking on the phone to Creeley, so as not to upset Robynn, Althea had overheard him. As soon as he had hung up she gestured for him to come out into the hallway. Seeing that Robynn was happily engrossed in *Dora the Explorer*, with Dani keeping an eye on her, he slipped out.

"Maybe I can help," Althea said quietly.

"Do you really know what the problem is?" Jack asked.

"I watched your face turn pale and heard enough to know you're worried about Robynn and need to send her somewhere out of harm's way. My grandson might be able to watch her. Timmy, he's the one who sent me the journal. He lives in Portland."

"Does he have other kids?"

"No, he's not even married, but whenever we have family gettogethers, it always seems like Uncle Tim is the most popular amongst my great-grandchildren. More importantly, he's a good boy...I mean, a good man. He's completely trustworthy."

"I appreciate the offer, Althea, but I'm a little hesitant about turning Robynn over to someone I've never met."

"Then you'll meet him. He included his cell phone number in the package and said I can call him at any time."

Jack sighed. "I don't know, it seems like an awful lot to ask of someone."

"Well, it probably is, but if I know Timmy, he'll come," she replied. "See, we have something that he's always on the lookout for—a story."

"It's a story all right, but would a newspaperman really believe it? Would anyone?"

"Why don't we find out?" Althea went back into the room and got envelope in which the journal had arrived, and from it pulled a note. Adjusting her glasses she read its contents then returned to Jack. "Should I call him from the room phone, or can I borrow that cellular thing of yours?"

* * * * * * *

Tim Kinchloe was trying to come up with a synonym for *foreboding* when his phone rang. Picking up the call, he said: "*Leader and Press*, Kinchloe."

"Hi, Timmy, it's Noni again."

He sat up, alert. "Noni, hi. Is everything okay? Did you get your package?"

"I did, and thank you so much. But now I have an even bigger favor to ask you. I need you to come down to San Simeon."

Tim had wanted to go down to her yesterday, but she had rejected the idea. Now she wanted him to drop everything and head down. Something was seriously awry. "Noni, please tell me the truth. Are you all right?"

"Yes, Timmy, yes, I am all right, but I need your help. I have friends down here and one of them has a little girl, who's just the sweetest little thing imaginable, but we need someone to take care of her."

"And your friend can't because...?"

"I'll explain when you get here. At least I'll try. You may not believe it when you hear it, but it's quite a story."

"Does it have to do with that journal?"

"Yes."

"Noni, this is really...." He lowered his voice so no one in the newsroom around him would hear. "It's insane is what it is, but I need to tell somebody. When I went to get the journal, the guy who wrote it, your friend, Howard, he, well, he—"

"Did he speak to you?" Althea said, so matter-of-factly that it took Tim's breath.

"He left a message for me in that book."

"Oh, that makes sense, dear. You're a writer, so it stands to reason he'd write to you."

Yeah...that makes all the sense in the world, Tim thought.

"It's okay, Timmy, he's on our side."

"Our side of *what*, Noni?"

"I'll try to explain it when you get here."

Tim Kinchloe sighed. "I'll get there as soon as I can, Noni."

"Please hurry. We don't have a lot of time."

She was gone even before he could say anything else. Nothing he had heard in the last two days sounded as ominous as that fatigued *We don't have a lot of time.* If he was going to get there within the day—and from the sound of her voice, he needed to—he was going to have to fly, then rent a car in California. He was also going to have to explain to Crazy Madonna why he would be out for at least Monday. It had better be good, too.

Hundreds of miles away Althea handed the cell phone back to Jack. "I'm glad I don't carry one of those things," she said. "I'd never be able to figure it out."

"I'm sure you'd find a way," Jack said, smiling at her. What worried him as he walked back into the motel room was finding a way to tell Robynn that he was, in essence, going to abandon her for awhile. It was probably going to be the hardest thing he'd ever done, but it had to be done. Robynn was ultimately the only that mattered, really mattered, to him. She *had* to be safe, no matter what. "Hey, punkin, can I talk to you?" he said, sliding down onto the floor so that he was on her level.

"Can it wait for a c'mercial?" she asked, and Jack agreed. It was the least he could do. When the commercial came, he asked her to sit next to him and put his arm around her. "Punkin, I'm going to ask you do to something that's going to be really hard, but really brave. And I think it's really necessary, okay?"

"'Kay, daddy."

"Robynn, I need to go do something, and I can't bring you along with me. So I'm going to let you stay with a nice man named Uncle Tim."

"But I don't want to," she whimpered. "I want to stay with you."

"I know, I know, punkin, and I wish you could, but you can't. I'm sorry."

"How 'bout Noni? Can I stay with her?"

Althea's head dropped down and she shook it sadly, knowingly.

"No, Robynn, I'm sorry."

"Dani?" Her voice was a mouse's now.

"Robynn, punkin, I need to send you away."

"I don't wanna leave you and Noni and Dani!" the girl blubbered out, and Jack could not help but notice that she made no mention of her mother.

"I know, Robynn, but I have to."

"*Noooooooooo!*" She launched herself at him and nearly cut off his wind with her arms.

It always pained Jack to see his daughter crying, not pain in the metaphoric spiritual sense, but real, physical pain. His stomach felt like he had been punched, and his legs had a numb wobbly feeling to them. It particularly pained him to know that she was hurting even more by his words.

"Robynn, I don't want to be away from you," Jack said, hugging her back, "but I'm afraid we have no choice."

"How c-c-come?"

"Noni and Dani and I all have to go someplace and do something that wouldn't be safe for you. I'm really, really sorry, but we need you to stay with Noni's grandson while we're gone."

"I won't!" Robynn cried, stamping her foot. "You just want to go off and drink beer!" Then she rushed back into the bathroom, slamming the door behind her. Jack stood there, stunned. This was the first time Robynn had ever, ever, acknowledged that she even noticed Jack's drinking.

It was also the moment Jack Hayden vowed he would never take another drink again.

"Do you want me to go to her?" Althea asked.

"Not yet," Jack said, forcing the words out. "Let her cool down first." He gazed up at his friends, two women whom he had only known for a short time, but whom had he had grown to love and trust above practically all others. "Anyone else here wonder why us?" he asked, weakly.

"Why us what?" Dani asked.

"Why are we the ones who are being thrown into all this? Why are we the ones having the dreams and getting visits from

Howard? I mean, I understand it in your instance, Althea, since Howard had a connection with this Igee, as well as with you, but why the rest of us? Why Robynn? Why were we chosen?"

"Perhaps it's because we know the difference between right and wrong," Althea offered. "Maybe I'm just a foolish old woman, but I look around at the things that are happening today, not just here, not simply to us, but everywhere, all over the world. Wars, intolerance, poverty, some people facing starvation while others sit on inconceivable wealth...this is what things were like when I was a young woman. Back then we thought we were fighting assorted demagogues, including a horrible little man who looked like Charlie Chaplin. But it was this Legion then, just like now. It's back, and we can see it while others can't. Or maybe the others can, but they accept it, which is even worse. But that's why us. Whether we like it or not, we're part of our own legion, a legion for good. We just don't know what to call ourselves. Oh, heavens, I have to lie down." Althea Kinchloe stretched out on the bed and closed her eyes.

Neither Jack nor Dani said anything, in part because Althea seemed exhausted and they did not want to disturb her rest. Had it been convenient, Jack simply would have left and gone into the other room, but there was still Robynn to contend with. She remained in the bathroom with the door closed, and he could hear the sounds of soft, weary sobbing coming from the inside. She would probably cry herself to sleep and then he could go in and get her.

It was Dani who broke the stillness of the room by walking toward him and holding out her arms, in an unmistakable invitation, which Jack accepted. They stood in the middle of the room, holding each other, not really knowing what the embrace meant, but understanding that their shared warmth and energy was in some sense revitalizing them both. It was not a romantic exchange, it was a human one. They continued to hold each other until a soft voice broke their embrace. "He was wrong," Althea Kinchloe said weakly.

Jack rushed to her. "What's that, Althea? Do you need something?"

She looked at him and smiled. "I need you to know that that man, that horrible man, is capable of making mistakes. He told me when I would die, but he was wrong. It's a day early. I've beat him. Remember that, dear, he can make mistakes." Still smiling, she closed her eyes.

Leaping up, Jack said, "We have to get a doctor." He ran to the room phone.

"Jack, wait," Dani said, listening at the bathroom door. "Robynn's talking to someone."

"To herself," Jack said, starting to dial the front desk.

"No, I can hear two voices!"

Putting the receiver down, Jack ran to the bathroom door and listened. He heard Robynn's voice, and then heard the response from the other voice. One he recognized. He looked back at Althea, who was lying on the bed silent as death, but still smiling. "She's dead," he said.

"You haven't checked for a pulse."

"I don't need to. I know she's dead because I just heard her voice in the bathroom, breaking the news to Robynn."

CHAPTER THIRTY-FIVE

Jack and Dani said nothing. Finally, Dani crept over and checked for a pulse, finding none. She carefully laid her arm back over her body. A look of peace had settled on her face.

All of a sudden Jack missed her terribly, this woman he had met only a few days earlier. But he understood that she had fulfilled her role in this bizarre drama, and that it was the proper time for her to exit. Her function, he believed, was to give them the important news that Igee could make mistakes.

The bathroom door opened and Robynn walked out. Jack rushed to her and hugged her, and she hugged back. "Daddy," she said in a whimpery voice, "Noni's dead."

"Yes, punkin, Noni's dead."

"She told me so. In the bathroom."

"I know she did, honey."

"She was a ghost."

"I know."

"I thought ghosts were s'posed to be scary."

"Some are, but Noni isn't," Jack said, looking deep into his daughter's eyes. "Just like her friend Howard isn't. They're good ghosts, I guess."

"I love Noni."

"So do I, Robynn."

"But she told me I had to do what you said, and that I needed to go with Uncle Tim."

"I'm glad she told you that, punkin," Jack said. "She knew Uncle Tim better than any of us, and she wouldn't have asked you to go with him if she thought there would be any problem with it."

"But I don't want to go."

"I know, and it hurts me to have to send you away. But my biggest job as a dad is to keep you safe, and sometimes I have to make hard decisions to do that." He hugged her like a dying man clutches a life preserver. "Robynn, do you want to see Noni?" he asked her.

"You mean see her dead?"

Jack nodded.

"Okay."

Jack led her to the bed and Robynn stood beside it, studying the body of the old woman. Any emotions she was having were unreadable on her face. "She's somewhere more fun, isn't she?" she asked.

"Yes, I think she is."

Robynn wrinkled her nose. "She doesn't smell very good."

"I know, punkin. That's one of the things that happens when you die. But we're going to take care of that. Do you think you could go with Dani over to the other room?"

"Okay."

The two left to go next door while Jack contemplated his next move. He should, of course, call the front desk to let them know immediately, but he knew that their first move would be to call the closest police station, so he decided to cut out the middle man and go straight to Creeley himself. He'd let the desk clerk know afterwards. Pulling out his cell phone he punched in Creeley's number and waited. It was ringing an inordinately long time, and for a moment he was afraid that Creeley was unavailable, which seemed odd for a policeman. Finally the line picked up, but instead of the policeman's voice saying hello, all Jack heard was an empty silence.

"Hi, Cree? Are you there?"

"There's no Creeley here, Jack," a man's voice said.

"That you, Carl?"

The response was a laugh, one that made the skin on the back of his neck bubble. Suddenly Jack knew who it was.

"Elley says hello, and she can't wait to see you," the voice of Louis Norman Igee said. "You and that split-faced little bitch you claim to have fathered. But we know the truth, don't we?"

"Fuck you," Jack said.

Igee laughed. "In your dreams...someday. But we were talking of Robynn. You can try and hide her but it won't work. Elley will find her, and why not? She's her mother, after all. She brought her into this world, so who better to—"

"*Shut up!*" Jack roared. That drew only more laughter.

Don't let him get to you, Jack ordered himself. *He's trying to rattle you; don't give in. Remember what Althea said: he can make mistakes.*

Taking a deep breath, Jack said: "Are you quite finished, Mr. Igee?"

There was a pause, and then the voice said: "I see you know my name. You have done your homework."

"What do you think I've been doing, hiding under the bed?"

"Drinking would have been my guess."

He's trying to goad you. All you have to do is return the serve.

"Well, those days are over, Igee, and you know what? I have you to thank for that. But here's what I don't understand: why do you have to have Elley commit your crimes for you? Are you really so incompetent that you can't do it yourself? Or are you just too big a pussy?"

There was a sharp intake of breath on the other end of the line, and crazy though it sounded, Jack swore that the cell phone in his hand was getting warmer.

"You think you are a wit," the voice said.

"Not particularly, but I'm still a man. I don't have to have a woman do all my dirty work for me." Then Jack started meowing into the phone.

The line went dead.

Jack felt triumphant and degraded at the same time. He had stood up to the evil bastard, but did so on the taunting level of a playground bully. Yet it had worked. Why had it worked?

Jack jabbed in Creeley's number again, and this time the call went to the right place. "Cree, it's Jack Hayden," he said.

"Yeah, Jack, I'm afraid I don't have any more information for you," the policeman said.

"That's not why I'm calling. I'm afraid there's a dead body in my motel room."

A pause, then: "Oh?"

"She's an elderly woman, a friend of mine. She died of purely natural causes. She was in her nineties."

"She's in your motel room, you say?"

"That's right, at the Tide Pool Inn."

Even though it wasn't really necessary, Creeley told Jack not to leave the premises, and also recommended that he go ahead and notify the front desk, telling them that he was already on his way over, and then hung up.

Jack reported Althea's death to the horrified young clerk at the front desk, who started to resemble an untied balloon that one lets go of until Jack told her that he had already called the police and that they would be there momentarily. Then he went back to Dani's room, where Robynn was happily watching television while Dani looked like a wreck.

"It'll be okay," Jack said, gently rubbing her back.

"Will it?" Dani asked.

"Promise," he said.

"Shouldn't we notify Althea's family?"

"Her grandson is probably on his way down here," Jack said. "I guess we need to wait for him. I'm sorry to have to dump all of this on him, but what choice have we got? She's not our relative."

"Did you talk to Creeley?" Dani asked.

"Yeah, he's on his way over. Dani, could you take Robynn to the pool, or somewhere?"

"Can I get some à la mode?" Robynn asked, pronouncing the word slowly and carefully. "That's what I had the day we met Noni."

"That's right, you did, punkin."

"I'll see what we can do," Dani said, taking the girl by the hand. To Jack, she added, "We'll come right back afterwards," and then the two of them left.

Creeley arrived ten minutes later and Jack joined him in the room containing Althea's body. Creeley had his hands full attempting to calm the motel's manager, who was visibly stressed by the situation. "How fast can you get her out of here?" she asked nervously.

"Not until the coroner arrives," Creeley said. "But I've got a call put into him, so it shouldn't take more than an hour."

"An *hour*?" the manager cried. "We have to have a dead body in here for an hour?"

"I promise you, ma'am, she won't steal the towels."

As it turned out the coroner, who was also a doctor in the Paso Robles hospital, got there within twenty minutes, and verified that there were no signs of anything except a natural death by a woman of advanced age. Noting the slight smile on her face, Dr. Franklin Lee, who looked to Jack to be barely out of his twenties, said: "I just hope it's as pleasant as it seemed to be for her when it's my time to go. Are you next of kin?"

"No, no, I'm just a friend," Jack said. "Her grandson is on his way down here."

"You called him?"

"No, she called him, but not about this. Well, obviously not about this. I can call him right now if you think that will help. Althea had called him from my phone, to the record of the number is still there."

"Please do," Dr. Lee said.

Jack found the number for Tim Kinchloe in the phone's memory and redialed it. "This is Tim," a man's voice answered.

"Mr. Kinchloe, hi, my name's Jack Hayden."

"Whatever you're selling, I don't want it."

"No, no, I'm not selling anything. I'm a friend of your grandmother, of Althea."

"Does she need to speak to me again?"

"Um, actually, Mr. Kinchloe, I'm terribly sorry to have to tell you this, but—"

"Noni's dead, isn't she?"

"I'm so sorry, but yes she is."

There was a long sob-like sigh at the other end of the line, then Tim Kinchloe said: "I suspected as much."

"You did?"

"Mr. Hayden, I know my grandmother well enough to know that she would die before asking anybody for anything. That's not an idle metaphor. When she began calling me and asking me to send her things and then come down there, I sensed it was a life-or-death situation. Are you the father of the girl I'm supposed to be taking back with me?"

"Yes I am."

"So can you explain to me what the bloody hell is going on?"

"Mr. Kinchloe, I would give up a limb to be able to, but no, I don't think I can. Not to a reporter's satisfaction, anyway. What I would have to say wouldn't make the slightest bit of sense to you."

"Well, you're honest, at least. I suppose you need someone to deal with Noni."

"A family member, yes."

"All right. I'm on my way to the airport. I should be down there within about four hours, probably. I only ask one thing."

"What's that?" Jack asked.

"That you tell me everything you know, whether it's unbelievable or not."

"It's a deal. And Mr. Kinchloe?"

"Call me Tim, please."

"All right, Tim, and I'm Jack. I just want to tell you that your grandmother was an exceptional human being."

"I know that, Jack."

"I was with her when she passed away. She died with a smile on her face. If it's possible to die happy, I think she managed to. And she thought the world of you."

"Thanks. I'll be there as soon as I can."

The line went dead. Jack clicked the cell off.

"Okay, Doc, Althea's grandson thinks he can be here in about four hours," Jack said.

"We'll take the body to the hospital morgue in Paso Robles until he arrives," Dr. Lee said.

It took another half-hour to remove the body, after which the manager began to stress over cleaning, and maybe even being forced to replace, the bed. Jack was not in the mood and was glad when she finally left.

* * * * * * *

Tim Kinchloe was as good as his word; practically four hours to the minute after he had hung up on his call with Jack, he pulled his rental car into the parking lot of the Tide Pool Inn, went in and asked for Jack Hayden. "You gonna die on us, too?" the woman behind the counter muttered, as she buzzed Jack's room.

Jack soon emerged and sized up the man to whom he was going to turn over his daughter. There wasn't much resemblance to be found between he and Althea, though that was to be expected. Tim Kinchloe had sandy hair, and while not quite fat, looked soft. The two men exchanged awkward formalities, and then Jack went to get Robynn.

Althea had been right about one thing: Tim Kinchloe did seem to have a way with kids. Robynn took to him almost immediately. In fact, it proved to be Jack who had the bigger problem with her leaving. He had never before been forced to turn over his daughter to someone he knew so little about, not knowing when—or even if—he would see her again. He had felt nothing out in the parking lot earlier while transferring her car seat from his pick-up to Tim Kinchloe's car, but now back inside, the truth of the situation was caving in on him. "This is only going to be for a short while," Jack explained to her. "Then we'll come and get you, okay?"

"All right, Daddy," she said, with heartbreaking maturity.

Once she was strapped into the rental, Jack attempted

to explain the happenings of the last week to Tim Kinchloe, and surprisingly, Kinchloe had appeared to accept that Jack was speaking the truth. Jack had stressed the part about his wife having suffered some kind of mental breakdown, which rendered her dangerous to be around, and that served to make Tim understand why he was being asked to whisk Robynn away.

Looking up at Kinchloe, Jack tried to smile, though what his expression actually conveyed was, *please keep her safe*! Tim acknowledged it with a nod.

It was time for her to go, and Jack Hayden was having a hard time holding the tears back as he gave her one last hug in the car seat. Creeley, meanwhile, took the opportunity to pull Tim Kinchloe aside. "I've talked with your father," the policeman said, "and he's taking care of the arrangements to get your grandmother's body up to Vancouver. I told him that you were already down here, that she called you and asked you to come, but that you weren't the person to deal with the body, because you're not the next of kin. That will give you the opportunity to clear out and take care of the girl."

"Did you mention Robynn to my father?" Tim asked.

"No, I'm afraid I'm going to have to let you handle that one." Creeley lowered his voice so Robynn couldn't overhear. "Hopefully the girl's mom will be apprehended quickly and the task that Jack and I are facing will be accomplished soon, so with luck you'll only have her for a couple of days."

"And without luck?"

Creeley ran his hand through his hair. "Without luck, I'm not sure it matters much." Pulling out a business card, the policeman handed it to him. "Call if you need anything."

Tim Kinchloe nodded stepped back over to the car. "Okay, Robynn," he said, "I guess we'd better get going."

"Punkin, Uncle Tim is going to take real good care of you," Jack said.

"I know," she replied. "I love you, Daddy."

"I love you, punkin."

Then Tim closed the car doors and while Jack watched, with

a boulder in his throat, the car pulled out and headed for the freeway. "Tell me it's worth it, Cree," he said.

"She's safe, Jack," the policeman said. "Just keep focusing on that."

Rob Creeley's cell phone rang and he grabbed it, barking, "Yeah, Creeley, what'cha got?" He paced back and forth while listening for about a minute, then said, "Okay, good, keep on it," and hung up.

"Did they get Elley?" Jack asked.

"No, but we might have picked up her trail. A waitress in a restaurant called the station to report a woman whose description resembles your wife stopping in for dinner late last night. She was seen getting into an old station wagon."

"Where the hell'd she get that?"

"The cashier, god bless her, got the license number and it was traced to a guy living in a hippy hideaway up the coast at Big Sur. State police are on the way up there to talk to him, if he's still there."

"You mean if she hasn't murdered him?" Jack asked.

"Look, Jack, I know this is difficult to accept—"

"I've accepted it, Cree. I just sent the most important person in the world to me away with someone who is one step removed from a total stranger because I've accepted the situation only too well."

Dani Lindstrom now joined them in the parking lot. "Is Robynn gone?" she asked, and Jack nodded. "I figured you didn't need me in the way while you were saying goodbye." She reached out and rubbed the back of his shoulder in an intimate way that did not escape Creeley's notice. "You going to be okay, Jack?" she asked.

Jack shrugged. "It's not like I have the luxury of falling apart. None of us do now."

They walked back into the motel. Once in the lobby, Jack's cell rang. "Now what," he muttered, pulling it out and answering it. It was Yolanda back at the office, a place he had all but forgotten about. "Guys, I'd better take this," he told Creeley and Dani. "I

was supposed to be checking in at the office and I haven't been."
Walking back out into the open air, he said: "Sorry, Yoli," he
said. "I guess I haven't kept in contact, have I? What's up?"

"After what happened to Mr. Broarty, I wanted to make sure
you were all right," the receptionist said.

"I've been better, truth be told, but I'm still here."

"Good, because there's something else."

"God. What now?"

"We're been slapped with a ten-million dollar civil suit from
Resort Partners over the probable fall-through of the Wood City
project as a result of the killing of Mr. McMenamin."

"Shit. And how nice they have their priorities in order.
Business first, and then we'll get around to the matter of
murder, if we have the time. But why the hell are they suing the
company? Marc's the one who went nuts and killed Emac."

"The suit charges us with criminal negligence and incompe-
tence."

"Great. What's Greenberg got to say about this?" Mitchell
Greenberg was the chairman of Crane Building Inspections,
Inc., and the husband of the late Marcus Broarty's aunt.

"He's raving like a crazy person," Yolanda answered. "Mrs.
Greenberg become hysterical and had to be hospitalized, and
he only just got back. In fact, that's the reason I'm calling you."

"Let me guess: he wants me back in the office ASAP so he
can grill me about what really happened."

"You got it."

"Well, the answer is no. Tell Greenberg that I will return to
the office as soon as I am ready to, and I'll talk with the lawyers
or whoever else he wants, but it will be on my schedule, not his.
I will not be down there today and probably not tomorrow. I
may not make it this week. I'll be there when I get there, and if
that's not good enough, than he can go to hell."

"He's not going to like that, Jack."

"Well, then I quit. It's simple as that. From this moment on,
he has no power over me, because I swear to you you, Yoli,
nobody is going to like what happens if I just abandon what I'm

doing up here. I'll take my lumps from Greenberg and whatever formidable law firm Resort Partners has engaged when I get back, but not before."

"Jack, what have you gotten yourself into up there?" she whispered.

"Something that would make the worst Greenberg could possibly throw at me feel like getting snapped with a rubber band. I'll call you and let you know when I'm coming back." He shut off the phone and stood there for a moment, looking at the otherwise normal blue sky and the otherwise normal ocean off in the distance. He went back inside to find Creeley and Dani loitering in the lobby, which made the manager very nervous.

"I filled the Chief in on what was in Howard's journal, Jack."

"So, Cree, what do you think?" Jack asked.

"I think I need some coffee. Why don't we go into the coffee shop."

The Tide Pool coffee shop was all but empty, which was good for them. After the waitress appeared to take their order—a coffee for Creeley, a hot chocolate for Dani, and a large iced tea for Jack, who even though he desperately wanted a beer, remembered his pledge—they began to talk. "How do we fight this thing?" Jack asked. "It's everywhere."

"I think we're all agreed that the nucleus of it is that damned mural," Creeley said, and the other two nodded in acknowledgement. "Well, then, it doesn't take genius to figure out that we have to destroy the mural."

"But how?" Jack asked. "More holy water? According to Howard's diary, that was a bust. Fire didn't seem to do anything either, and painting it over worked for a while, but then the started to chip away. So what do we do? Get pickaxes and scrape it off?"

"How about solvent?" Dani asked.

"Solvent?"

"Back when I was studying art there was someone in my class who had worked incredibly hard on a painting, and then when it was nearly done, she accidentally dumped some paint thinner on the canvas and ruined the whole thing. She wanted to kill herself, because there was no way to fix it, the solvent had run the colors and impregnated itself into the surface of the canvas. So, yeah, maybe solvent, paint thinner."

"What if it's a special kind of paint created by Igee to resist any kind of solvent?" Jack said. "The idea's right, but we need something stronger, like acid. But I don't suppose you find that at Walmart, either."

"Acid is used for making etchings," Dani said. "Glenowen is an artist's community. Surely someone up here has to be into etching."

"Sulfuric acid is also used to make fertilizer," Creeley said. "There're places within driving distance that use it by the drumfull. I'd say I could get as much as we need."

Jack sighed. "There's something I have to say, Cree, and I hope you don't take it the wrong way."

Creeley held up a hand. "Jack, I hope that you're not going to give me any crap about how this is your problem and not mine, and how I can't take the risk of helping you go after this Legion thing. You're not going to do that, are you? 'Cause I've gotten kinda fond of you, and I don't want you to insult my intelligence by loading that pile of pigballs on top of my head."

"I just don't want to get anybody hurt that doesn't have to be."

"Neither do I. Let me remind you that on top of whatever this asshole is planning to throw at us we still have a mentally unbalanced, dangerous, probably armed woman running around. Do either of you know what to do if someone suddenly pulls a gun on you?" He let that sink in for effect. "And yeah, she got the better of me once, but now I'm expecting trouble so I can prepare for it. Besides, I kind of owe her a little payback."

"Cree, whatever it is that's happened to Elley, she's still my wife," Jack said. "I don't want you to just gun her down."

"I have no intention of gunning her down, Jack. But if I can get the better of her this time, maybe I can defuse the situation before it becomes lethal. Sorry, but I'm in this to the end, so just put any conflicting thought out of your mind. So, you want to go get some acid or what?"

"Yes," said Dani. "Let's get it over with."

"All right," Jack said.

"Fine," Creeley said. "I'll go home and get my truck, and then head out to get some acid. I'd suggest that you two go on down to the station and don't leave until you hear from me. Carl should be there, he'll keep you company. Oh, and tell him he's in charge until I return. He won't like that, particularly, but he'll go along with it."

After Jack paid the bill, which emptied his wallet, the three walked out of the motel. "Leave your car here," Jack said to Dani. "We'll take my truck to the Glenowen police station. It will do better on the road to Wood City. As he approached his truck in the parking lot, he could see that the passenger door was ajar. "Dani, don't move!" he ordered, and she froze. "Cree, come here," he called, and the policeman trotted over. "Look at that," Jack said, pointing to his pickup. "I never leave the doors open like that, I always leave it locked. Someone has broken in."

"Stay back," Creeley said, drawing his gun as he crept slowly toward the truck. "If someone is inside that truck, you'd better come out. This is the police."

There was no reply.

More cautiously now, Creeley knelt down and scanned underneath the truck, then rose again. "I'm locked and loaded, so don't do anything dumb." A couple other people in the parking lot now backed away as Creeley slowly stepped toward the cab of the pickup, his gun poised in front of him, stopping when he was close enough to see inside through the back window. Then Creeley dropped the gun and opened the door. "All right, Jack, it's safe," he called back.

Jack trotted up and saw the policeman examining the passenger door window. "Probably used a slim jim," Creeley said. "Check and see if anything's missing."

Jack looked through the cab and found his papers and note-books intact. His microcassette recorder was on the seat. Looking through the glove compartment, he discovered nothing missing. Even the small cloth bag filled with several dollars worth of change for parking meters was still there. "Everything's here," he said. "Why break into a truck and not take anything?"

"Maybe someone wanted to leave something, not take it," Creeley suggested.

Jack looked through the cab again, even checking behind the sun visors and under the seat, but found nothing that should not be there. He shrugged and started to close the door, but then said: "Wait a minute, I know what's gone now." Searching the cab yet again, he told Creeley, "I had a small video camera in here. That's what's missing. I must have left it in plain sight and someone got it."

"Was it valuable?" Dani asked.

"Not really. It was a couple of years old, and not that fancy. The last thing I used it for was to videotape the mural. Oh, god...."

"What?"

Jack gave a mirthless laugh. "I photographed that mother when it was at it's nastiest," he said, "so whoever took the camera is in for a hell of a shock if they happen to hit playback."

* * * * * * *

Betty Dorgan thought she heard a knock at the front door, but had not been sure. Carl was at the station—something unusual was going on in the village, though he would not tell her what—and Kevin, her beautiful, loving Kevin, was still setting up his own household, so she was at home alone, which felt strange. Imagine, not experiencing empty nest syndrome until the age of fifty-five. Her own mother had already shooed the last chick away by the time she was forty.

Betty answered the door but found no one there. Maybe it had been her imagination, or perhaps simply the fact of having an empty, quiet house was introducing her to little noises and bumps that had always been there, but had been obscured the sounds of daily life. She was about to close the door when she noticed the object lying in front of it. It looked like one of those palm-sized video recorders.

"That's certainly strange," Betty muttered to herself. She was not the most technologically advanced of people in her circle, certainly not like her friend Helene, who even had one of those iPad things, or Pod, or whatever they were—the kind of contraption that totally confused her. Carl knew about some of this stuff, though the smaller the devices got, the harder a time he had with them, given the size of his hands.

Betty knelt down and picked it up, and saw that there was a note attached to it. Adjusting her glasses, she read: *Carl Dorgan must watch this—urgent!* Heavens, it must be a clue to some case he's working on. Taking the recorder and the note, she turned to go back inside, but stopped when she felt wetness on her thumb. The ink with which the note had been written was still wet, and she had smeared it. "Oh, shoot," Betty Dorgan said, careful not to wipe it on her dress, particularly since it felt not like ink at all, but rather paint.

Whoever had written the note and left the video recorder must have been in a real hurry. Whatever this was all about, it must be important.

* * * * * * *

Robynn was tired.

She was tired of riding in cars. She was tired of living in rooms that weren't hers. She wanted to go home. She wanted her daddy. She wanted Noni.

She wanted her mommy, too, even though she was a little bit afraid of her now.

But Uncle Tim was nice. He wasn't like that other man who had taken her from school, who was always mad, and then started acting really funny when she had to go pee.

She just wanted to go to sleep and wake up and have her life like it had been before—except she wanted Oyster Cracker to be there, too. She wanted to go back to school. She wanted to see her teacher again. But she also wanted to stop having those dreams that scared her, which meant that she didn't really want to go to sleep.

But she was so tired; tired enough to start crying.

"You okay back there, honey?" Uncle Tim asked from the front seat.

"Mm-hmm," Robynn said, closing her eyes.

"That's all right, you can take a nap if you want."

Robynn didn't know how he could see her in the front seat, but she was too tired to try and figure it out. The movement of a car rarely lulled her to sleep, but today she was just too tired to resist.

But please, she thought before drifting off, *don't let that man, the muverfucker, near me.*

Tim Kinchloe meanwhile had spent the last eleven miles wondering exactly what he had gotten himself into. He was on his way to the San Luis Obispo airport with a little girl he had only just met, to whom he could establish absolutely no relationship or even prior contact, should anyone ask, and then he would fly home with her and put her up in his apartment, not having the faintest idea how to take care of a five year old. That's providing he even got her on the plane here and off the plane in Portland without being stopped by a Transportation Safety officer.

If he was stopped by the authorities anywhere along the way, all he had to do was have them call Chief Creeley, who would explain everything, or at least give a good cover story. Still, that did little to wipe away his present visions of headlines reading: *Portland journalist arrested on suspicion of kidnapping.*

But it was too late to turn back now.

Behind him, the girl was muttering something. Adjusting the rearview to glance back, he saw that she appeared to be sound asleep. Maybe she talked in her sleep. Lots of kids did. From what Tim had been briefed on, she'd been through a lot lately, so it would not be surprising if she was having a nightmare.

And Robynn Hayden *was* dreaming, but it was not a night-mare. She was at her school, playing in the sandbox, and the shadow of someone came up to her. Robynn looked up and saw who it was. "Noni!" she cried, getting up and giving the old woman, who had knelt down, a sandy hug. Robynn knew it was Noni, but this Noni looked different; younger.

"Hello, punkin," Noni said.

"I miss you."

"I miss you too, but we're here now. Only for a minute, though. Robynn, there's something I need to tell you."

"What?"

Now they were in the back seat of a car. Robynn wasn't strapped in to a car seat. She liked that, being able to ride like a big person. Noni was seated next to her."

"It's something very important, and you need to remember it."

"Okay."

Althea leaned closer to her. "Always remember, punkin, it's harder for somebody to hurt you when you're not scared."

"What does that mean, Noni?"

"Just that. Some people may try to scare you, but if you don't let them, then they have a lot less power over you. Can you remember that?"

"I think so."

"Well, here, maybe this will help you remember." Noni reached behind her neck and unclasped a necklace, then held it out in front of her. It was a silver chain and it had a matching locket on the front. She carefully opened the locket, doing it slowly so that Robynn could see how to do it, and showed her a picture inside. The picture was of a young man.

"That's Howard!" Robynn said.

"That's right. I never took that picture out, and nobody ever opened this locket except me, so I've carried his picture around with me my whole life with no one any the wiser. It has given me strength at times when I needed it, so now I'm going to give it to you." She dropped the necklace into Robynn's small hand.

"Thank you, Noni! Can I put it on?"

"Yes, punkin, and remember what I said about not letting people scare you. If you start to feel frightened, just hold onto that locket. It will be like having me there with you, holding your hand. You can even open it and look at the picture if you like."

"Okay." Not so expertly as Noni, but still carefully, Robynn opened the locket and looked at Howard.

"I have to go now, punkin. Bye-bye."

"Noni, will I see you again?" she asked, but Noni was already gone. Then Robynn Hayden closed her eyes.

When she opened them again, she was in her car seat in the back of Uncle Tim's car. She was awake again. They weren't driving, though. They had pulled over onto the shoulder of the highway. Tim was looking back at her, his face ashen. "How come we're not going?" she asked.

Tim Kinchloe was breathing into a baggie, which he removed long enough to say: "I had to stop for a minute. I need to rest." She could see that his hands were shaking. He breathed in and out into the baggie for a few minutes, then took it down from his face.

"Are you gonna barf?" Robynn asked.

"No, I'll be all right. It's hard to explain what the bag's for, but sometimes I need it."

"Okay," Robynn said, letting go of the locket, which fell down onto her lap.

Tim Kinchloe took several deep breaths, holding the last one, and releasing it very slowly. "My grandmother wore that necklace for as long as I can remember," he said.

"She gave it to me," Robynn said.

"I know, honey. I know she did." Tim knew that because when he looked in his rearview mirror, he saw his dead grandmother sitting back there with Robynn. He saw her hand the locket to the girl and smile. That was why Tim had nearly run the car off the road, screeching to a halt on the shoulder. That was why he had to use the baggie in his pocket to keep from hyperventilating.

And having to use the baggie to keep from hyperventilating, to get over the shock of seeing Noni in the backseat of his rental car, is why Tim Kinchloe did not notice that an old beat-up station wagon, driven by a woman, had just pulled up on the narrow shoulder behind him.

CHAPTER THIRTY-SIX

"Must be a big sale day," Jack said as he slowed his pickup down to nothing to look for a parking spot in the middle of Glenowen village. They had already slid past the police station, and even on the side streets, the village seemed parked to capacity. He went up to the next block, only to find it parked up as well. "I take that back, it must be free beer day," he said. He had drive past antique shop row at the outer edge of the business district before finding an empty spot. "Good god," he said, irritably, throwing the truck into park with a bump. "We're damn near out of town."

"The walk might do us good," Dani reasoned. "Give us something to do, anyway."

They got out of the truck and started back toward the police station, several blocks down, trudging on in silence, each knowing that if they started to talk with each other, the conversation might lead to questions of just what in the hell they thought they were doing fighting this nightmare, which in turn might weaken their resolve.

While he was not speaking out loud as they walked, Jack became lost in thought. *Why did the stupid schoolyard taunts bother Igee so much?* he continued to wonder. Then understanding flooded over him like a tsunami: *because his arrogance was punctured; his ego.* That was the secret. That was Louis Norman Igee's weak spot. Maybe that was the weak spot of every evil person, the belief in their own invulnerability! All he had to do was keep pounding on Igee's vanity, his arrogance, and—

"Daddy, help me!"

Jack pulled up so suddenly he nearly fell over, instantly shaken out of his self-imposed trance

"Owwww, they're hurting me! Daddy, please!"

"Robynn?" he shouted, looking around.

It was all different now. Every foot of downtown Glenowen was different. The buildings and stores were not the same as they had been earlier, and there were no cars parked alongside the curbs. In fact, the streets weren't even paved. There were no people either, no pedestrians. There was only one prominent building on this block, and Jack recognized it immediately.

The Saddleback Inn.

"Daddeee, help me!" his daughter's voice shrieked from inside the building.

"I'm coming, Robynn!" Jack shouted, running up to the building and disappearing inside.

On the street behind him, Dani called out, "Jack, what are you doing?" but it was too late. He was already inside, only it was not a saloon that Dani had watched him race into; it was a public toilet structure. She had heard him call Robynn's name right before entering the facility, and feared that something was playing with his head. She needed to get Jack out of the public building and shake him out of his delusion.

Somewhere in the village, a clock struck four.

Dani ran over to the small cinderblock building and knocked on the door of the side marked *Men.* "Anyone in there?" she called, and no one answered, not even Jack. That was not a good sign. Knocking heavily on the door and calling again, receiving no reply, she decided to brave it and pushed her way inside. Dani had not been inside a men's bathroom since high school, when she did it on a dare, so she had no way of knowing if the drab, foul-smelling place was representative of the breed. She hoped not. The room had two stalls, one regular sized and one made to accommodate wheelchairs, and two brown-stained urinals fixed to one wall. On the same wall were two sinks, separated from the urinals by a rusting partition. The corners of the place were filthy and the floor was sickeningly damp. The place reeked of urine.

The door of the regular stall was closed, indicating someone was inside. "Jack?" she called, hearing her voice echo slightly as it bounced off the austere walls. "Jack, are you in there?"

No answer came.

Crouching down, Dani looked under the rusting-out cubicle walls of the toilet stalls for feet and found none. "Shit," she muttered. Scanning the place for any kind of escape route, she saw a small window at the top of one wall, but it seemed hardly big enough for someone Jack's size to squeeze through, and would have been damned difficult to reach anyway. Clearly he did not flush himself down the drain. So where was he?

She turned around and faced the scratched mirror over the dripping sink, which enabled her to see most of the rest of the reeking bathroom behind her. She knew she could not stay in here much longer, since someone would eventually come in and wonder why there was a woman in the place, but she hated the idea of leaving without knowing what had happened to Jack. Could it be that he really went into the women's side, and she only thought it was the men's? It didn't seem likely—she had seen what she had seen, after all—but at least that made more sense than his disappearing off the face of the earth. Besides, she could check in the women's side without any fear of discovery.

Still looking in the mirror, Dani ran her hand through her hair to straighten it, and then smiled at her folly. Everything's turning to shit and she's worried about her hair being messed up. She had no sooner turned to leave when she heard a man's voice say: "Danica."

She spun back around. "Jack?"

"No, Danica, it's me."

The voice sounded faintly familiar, but she could not place it. But now she noticed that there were feet and legs visible under the partition in the small toilet stall; hairy legs that were partially bare because the man's pants were around his ankles.

"It's so nice to see you, Danica," the voice said.

"Who are you? How do you know me?"

"I was the first one who tried to know you, don't you remember? I called you my little tulip."

Dani Lindstrom clapped her hand over her mouth to stifle a scream. That voice...now it was all too horribly familiar. It was Mr. Maurison, her sixth grade teacher, who had attempted to molest her.

"Remember, Danica? It was in a bathroom back then, too, all those years ago when I introduced you to Mister Six-Incher. Remember?"

Frozen, Dani watched what appeared to be a very, very old hand reach down and pick up the pants, lifting them up. She heard the jangle of a belt buckle followed by a loud *zip* sound, and then the sound of a toilet flushing.

"I made it a math problem for you," the voice said from inside the stall. "'How many times will six go into eleven?' But you failed, didn't you? You wouldn't let six go into eleven at all. All you let me do is touch you. Juanita Cordero, now she let me give her math lessons. You remember Juanita, don't you?"

Dani choked back a sob. Juanita Cordero was a name she had not heard in more than twenty years, but she remembered Juanita, who had been a special-ed student at the school. One day she simply snapped and attacked another student, hurting him badly. The rumor at the time was that the other kid had exposed himself to her on the playground, but not everyone believed that. No matter what really happened, Juanita was gone from the school almost overnight, having been transferred to a special institute better equipped to deal with special kids.

"*Retards* is what you kids used to call people like her," Maurison said, "but not me. I called her pure honey."

"*Bastard*!" Dani screamed. "You piece of filth! Do you know I was actually glad when I read that you died!" She stopped for a moment, and then continued: "You are dead, Mr. Maurison, you're not really here."

The door to the stall started to swing inward. "Oh, I'm dead, all right, my little tulip, but I am here."

Dani Lindstrom shrieked at the sight of the gray, rotting thing that shambled out of the stall. As the corpse of her former teacher advanced, she inched backwards and soon hit the entry door. Spinning around, she pulled on the handle, but the door wouldn't open.

Dani felt something on her shoulder, something that smelled like rotting meat, and she turned back around. It was face to face with her now. Even though the thing had no lips, it spoke perfectly clearly: "You never gave me the answer to my math problem back then, but now we're back together. We can make up for lost time." With a bony, maggoty hand, the corpse of Eugene Maurison undid his zipper, letting out a pale, gray, decomposing six-inch battering ram. Dani screamed again and pushed against the corpse as hard as she could, propelling it backwards. What was left of Mr. Maurison went down onto the filthy floor, and Dani turned back and pulled on the handle of the door again, this time as though her life depended on it. The handle ripped off in her hands, leaving a hole in the door.

The corpse was starting to get up again, using the sink basin to try and pull itself up to its feet. Panicked, Dani ran to it and kicked the dead creature in its head as hard as she could, caving in its temple. Maurison's corpse did not scream in pain as much as frustration, but the move was enough to send it rolling toward the wall.

Dani charged the door and threw herself against it as hard as he could. The door gave way and she found herself literally flying through the air outside of the public toilet before crashing down onto the concrete walkway on her right shoulder and rolling. She came to rest on grass, and cried out in pain, clutching her shoulder. There was blood seeping through her blouse and reaching in to touch it, it felt hot and raw, but it didn't seem to be broken. But Christ Almighty, how it hurt! Dani managed to get up to her feet and now felt like she was going to be sick. She'd just have to do it on the grass since there was no way she was going back in the public toilet and using one of the bowls. After a minute or so, though, the feeling went away. Then she heard a man's voice: "Hey, lady, you okay?"

She recoiled at the sound, fearing it was once again her long dead assailant, but the voice was instead coming from a complete stranger. He was a bearded, middle-aged man in an outback hat, jeans and a vest—a not uncommon look for the village. "Do I need to call someone for you?"

"Thank you," she gasped. "Please call someone from the police. Chief Creeley or Deputy Dorgan, if they're there."

"Lady, you're bleedin' pretty bad, you need an ambulance too?" the man asked.

"I'll let one of them decide," she replied, "but I was attacked in that public toilet."

"In that what?" the man said, pulling out his cell phone.

"In that public—" Dani looked over at the building she had just burst out of.

It was not a public toilet.

Its signage declared it to be Linder's Gallery. What's more, there was no door on the side through which she had escaped, broken or otherwise. "Oh, my god," she said, sinking down to the ground.

"Yeah, send somebody out to Main and Quarry," the man was saying into the phone, "there's a woman here who's been hurt. She says she was attacked, but she's not makin' the most sense. Yeah, I'll stay here."

Within three minutes Carl Dorgan pulled up and hurried over to Dani, who was still seated on the ground. "Can you get to your feet, ma'am," he asked. Dani nodded and with Dorgan's help, and a lot pain, rose. Turning to the passerby in the hat, the Officer asked, "You see what happened to her?"

"No sir, I just saw her laying there yelling. It was almost like she wasn't there, then a second later, she was."

Dorgan only nodded and thanked the man, telling him he could go on his way now. Walking slowly, he helped Dani to the police car. A few other pedestrians stopped to watch what was going on, but quickly dispersed when it appeared to be nothing.

"Where are we going?" Dani asked.

"To the station," Dorgan replied. "Before he took off this morning, the chief told me something might happen involving you and Hayden, so I've kind of been expecting it."

"Where is Jack? I have to find him?"

"First thing we need to do is get you safe and get you some medical treatment if you need it, and then I'll find him."

Dani's shoulder radiated white hot pain as she got into the police car, but she managed to keep from whimpering. She had no doubt that things were going to get worse before they got better, so there was no sense giving to anything in now.

* * * * * * *

Jack heard a clock from somewhere out in the village strike four.

The interior of the Saddleback Inn looked different this time. There were no neon signs, and the place looked newer, less rundown, a little bit more like the Western saloons that Jack used to see on television and the movies. There was sawdust on the floors and no refrigerators behind the bar, just an old ice box. The beer taps were unidentified as well, indicating that it didn't really matter what brand you chose, beer was beer was beer. It had only taken a second for Jack to feel like a fool after rushing through the door and racing to the spot where he had seen his daughter screaming through the window, because Robynn was not there.

Of *course* Robynn was not there. Had Legion not been pushing his buttons so skillfully, he might have rationalized that there was no way she could be there. But he was here, here inside the Saddleback Inn, wondering what was going to get thrown at him this time.

The place appeared to be deserted; no one bellied up to the bar, no one was at one of the round tables, and no one was behind the bar. It was though the place was waiting for him to make the first move before it came to life, and how it wanted him to make the move was evident: lining the entire length of the bar itself were pint glasses of ale, their heads frothing over the tops of the glasses seductively. An inviting malty smell filled the bar, and Jack actually began to salivate.

"No, no, *no!*" he shouted, shoving the full pint glasses off of the bar. He would not take a drink. He would not.

Jack forced himself to turn around and was about to go back out when he heard a voice softly calling his name. It seemed to come from the behind the bar. Looking over, Jack noticed for the first time the painting of the woman up on the wall. It was a different one that the painting he had seen during his earlier "visit" to the Saddleback, but no less provocative. If anything, this one was worse, since it looked like a Vargas painting from an old *Playboy* magazine, a skillfully rendered picture of a half nude woman who was thrusting her crotch forward like a business card. When Jack's gaze moved up to the face, he gave an involuntary start.

It was the face of a woman about twenty-five years old, but it was a very familiar one, right down to the scar on the lip. The face in the painting moved. It winked at him. The scarred lip stretched into a leering smile. The woman's vagina thrust forward toward him. "Put it there, Daddy," she cooed. "Let's get dirty together."

Instead of being sickened or outraged, Jack felt strangely confident. This time the demonic force that was trying to get to him had gone too far. Taking a deep breath, he slowly turned around from the bar and in a loud, commanding voice, shouted: "You were better off trying to convince me that she was in danger, you know. You've overplayed your hand, Igee. You're demonstrating the fact that you can miscalculate. Not a smart idea." Jack stopped speaking for a moment to see if there would be any kind of response. There was not. "By the way, that painting doesn't look anything like her," Jack went on. "If you're the one who painted it, maybe you should go back to coloring books."

One of the remaining pints of ale on the bar suddenly flew

off and shattered against the wall, sending amber liquid and glass shards all over. Clearly, he had struck a nerve with the monster. Feeling strangely satisfied, Jack nonetheless realized it was time to leave. He made a run for the door and dashed through, praying that he would reemerge onto the main drag of present-day Glenowen.

No such luck.

Now Jack was in what appeared to be late a nineteenth- or early twentieth-century version of the town. Standing only a few yards away from him in front of the place was a man in old-fashioned clothing with his head under a black cloth that backed and antique camera. The man's left hand held a mortarboard heaped with powder. Before Jack could say, or even think to say, anything, the flash went off, startling and momentarily blinding him. He heard a man's voice say: "Like to have a shot of you, for future reference. Never know when it might come in handy."

"Who are you?" Jack asked.

The man said something that Jack could only make out as *filled Oregon*, which made no sense. "Don't worry, sir, I'm a friend, here to reassure you that what you're doing needs doing," he went on. "I can't help you none, not anymore, but we're with you." The last thing Jack heard was a very indistinct *it's up to you now.*

Jack Hayden realized his eyes were shut. When he finally opened them, present-day Glenowen was back, and all traces of the Saddleback Inn were gone. He was standing in front of the same shop he had been found leaning against earlier. Taking a quick survey of his clothes, he was relieved to find that he was still dressed and nothing was exposed. His next thought was to look around for Dani, whom he left rather abruptly standing in front of the Saddleback, but she was nowhere to be seen. Was that the prime objective of his being yanked into the past and tormented, to separate him from Dani? They really must be getting desperate.

"Jack Hayden?" a voice called out, and Jack looked up to see Carl Dorgan walking briskly toward him. "You all right, Jack?"

"Yeah, yeah I'm fine."

"Good. Miss Lindstrom's up at the station. She said you kind of got away from her. I'll take you to her."

Even though the Glenowen police station was well within walking distance, as was everything else in the village, Dorgan led Jack to his police car and they drove the short distance.

"Thanks for finding me, Carl," Jack said.

"Chief asked me to keep tabs on you," Dorgan answered, clicking on the blinker to turn and pull into the designated reserved parking space near the stationhouse trailer.

"How much do you know about what's been happening?" Jack asked.

Dorgan shut off the ignition but stayed in the car. "No details," he said, "but there's kind of a history of things happening around here. Why, I don't know, but there is. My grandfather used to talk about some strange people and problems way back when. He used to complain about a group of people he always called 'Legionnaires.'"

Jack Hayden suddenly grew cold, but he said nothing, letting the policeman continue.

"When I was a kid," Dorgan went on, "I'd get visions of guys in foreign legion hats running around creating mischief, but I don't think that's what he meant. I think they were a lot more dangerous than that, kind of like the KKK. One time Granddad said he had to run from a mob of 'em like a jackrabbit running from a coyote, and barely got away with his skin still attached. Course, you have to understand that Granddad did always have a tendency to make a good story better, for whatever that's worth. He should have been down south making movies, instead of being a small town photographer."

Once inside the police station Jack went to Dani, who was leaning against a wall, and tried to embrace her, but backed off after she winced from the pain. "What's wrong?" he asked.

"I managed to hurt my shoulder," she said, gingerly putting her arms around him. "I had another experience, Jack. This one was almost as bad as the one at Wood City."

She was hesitant to relate her experience in front of Dorgan until Jack assured her that it was all right. After hearing what she had gone through, whether hallucination or not, Jack realized he had gotten off easy this time. He told of entering the bar and seeing the painting, but how he had managed to keep it from getting to him. He considered adding the part about the photographer, which Jack now realized was the solution to the mystery of how his image ended up in a century-old picture. But neither Dani nor Dorgan knew about that picture, so he kept it to himself. But then something else struck him. "Carl, didn't you say your grandfather was a photographer?"

"Yeah. Had a shop in the village."

"Was his name Phil, by any chance?"

"That's right, Phil Dorgan. How did you know?"

The man with the camera had not said *filled Oregon*...he'd said *Phil Dorgan*. "I guess you could say he told me," Jack replied.

Carl Dorgan started to shake his head, as though trying to dislodge an idea. Finally he said, "I don't pretend to understand all of this, I'm just trying to carry out my orders."

The door of the police station suddenly swung open and Rob Creeley entered. "Good, everybody's here," he said, surveying the crowd. "I was worried we'd all get split up somehow."

"They tried," Dani said, shivering. "They tried like hell."

"I've got the stuff we talked about earlier out in my truck," Creeley said. "When do you want to do this?"

"Sooner is better than later," Jack said. Then, turning to Dani, he added: "But if you're not up for it, you can stay here."

"I'm going," she said. "I owe this bastard something."

"You need me to come along, chief?" Dorgan asked.

"No, Carl, you stay here," Creeley responded. "If we need you, I'll be sure to call you, though. Okay, Jack, Dani, let's go."

They got up and started for the door, but before they had left, the station phone rang. Everyone instinctively stopped as Carl Dorgan picked it up. Then covering the mouthpiece, he said: "It's all right, it's just the missus." He added: "It's the

Legionnaires you're going to go fight, isn't it?"

"Yeah, Carl, it is," Jack said.

As the three of them left the station, Dorgan turned his attention back to the phone and said, "Okay, hon, what's up?"

* * * * * * *

Jack, Dani, and Creeley strode out to the policeman's truck, which was much larger than Jack's and looked like it had actually been used to haul a small payload or two in its time. Lined up against the side of the truck bed, held fast by hooked bungee cords, were six glass gallon bottles each filled with a clear liquid. "Is that the acid?" Jack asked.

"That's it," Creeley said. "Had to give them a mighty fancy story to get it all, but there it is. I guess we'd better do this before one of us gets cold feet. We should all be able to sit comfortably in the cab."

"Cree, maybe I should ride in the back and keep and eye on the bottles," Jack said. "I'd hate to have one fall over and break on the way."

Creeley looked skeptical at first, but finally relented. "Well, all right, but if one does happen to break or start leaking, you stay the hell away from the contents and start pounding on the top of the cab, and I'll pull over. Okay?"

"Got it."

Creeley and Dani got inside the cab while Jack climbed into the back. As they pulled away and headed down Main Street, the glass bottles rocked and jiggled noisily, making Jack wonder if riding back here wasn't a stupid idea. But it was too late to worry about that now.

He began to tense up as they came got to the turnoff onto the dirt road that would take them to Wood City, probably for the last time. That tension might have been what saved him from injury when he suddenly lurched forward as the truck swerved onto the shoulder and screeched to a halt. "Hey!" Jack cried, bracing himself with his hands. "What are you doing, Cree?"

"Jack, look, in front," the policeman's voice called. Rising over the cab, Jack saw a vehicle stopped by the road, right across from the turnoff to the forest road leading to Wood City. It was a battered old station wagon.

"What about it?" Jack shouted, getting the message a second later. "Oh, god," he groaned, remembering that the last time Elley had been sighted, she was getting into a strange vehicle.

An old station-wagon.

CHAPTER THIRTY-SEVEN

As soon as the traffic allowed Creeley to make a left turn, he steered the truck into the woods. But immediately Jack Hayden saw that things were different. The trees were thicker, the roadway all but overgrown. "What the hell?" he heard Creeley say.

The truck was only able to penetrate the woods by about fifty feet, and then the road appeared to end. Jack jumped out of the back and looked at the trees and brush. "It was here, Cree," he said. "The damned road was here!"

"I know," the policeman replied getting out of the truck, "but it's not here now. Where the hell'd it go?"

Dani got out of the truck, too, and examined the near-solid wall of vegetation that now obstructed their path. "It looks like these trees have been here forever," she said, her voice shaking. "How can that be?"

Creeley was now kneeling on the ground. "Hey, take a look at this," he said. "Whoever's in charge of this nightmare covered up the road, all right, but they missed these." Jack and Dani squatted down on both sides of the policeman and saw the unmistakable pattern of rubber tires in the dirt. They could also see that the tracks stopped at the very edge of a thick wall of vegetation and trees, so thick that no vehicle could possibly pass through. "What do you make of that?"

"Can we make it through this on foot?" Dani asked.

"Yeah, I think so," Creeley said, rising. "But that'd mean we'd have to carry those jugs of acid with us."

"Let's get going, then," Jack said. Climbing back into the

truck bed, he carefully unhooked the bungee cords that were holding the bottles, and then two at a time, handed the gallons of acid to Dani and Creeley. "Remember," he said, jumping down, "we need to be ready for anything."

They began squeezing through the tangle of brush and branches. With each step the thicket became even denser, like a deliberate hedge, and right about the time Dani was beginning to wonder if they were really going to make it through, the vegetation began to clear. Soon they were standing on the road itself, looking back at the wall of green through which they had managed to pass. Creeley was kneeling down again, examining the road. "More tire tracks. We might not be alone in here."

He set down his acid jugs and pulled out his gun, then carefully picked the jugs back up with one hand. As loudly as he was able, Creeley shouted: "If there is anyone within the sound of my voice, I want you to know that I am an officer of the law and I am armed." When he stopped, the forest swallowed his voice. "I will use my firearm any time I need to. I would advise you to present yourselves immediately." There was no response for a moment, and then a sound was heard, far up the road.

"What was that?" Dani asked.

"Might have been a hawk," Creeley said.

"Didn't it sound like a voice?"

"I don't know. Helloooo!"

The sound came again, stronger this time.

"That was a voice," Dani said.

Jack Hayden said nothing. He was trying with all his might to dissuade himself from the terrible notion that the cry sounded like Robynn. But like her image inside the Saddleback, it had to be an illusion. Robynn was safe with Tim Kinchloe.

"Well, if someone's here, we warned them," Creeley said. "That's about all we can do. Let's go." The three trudged up the dirt road, penetrating the woods more deeply with each step.

"Has this road gotten steeper, too?" Dani said, panting.

"No, but we're usually able to drive on this part of it," Jack said. "It levels off closer to the town."

Not only did it level off, the road was now wider than he had ever seen it, and not as much of a washboard. "Goddamn," Jack said. "It's like the road itself has been re-graded."

After what was starting to seem like an endless trek, the first of Wood City's houses came into view. Jack stopped dead and stared at it. It was as new. Four solid walls on a sound foundation, newly painted windows and doors, and on the roof perfectly straight rows of wood shingles topped by a sturdy brick chimney, from which a wisp of smoke was emerging.

"It's come back," Jack whispered. "The whole town has risen from the dead."

"There are more houses up ahead, Jack," Creeley said. "A whole slew of them, from the looks of it."

"They appear to be inhabited," Dani said.

Jack nodded. "Welcome to Legion City."

"Do you think anyone's really inside?"

"I don't know, but just for safety's sake, let's assume so," Creeley said. "If either of you see a door or window move, even a crack, even peripherally, shout."

"I'll watch the houses on this side of the road," Jack said, jabbing left. "Dani, you watch those."

She nodded and they proceeded.

Each house the passed looked the same: they had identical designs, were painted the same colors, had similar tiny vegetable and flower gardens out front and each one had a wisp of smoke coming from the chimney. "Smell that?" Creeley said, as they walked past a cluster of the small houses. "It's like the smell of a lit match."

"It's sulfur," Jack said. "Brimstone, if you'd rather. It's faint, but it's there."

"Guys, can we stop for a second," Dani asked, setting down her jugs of acid. "Carrying this thing is playing hell with my shoulder."

"Oh, sorry," Jack said, having forgotten about her injury. "Let me take one." He rearranged his two jugs in one hand, as Creeley had done, and then took one of hers. "Can you manage the one?"

Dani nodded, picking it up, and they started up again.

Soon they were in the main part of the residential district. "Jesus, if Resort Partners could only see this they'd piss their pants with delight," Jack said. "This is exactly the kind of development they were planning on doing here. The houses aren't as log-cabin rustic as they wanted, but it's already here."

"And what a great place to spend a holiday," Dani added.

"I can see their brochure now. 'What happens in Legion City stays in Legion City...especially the souls of the dead.'"

"I'm glad you two can laugh about this," Creeley said sourly.

Jack stretched out his left arm, which was carrying two of the jugs, now fully understanding Dani's complaint about what it did to one's shoulder, even an uninjured one. "Laughing at evil may just be the way we survive this," he said.

They were now approaching the business area of Wood City. Their destination, the City Hall building, could be seen up ahead. In the dappled light of the forest, it appeared to be glowing, so new and bright was the white marble from which it was made. The three stood in silence and took in the building. "Are either of you as scared as I am?" Dani asked.

"Probably," Creeley answered.

"Do we really have the strength to fight this thing?" Jack asked.

"We'd better," Creeley responded, "because I didn't arrange for any backup."

Jack was thinking. "Maybe we should make our own backup, then."

"How so?" the policeman asked.

"Let's leave some of these jugs behind, just in case," Jack said. "That will be our backup. If we go marching up there with all six, and something happens to each one of them, they break or don't hit the target, we're out of ammo and Legion hasn't even begun to fight. This way we would have at least the hope of a second wave of attack."

"Works for me," Creeley said. "Where to you want to stash

them?"

"Somewhere around here, I guess," Jack replied. Spotting a thicket of brush that would make good cover, Jack carried his three jugs over to it and tucked them behind the branches, to the point where they were completely obscured. "Now all we have to do is remember where they are ourselves." He had an idea: Jack pulled out his cell phone and set it down by the bottles. "If we can't find the bottles, just call my number, Cree, and we'll follow the sound of the ring."

"Your cell works in the middle of the woods?" Creeley asked.

"That's the most unnatural thing of all," Jack replied. "If we come out alive, I'm going to call my carrier and offer a testimonial."

"Maybe it's not the carrier," Dani said. "If the other side can make paintings change and write things on mirrors, maybe our side can offer phone service in a forest."

Divvying up the three remaining jugs of acid, one each, they strode toward the city hall. When the reached the gleaming marble steps, Dani stopped and called out: "There's a car over there." Following the direction of her finger, Jack and Creeley saw a cleared spot in the forest a couple dozen yards away from the side of the stone building, and the abandoned car that sat it in. The driver's door was hanging open.

"Doesn't look like anyone's there," Creeley said, pointing his gun in the general direction, just in case.

"Who's is it?" Dani asked.

"It almost looks like the one that...oh my god, no, NO, *NO!*" Jack screamed, breaking and running towards the car.

"Jack!" Creeley screamed, but he showed no signs of stopping, so Creeley charged out after him, with Dani right behind. When they got close enough to the car, they realized why Jack was so alarmed.

It was Tim Kinchloe's rental car. The vehicle in which Robynn had last been seen.

"Robynn!" Jack screamed. "Robynn, are you out here? It's Daddy, punkin!"

Dani screamed then, and Jack jumped, dropping the acid jug, which bounced on the soft moist earth but did not break. Dani was pointing at something under the car.

Feet.

"Get back," Creeley commanded, setting down his jug while he got on his hands and knees and examined the body that was underneath the rental. Reaching under, he found and arm and put his fingers on the wrist, but the temperature of the flesh told him all he needed to know. Grabbing the arm as best he could, he began pulling, dragging it out from under the car. When the face was revealed, Jack sank to his knees. "Oh, my *god*," he moaned.

It was Tim Kinchloe, his glazed eyes staring straight up, his shirt drenched with blood from the gash that nearly separated his head from his torso.

Dani screamed: "Jack, she's here!"

"Robynn? Where?"

"Not Robynn!"

Jack looked past the car to see his wife standing there. Her left temple bore a nasty bruise, and in her right hand was a long, lethal knife, dripping crimson.

"Hello, darling," Elley said.

CHAPTER THIRTY-EIGHT

"Ma'am, drop the knife and put your hands up," Creeley said, leveling his gun at her heart. "You are under arrest."

Elley looked toward the policeman with an absent, and said, "Lick me, Smokey."

"I could shoot you right now and save the country the cost of a trial," Creeley said.

"You could do that, but if you did, how would Jack ever find out what happened to Robynn?"

"What have you done with her?" Jack demanded, his fists clenched so tightly that his nails dug into his palms.

"My guess is she's in the City Hall," the policeman said.

"Maybe, maybe not," Elley said, smirking. "But there is definitely something in there you should see."

"All right," Jack said, "we'll go inside."

"Wise choice," Elley responded. "Only choice, actually. And to prove my sincerity...." She dropped the bloody knife on the ground.

"I've still got this," Creeley said, gesturing with his gun.

"Woop-de-doo," Elley muttered, unconcerned. "What I've got is the knowledge of what's going to happen out here, and it doesn't involve those jugs. So drop them." No one made a move. "Or else," she added. Slowly, Creeley bent down and set his jug on the ground. Dani similarly left her jug on the ground, but Jack refused to drop his.

"I said drop the gasoline, Jack," Elley demanded.

Gasoline! Jack thought. *She doesn't know what's in here*!

"Fine," he said, desperately trying not to reveal his elation.

"I'm surprised the juice made it this far before Jacko drank it," Elley said. Then turning to Dani she added: "Or haven't you figured out yet, Hedwig, that Boytoy here is a barely functioning alcoholic?"

"Maybe someone drove him to it," Dani said.

Elley gave an unintelligible, mimicking response that sounded like Beaker from The Muppets. "Okay, let's go, kids," she added, turning and walking to the City Hall building. The three followed, but before they entered, Jack rushed to keep apace with his wife.

"Elley, I'm only going to say this once," he uttered. "I know you cannot be held entirely responsible for your actions. But if you have done anything to harm Robynn, I will kill you with my bare hands."

Elley Gorman Hayden ignored him.

The knob of the great brass door to the City hall building turned and the door slowly swung open, without any of them touching it. Then Elley, Jack, Dani and Creeley went inside.

* * * * * * *

Robynn had finally stopped crying, not because she was no longer scared, but because there were simply no tears left in her to come out. She was inside one of the small houses that were out in the woods, lying on the floor. Her mouth hurt because the handkerchief had been shoved inside it and she felt like throwing up, but managed to keep from doing so because she didn't want to keep tasting it on the cloth. Her chest ached from all the sobbing she had done while locked up in this house and she could feel the boogers running down from her nose. What really hurt were her wrists and feet, where she had been tied up. And she had to go pee. Robynn desperately tried to think of something happy, anything, like Dora the Explorer or Elmo, but the images would not pop into her mind. She couldn't cry out, she couldn't move, she was stuck in a strange, dark house, and worst of all, it was Mommy who brought her here.

I'm supposed to kill you, Mommy had said. *I should, too, but....* Then she said a bunch more words that Robynn didn't really understand, but it sounded like she was arguing with herself. Then Mommy tied her up. Robynn cried when she did so, and mommy stuck the handkerchief in her mouth, and then left.

Robynn whimpered when a brand new thought flooded her mind: she was stuck in the middle of the woods...what if a bear showed up and found her and wanted to eat her? Oyster Cracker was lying on the floor, but he couldn't protect her. She closed her eyes and squeezed them tight, hoping that when she opened them again it would all be just a bad dream. But deep down inside she knew better, and wondered what she had done to be punished like this.

That was when she heard a voice saying: "Who are you?"

Robynn opened her eyes and saw someone standing over her. It was a girl, a little older than herself, maybe a second grader, with long blond hair and a very plain blue dress. She looked sad.

Robynn tried to say something but could not, because of the gag.

"You must have done something *really* bad to get tied up," the blonde girl said.

Robynn shook her head forcefully. *I didn't!* she thought. *I didn't do anything that bad!*

"Here, let me help you," the girl said, walking around behind her. Robynn felt herself being lifted up to a sitting position, and pretty soon, the handkerchief that was all but choking her was taken away. "Take the ropes off," Robynn pleaded.

"I'm trying," the girl said, "but I'm not very good with knots."

It took a few minutes, but finally the girl had managed to get the ropes that were binding Robynn's arms and feet loose. She tried to stand up but felt dizzy, and sat back down.

"Who are you?" the girl asked.

"Robynn Lee Hayden," she answered. "Who are you?"

"My name's Victoria. I used to live here."

"I have to pee."

"There's a bathroom over there."

Robynn made it into the tiny bathroom, which was barely big enough for the tub, and closed the door. She sat down on the potty and tried very hard not to start sobbing while she peed. She didn't want to act like a baby in front of Victoria, who was nice and who had helped her. When she was finished she went back into the room where she had been tied.

Victoria was still there, but now she was holding Oyster Cracker, who Robynn had clung onto while her mommy had dragged her here.

"Hey, that's mine!" Robynn said.

"I know," Victoria said. "I just think it's neato. I've never seen a toy like this one. I have a dolly."

"I have lots of dollies."

"Really? I just have one."

Robynn didn't know any other kids who had just one toy. "His name is Oyster Cracker," she said.

"Oyster Cracker. That's funny."

"You really like him?"

"I think he's the cute."

Robynn thought very seriously, and then asked: "Do you want him?"

For the first time, a wide, beaming smile broke out on Victoria's face. "Really? You'd give him to me? Just like that?"

"Yeah. You let me loose."

"You're nice," the blonde girl said. "I wish I'd known you when I was alive."

Robynn did not know what to say, or even what to think. The girl in front of her certainly *looked* alive, but she said that she wasn't, and she did not seem like the kind of person who lied. Besides, Noni had come to her when she wasn't alive anymore.

Then with a small wave, Victoria vanished, like she had never been there, taking Oyster Cracker with her.

Robynn didn't want to be in this house anymore. She wanted to find Daddy. She walked outside and saw that there wasn't anybody standing around. Not even her mommy. She didn't really want to see her mommy anyway. Way off in the distance she could see Uncle Tim's car, but she knew that Uncle Tim wasn't going to help her. Not anymore. She was sad about that, but she wasn't sad in the same way she would have been if Mommy had killed Daddy.

Don't even think things like that about Daddy! she ordered herself.

Robynn knew there was a highway somewhere nearby. Maybe she could get to it and get out. Maybe somebody nice would pick her up and help her. She knew the road that ran through the woods would eventually lead to the highway, so she started down it. She really wished she still had Oyster Cracker for company, but Victoria really, really liked him. She wasn't sorry she'd given him away.

As she walked, it seemed like the forest was never going to end, and Robynn started to get scared. Maybe she should just turn around and go back to the house. Maybe another friendly ghost would show up and play with her. She stopped and turned around, surprised at how far she had walked already. But it seemed like there was so much more forest between here and the highway.

Robynn was about to take the first step back when she heard a sound that she'd heard lots of times before: it was Daddy's cell phone. But what was it doing out here in the woods? Following the sound, she finally came to a bunch of brush, and lifting part of it up with her hand, saw the three bottles, and the phone sitting next to them. She picked up the phone and pushed buttons until the ringing stopped, then said: "H'lo?"

"Hi, punkin!" a familiar voice said.

"Noni!" Robynn cried. "Noni, I miss you!"

"I miss you too, dear."

"Noni, something real bad happened to Uncle Tim."

There was a long sigh at the other end of the phone. "I know, Robynn, and I'm heartsick over it, because in a way it was my... well, never mind. Now we have to work to make sure that your daddy finishes the job he has to do, okay?"

"Okay."

"Your daddy is going to need your help, and it's not going to be easy, but I know you're a big strong girl. Do you see those big bottles hidden in the bushes?"

"Uh huh."

"You need to carry them back to the big white building past all the houses, the one that's made out of stone. You need to find a place to put them where they can't be seen, okay? You might have to make three trips, one for each bottle. It's really important that you do this. Okay?"

"'Kay."

"Can you pick them up?"

"Let me see," Robynn said, laying down the phone and reaching for a glass jug. It was awfully heavy, but she managed with both hands. Setting it back down, he picked the phone up again and told Noni, "It's *really* heavy, but I think I can do it."

"I know you can, punkin," Noni said. "So you hang up now and take those up to the building, and be very, very careful, all right?"

"All right."

"You still have my locket, right?"

"Uh huh." Robynn fingered it as she spoke.

"Good. Goodbye, punkin."

"Bye-bye, Noni." She tossed the phone to the ground and held the locket once again.

It seemed like it took forever for Robynn to get the first heavy jug of stuff all the way up to the white building since she had to stop and put it down and rest every so many yards, but she made it, setting it down at the front of the steps, just like Noni had told her to do. Then she went back. By the time she had gotten back to the hiding place, she was tired and sweaty, but most of all thirsty. She should have gotten a drink while she was in the bathroom of that strange house, but she hadn't been as thirsty then. As she pulled out the second jug she looked at it closely. It looked just like water, and it had a screw-top cap on, like the kind on the orange juice bottles, which she was able to open on her own.

And she was *so* thirsty.

CHAPTER THIRTY-NINE

Dani Lindstrom stared at the painted wall, speechless.

"Motherfuck," Rob Creeley muttered as he surveyed the mural, which was now completely uncovered, its vibrant wet colors—mostly reds, browns and greens—glistening in the dim light.

Jack Hayden saw that the painting was different than the last time he had seen it. In one corner was a scene of an angry mob armed with pitchforks, torches, and a tar barrel, storming the front of a building labeled *Photography*. Jack had a good idea whose shop it was, and also had a pretty good idea that the image was placed there as a warning to Jack, that this was just a taste of what happened to people who crossed Legion.

Lower down, the abattoir scene was gone, though the image of Marcus Broarty remained. He was no longer butchering Egon McMenamin, as Jack had seen earlier; now he was with Robynn. The two figures were in a depicted in a grassy, weedy area, and both were naked. Broarty was wearing an expression of demented joy as he sodomized the girl. Robynn's face was shown in anguish, her mouth stretched so wide in terror that blood was coming from her scar.

Jack turned his head away and swore.

"Fun stuff, hey kids?" Elley said with a smirk.

"How can you—?" Jack couldn't finish.

"She can because she knows it's not true," Dani said. "She knows the mural is lying."

"Think so, Hedwig?" Elley said. "How about that, then?"

She pointed to a particular corner of the painting which showed Dani and Randy Mount. Dani looked at her painted self taking Mount's penis inside her.

"That never happened," Dani said.

"Oh?" Elley said. "You know that for a fact?"

Dani had been unconscious when Mount undressed her and climbed on top of her. For all she knew, he might have stuck his miserable thing inside her. In fact, the thought that he might have done more than simply ejaculate on her stomach had quietly haunted her, even though there was no proof one way or the other. It was the uncertainty that tormented her. Then, miraculously, the uncertainty disappeared, and she knew. She knew.

She snapped her head sideways to face Elley, brushing a wisp of her white hair over her ear. She wore a triumphant expression. "I was wrong," she said. "The mural isn't simply lying to us, it's visualizing our fears. I don't know exactly what that bastard did to me, so the mural is presenting me with my worst case scenario, hoping I'll succumb to the fear that that is what happened. And it's the same for you, Jack, you were afraid your boss had done something to Robynn, so the picture is showing you the most horrible possibility. But it didn't really happen."

Slowly, reluctantly, Jack turned back to face the mural. The image was still there, in all its grotesque horror, but the colors now seemed a bit muted.

"What about you, Cree?" Dani asked. "I don't see your picture in the mural at all."

"You're right, I'm not there," Creeley answered, "but my wife is. That's her there." He pointed to the painted image of a dark-haired woman going down on the priest. "I recognize the priest, too: Father Mendes. Maria has been seeing a lot of him lately. She visits him often."

"Have you been concerned that something was going on between them?" Dani asked.

"Not concerned, exactly."

"Just a lingering fear that attacks you late at night and won't let you sleep, like some kind of virus, and there's nothing you can do about it short of coming out and asking your wife if she's cheating on you," Jack said.

"She wouldn't cheat on me!" Creeley said with some heat.

"I know that, Cree. I also know this damned painting is playing us like violins. That journal we read from Althea's old boyfriend talked about how the mural revealed deep dark secrets, the kind that you'd almost kill to keep hidden. That was their greatest fears, Howard and his friend, that those secrets would be revealed. My guess is that none of us have anything in our backgrounds quite that bad, so the damned thing is preying upon our fears of the things we *don't* know."

Elley began clapping her hands slowly, sarcastically. "Isn't Jack a clever boy? Don't get the idea that you're winning, any of you, because you haven't seen anything yet."

"The only thing I want to see is my daughter," Jack said. "You said she was in here."

"I said nothing of the sort," Elley replied. "Your friend Sheriff Lobo said she was in here. All I said is there was something in here you should see."

"*Where is she, goddammit?*" Jack roared.

"You'll just have to find her, won't you, lover?"

All at once Jack was so sick of her voice that he wanted to choke her. *But that's what it wants,* he thought a moment later; *that's how it works. The evil, the mural, Legion, whatever form it takes, did not actually harm people itself. It got people to harm each other, or themselves. If he lost it and choked her, the painted depiction of it would appear immediately in the mural. Don't give in to it.*

"Besides, Jack, I don't know why you're so worried about Robynn now," Elley said, her voicing digging into him like a homemade shiv, "you're the one who let her go off with a stranger. Who knows what he might have done to, or with her? A single man in his mid-thirties...hmmm. If you really cared for Robynn you would have called my mother to come and get her."

"Your *mother?*" Jack cried. "Please! When has the great

and social Lois Eunie Gorman ever shown that she cared about anything, except...oh, my god...your mother's maiden name was *Morgan*, wasn't it? Jesus, it works both ways."

"Ladies and gentlemen, Jack's mind has left the building," Elley taunted.

"You don't even know, do you?" Jack went on. "You're stuck in the middle of this, about as deep as it's possible to get, and you don't even know why. You have no idea the true nature of your mother. My god, that's why Igee has such a grip on you! That's why he's been able to turn you into such a monster. You were *born* into Legion and you don't even know it!"

"What are you babbling about?"

"Your mother's name! I don't even need to work it out on paper to know that Lois Eunie Morgan is an anagram of Our Name is Legion! She's one of them. She's always been one of them."

"Oh, go fuck yourself," Elley spat, but with considerably less assurance than she had exhibited minutes earlier.

"Look, dammit," Creeley broke in, "we came in here because you led us to believe the girl was here, but she isn't, which means she's somewhere out there, so I'm going to go look for her. But first, I'm going to have to deal with you. Put your hands behind your back, ma'am." He slipped his handcuffs off of his belt.

"Whatever you say, officer," Elley said meekly, slowing putting her hands behind her. Then in a lightning move, she whipped her hand right back around, now holding the .38 that had been tucked in the back of her pants and covered by her shirt, and rapidly fired three shots at Creeley before he could even move.

With a scream of pain and shock, the policeman went down on the hard, cold marble floor.

"What kind of a moron cop doesn't even pat down the suspect?" Elley sneered. "You bozos are making this entirely too easy."

* * * * * * *

The loud *bangs* that came from the inside of the white building scared Robynn so much that she nearly dropped the second jug of liquid on the stone steps. But at the last minute she managed to catch it, standing still, breathing hard, and listening to the liquid inside slosh back and forth. She knew that if she had dropped and broken it, it would have been bad.

She knew that because back at the hiding spot, when she realized how thirsty she was, she had started to unscrew the cap to this jug. Just as it was loosening, she heard a man's voice command, *No*! She whirled around to see who was behind her, but there was nobody there. She looked around in the woods, but didn't see anyone. Then looking down at the jug, which had fallen over on the ground, but had not come uncapped, she watched the liquid swirl around until it appeared to form a shape. It was an image she had seen before, and one that always scared her: a skull with crossed bones underneath. She only saw it for a moment before it disappeared, but she knew what it meant, since several of the bottles that Hortensia used to clean their house had that same picture. The stuff inside the jug was poison.

If she had dropped and broken the glass bottle when she heard the bang sound, then the poison would have gotten out and she might have gotten some on her. Carefully, she set the jug down next to the first one, which she had hidden behind a stone railing where it couldn't be seen, just like Noni had asked. Then she sat down on the steps. Robynn was tired. This was a really silly thing to be doing, but Noni wanted her to do it. But she was still really thirsty. She thought she remembered which house she had been tied up in, and headed for it so she could get a drink out of the sink before going back for the third bottle.

Walking to the front of the little house, she went up to the door and pushed it open. This was the place, all right. The ropes were still in the middle of the room, and so was that handkerchief that had covered her mouth. Robynn walked past them all on her way to the tiny bathroom, and once there, she turned on the cold water started cupping handfuls of it into her mouth, slurping it up until she was no longer thirsty. There was no towel anywhere to wipe her wet hands on, so she just wiped them on her pants. But there was, a small mirror above the sink, which Robynn wasn't tall enough to see into. That was frustrating because Robynn liked looking at herself. She had that thing on her lip that other kids, even other grownups, didn't have. She thought it must be something special, since no one else had it. She tried standing on her tiptoes, but all she could as she looked up into the mirror was the very top of her head.

Maybe if she stepped back.

Robynn took a step back, keeping her eyes on the mirror, and slowly, step by step, her reflection came into view. She had backed herself all the way up against the wall. The room was dark, so she didn't have a good look at herself, but it was enough. She smiled, showing off her front teeth, and waved at herself. Having satisfied both her thirst and her desire to see herself, Robynn was about to take off and get the third jug when noise coming from outside the bathroom made her freeze in place.

She looked in the mirror again, and this time saw a figure coming right up beside her. It was a man.

* * * * * * *

Jack had not even thought for a second before he launched himself at Elley and football-tackled her to the floor. Had he, he probably would not have tried it. Jack Hayden may be a lot of things, but he never really considered hero to be on the list. Then again, physically assaulting a woman carrying several less inches and thirty fewer pounds probably would not qualify it for a future list. Elley's right elbow had made a sickening thud as she hit the floor and her gun flew out of her hand, skittered across the polished surface and ended somewhere against a wall. Jack had rolled her roughly onto her stomach and sat on her back while he twisted her arms behind her. Had her elbow been broken, she would have screamed much more loudly than she did. She bucked like a bronco as he held her arms tight and screamed to Dani, "Get the handcuffs!" Dani rushed to the fallen policeman and retrieved the cuffs, and while Jack continued to hold tight the wrists of his screaming wife, Dani fastened on the cuffs.

"*I'll fucking kill you!*" Elley was screaming, as Jack got off of her.

"Like you did Cree?" he spat back.

"I don't kill that easy, Jack," the policeman said in a weak voice.

"Thank god!" Dani cried as she ran toward him to examine his wounds. Either Elley had not intended to kill him or she didn't know what she was doing with the gun, because only two of the bullets seemed to connect at all; one had torn past his shoulder, ripping his shirt and drawing blood, but only as a flesh wound, while the other had lodged in his abdomen. "Jack, he's still hurt pretty badly," she said. "We have to get him out of here."

"Let's just do what we came here to do and then find the girl and get the hell out," the policeman said, his voice tinged with pain.

Jack, meanwhile, had removed his belt and used it to strap Elley's feet together, so she could not rise. Then he managed to get enough of a handful of her hair to yank her head back uncomfortably. "I'll give you one more chance to tell me where my daughter is," he said.

"Fuck...*you!*" she panted.

"Jack, for the first time we've got the advantage," Creeley called out in a pain-soaked voice. "Get the damned jugs and take care of the mural. If it's destroyed, maybe she'll turn back normal, and then you can ask her where the girl is."

Jack took a moment to let that sink in. "Right, okay." He let Elley's head go. She groaned as it snapped downward, her forehead nearly hitting the floor, and whispered, "Cocksucker." Jack stood up and told Dani to get one of the guns, either Elley's or Creeley's. "Then you come here and keep her covered. If she looks like she's going to get loose enough to get up, shoot her in the knee. I'll go get the acid and come back."

"*Acid*?" Elley screamed.

"That's right, *lover*," Jack spat. "Not gasoline, acid. We're not going to try and ignite that monstrosity. We're going to sizzle it right off the wall!"

Elley started ranting madly, spitting threats and thrashing on the floor, and Jack ignored her as he moved to the heavy metal doors of the building. Pulling them open, he started out, but then stopped dead. Carl Dorgan was standing there, just outside, a shotgun in his hands, its barrels pointed straight at Jack's chest, a look of stone cold hatred on his face.

"Carl, it's okay, we've subdued her, you can put the gun down," Jack said, but Dorgan refused to lower the gun. He forced Jack to walk back into the building. "Carl, what the hell's wrong with you?"

"Deputy," Creeley called weakly as soon as he saw him, "drop the weapon now."

"I have a gun, too," Dani called out. "Drop the rifle or I'll fire."

"Lady, before you even had the chance to aim I could blow this bastard's heart clear out of his chest with one barrel, and yours with the other one," Dorgan replied. "You don't think I can, then try me."

"He's right," Creeley said. "Don't test him. Carl, what's wrong with you?"

"He's under the same sort of control that's affected all of us and made us do things we normally wouldn't," Jack said. "What is it, Carl? What did they show you to make you do this? Whatever it is, it's a lie."

"I know what I saw on that videotape," Dorgan said, "the whole sick, filthy thing!"

"We don't know what you're talking about!" Dani cried.

Dorgan swung the gun around to face her and barked: "Don't get smart with me, lady!"

"Jack, grab the gun!" she cried, but Jack was not quick enough. For such a large man, Dorgan was fast. He whipped the barrels around so rapidly that he caught Jack in the side and knocked him to the floor.

Dani screamed.

"Carl, you have to listen to me," Jack panted painfully.

"The hell I do!" the policeman roared. "You stated your case on that videotape, you rat bastard! You sent me the goddamn camera you shot it with! Don't think I didn't examine it either. It had a tag with your name on it, Hayden!"

"Oh, Christ, my camcorder," Jack said. "Someone stole it from my truck. Carl, you have to believe me."

"I believe my own eyes," Dorgan growled, leveling both barrels straight into Jack's face. Behind them, Elley started laughing.

"For Christ's sake, listen to me!" Jack hollered, slowly rising, his hands held defensively in front of him. "I taped the mural with my camcorder. That's what was on the tape. I don't know what the mural has shown you or what it's saying that we did, but it's a lie! The mural is part of Legion!" Jack stopped then, having suddenly realized just what it was that had been seeded in the Officer's brain. "This has something to do with your son, doesn't it?"

"You know goddamned well it does! You killed him, you and the girl! But killing him in a normal way wasn't enough, was it? Just taking the life of a developmentally disabled kid wasn't a high enough kick for you, was it? You had to...to...*Christ.*"

Dorgan looked like he was going to break down and cry.

"Listen to me, Carl," Jack said. "You're a good cop. You have to use reason and logic to do your job. Why on earth would any of us want to hurt your son? What would be our motive?"

"You're sick, that's why," Dorgan said, but his voice was weakening.

"Okay, fine, let's use that hypothesis, Dani and I are demented psycho killers. Why would we be so stupid as to videotape ourselves committing the crime? Even if we did, why would we send you the tape? Not only the tape, but the camcorder?"

"Some criminals want to get caught."

From the floor, Elley said: "And you have caught them, officer. They are maniacs. Look what they've done to me? Nobody can help your boy now, but you can help me. Free me so I can get away from here, and then you can do whatever you want to them. Or kill them first, I don't care."

Dorgan's eyes narrowed, but he made no move to remove her cuffs.

"Carl, reason this through," Jack said. "How did you get this tape? Was it delivered? Was there a drop of wet paint on it? And did it tell you where to find us?"

"Damn," Carl Dorgan said, lowering his shotgun. "Goddammit to hell."

"Thank god," Jack panted. "I know all this is hard to accept, but you have to believe us. It's the mural that's doing this, or what's in the mural."

"Don't fall for his lies, officer!" Elley shouted. "How can a painting do anything to anyone? They're the ones doing this!"

"Carl, what did that tape show you?" Jack pleaded.

Carl Dorgan looked twenty years older than when he had stepped inside the building. "It showed you and the girl throwing acid all over my boy until he was...."

Elley looked momentarily startled, and then shouted: "Yes! You see? The proof of their guilt is right outside! Three jugs filled with acid, the same stuff they used on Kevin! They were planning to use it on me, too, until you came in."

Wearing an inscrutable expression on his weathered face, Carl Dorgan stepped to her and knelt down. He unlocked the cuffs.

"Thank you," Elley panted, sitting up. "Now arrest them."

"No," Dorgan said, pointing the shotgun barrels at her head. "Not until you tell me how you knew my boy's name was Kevin."

"I heard Jack say it," Elley replied quickly.

"Carl, I never knew your son's name," Jack said. "You never told it to me. When you showed me his picture, all you said was my youngest."

"You're not going to believe him, are you?" Elley cried.

"I am," Dorgan said, "because he's right. I never told him my boy's name." Then he dropped the shotgun again. "Jesus Lord, what have I done?"

"It's okay, Carl, no one's hurt," Jack said. "You didn't do anything bad."

"The hell I didn't. Those jugs out there...."

"They really are filled with acid, Carl. We're going to burn that thing off the wall and end this nightmare once and for all."

"No you won't," Dorgan said, looking again like he was about to cry. "I broke 'em."

Creeley moaned.

"Hell, I saw those bottles in that goddamned videotape. I saw what the acid did to my boy. At least I thought I did. When I saw those jugs sitting there, I threw 'em against the trees and watched the stuff sizzle down."

"All three jugs, Carl?" Jack asked.

"There was more than three. I found 'em in a couple different places—"

"Oh, god," Dani moaned. "The reserves, too."

"Damn it, chief, I...." Now Deputy Carl Dorgan did break down in tears.

"*I've always felt a man's tears were a sign of weakness,*" said a voice that filled the entire building. All of them looked around for the source of the voice, but it was Dani who first discovered it.

"My god, the mural's *alive!*" she cried.

All of the painted figures now seemed to be moving, or at least pulsating, as though they were live figures trying to hold their poses and not doing a very good job of it. In the very middle, though, was the figure of a man who, even though rendered in pigment in a stylized art fashion, was moving like a character in an animated cartoon. His dark hair was bushed up on top and his eyes were black pits. In one hand was a paintbrush and in the other a palette.

"Louis Norman Igee," Jack said, and the figure smiled and bowed.

CHAPTER FORTY

"It's just one more illusion," Jack said, watching the figures in the mural writhe and move. "Like all the others."

"There you're quite wrong," Igee said. "In the confines of my life's work, I'm as real as I've ever been."

"Right, I remember now. Howard's journal theorized that your spirit entered the mural, even as your body burnt to a crisp on this floor. And if that's so, that means you can't leave the mural, either, except as an illusion. You're stuck there."

"But my powers remain formidable, I think you'll agree."

"Your supernatural powers, arguably. But your artistic powers are dog crap."

There was a momentary flash of anger from Igee, revealed by his skin tone's sudden flush, but then it passed. "A good try, Mr. Hayden, but that sort of thing will no longer work. You see, I believe in learning from my enemies, and what I have learned from you is that *you* will try to goad *me*. You think it is the only power you have over me. I, on the other hand, have many, many powers over you. It is my power that has kept this mural alive all these years. I confess that I did not plan it that way. It was through Lenore that I first discovered the possibilities, but I am not displeased with the results.

"Who's Lenore?" Jack asked.

"Really, Mr. Hayden," Igee said. "Surely you remember Lenore Imaginous...my muse." Igee's painted image smoothly glided across the mural until he came to the figure of a woman. She had red hair and features that Jack did indeed know well.

It was the woman from the Saddleback Inn and the photograph in his motel bathroom. It was the face he had first seen in a flash through the lens of his digital camera several days and a seeming lifetime ago.

The painted form of Lenore Imaginous winked at Jack and smiled.

"She was the first to actually enter the mural. Others followed. Many others. And there will be many more to come."

"Jack, I think Cree's in trouble," Dani suddenly shouted. Without any warning, Dorgan tossed the shotgun to Jack, who managed barely to catch it, and raced to the prone figure of Rob Creeley.

"He's lost a lot of blood," Dorgan said, putting an old, soiled handkerchief over his gut wound. "We gotta get him out of here."

"Quite out of the question," Igee stated.

Dorgan stood up with surprising speed and forcefulness and began walking toward the mural. "Goddammit to hell, I'm sick and tired of this!" he shouted. "I've taken orders on behalf of my flag, and I've taken orders from commanding officers who didn't have the brains God gave a mule, and to my eternal shame, I even started to take orders from a goddamned video-tape. But I've never taken orders from a painted pissant on a goddamn wall, and I'm not about to start now! So shove your opinions up your ass!" Turning his back on the mural, he went back to Creeley and started to pull him to his feet. "Let's get you the hell out of this nuthouse," he said.

"No, Carl, leave me be," Creeley moaned, and Dorgan set him down again. Keeping his voice quiet, the chief went on: "Go out there and find Jack's girl. She's out there somewhere. Don't worry about me." Dorgan turned back to the mural, and saw Igee laugh.

"Go ahead, go get the brat," he said. "Bring her in her. You might as well all be together for the final defeat."

"Screw you," Jack said. "I'm not conceding anything."

"Oh, of course not," Elley said. "You never concede to

anything, not your dead-end job, not your personal failure, not your drinking. You've always lived in Jackland, haven't you? A place where there is no problems that can't be solved with a twelve pack and a promise to do better, someday."

"Maybe I have, Elley," Jack said, glaring at her, unable to stop his tears. "Maybe I am a loser who's taken the easy way out whenever possible and drunk too much and pissed away the years that I could have used to make a success of myself. Maybe everything you've ever said about me is true. But this isn't about me."

"Oh, but it is," Igee's figure said, "It *is* about you now, particularly how you are about to lose everything." Igee smiled and at once, all of the painted forms from the mural, even the animals, turned their heads and looked straight at Jack. Broarty's painted image looked at him with a particularly violent hatred, and behind Broarty, staring into his soul, was Lenore. Slowly they turned their gaze to Dani and then Dorgan and Creeley, as though surveying the room around them. "It's Judgment Day, ladies and gentlemen," Igee said with a laugh, and in unison, all the figures—men, women, children, those close to the imaginary proscenium of the painting, and those far away on the horizon line, began to move, to shamble, to enlarge, to come closer.

"Carl," Creeley said, "go find the girl, but don't bring her in here. Take her away."

"But—"

"That's an order, deputy."

"Don't bother, officer," Igee's figure said. "The truth is the girl is dead."

"No," Jack tried to say.

"Oh, yes. Thanks to her mother."

Jack looked at Elley with black hatred. He took a step toward her and raised Dorgan's shotgun, holding every intention of blowing her brains out, but Elley looked at him and slowly shook her head. She did not do it with a smirk or any other indication of arrogance. She did it the way they used to silently communicate in the better days of their marriage. Jack stopped and examined her face, and saw her mouth, *I didn't*. He stepped back, and as he did, Dorgan wrenched the shotgun out of his hands.

"I'll do it," Dorgan said. "If someone's got to go down for murder, it'll be me."

"Carl—" Jack began.

"No, this is all my fault! If I hadn't broken those five goddamn jugs that girl would still be alive, and this would be over by now!" He leveled the shotgun at Elley.

"*Carl, wait!*" Creeley shouted so loudly that a jet of blood spurted from his midriff. "How many jugs did you break?"

"All of 'em. Five."

"Jesus!" Jack cried. "Carl, there were *six* jugs! One's still out there. And so is Robynn. There's still hope!"

"I told you, the girl is dead," Igee said.

Jack's eyes locked on Elley's. "I don't believe it."

"Then tell them," Igee instructed her.

Elley looked back and forth from Jack to Igee, then bowed her head. "I know what you wanted me to do," she said, finally, "but I'm still her mother, for god's sake. I didn't kill her. I left her tied up in one of the houses to keep her out of the way."

Hot anger flared from Louis Norman Igee's painted face, which was looking at Elley. "*I told you to kill her!*" he roared. "*You deliberately disobeyed my orders!*"

"She's my child," Elley moaned. "She's not yours to kill!"

"But you are," Igee said.

"Elley," Jack said, starting toward her, but coming to a halt when the arms of the figures closest to the front of the painting broke through the surface of the mural. They were now emerging from the wall, dripping wet with colors. "Good god...."

"Carl, get out of here!" Creeley shouted again. "Find the acid and find the girl!" He felt weak from the exertion. This time Dorgan sprinted for the front entrance, but the heavy brass doors refused to open for him. He pulled on them as hard as he could, and then tried pushing, but they held fast. "Can't get it open!" he said.

"Use the window," Creeley ordered. Dorgan took up his rifle and trained it on the window in front of the building, then fired and blew to atoms. He found it was just large enough to let him through, and after carefully hoisting himself up so as not to cut himself on the glass shards, he leapt through.

"He won't get far," Igee commented, but his face showed displeasure at the escape.

The first row of figures were now completely through the surface of the mural and were freestanding on the floor, drizzling red paint on the marble surface that was indistinguishable from the blood seeping out of Rob Creeley. Jack and Dani backed up until they were next to Creeley. "We can all get out through the window," Jack said. "We'll carry you."

"No, Jack, you and Dani get out of here while you can," the policeman said. "I'd only slow you down. Just leave me here."

"Like hell," Jack said.

The figures started toward the three of them, but then stopped suddenly, as if reacting to a silent command. In perfect unison, the heads of the figures turned toward the right and set their gazes on Elley. Then they started to shuffle towards her.

"What are they doing?" Dani cried.

"They're going for Elley," Jack said.

Seeing the figures coming closer, reaching for her, Elley screamed: "Get them away from me, dammit!"

"Nobody escapes Judgment Day, my darling," Igee said.

Elley screamed as the painted forms bodily picked her up from the floor, drenching her in running colors in the process. "What are you doing to me?"

"I was going to kill you, I admit it," Igee said. "But I've changed my mind. I've decided to give you eternal life in here with me."

Elley was now so completely covered with paint from head to foot that she looked no different from the moving figures, but she continued to scream as the figures dragged her back toward the wall. When they got close enough, Igee himself pulled her bodily into the mural. Once there, she no longer screamed and her hands were no longer bound behind her, the handcuffs having melted away like running pigment, but the look of trapped agony and fear on her now-painted face was so extreme that Jack had to turn away.

The army of figures was now shuffling toward the rest of them slowly, quietly, wetly. "Cree," Jack said, "we have to get you up and out of here. Help me, Dani." Dani, however, was too horrified by the sight of the approaching nightmare army to do anything but stand and shake. "*Dani!*" Jack shouted, but she refused to snap out of it. *She's in shock*, he thought.

Somehow, he had to get them both out.

Jack lunged for Dani and yanked her out of the way of the first wave of reaching arms, and pushed her against the wall. He'd have to pick her up and shove her head-first through the window, and she would probably come out of it with her mid section cut up like an onion from the glass. But was that really worse that what was going to happen to them if they stayed? Jack picked her up like a baby and had started to lift her to the window, when he heard the voice outside.

"Anybody still in there?" Carl Dorgan was calling.

"Yes!" Jack called.

"Here, take this!" Dorgan said, and Jack saw a jug of acid being thrust toward him.

Jack quickly set Dani back down, grabbed the jug and uncapped it. Jack had never really had any experience with sulfuric acid so he was not prepared for the acrid smell, which hit his sinuses like a prizefighter's jab. Taking a chance, he sloshed a little on the closest figure to him, and watched with satisfaction as it bubbled and melted away. A slight trace of sulfur odor replaced the acid scent.

Just like the Wicked Witch of the West!

The other figures stopped, and Jack couldn't tell if they were repelled by the odor of the liquid, or the realization that it was lethal, or by another unheard command. He took a step closer and sloshed a little more, hitting three figures—two men and a woman—each of which began to bubble.

The crowd now started backing up. Behind them, the figure of Louis Norman Igee was displaying a cartoonish expression of rage. Jack expected to see painted smoke coming out of his ears, and just the thought of that brought up a laugh from deep within him. But once that was finished, he realized he probably did not have enough acid left to destroy the entire mural. Maybe if he could get the figure of Igee, the rest of the painting would go with him. He splashed a little on each figure in front of him, and before long they were all but stampeding back into the mural! "*Cowards!*" Igee shouted, but still they fled, pushing past him.

Jack stood as close to the wall as he dared, given the probable splash back, and got ready to throw the acid on Louis Norman Igee. But before he could, the painted figure with lightning speed reached out and grabbed the figure of Elley and pulled it in front of him.

"Who's the coward now?" Jack asked.

"She dies if you throw that!"

"She's dead already," Jack said.

"No, she's not," Igee said. "I can send her back. Her soul is still intact."

"Such as it is."

"If you throw that acid, you will be killing your wife, not me."

Jack stood there, his mind spinning like a CD that wouldn't play, his breath short and harsh. Was Igee telling the truth? Would he really be killing Elley? Everything she had done had been done under the control of this monster of Legion. If he could get her back and destroy Igee, then she would be free of him.

God, he wanted a drink!

"*Jack,*" the figure of Elley moaned from the painting, her voice faraway and distorted. "*Give it to me.*" With a sudden thrust she wrenched her right arm free of Igee's grip and reached through the painting. Jack yelled and stepped back, but not out of Elley's reach. She grabbed the jug from him and, with her arm still protruding out from the wall, swung it forcefully against the mural, just over her head, where Igee's face was now visible. The jug shattered and Jack leapt back to avoid an acid shower. Igee took the full force of the liquid. His mouth as wide as the entrance to Hell, but no sound came out. The painted skin on his face boiled and then dissolved, leaving only bare plaster and a gag-inducing stench of sulfur. The acid then spread downward to Elley.

Even as she was being burned by the liquid, the figure of Elley Gorman Hayden managed to raise her head to face Jack. She tried to speak, but could not. She mouthed a word. Jack wasn't sure, but he thought it might have been *Robynn*.

Then she was gone; melted away.

All of the figures around them stopped moving, like as though a film had suddenly freeze framed. The colors on the wall began to fade, the wetness began to dry, and the figures now appeared aged and cracked. Bit at a time, little pieces of ancient paint flaked off and fell to the floor, as the mural began to collapse. Light streamed into the interior from the now-opened doors.

Jack staggered backwards, exhausted, and stumbled into Dorgan. "You okay, Jack?" the officer asked.

"Yeah. Yeah, I'm okay. But now we have to find Robynn."

"She's right outside, Jack. She was the one who led me to the last jug of acid. She's the one who saved all of us."

Jack raced through the doors and saw his daughter was standing at the base of the steps. "Daddeeeee!" she cried.

"I'm here, punkin!" he cried, leaping down to her and picking her up in a tight embrace.

"Daddy, I was so worried!"

"Me too, punkin, but everything's okay now."

"What about Mommy?"

Jack sighed and held her tighter. "Mommy's not okay, honey," he said. "Mommy's gone."

"She changed, Daddy," the girl said. "She wasn't like Mommy. But I don't want her to be gone." She began to cry.

"I know, punkin, I know. I don't want her to be gone either."

Robynn rubbed her runny nose on Jack's shoulder.

"I met another girl, Daddy. Her name is Victoria. She was a ghost. She untied me."

Jack felt chilled, but he kept listening as Robynn went on to tell him how Uncle Tim had suddenly appeared in the bathroom of the house. At first she was scared, but when she saw it was Uncle Tim she was okay. Then he told her that she needed to wake up and get that last big glass bottle that Noni had told her she needed to bring up to the building, so that the big policeman could come out and get them. "And you know what, Daddy?" she went on. "Until Uncle Tim told me I had to wake up, I didn't even know I was asleep."

Jack was still hugging her tightly when Dorgan rushed outside. "We have to get them out of here, Jack," he said. "The whole place is breaking up in there."

"I have to put you down, punkin'," Jack said, "but don't move. I'll be right back."

He accompanied Dorgan back inside and that Creeley had been propped up against the wall, and looked barely conscious, and Dani was sitting next to him, still in shock. "I've radioed for backup and an ambulance already," Dorgan said. "But we have to move them. Look."

The wall that had once contained the mural was now flaking and crumbling onto the marble floor. At that moment a loud cracking sound came from the ceiling, and both men jumped back as a chunk of plaster fell down. "It's reverting to ruins," Jack said. "We've got only a minute or so." Dorgan handled Creeley and Jack took Dani, who was as easy to lead around as a child, and ran outside where Robynn was waiting for them. A siren could be heard in the distance. "Head for the highway, stick to the road, and be careful," Jack said. "You going to make it, Cree?"

The chief's good arm was draped around Dorgan's shoulders, and his face was ashen and sweaty, but he smiled and asked: "You know of a better option, Jack?"

Behind them another crack came, this one louder, and the entire roof of the City hall caved in. As quickly as possible with an injured man, a little girl and a woman in shock, they raced down the roadway, listening to the destruction behind them. Each building and house of Wood City, as they passed them, would give way and fall in on themselves, leaving nothing but rubble.

When they passed one of the last ruined houses, Creeley suddenly cried out: "Shit, there's a baby over there!"

Jack looked over, but recognized the house in question. "No, Cree, don't worry," he said. "It's a doll. I saw it days ago."

"It's Victoria's!" Robynn said. "She said she had a doll! And look, there's Oyster Cracker!" The girl pointed at the remnants of the building, and Jack saw the ruined toy he had bought for his daughter only days before, once plush and furry, but now threadbare, sodden and leaking stuffing, destroyed by exposure to the elements for seventy-five years.

"I love her, Daddy," Robynn said. "I love Victoria."

"Then I love her too, punkin," Jack said, taking his daughter's hand and running away.

By the time they got back to Rob Creeley's truck, where they were greeted by paramedics, police and firemen, Wood City was dead. Jack Hayden silently prayed Wood City would stay that way.

EPILOGUE
SEVEN YEARS FROM TODAY

"Jack, what are you doing?" Dani called from the other room, while Jack Hayden scanned the headlines on his iLynk. *Child porn scandal forces candidate from race*, the top one read, and Jack clicked on it. "Good morning, Jack," said a pleasant looking hologramic woman whose face appeared on the tiny screen, "here is the story you ordered. A spokesman for Senator Matt Comingore's campaign committee confirmed that the candidate will drop his bid for the White House in the wake of the scandal that resulted from the senator's attempt to buy child pornography from an undercover FBI agent. Comingore is expected to make the official announcement before the week is out. Sources close to the senator deny that he has been placed on a personal suicide watch by family and friends. Our iLynk poll, taken early this morning, confirms that only fourteen percent of users feel that Comingore should retain his Senate seat during the course of the investigation, while eighty-six percent believe that he should be expelled immediately."

The face on the screen now switched to that of a middle-aged, gray-haired man who was identified in a crawl as *User docjay*. "I simply do not understand the constant stream of these scandals from the rich and powerful," the man declared to the camera. "They know the world is watching, what on earth could make them do something this blatantly stupid?"

Jack knew what on earth only too well.

He switched the pod off as Dani came into the room. "Are

you just ignoring me?" she asked.

Jack looked up at her and smiled. Her new hair shade of strawberry blonde suited her extremely well, better than the light brown she'd been wearing. "You know I wouldn't ignore you."

"Then help me with the invitations. Who do you want to invite from your office?"

Jack thought for a minute. Dan Killough, would be expecting an invitation, and even though a little bit of Dan went a long way, it was the politic thing to do. Frankly, Dan had been more responsible than Jack had for the success of Prestige Construction Engineering, which Jack had struggled to form out of the ashes of Crane Commercial Building Engineering after Crain had completely imploded, once the revelations came out about how much Marc Broarty had been dirty-dealing clients. Dan was a go-getter with sharp business acumen, but also the kind of hyper-drive personality that wore Jack out even after short periods of time. Of course Yolanda, one of the few carry-overs from Crane, and her husband Ramón, would be invited too, but Jack didn't know how many others to include. Then there was Rob Creeley and Carl Dorgan, with whom he had kept in touch over the last seven years, but they weren't part of the office. Besides, Cree and Maria's second child was only a couple of months old, so he might not be able to make the trip. This was getting complicated. "I may have to get back to you on that," he told Dani.

"Don't take too long," she said. "The wedding's only a month away."

"I know."

Dani sat down next to him. "Jack, forgive me for asking this, but I have to. You really *do* want to get married, don't you?"

"Of course I do," he said. "Why wouldn't I?"

"It's just that you've really been in a fog lately, almost like you're deliberately putting things off."

Jack put his arm around her and she rested her head on his shoulder. "Sorry," he said. "I don't mean to. But the reason we're able to get married in the first place is weighing me down a little."

Dani squeezed his hand. Having to wait until Elley, who officially had vanished and was presumed dead, could be declared legally so by the courts, had not been easy for her, either. At least Lois Eunie Gorman's ongoing persecution of Jack over Elley's disappearance had come to an end after Lois had been killed in a freak highway accident involving a paint truck.

The front door of the house banged open and Robynn bolted in. "Hi, Dad," she called out before coming into the living room. Seeing the two of them on the couch, she wrinkled her nose and said, "Jeez, you two. Get a room!"

"I refuse to apologize," Jack said.

"Me too," Dani added. "So there."

Robynn rolled her eyes dramatically and then bounded into the kitchen.

"She's so grown up," Dani said.

Jack nodded. She was beautiful, too. Robynn's had undergone reconstructive surgery two years ago and while it had left the tiniest trace of a line on her lip, you really had to look for it.

Robynn came back into the room munching on an apple. "By the way, I talked to Ronni at school and she said her father would be happy to stream the wedding."

"Okay, good," Jack said. Turning to Dani, he added: "See? That's one thing I got accomplished."

"One down, thirty-five billion to go," she replied. Dani wanted to ask Jack if it would bother him if she had champagne at the ceremony, but that was a question for later, when they were alone.

"Hey, maybe I could take pictures," Robynn said. "I've got that camera."

"Have you tried it yet?" Jack asked. "That was the thing I was using back when—" He didn't finish. It was the camera he had used for the whole Wood City episode, but he didn't want to risk any trigger words. Robynn had emerged from the nightmare with no memory of anything that had happened during that week seven years ago, including, blessedly, her mother's insanity. While for Jack it still manifested itself in difficult, sleepless nights every now and then, which alternated with times when he was convinced that it never happened, couldn't have happened (until the next nightmare changed his mind back), he was happy to accept the brunt of the memory of that day alone and spare his loved ones.

He had found his old digital camera in the garage about five months back, and had passed it onto Robynn, more as a toy than anything else. "I'd be surprised if it still worked," Jack said.

"I can find out," she said. "Pleaaaase!"

"I'll tell you what," Dani said. "If it works, you practice with it and get good, and then you can cover the reception. How about that?"

Robynn smiled again. "Sweet! I'll go up right now and start!" She ran up the stairs to her room and from below, Jack and Dani could here the sound of her closet sliding open and a ton of stuff being drug out.

"She's so impetuous," Jack commented.

"She's so twelve," Dani said. "But she's so good that I think we can cut her a little slack, okay?"

"Okay. I just hope she won't be too disappointed if the camera doesn't work."

"You know if there's anyone who could coerce it back into action, it would be her."

"Got that right." Jack stood up. "Since you brought it up, tell me what other thirty-five billion things you want me to do are while I'm still in the mood."

"Number one's shot, because Robynn's home now," Dani replied with a grin. "Your loss."

"Yeah?" he grinned back. "Well, wait until tonight."

Upstairs, Robynn Hayden dug out the shoebox containing the camera that her father had given her and switched it on, not sure if the battery was still good. She was happy when it quietly jumped to life. Looking through the viewfinder, she lined up a series of shots of her room, but when she tried to take one, a flag popped up telling her that there was no memory card. She went back into the shoebox and pulled out a small, stamp-sized plastic wafer and, after poking around, found the proper place in which to insert it. She tried snapping again, but the camera told her that the memory card was full and that she had to get rid of some images.

"Maaaan!" Robynn sighed, turning the control switch on the camera to view. Looking through the viewfinder, she saw picture after picture of a forest. It looked faintly familiar, like some place she might have dreamed about once.

Fishing back through the box once again, she found the cable that connected to her computer, which was almost as old as the camera, her dad being too cheap to get her a new laptop. But in this instance that proved to be a good thing, since the camera still able to connect to it. Since her school computer class had spent one whole day on downloading digital photos she had little trouble in getting them from the memory card onto the computer.

Paging through them, they each seemed to be of trees and woods and occasional tumble-down buildings, except for one that was pretty much intact. It looked like an official building, like the post office downtown.

The sight of it also stirred a tiny little uncomfortable worm within her brain.

The last picture startled her. It was the face of a woman. A painting of a woman, actually. Robynn stared at it, wondering who it was, and why her dad had taken a picture of it. She decided to print out a copy.

Because her color printer was also pretty old, it took a couple of minutes to zap the picture out. Taking it off the tray, Robynn looked at it again, now with new understanding. Enlarged to a full page size, she could see that it was not simply a painting of any woman.

It was her mother.

Seeing her mother's face so unexpectedly forced a flood of conflicting emotions to rise to the surface, and she had to look away. She just didn't want to deal with that stuff right now, not right before the wedding. Dad and Dani had enough problems without her suddenly developing "Mommy" issues.

She had always been good at compartmentalizing problems and putting them away for awhile, like folded clothes.

Now, though, she began to worry that maybe she shouldn't have deleted it from the memory card; maybe Dad wanted to keep the picture. On the other hand, he had given the camera to her without even looking to see if there were any pictures with it, so maybe he had forgotten all about it. Anyway, the picture wasn't gone. It was still on the computer. She reached over and made sure all of the images on the memory card were saved. Then she forced herself to look again at the picture she has printed out, and felt immediately foolish.

The woman in the painting was *not* her mother. It was not even close. For one thing, pictures of her mom show her with brunette hair, and this woman was a redhead. Jeez, was she spazzing? Robynn held the picture at different angles trying to understand how she could have been so mistaken. Maybe she was starting to lose it like Loony Linda in her class, who was constantly telling people about seeing things that anyone with a brain knew weren't really there.

Robynn took a deep breath. She'd have to worry about it all this later; she had things to do now, namely practice with the camera. Standing the picture up in front of her computer screen, Robynn then reached for the camera and noticed something on her thumb. It looked like colored chalk or something. Noticing a smudge on the printed picture, she realized what it was: toner from the color printer. It was probably too old to use.

"Jeez," she muttered, grabbing a tissue to wipe it off. She'd really have try and persuade Dad to get her a new computer some time, or better yet, Dani. Dani wasn't as big a cheapskate as her dad.

Taking up the camera, she lined up a shot of her bookshelf and clicked one off, seeing it appear on the viewfinder a second after the flash. Turning to the other side, she snapped a shot of her dresser. That one came out a little blurry. This was going to take some work. Maybe she should go find Claude, the family's orange tabby cat, and use him as a subject. If she could get some good shots of Claude, she could surely get some good ones of people at the reception.

Standing with her back to the computer screen, Robynn could not see the printed-out image of the woman's face behind her.

Nor the way it turned to watch her as she left the room.

ABOUT THE AUTHOR

Michael Mallory is a short story writer, novelist, journalist, and occasional actor. He lives in the Greater Los Angeles area. You can visit him at:

www.michaelmallory.com